BY SUN AND CANDLELIGHT

BY SUN AND CANDLELIGHT

Susan Sallis

CROWN PUBLISHERS, INC.
NEW YORK

Published by Crown Publishers, Inc., 201
East 50 Street, New York, New York
10022. Member of the Crown Publishing
Group. Originally published in Great
Britain in 1989 by Bantam Press, a
division of Transworld Publishers Ltd.
CROWN is a trademark of Crown
Publishers, Inc.
Manufactured in the United States of
America

Quality Printing and Binding by:
Berryville Graphics
P.O. Box 272
Berryville, VA 22611 U.S.A.

FOR
MY
FAMILY

BY SUN AND CANDLELIGHT

Prologue

*O*n V.E. day, Carol Woodford crossed the summer-dry fields and went into the tumbledown cottage she and her friends had christened the Haunted House. Her long sixteen-year-old legs straddled the hole at the bottom of the stairs with practised ease, and she climbed the rotten treads to the bedroom as she had done so often. But before, she had always been with the others: now, on this day—long-awaited, historic—she was alone by choice. Everyone else would be in Northfield village, or at church, or with their families. She had told her mother she was going for a walk. She couldn't bear to see the beloved, bereft face any more. Her mother's courage was too much for her to bear. Carol's father had died only three weeks ago. He hadn't seen the end of the war; he hadn't even been there when Carol finished her school exams.

She sat on the rusty bed in the first-floor bedroom where the four girls always came together, and stared blankly out of the window. She was reminded of the constantly moving atom. Were there enough atoms out there to reincarnate her father? Why

1

couldn't she and Mother have supplied some from their over-subscribed bodies to repair his disintegrating heart? Why was death "the end"? Why couldn't you do anything about it?

She said aloud, "I believe in you, God. But I hate you. All right, I know you gave us free will. I know all that. But you can intervene to change the course of events if you really want to. And you didn't. I asked you. Mummy asked you. And you didn't."

After a long time her eyes focused properly again and she saw Monica crossing the field. She wished she could go on being alone for a bit longer, but if there had to be someone, she was glad it was Monica. Unemotional, practical Monica, who would refuse to weep with her like Myrtle and Liv might have done. Perhaps Monica would come home with her. Mother liked Monica.

Carol went to the raised stair lid as Monica passed beneath it. She said, "Don't jump. I'm here." And Monica replied, "I know."

Monica often did know things like that. She knew how Carol's mind worked. It wasn't always good to have someone so sentient around. But it was a two-way thing; when Carol saw the black hair in a million carefully contrived curls beneath the saucer hat; the make-up; the American nylon stockings; the long, pre-War gloves, she knew something enormous had happened.

She waited while Monica dusted down her dress ostentatiously. Monica was nearly seventeen; she was beautiful, like Rita Hayworth. Carol smiled without envy. She was not beautiful herself. Liv had told her once she looked like a horse.

Monica said edgily, "What are you laughing at?"

"Nothing. Thinking maybe your Victory outfit isn't quite the thing for the Haunted House."

"Not meant to be. I just slipped in to say goodbye to you."

"How did you know I'd be here?"

"Well. You weren't at home. Where else would you be?"

"Nowhere." Carol peered out of the window so that Monica could not see her face. "Why goodbye?" she asked. "Where are you off to?"

"London. Trafalgar Square, I think."

None of the girls had ever been to London; for so long it had been completely beyond the pale, a war zone.

Carol said incredulously, "Mon. What has happened?"

"I'm having a baby. I'm going to pick up the first rich-looking Yank I see in London, and make him marry me and take me back to America." She shoved out one hip and put a hand on it. "I look all of twenty-two or three, don't I? Don't I, Carol?"

"Oh . . . Oh my God . . ." Carol turned from the window and stretched out her arms. "Oh, Mon—oh God—who—"

"Keep away!" Monica's voice was sharp. "You'll mess up my hair or make me cry or something! Just keep away."

Carol fell back.

Monica said, "I shouldn't have told you. Damn fool me. That's what I am. A damn fool. You were always soft! God, it's not the end of the world! Other girls have . . . other girls have . . . other girls have . . . ."

Carol interrupted helplessly, "Can't you marry the father? I know Miss Edgeworth says they don't respect you afterwards. But surely—"

"No, I can't marry him."

"Your father would make him. He'd make him, Mon! It's his duty—oh, he must be horrible to do this to you and then leave you to take it all by yourself!"

"He's not very nice. But then, neither am I. And if Dad knew about it, he'd kick me out. I'd rather go under my own steam, thank you very much."

"Oh, Mon. Don't be daft. As if your dad would kick you out!"

Monica sighed sharply and looked at her friend. They were almost the same age, but although Carol was six inches taller, she was unmistakably years younger in experience.

"All right. You may as well know. Then you'll want to see the last of me too." She smiled slightly. "I've always been honest. You've got to admit that, Cass. Not wise. Not a bit clever. But honest." She stopped smiling. "I found out . . . last year actually . . . I'm adopted."

"Oh." Carol wondered what her reaction should be. She said, "Well . . . that means your parents actually chose you. You're more special than the rest of us."

Carol had once told her own parents that the Cooks, Monica's parents, were like a couple of shunting engines, pulling and pushing their two sons here and there and vainly trying to get stubborn and wilful Monica on to the rails in order to start chivvying her likewise. Monica's abrupt disclosure explained a lot. She wasn't like them; not a bit. They were all rough and tough and uncaring. Monica could be tough, but it was just a veneer.

Monica said brightly, "Not really. They already had Gus and Giles, they didn't want any more kids. My real mother paid them.

And they needed the money. Dad had been out of work since the last war with his chest. They had to do something."

"Oh." Carol searched her mind for something to say. "I can understand that you feel odd. But you must be fond of them and they must be fond of you. You can't run away."

"Watch me."

Carol said, "Are you going to look for your mother? Your real mother?"

"She died a long time ago. When I was ten. And she never told Mum and Dad—the Cooks, I mean—she never told them who my father was. Maybe she didn't know. Maybe she was a prostitute."

"Oh, Mon."

"Well, you never know." She attempted to smile. "I don't know her, so I can't grieve for her. Do you realise how lucky you are to be able to grieve for your dad? Grieve properly?"

"No. I suppose I don't."

"Oh, Carol. I'm sorry. Going on like this. I just wanted to say goodbye. That's all."

"But who was it, Mon? Surely you don't have to run away."

Monica's eyes slid past Carol's head and into a future that did not hold anyone she knew.

"It was Giles. Gilly. The one I've always loved best."

"Your . . . brother?"

"Quite. And Dad's favourite, too."

"But how could you, Mon? Was it when you found out—about the adoption? You had always loved him, and when you knew you weren't related, then you discovered your love was—"

"For God's sake, Cass! Shut up!" Monica gave a small sob and turned away. "It wasn't a romantic film. Nothing like that. He was the one who told me I was adopted. That I'd been sold. That I'd got no-one to call my own. Then he said that I could very easily have someone of my own. My very own." She banged her head on the wall and her hat was pushed high on her curls. "Yes, you're right, it was like that. I've always loved him. We used to mess about when we were little kids—oh, I can't tell you, you've got no brothers. Disgusting, it was. And then I got older and knew it was disgusting and stopped it, and . . . that's what happened. I was seduced because I wanted a brother again! And I couldn't have been seduced if I'd known he was my brother! Oh, it's too difficult, too complicated. And I'm so tired. I'm so tired, Cass."

She let Carol approach her and hold her awkwardly in her long arms.

She sobbed, "Admit you're sick to your soul. You're so—so—perfect. I shouldn't have told you—"

Carol said, "You told me because we're friends."

"I don't want the others to know! Liv and Myrt. Don't tell them. Ever. Please, Cass."

"Of course I won't tell them. One person is enough."

"But you're not the right person. You can't bear it."

"I wouldn't have been able to. Before. But now . . . it's different now. It's something to do with atoms and putting life back together."

"What are you talking about?" The sobs increased.

"I'm talking about my father. I can't do anything about that. Can't you understand, Mon? Something can always be done with life. But death . . . nothing. Nothing."

Monica allowed herself a small gasping laugh. "Nothing much to be done about this life either, Cass. I've tried gin. And hot baths. And running a mile. It's still there."

"Oh, Mon. You shouldn't."

"No. Well, I had to try. Poor little devil." She pushed herself upright and unwound Carol's arms. "I'd better be off. There's a train at four-fifteen, and if I don't get a bus into town in the next half-hour, I'll miss it."

"Mon. You can't. You know you can't."

"Listen, innocent. I know I can. I know what to do." She shook her head at Carol's expression. "It need not mean a thing, Cass. The actions. It's up here it counts." She touched her forehead. "All I have to do is get off the train and join in with everyone else. I pick the nicest-looking American I can see, and we start dancing. Who knows, he might make a marvellous husband, as well as a father for Gilly's baby!" Her defiance crumpled again and she fumbled for her handkerchief. Her gloves were already grubby. "Oh, Cass. I'll never forget this place and our happy times."

"Of course you won't. We'll come back—often. Together. Listen—" Carol felt herself change, felt energy course through her. "I've got a wonderful idea. You'll come to us. Mummy will think of something. She will honestly. She'll do it for you and me and Daddy. I can't explain it. I know you think I'm stuffy—"

"I don't. I think Liv is stuffy. Not you."

5

"Come home with me, now. Please. We've got Daddy's insurance . . ." Her voice petered out and she cleared her throat and went on loudly, "Mummy thinks she can't be of use to anyone any more. She wants to go on holiday. We can all go. No-one need know. She will think of something."

Monica did not immediately repudiate the idea. She kept swallowing and looking at Carol as if she'd never seen her before. And Carol tried to explain why it was the only course of action . . . she reminded Monica of their closeness . . . she talked about their times in the Haunted House. And Monica listened.

When the two girls arrived at the big house in West Heath later that afternoon, Mary Woodford listened to them without interrupting once.

She knew within ten minutes what she would do if Monica would let her. And Monica was without will, without purpose. She handed her body with its baby into Mary's suddenly useful hands. And Mary smiled properly for the first time in a month, and went on making her plans.

The cafe where Mrs. Cook worked was still open at eight o'clock that evening, and Mary went in alone and asked Mrs. Cook if Monica could stay with Carol for a while to "cheer her up." Monica had already packed a case. There was no need for her to go back to the council house in Turves Green.

The summer was strangely idyllic. They went to Rhyl and were there when news of the Hiroshima bomb came through. And Mary, horrified and thankful, decided that now was the time to share some of her plans with the girls.

She had known Dilly Gosling for years; Dilly had made her wedding dress in the days when people considered their dressmaker as part of the family. When she married George "Gander" Gosling and went to help him with his small hotel near Paddington, Mary had continued to send Christmas cards and Dilly had written back effusively pressing for a visit from any of them. Mary thought the time had come to pay that visit.

When she returned, three days later, the plan was settled. Monica would stay at the hotel until the birth of the baby. If she liked it, she would be trained in management.

"I told her the truth, Monica dear. All of it. She is offering you a home and training. And it will be a good home, and excellent training. How do you feel about it?"

6

Monica turned white, then fiery red. She said painfully, "I suppose, if I'm to be . . . taken in by someone . . . they have to know."

Mary said gently, "Dilly Gosling comes from Selly Oak, Monica. She has been lonely in her time. She will look on you as a daughter. But, unlike most mothers—"she tried to coax a smile on the strained face opposite her"—she will be entirely without criticism."

"I didn't mean—I'm very grateful, Mrs. Woodford. I just haven't wanted to . . . look into the future. It's been marvellous with you and Carol. Marvellous."

Carol said, "And it will be marvellous again! We'll be with you. Don't worry about that."

Mary said, more practically, "We'll stay the first week darling. Then we'll come back when the autumn term finishes. In time for the birth."

Monica was suddenly terrified. It was September and she had the tiniest lump above her knicker elastic. She had almost forgotten that some time around Christmas there would be a birth. It was then that Mary put the rest of her plan to her.

"I wondered . . ." it seemed, suddenly, an enormity. "Only if you thought . . . I mean, you don't have to make up your mind now or anything. But—Monica, dear, could we take the baby?" Mary swallowed. "You see, I expect I seem old to you, but I'm not really. I'm not forty yet. And . . . I don't seem to have much to . . . to do. And we'd hold him in trust for you. I mean, it would have to be an official adoption of course, but he'd be there if ever you wanted . . . your circumstances permitted . . ."

Her voice petered out. She stared at Monica and Monica stared back. Then slowly the girl's eyes filled with tears. She almost never cried. She dashed angrily at her face and blurted, "It would be the most marvellous thing . . . it would kind of . . . make my adoption okay. If you know what I mean. It would make everything . . . okay."

Carol said, "Mummy! It's a wonderful idea! Oh, Mon—Mon— we're going to share this. Properly. Aren't we?"

Monica could only nod.

It worked out as Mary had said. The Goslings took to Monica immediately and—fortunately—Monica took to them. And a week before Christmas, after a terrifying labour lasting thirty hours, a baby girl was born.

Monica's first words were, "I don't want to see her. I don't want to get fond of her."

But Carol, who had been there all the time and was euphoric with relief, merely laughed.

"Oh, Mon. Don't be silly. You know you can see her when ever you want!" The midwife was busy with olive oil and a binder. She wrapped the baby tightly and held her out. Automatically, Carol took her. "Baby . . . baby . . . you're all right with us . . . no need to cry. . . . We're all going to look after you."

Monica was not well for nearly a week afterwards. The doctor used some of the very latest drug and told Mary there was nothing to worry about. "A few years ago, this sort of thing was extremely dangerous. Not any more."

Mary was worried. "What is it, Doctor? She hasn't got septicemia, surely?"

"There is some infection in the Fallopian tubes, Mrs. Woodford. As I said, with penicillin there is nothing to fear."

And he was right. Before the week was out Monica was going to the bathroom under her own steam and looking almost the same as she'd done a year ago.

At first she refused to choose a name for the tiny girl, but after pressure from Carol, she said carelessly, "All right then. Elizabeth. After the princess." She looked out of the window. "I'm not coming to the christening. Nothing like that."

"You might change your mind," Carol said. "We won't have her christened for ages. Will we, Mummy?"

"I won't change my mind. I don't want to see her. You will be her family. And you're more my family than the Cooks."

"You'll have to come home sometimes," Mary protested.

"I don't think so. I'm going to work really hard for the Goslings. I never thought I was domesticated, but I'm quite excited about it. A new life. I'm going to start a new life."

"We shall come to see you," Carol said.

"Please don't. Not for ages anyway. Let me get going properly." Monica held Carol's arm. "You know I'll be all right. I'm much tougher than you. Don't come to see me. Promise?"

Monica could hardly wait to get rid of them. She hurried through the legalities, signing away her child without reading the document. She did not see them off at Euston. But after Carol had carefully handed Elizabeth into the taxi and on to Mary's lap, Monica planted an unexpected kiss on her cheek.

"Listen, Cass. You'll never breathe a word . . . I mean, I know

8

you won't, but Liv and Myrt might try to guess, and the kid is so like me—dark and swarthy. You'll fob them off somehow. Won't you?"

Carol grabbed a handful of Monica's jumper, and squeezed it. "No-one knows except us. And no-one will ever know."

Monica pulled away the gloved fingers and shook them, as if they'd made a bargain. Then she turned and fled back up the steps of the boarding house.

I

The church was packed. The Dennings were well-known in Northfield and since Dr. Denning had come home covered in glory from his last-ditch heroism in the Far East, his list of National Health patients was the longest in the area. He was wearing full uniform for the wedding, though it was doubtful whether he was entitled to do so.

Liv and Carol waited in the church porch, holding Bessie between them. Myrtle had insisted on traditional bridesmaids' dresses, and Liv, who had wanted to wear a New Look dress with a saucer hat, had sulked for ages, then chosen something which would outshine Myrtle and look ridiculous on Carol. Now she realised that whatever she had worn, Bessie Woodford would steal the occasion. At nearly six years old she was as pretty as a picture with long black hair to her shoulders, luminous dark eyes set in perfect olive skin, and a nose, mouth and chin that seemed brushed gently upward in perpetual laughter. Today, Liv noted, her ears were suddenly revealed by the flower circlet on her head which pushed her hair back. They too were perfect. Twin pink shells giving a mother-of-pearl effect as the sun shone through them.

The sun was everywhere. Blazing into the porch, sending beams through the side windows, striking patterns over the congregation who sat beneath the stained glass.

"Myrtle's always been so damned *lucky*," Liv murmured to Carol. "Fancy landing that gorgeous surgeon! I mean . . . *Myrtle!*"

"He's an osteopath, Liv. Not a surgeon. And Myrt is an osteo-path too. And she deserves to be happy."

"Oh . . . you! Myrt's going off to Bournemouth. You're going to Paris. We've heard nothing of Mon since she finished her hotel training. You're all leaving me in this dump!"

Carol looked sympathetic. "Poor Liv. Anyway I'm not going away for long." She smiled down at Bessie. "Can't leave you and Grannie for long, can I, Baby?"

Bessie beamed and rubbed her cheek against Carol's fingers. Everyone knew that the two of them were inseparable. Everyone knew that Bessie called Mrs. Woodford "Grannie" though she was the child's adoptive mother. And Liv and Myrtle had seen nothing of Carol after that October farewell in the Haunted House. They could not help but dally with the outrageous idea that Bessie might belong to Carol. So much for Cass and her peculiar inhibitions. They both wanted to know how it had happened and dared not ask.

But Liv, suddenly provoked, couldn't resist a little dig.

"I'm surprised you could go to university and leave Bessie when she was so young. It's not so bad now she's started school."

Carol looked up, surprised. "She had Mother. They're the best of friends."

"Oh yes, I forgot. Grannie," Liv said.

"Where is Grannie?" Bessie interrupted. "Is she sitting with Mrs. Denning? Will she be all right?"

"We can peep and look at her if you like." Carol drew the child forward to the inner door and there was Mrs. Woodford sitting by the Bakers in the middle of the church, twisting her head like an owl to get a glimpse of the bridesmaids. Bessie waved and she waved back delightedly. Carol thought she looked younger as the years went by. Mrs. Woodford was not as tall as Carol but she was just as unbeautiful, and when her husband had died six years ago she had shrivelled into an elderly woman overnight. Bessie had changed all that.

"I wanted her to sit in the front with Mrs. Denning," the child whispered now. "Then we would have been by her and she could have smiled."

Carol wanted to hug her. She was still five years old and her prime concern was "Grannie."

Liv said at her shoulder, "My God. Look at him. He's so handsome."

Carol switched her gaze to the front right-hand pew where Malcolm Chester Lennox waited for his bride. She knew that her father would have turned down his mouth at the obvious good looks, the ridged waves, the toothbrush moustache. But maybe that was unfair. This man's personal presentation was important in his job. Outside regular medicine, outside the new and revered National Health scheme, he had to use all his assets.

She turned away. "He certainly is."

"Well, Myrt might have nobbled him, but the best man is definitely mine!" Liv continued to stare down the church and as if her gaze was magnetic the best man turned and looked towards them, and smiled. He was not as obviously handsome as the groom. He was fair and nondescript until he smiled. Then there was something rather special about him.

"I like him best," Bessie declared. "Is that why he is called the best man?"

Liv started to explain as the bridal car drew up. There were people waiting at the lychgate and a little cheer went up as Dr. Denning alighted and handed out the froth of white net beneath which was Myrtle. She joined her bridesmaids and stood still while Liv dealt with the train, bouquet and veil.

"Now you know what to do." She was in her element. "The veil goes up and back, over the combs. It will give you more height. And take it slowly. Those platform shoes are lethal. And give me the bouquet when the vicar says—"

Dr. Denning said smoothly, "I think we remember last night's rehearsal. Don't we, honey?"

Myrtle managed a single nod. Then the organ struck up and everything started. "Here comes the bride . . . all fat and wide . . ." But Myrtle knew now that she wasn't fat. She was plump and desirable. When she had gone to Malcolm's treatment room with three other students to "observe," she had known he wanted her straightaway. But she had held out for marriage. For two years she had held out, smiling gently when he boasted of his other conquests. And in the end he had been forced to ask her to marry him.

She moved her laden head with difficulty to look at her two friends. Liv Baker, the pretty flirt. Carol Woodford, the romantic—as plain as Myrtle in a different way. Myrtle has always paired off with Carol until V.E. day when, inexplicably, Monica Cook had moved in to console the Woodfords after the death of Carol's father. It had been Myrtle and Carol who had stolen a precious can of paint from the school store and daubed the Post Office wall with the then-familiar slogan "OPEN SECOND FRONT NOW!" Myrtle smiled and remembered burying the can in the garden of the Haunted House. They ought to go back and dig up that paint can. It symbolized all their escapades. Then she remembered being jealous of Carol; it had been amazing, quiet Cass having an illicit affair, and an even more illicit baby. Carol had the best of all worlds: her mother taking care of the sin itself, Carol off to university and then landing this job with a firm of publishers who were sending her over to Paris. But now . . . now Myrtle was glad she had waited. And she was glad she was getting married before Liv. Carol and she might have been the ugly ducklings of the quartet, but they'd made it before Monica and Liv. Carol. Dear Carol, looking anxious, putting out a hand which Myrtle could not take because one arm was in her father's and her other cradled the massive bouquet. But she smiled a special smile, and said, "I wish Mon was here." And Carol nodded. And Liv said, "Bessie darling, you in front." And Dr. Denning said, "Let's get the show on the road," and they were off.

Myrtle knew the devil was in Malcolm when he merely brushed her cheek with his lips after the ceremony, then murmured in her ear, "I see what you mean about your sexy friend. Games-captain type on top, and molten lava underneath." But she wasn't going to let it spoil her day. Instead, she glanced at Bessie standing there like an angel, and murmured back, "And molten lava burns. As you see."

But maybe it sounded like a warning, because he wasn't smiling when he gave her his arm, and when they all stood about in the vestry for the signing he kept glancing at Carol and Bessie with that still, aware look that she'd seen on his face before when he'd got a woman patient he fancied.

It was all right again in the car. There was a glass partition between passengers and driver which gave an illusion of privacy,

13

and taking his hand she slid it under the net and along the smooth satin of her dress.

"Can you feel my heart beating?"

"No." He cupped her breast hard and pushed it up until it was almost beneath her chin. Then at last all his repressed passion came to the fore and he kissed her madly until the car drew up outside the hotel. The driver got out with slow tact, keeping his eyes averted from the mirror. Myrtle gasped, "Malcolm—darling—we're there!" "Not quite." He lowered his head to the satin. "Oh, baby . . . bunny rabbit . . . do you know what these do to me?"

She smiled. It was the realisation two years ago that he thought her breasts were beautiful that had made her start to stand up straight again.

"That was when I fell in love with you," she admitted, kissing his waves which, amazingly, remained undisturbed.

The car door was opened by her completely tactless mother, and with Malcolm's body on top of her she almost fell into the gutter. It did not help when Mrs. Denning, flustered out of her wits, tried to make light of the matter by blaming her daughter.

"Come on now, Myrt! Enough of that! You're not allowed to start on the main course until this evening!"

It was all so utterly tasteless. How could Malcolm know that poor Mother had had to learn this kind of defence because Daddy was a philanderer?

Myrtle scrambled out of the car without a bit of dignity, and had to wait while her new husband straightened his tie and emerged unruffled and smiling urbanely. And—almost without pause—looking around him until he spotted the arrival of the bridesmaids.

Myrtle watched her parents going up the steps to the hotel, and knew that she and Malcolm were younger replicas of them. Mrs. Denning, tiny and plump, was clinging to her husband's arm as if he might shake her off at any moment. And he was smiling and smiling. But not for his wife.

Myrtle thought wildly, "Mother's had to put up with it all these years—but I won't—I won't—I won't!" And she too smiled up at Malcolm and said, "Look at me, my darling. Just look at me. No-one else."

Mrs. Woodford said, "I don't really like Bessie being shown around like an expensive doll, darling. It won't do her any good."

Carol, who had done the rounds as quickly as possible, was

sitting by her mother drinking a cup of tea.

"This is lovely. How did you get it?" she asked, looking for Bessie over the rim of the cup.

"I know one of the waitresses. She was in the Girl Guides with me. Many years ago."

The waitresses were mostly in their late forties; some were even older. These days young girls were used to working alongside men in factories and earning good money.

"Trust you. Everyone thinks you're so quiet and reserved. It turns out you know more people than . . ." Carol put down her cup. "Oh, there she is. Look at her, Mother. She's so *pretty!*"

"Like a little doll?" Mrs. Woodford asked quizzically.

"Well, I suppose so. But, just this once . . . she is so enjoying herself."

Mrs. Woodford smiled. "Not much we can do about it anyway. Wasn't she marvellous? The way she held the train and stood so quietly. Reverently, almost. I could have burst with pride."

Carol said softly, "She's made all the difference to our lives, hasn't she?"

"Oh yes." Mrs. Woodford never dissimulated. She nodded. "She was a gift from heaven. Literally, I felt." Her smile broadened to a grin and she looked very young again. "But I couldn't have coped with her on my own, Cass. How we scrambled through that first year I'll never know. You were wonderful."

"I loved it. I didn't want to go to Bristol. Thought she'd forget me. Thought you'd be frazzled out! But she . . . sort of . . . grew up, all at once, didn't she?"

"Anyway, you were home so often." Mary Woodford's smile became wry. "I'd have hated it—you going away to university—if it hadn't been for Bessie."

"I don't think I'd have gone. Strange. Everyone thinks we made a prison for ourselves, taking her on. It worked the other way really."

"Yes. I wonder if Mon . . . how Mon feels about it now."

"She's ours, Mother."

"Oh I know, darling. But . . . oh, look at her now. Just look. Miss Pears of 1952."

Bessie was shaking hands gravely with a boy of ten or eleven. He was Myrtle's young brother, and though they lived quite near each other Bessie did not meet him often and was rather in awe of him.

He wore long trousers and a Norfolk jacket, and his hair was so slicked down with brilliantine that his head looked flat on the top. He was not quite old enough to be tongue-tied, and Bessie was too young to cause him any inhibitions.

He said frankly, "You are very pretty. I didn't want to come actually. But I've got to admit, it was all very pretty."

Bessie said politely, "You look nice, too."

"It took Ma ages to get me up like this. She borrowed the jacket from someone. But the trousers are mine." He spoke with quiet pride.

"Oh." Bessie did not understand the importance of long trousers, but she knew she loved the feel of her dress whispering about her ankles.

She said, "You'll miss Aunt Myrt, won't you?"

"Not really. She's never at home."

"I miss Cass when she goes away. She's going to Paris in September."

"I know. Myrt's as jealous as anything."

"They're friends!"

"That makes it worse. What, between you and Paris, Myrt grinds her teeth in her sleep!"

Bessie laughed, realising it was a joke, or one of the strange grown-up compliments.

She said, "Paris is over the sea."

"Yeah. It's in France."

"Cass will be a long way away."

"Yeah." He couldn't think of more to say on that subject, so he changed it. "Why do you call her Cass?"

Bessie was surprised. "It's short for Carol. Aunt Myrt calls her that too."

"Yeah, but you call Mrs. Woodford Grannie. So Cass must be your auntie. But you call her Cass."

"She's my sister, silly."

"Oh." It didn't make sense, but it wasn't that interesting. He heard his father's voice and looked around apprehensively. "Oh, lord. They've cleared the tables. You know what that means, don't you?"

"What?"

"Dancing. I hate dancing."

"Don't worry. I'll dance with you if you like."

"Oh. Will you? Thanks a lot, Bessie."

She remembered a line from her story book. "It will be a great pleasure, Boris."

Myrtle said, "Well girls, what do you think?"

"He's a dish," Liv said generously. "Handsome, successful. A dish."

"It's good that you're in the same profession, too," Carol added. "You'll understand each other's problems, be able to talk about your work—"

"He's no talker," Myrtle giggled. "He's all action. You should have seen him in the taxi here! He almost had my dress off!"

Carol flushed slightly. Liv said, "He must be mad for you, Myrt. Well, you're the first of the four. Who would have thought it?"

Myrtle was conscious that the compliment had a sting in its tail. She tried to pass it on. "Carol was the first, don't forget!"

Carol was completely uncomprehending. She said, "To go away from home, d'you mean? Well, it was Mon actually. If you remember, she started her course while I was still at school."

Liv giggled senselessly, and Myrt said, "Oh come on, old thing. You can come clean with us, surely?"

Carol still stared wide-eyed, and Liv stopped giggling and said, "My God, Mon said you'd never be an old maid even if you never got married. And she was right. You're a dark horse, Cass!"

Carol felt a tide of colour start from the base of her neck. She looked to where Bessie was dancing sedately with Boris Denning. "You don't mean . . . you surely don't mean *Bessie?*" she asked incredulously.

Myrtle might well have passed it off then, because after all she and Carol had always been paired off when Liv and Mon went boy-hunting, but Malcolm and his best man arrived, both—incredibly—making a bee-line for Carol. She managed to get her shoulder between the two of them and laughed up at her husband.

"All right, darling—we were just having a final gossip before life sweeps us away for ever! Such a pity Mon couldn't be here to complete the quartet. We were inseparable at school, weren't we, girls?" She did not wait for an answer. "Come on then. Let's dance."

The best man stared deeply into Carol's bewildered face.

"You've forgotten my name. It's Reggie. And you're Carol. Myrtle's very special friend. Shall we dance?"

Carol looked at Liv. Her grey chapel eyes were veiled. But Carol knew her so well.

"Won't you dance with Liv? I really should talk to some of these people."

And she moved back and away towards her mother, knowing she had done nothing to endear herself to Liv. The glorious curly hair fitted neatly beneath the best man's chin; they were perfect together. But Carol had given him to Liv and that was simply not good enough.

Feeling sick and shaky she suddenly decided to avoid her mother, and made for the ladies' room.

Malcolm said, "Oh really, Myrtle! What's all the fuss about? I wanted to dance with your friend, that's all.'

"You've been looking at her all day. You're married to me. Just now. Remember?" Myrtle knew she sounded shrewish, and could not stop herself.

"You're not going to let me forget it, obviously. Shall I pop along to an ironmongers and get some chains or something?"

"Childish."

"You're the one who is being childish. And stop shoving yourself against me like that. It's too hot for that sort of thing."

Myrtle felt tears burn her eyes. "I thought you liked my breasts?"

"I do." He looked down at her. "Oh, darling, I do. Are we having our first row?"

"I think so."

"Kiss me."

He bent his handsome head and kissed her ardently. One or two people clapped. Myrtle felt her spirits lift. He might be a wanderer, but he'd always come back to her. She was certain of it. She must make certain of it.

Liv tried to quell her sudden dislike of Carol. It was so ridiculous and petty. She searched her mind for one of her provocative remarks the opposite sex usually found so enchanting.

"Reggie? Is there another name to go with Reggie?"

It sounded ridiculous. As if she were talking to her grandmother's canary. She tried tipping her head right back so that he could see her wonderful teeth.

"Reggie Bradbury."

He really was good-looking. Not so obvious as Myrt's Malcolm, but longer-wearing. She'd noticed him straightaway. It was so unfair he'd been attracted to Cass. After all, she didn't want him.

"Reggie Bradbury." She rolled the syllables out as if they had some extra significance. Reggie Bradbury. Olivia Bradbury. Well, Olive Bradbury really. She invariably tried her name with the surnames of new men friends. She very much liked Olivia Bradbury.

"That's right," he replied, as if she were stupid, or deaf, or something.

"It sounds like a film star."

"Malcolm tells me it sounds like a cabinet-maker. Actually, I'm an auctioneer. With my father's firm."

Well, it was better than a furniture-maker. Though with Myrt marrying as-good-as-a-doctor and Cass about to take up a post in Paris, it could have been better.

"I'm just a little clerk. With the post office."

"Civil servant. Good job."

"Well, it is, actually. But it sounds so dull."

"Not at all."

"I'm a real small-town girl. Myrtle and Malcolm are going off to Bournemouth. Cass is away to Paris. All I want to do is stay here and get married."

"And what's wrong with that? It sounds very . . . womanly."

He was looking at her properly now. And yes, he was the sort of man she had known he was when she saw him first. She lowered her lashes.

"I shouldn't have said it, though. Sorry."

"I don't see why you shouldn't tell me how you feel. I take it as a great compliment."

"I feel as if I could tell you anything." She laughed breathlessly. "I've never felt like that before." And dammit, it was true. That was why she'd disliked Carol. Because this man meant something to her. Maybe he was the one.

He cleared his throat. "Anyway, I wouldn't call Birmingham a small town." He tried to make the conversation less personal. "It's the second biggest place in the country, you know."

"But Northfield is still a village, really."

19

"Yes. I knew what you meant. Sorry. I was just . . ." He tried to laugh and sounded as breathless as she had. "You're so simple. I didn't mean that either." He was rushing into things more quickly than she could have hoped. She lifted her lashes, let him see right into her transparent grey eyes for a moment, then lowered them again. "You're so *sweet!*" he amended.

"*And* silly. Like you said."

"I didn't say silly. I said simple. And that is something quite different. It's real. And basic. And good."

"Oh, Reggie."

Carol sat in a small side room, trying to compose herself. She wanted desperately to run away; go outside, find a taxi and go home to the old, ivy-covered garden behind the trellis screen. The three years at university had been hard for her; she was not brilliant and had had neither time nor inclination for the social life. She recalled endless hours in her room at Bristol, trying to force her mind to grapple with ancient historians who all saw events from different angles. She remembered the efforts of kind fellow students to integrate her into the social life of the university. She hadn't wanted that. She had wanted to keep the inner core of her mind free for Bessie. She loved Bessie with a protective force that surprised herself. She loved her . . . as a mother.

The discovery, forced on her by Liv an hour ago, shocked her. Both she and her mother looked on the adoption as a trust. They were holding Bessie in trust, as it were. Until when or for what, they did not know or ask. The head of their small family had been taken away from them, and Bessie had come. It was ordained that way. On the advice of the local vicar they had told the child she was "chosen" long before it could mean anything to her. But she knew she was special. That was what mattered.

Carol closed her eyes. She and her mother had been in a room like this when Bessie had been born. It had even smelled of roses like this one did, because the private nursing home made a point of overlaying their disinfectant smells with serried vases of flowers. And Carol had seen Bessie before Monica herself. It was no wonder she had felt like Bessie's mother. She had spent so much time with Mon during the pregnancy. She had shared *everything*.

Not quite everything. It was after all Monica who had conceived and borne Bessie. Carol forced the thought of Monica and Giles into her mind, though she had spent long hours all that time ago trying not to do so. Now she thought quite deliberately . . . Monica and her adopted brother begat Elizabeth Woodford. That was how it had been. Begat. Adopted. Two completely different processes. Carol kept her eyes tightly closed. She knew that there must be something wrong with her. She was conscious at times that her whole being was filled with love; not just for her mother and Bessie and Mon. For the whole of humanity. And then . . . then she would come up against a brick wall. It was as if her love bounced back at her, unwanted and ridiculous. Only her mother and Bessie continued to shine with a kind of reflection of her own feelings. And now, even Bessie's presence was tarnished.

She stood up abruptly and moved to the window as if to escape her own thoughts. The sash had been lifted and the smells distilled by the heat of summer drifted through into the small room. Hot grass and hot leaves and hot cars and hot bodies came at her like sensual gunfire. She said aloud, "I hate August. It's too brazen," and then drew back, embarrassed, as Liv and the best man walked across the gravel, possibly within earshot. But Liv was talking herself, so could not have heard.

"Let's find some shade. Somewhere natural. Oh, look at that weeping willow. Like a little house!"

And the best man said, "It's made for you. It grew there just for you."

"Rustic, d'you mean?"

"Pastoral. Pastoral and real. And so innocent."

They crossed the lawn and Carol found herself smiling at last. So Liv had accepted the "gift." She had conquered for herself. What a relief. It meant Carol could talk to her properly and convince her that Myrt's ridiculous assumption about Bessie was . . . ridiculous. Not that Myrt really believed it, of course. Myrt said things just to be outrageous, and she was completely loyal. But Liv was different; Liv might say something to others. Carol felt herself growing hot again.

A sudden breeze across the room told her the door was open. She looked up and saw that Myrt's new husband had come into the room and was standing holding the door and swaying gently. For an instant Carol considered climbing through the window, then realised she was being childish and turned into the room, smiling.

Malcolm said, "It's you. I've been looking for you all day. Were you waiting for me? Here? For me?"

He was obviously drunk. Carol said, "Where is Myrtle?"

"Talking to Mumsy. While that ghastly Mrs. Baker gets off with Dadsy. So we're safe."

Carol smoothed her long skirt. "It must be time for you to change. I must go. I promised I'd help Myrtle. Everything is laid out upstairs. Her suit. And her hat."

"Are you frightened of me? You're as pink as a rose. You remind me of a rose. Not opened. All closed up with thorns at the ready. But when you open up . . . wow!"

"Of course I'm not frightened. You've just married my best friend. How could I be frightened—"

"You're trembling. Just like a rose when the rain starts!"

"Oh, Malcolm. Really." She wanted to tell him he sounded like a soppy film hero, but couldn't quite do it.

He took her prudish protest at face value.

"Yes. Really. You're different. You're special. You're interesting, dammitall! I'm interested in you." He took two lurching steps towards her and she backed against the wall. It was a mistake. He went on lurching, and ended up leaning on the wall too, an arm either side of her. He smelled of whisky and brilliantine. She closed her eyes.

"Oh, Carol . . . Cass they call you, don't they? How old were you? Sixteen? Was it a bloody Yank? Did he hurt you? Oh Cass . . . Cassie . . ."

She opened her eyes and saw his face looming nightmarishly. Then she made her biggest mistake of all. She opened her mouth wide to yell for help. And he was literally inside it.

She thought she would choke. Her hands clawed at his shoulders, but he was a big man and he simply stopped leaning on the wall, and leaned on her. His tongue was a solid six ounces of liver pushing into her throat. It was the most ghastly physical experience of her life. She left his shoulders and tried to scratch his neck above the stiff shirt collar. They swayed from side to side. They were both making animal noises.

And then, unexpectedly, he left her. He was wrenched from her. There was a horrid sucking noise as of a bath plug being pulled out, he went staggering backwards, and Myrtle's furious face was visible beneath his flailing arm.

Carol sobbed and tried to say thank you. But apparently Myrtle held her responsible.

"You—you—*bitch!*" she screamed, her voice ripping through the window and alerting Liv and Reggie beneath their pastoral arbour. "You absolute bitch! My wedding day—on my wedding day—can't you keep your hands off—good God almighty, is no man safe from you—should have known back in the Haunted House—pretending to be—never want to see you again! Never! D'you hear me? I never want to—"

Malcolm, suddenly sober, managed to free himself.

"I should think every bloody person in the bloody hotel can hear you! What the hell is the matter with you? Groom's prerogative to kiss the chief bridesmaid!"

"The best man—the best man's prerogative! Not yours—and certainly not Carol Woodford! My God, I've told you about her, and you should know—"

Carol found her voice at last with a giant sob.

"Myrt! Please stop—please don't go on! Malcolm is drunk—he didn't know what he was doing!"

It was her final mistake. She lost the remnant of chivalry Malcolm was throwing in her direction. He made no more protests. He allowed Myrtle to denounce Carol in front of crowding guests. He stood with bowed head while she tore apart the friendship of schooldays, stripping herself as well as her friend. Perhaps if Monica had been there it would never have happened. Or if Mrs. Woodford had arrived on the scene sooner, she could have stopped it. But Myrtle ceased ranting at last because she ran out of steam, and in that moment of silence which followed the tirade, the farcical quality which had somehow hovered over the whole wedding day was gone.

Certainly Myrtle had lost her dignity and plump prettiness, and stood there almost indecently naked without them. And Malcolm, his scratched neck beginning to seep blood, was revealed as most definitely drunk. But Carol, silent under her friend's whipped-up scorn, was not ludicrous or overdone in any way. She was no tragedy queen, nor a victim. Embarrassment seemed to have shrunk her so that the dress, chosen by Liv, appeared ill-fitting. But for the first time in her life Carol was beautiful. Her hair had been shaken out of its set by Malcolm's rough handling and haloed her face, making it look smaller than it really was. All her make-up had gone long since, but her fiery skin and sore mouth highlighted the intense blue of her dilated eyes. She stared at Myrtle as if trying to photograph her for posterity. Her throat moved occasionally but she did not speak a word.

Into this appalled silence, Mrs. Woodford arrived with an uncomprehending smile. She looked at her daughter, then at Myrtle and her new husband, then she crossed the floor and took Carol's arm.

"Bessie's tired, darling. I think we should go home now." She looked at Myrtle and her smile had gone. "Thank you for everything," she said with great deliberation. Then she led Carol past the gogglers and gawpers to where the music still played and Bessie and Boris were polka-ing, perspiring, and enjoying themselves like young puppies. Surprisingly, it was Liv's father, Mr. Baker, who found their coats and offered his car to take them home.

"How very kind," Mrs. Woodford was smiling again, tucking Bessie into one arm and Carol into the other. "I'm afraid these occasions are a little much for the very young and the old."

Bessie laughed comfortably. "You're not old, Grannie. And I'm not very young." She peered around Mrs. Woodford at Carol. "Cassie, guess what? Boris Denning says I'm the beautifulest creature he's ever seen and he wants to take my photograph." She giggled with delight and snuggled back into the leather upholstery of Mr. Baker's new Armstrong-Siddeley. "This is the first wedding I've been to. I specks it will be Aunt Liv who gets married next."

Carol made no reply, and Mr. Baker guffawed from the driver's seat. "D'you want me to book you in as bridesmaid for our Liv then?" he asked in his slight Welsh accent. Then with misplaced gallantry he added, "It will probably be your Aunt Cass who gets married next!"

Mrs. Woodford felt her daughter's shoulder tighten beneath her hand, but Bessie said comfortably, "Oh no, not yet. Cass is going to marry me when I grow up."

Back in the hotel, Mrs. Denning, incensed by Myrtle's inexplicable command to "get lost," approached her husband and Mrs. Baker.

"You chapel people are all the same!" she snapped, wedging her plump backside between them with great ostentation. "Give you half a chance and you're up to your tricks!"

She did not explain the nature of the tricks, but Mrs. Baker, flustered and furious, stood up and left without more ado. Dr. Denning said in a bored voice, "Oh really, Sylvia. More histrionics? Sounds as if your daughter has taken over in that department."

"Shut up, Ivan. The whole thing is ruined."

"And it's my fault."

"For once, no. It's Carol Woodford's fault. She's been flirting with poor Myrtle's—"

She was interrupted by Dr. Denning's laughter. Once started, he seemed unable to stop. He leaned his handsome head back exposing the manly throat, and laughed and laughed.

Outside, Reggie Bradbury lifted his head hurriedly and listened in astonishment and mounting horror to Myrtle's explicit denunciation of her friend.

"I say," he murmured. "Is she really . . . I mean, it's a bit steep, isn't it? Wedding day and all."

"Well. Perhaps Carol went too far." Liv did not want to be interrupted at this stage in the proceedings, but she was not entirely displeased at what was happening. It might precipitate events. She suspected that Reggie Bradbury would not be averse to following in his friend's footsteps quite soon, and she knew that she had already made a big impression. A few years ago he would have been another cross in her school rough note book. She waited until Myrtle's voice died away, leaning on Reggie as if her legs could not support her, gazing through the shifting curtain of willow in case anyone decided to come into the garden.

He said uncomfortably, "Look. Perhaps we'd better go inside now. It sounds as if there is a situation to be retrieved." He tried to laugh. "And as best man, I suppose I should be the one—"

"All right, Reggie." Liv sighed deeply. "Dear Reggie. So thoughtful." She leaned more heavily. "I knew immediately that you were the protective dependable type. What I didn't know was that you would be able to deprive little me of the use of my legs!" She laughed and let her knees sag. He had to hold her up and then she sort of fell back at the waist and her chest pushed against him, almost out of the sweetheart neckline of her bridesmaid's dress. He breathed quickly and suddenly kissed her again, less circumspectly.

And then the unthinkable happened. A breeze lifted the curtain of willow, and there was her mother crossing the lawn purposefully. She saw them. She stopped. Then she advanced very quickly.

"Olive! What are you up to? How dare you! My God, your father has gone off with—with that woman, and now you—!" She grabbed Liv's arm. "As for you, young man, all I can say is, if you go around practically ravishing every young girl you've just met, you're asking for trouble!"

Reggie stammered, "Mrs. . . . er . . . Baker . . . I do assure you I've never done anything like this before in my life!"

Liv put her hands to her face and began to cry.

Mrs. Baker said, "Then I hope your intentions are absolutely—"

Liv removed her hands and moaned, "Ma . . . *please!*"

But Reggie said, "Absolutely. Completely. Absolutely."

Mrs. Baker said, "Then in that case, I suppose . . ."

The curtain of leaves fell into place like a trap. For a while Liv's weeping was audible. Then it grew less and finally only Mrs. Baker's voice could be heard.

2

Bob Gallagher came to Britain from the States in 1951. He had spent some time in London during the war, and remembered the Albion where some of his fellow officers had stayed. So he booked in there.

Old Man Gallagher had died during the war, and Bob had returned home to find his mother trying to carry on the business—which she had started anyway. Bob had taken over immediately and in seven years had made Ideal Patterns the market leaders throughout the States. Now he wanted to go international.

His father had been brought up in the Bronx by his Irish family, and would have been content to live and die there. But he had taken a brawny and unbeautiful Scottish girl to a dance because his mother had known her mother when they were girls, and had been seduced by her in her tiny back kitchen when he took her home. When she announced that she was pregnant, he immediately volunteered to go to Europe and fight in the Kaiser's war. It made no difference. Her father was red-haired and enormous, and the Gallaghers were much too easy-going to put up a fight anyway, in spite of their Irish blood. Liam Gallagher married Kirsty Donaldson in 1917 just before he embarked for Europe, and Robert was born six months later.

They would have stayed poor all their lives just as the Gallaghers had always done, except that Kirsty had a talent and an energy inherited from her Scottish ancestors. The talent was in making clothes. She could cut out a dress with a few basic measurements, and the dress would fit perfectly, hang delightfully, and take less material than you would think possible. Kirsty supplemented the family income nicely until Hildie came along and soon after, Leone. Then it was all a bit too much for her and she began to make paper patterns for other people to sew. They sold like hot cakes. The family moved to Queens and then Connecticut. The children went to good schools. Bob married and divorced and had lots of love affairs. Hildie and Leone married well. Hildie and her husband, George, bought a farm in Connecticut and started to raise a family. Leone married an industrialist from Detroit and moved away. Bob went to war and had lots more affairs.

When he returned home he took his mother to see old Dr. Murdoch in the Bronx—the only doctor she trusted. He confirmed what they all knew: she had cancer of the liver. When she died, Bob already held the reins of the family firm. Suddenly, all he had achieved so far in life seemed pointless. He threw himself into making Ideal Patterns one of the success stories of the decade. He had inherited some of his mother's thriftiness as well as his father's wandering eye, and he decided to stay at the Albion because he realised it was value for money.

The first person he saw when he signed the register was Monica. She was then twenty-two; her gypsy good looks had settled into a kind of aristocratic sophistication. She reminded Bob of pictures he had seen of Winston Churchill's mother. It pleased him to think that he might transplant an English girl into American society, just as Randolph Churchill had transplanted American Jenny into his English background. Besides all that, he had to have her.

Dilly and Gander were still at the Albion, otherwise he might have won Monica during that visit. But they took their chaperonage very seriously, and although she virtually ran the hotel, she paid lip service to them in everything. And Monica seemed a cold fish. In spite of her Latin good looks and sultry eyes, he sensed the ice maiden in her. This made her more exciting than ever. A paradox; an enigma; an anomaly.

He lined up some appointments. Harrods and Liberty were out this time around, but there were other shops which could build up a reputation for him, and next year or maybe the year after, the others would come running. He concentrated on shops in Kensington High Street; small, select outlets glad to be associated with a large American company. And in the evenings, after dinner, he talked to Monica about his aspirations. And she listened. He thought it was because she was interested in his money, and he did not mind. After all, it was one of his interests too. She told the proprietress of the hotel about Ideal Patterns, and she was unexpectedly helpful. It turned out that she had been a dressmaker before the war and was able to put him on to some useful contacts.

By asking discreet and individual questions of Mr. and Mrs. Gosling, he could piece together some of Monica's background. She was an adopted child who had never got on with her family. That suited him well—he had no wish to support strings of hangers-on. Some good mutual friend had put her in touch with her employers when she was leaving school, and they had decided to train her to take on the hotel when they retired. So although she was interested in his money, she was by no means desperate for it. Old Mr. Gosling had a way of dropping hints, with one eye closed, that led Bob to believe Monica was probably the illegitimate offspring of a duke. Or maybe that was wishful thinking. She had style. And if Ideal Patterns were going world-wide, he would need a classy wife. And a good mother for his children. He wanted a family. He wanted . . . an establishment. Monica was ideal, in every way.

Monica resisted him without too much effort. Practically all the men who came to the Albion on their own made a pass at her, and she was adept at rebuffing them without giving offence. Even if they came back often, she rarely had any further trouble with them. What she did have was respect, and this was terribly important to her. She knew she was good at her job; she had suggested to Gander that some of the profits could be ploughed back swiftly into refurbishing the hotel after the long and arid war years, and the rooms at the Albion bore witness to her newly restrained taste. She never curled her hair or wore obvious make-up now. The colours of walls and carpets chosen by her were just as delicate as her own appearance. Gander got his licence; at her suggestion he extended the lounge into the long walled back garden so that guests could sit in the sun on the windiest of days. Monica saw him through it all; she insisted that he and Dilly should spend a week in Brighton when the builders were in. The decorators were practically locked in whichever room they were doing so that Gander would not be bothered by them. She cushioned the Goslings and the guests alike.

In 1952 Bob came back to the Albion. This time he had dinner with one of the directors of Harrods. He invited him back to the Albion and consulted Monica about the menu. After the meal, he introduced her to his guest.

"Miss Cook. She runs this place. It's kinda special—don't you agree?"

The V.I.P. did agree, and took a card on the way out. Dilly and Gander were impressed; Monica smiled coolly at Bob. But she too was impressed by his strategy, and before he went back to the States she accompanied him to the theatre to see *Oklahoma.*

The following year he came to England with most of the rest of the world to see the Coronation. At great expense he booked two places at a window on the route and asked Monica to come with him. He was put out when she declined.

"Surely you'll take time off to see the procession?"

He had thought she would have to show some gratitude if he'd bought her a seat, they were unobtainable on that special June the second. For the first time he began to wonder if she would ever succumb.

She said, "Of course. But I want to be with everyone else. I'm going to find a pitch tomorrow afternoon and stay overnight." She smiled at him. "You've lots more ladies to take to the Coronation, Mr. Gallagher."

"You're darned right."

But his annoyance could not hold out against those black eyes of hers, and he said ruefully, "But there's only one I want to be with for this special occasion. And please call me Bob."

"That would mean you'd call me Monica," she said. Her smile widened. "Why don't you come and pitch a camp with me? It will be much more fun than standing in a window. Bob."

His good-looking, open, Irish-American face split into a wide grin.

"Are you asking, Monica?"

She laughed assent.

"Then I'm coming," he finished.

And he managed to sell his window seats for twice what he had given for them. With some of the profit he bought her a pure silk scarf. She protested, of course—you could always tell a British lady by the fact that she refused presents from a man. He told her it was an old American custom—giving presents when it wasn't a birthday. "We call it an un-birthday present," he said solemnly. And she laughed. He was certain, then, that it would be all right.

Later he was to shock his sisters with the confession that he and his wife had slept together before they were married. He never made that kind of remark in front of Monica, however; her sense of humour was definitely lacking in that department. He might have had reservations about her mothering the large family he wanted to begin as soon as possible, except that as soon as the newly-crowned queen had gone by in her coach, Monica forgot herself enough to throw her arms around his neck and kiss him. And that kiss spoke volumes. She herself drew back from it, startled. Bob would not let her go. He held her by the waist, forcing her to be totally aware of him. And she was aware.

It made her defences all the stronger. Bob eventually gave in after three furious days of intense courtship, and asked her to marry him. Her reply was off-putting, to say the least. "I can't, Bob. I just can't."

"Why not? You can't deny we get on—"

"Oh yes. I like you. Enormously. But you see . . . you're American."

"You don't want to live in the States? Honey, you'll love it. And I'm making enough for us to live half the year there, and half here. Suits me."

"It's not that. It's something else. You wouldn't understand." She made a feeble attempt to explain. "After the war, so many girls got out of the country by marrying Americans. G.I. brides. You know."

"I don't get it. The war has been over for eight years, for God's sake."

"I nearly did that. Married a G.I. So that I could get out of England. Then I got this job with the Goslings. And things were better."

"You were that desperate?" He put an arm around her shoulders and felt her stiffen. "Poor kid. It must have been rough for you. But surely you're not going to make me suffer because you played around with a crazy idea for a couple of months?"

"Yes. No. I mean, I vowed I'd always look after myself. Not

expect a man to do it for me." She gave an embarrassed laugh. "You're too well off, Bob. If you didn't have a bean—"

"Can't you see that's why I want you? A lot of girls would be after my money. Listen, kiddo. You want to be independent and so do I. Can't we be independent together?"

"Bob. You're incorrigible. Can't you take no for an answer?"

"If I did, I wouldn't be a millionaire now."

She took a little breath. "A millionaire?"

"Sure. I could stay at the Ritz or the Savoy. I chose to stay at the Albion."

She was silent. Suddenly he wondered what the hell he was doing getting down on his knees to this little slip of a girl who had no background, no money . . . who the hell did she think she was?

He snapped, "Okay, honey. I'll not worry you any more."

He went out and found himself a girl and came back the next day just to say goodbye. She was white-faced and as jealous as all hell. He could feel it in the palm of her hand when she shook his.

He said, "No kiss, honey?"

"You can buy plenty of kisses, Mr. Gallagher. You don't need mine."

He forced a laugh. "True, Miss Cook. Very true."

He stayed away for four months, determined not to go crawling back. Then he did. It was no big soul-searing decision. He simply went into the office one morning and told his secretary to book him a flight. He spent three nights at the Ritz sleeping off the trip and making all the arrangements for a special marriage licence. On the fourth night he went to the Albion to seek her out. She was super-vising a Bonfire Bean Feast. Guy Fawkes was unknown in America, but he was glad he'd found her in the midst of another celebration. Her guard was less fierce at such times. When she saw him in the light of the bonfire flames, her face came to life for an instant. He went straight to her, took her hand, and led her into the deep shadow by the garden wall. She struggled against him, but she would not make a scene with so many people within earshot, and he kissed her until she began to respond. Then he held her away from him.

"I've got a ring and a licence," he said in a low voice. "If you won't marry me, say so now, and I promise you'll never see me again."

She was genuinely distressed. "Bob. Please. I can't make up my mind like that. Really."

"Do you love me?"

"I think so. I've missed you."

"Then that's the answer."

"It's not so simple. You've consoled yourself, admit it."

"All right. I'll admit it. But if I marry you, there won't be any others."

"How can I know that?"

"By keeping me happy."

He drew her to him and kissed her again. He hadn't been wrong. There was fire beneath the ice.

She pushed at him. "You're trying to rush me."

"Yes. It's now or never. I mean it, Monica. I've never begged."

"All right." She looked at him. In the shadow her eyes were black coals. "You don't have to beg now, Bob. I'm not sure about getting married, but you don't have to beg."

His face opened with surprise. "I don't get it. Most women *want* to get married." He kissed her violently, almost angrily. "I want to marry you, Monica. I want a wife. Kids. I want to found a—a dynasty!"

"Oh Bob. I know." He suddenly realised the black coals were shining. She was crying. "Listen. I have to see my family. I'm not sure. But I have to see them—"

"Why for Christ's sake? What hold have they got over you? I'll come with you. We'll blow them apart—"

"I must go on my own."

"Tomorrow. Will you go tomorrow?"

"Yes. Oh, Bob. Yes. Will you wait for me?"

"Tomorrow night. I'll wait until tomorrow night."

She was dismayed again. "They live in Birmingham! It'll take me three hours to get there. And then I've got to talk to them . . ."

"Tomorrow night."

He kissed her again. And after the party she took him to her room. He was disappointed to find she wasn't a virgin, but, after all, neither was he. He had never known anyone like her. He had thought by taking her by storm he was the victor in their odd little game. But as he lay in her bed, he knew the tables were turned on him. He would wait for a week—even a year—if she insisted.

Monica was under no illusions about Bob Gallagher. She found him very attractive and a good companion and a marvellous lover; but she knew that his energetic and optimistic attitude to everything stemmed from an innate superficiality. It was good to be with him when everything was going well; she wondered how he would be in an emergency. When he had told her that there would be no other women so long as she "kept him happy," she had sensed an underlying threat. She knew she could never tell him about Elizabeth and Carol; the Cooks and Gilly. He wouldn't be able to take that kind of emotional tangle; he'd run a mile. And he was attractive enough to make her hold her peace.

It was not his money. Strangely, Monica was not ambitious in a worldly sense. She wanted money, not for power, but for security against other people's power. She wanted quite desperately to be loved and cherished, and to belong to a family. And she wanted a suitable father for her children.

Bob could supply all her needs. He wanted to supply them. It seemed such a simple decision. But there was always Gilly.

She caught the Birmingham train at Euston by the skin of her teeth. She had left Bob sleeping; if she was back by dinner time as he had stipulated, she would make it up to him. If not . . . then it wouldn't matter because it would mean that Gilly still wanted her. And wanted Elizabeth too. He couldn't have known about Elizabeth, no-one could have known. Perhaps she had been unfair in not telling him. Maybe he had thought she didn't love him any more when she left home so abruptly and went to live with Cass and Mrs. Woodford. Maybe that was why he'd never got in touch with her, never even asked Mrs. Woodford for her London address. Maybe he'd retreated into silence because he felt hurt. When she told him . . . when she told him what had happened . . . surely everything would be all right again and she would thank Bob Gallagher for forcing her into this journey.

She took off the silk scarf Bob had given her for her unbirthday present last summer and slid it into the sleeve of her new donkey-brown coat, folded the lot neatly and put it on the luggage rack. She had packed a small overnight bag, just in case. After all, she would surely visit Mrs. Woodford whatever happened. And then she'd probably stay overnight. Or something.

She sat down and watched the telegraph wires swaying past the compartment window. She dared not think too much about the future. So she switched her mind to Mrs. Woodford and Cass. And Elizabeth.

She had said, right at the beginning, that Elizabeth belonged to the Woodfords; she would not take the role of mysterious and ubiquitous "aunt." Nor would history repeat itself yet again— Elizabeth would always know she was adopted, and she would know she had been chosen for love and not for money.

Monica caught herself in mid-sigh, and straightened her spine in the defiant way she had never lost. She remembered that on one of her rare visits to Northfield Mrs. Woodford had said hesitantly, "Monica dear, would you mind—be hurt—if Cass and I called Elizabeth Bessie? She looks like a Bessie. She's round and dark and giggly."

Carol had put in quickly, "Not Bessie Bunterish! She's just so cuddly!"

Monica had said, "Look. Both of you. She is yours. Legally and morally. If you recall, I did not even want to suggest a name." She looked straight at Cass. Dear Cass, flushed and anxious even then. "I like Bessie. But if I hated it, it's nothing to do with me."

They hadn't replied to that. Perhaps they had known that she would never be able to cut through the cord that bound her to her baby. She caught herself sighing again; it was no good, she didn't like the name Bessie.

The ticket inspector slid open the door of the compartment and she fumbled in her bag for her ticket. "Change at New Street," he intoned. "Stopper to Bromsgrove." She took back her punched ticket, feeling a rush of adrenaline to her heart. She was going home. That was the immediate future; she was going home.

The train was passing the university and she stood up to check her hair in the mirror. She dressed it in a "doughnut" on top of her head these days and sat her hats slightly forward. In the New Look black dresses she wore at the hotel she looked like a ballerina; in her new donkey-brown hat and coat she gave gave an impression of subdued sophistication that pleased her a great deal. She had left Northfield a frightened schoolgirl, prone to too much make-up and too many curls. She was returning a mature woman with un-mistakably good taste. She drew on her gloves, shouldered her bag, and picked up her case. Dammit, she wanted to be married and have a family, and she'd got two strings to her bow . . . most girls would envy her.

The train drew in at New Street. It was colder than in London, and it had been raining. Everything smelled of sulphur; it was a familiar smell that stoked the excitement inside her. She hadn't felt like this for years. She loved London, loved the fact that she had carved a niche for herself, but this place was where life had started.

She got on the Bromsgrove stopper and sat on one of the sideways seats that would give her a view of the canal and then the school. When she emerged on to the high platform and walked down the steps to Turves Green, it was as if she had never been away. The remains of the local bonfire charred the grass and the council estate spread around it like a small village. Every tree was familiar, the small row of shops where Gilly had had his hair cut each month was still there, and the brook which eventually meandered on to the heath and past the Haunted House. Children ran up and down the street collecting the dead fireworks from the night before; they were well wrapped up—quite literally—old scarves bound their necks and chests and were pinned at the back, and what looked like dirty crepe bandages were wound from wrists to fingers. Monica remembered reading somewhere that the Birmingham city council were involved in a big scheme to rehouse some of the slum dwellers from the blitzed city centre. Certainly, even with clothes rationing, the small children of her time had looked less deprived than these.

Number thirty-one was more run-down than she remembered, too. The gate had been propped open because a hinge was off and a bulbous Standard Vanguard was jacked up on the drive, one wheel missing. The front lawn was scuffed bare and muddy, and the holly hedge which she had loved was shrivelled and without a single berry. She hesitated, glancing at her watch, wondering who would be where. If her mother still had her job at the cafe along the Bristol Road, she would be there doing her morning stint. Perhaps her father and both boys would be at the Longbridge plant. That would be unusual; they tended to opt for differing shifts so that they could have the house to themselves when they were home. It was Saturday but they invariably worked at weekends to boost their wages with overtime.

There was only one way to find out. She eased her new coat past the Vanguard and knocked on the front door. The paint was chipped and the transom cracked. It had been like that when she left in 1945.

Nothing happened. She knocked again and heard, faintly, a bellow. Then someone's footsteps came down the stairs. The door opened and there was Giles.

He did not recognise her. She should have unbuttoned her coat or taken off her hat. Even then, with her black hair pinned up and her discreet make-up, she was so different from the flash young miss who had tried to look like Rita Hayworth. She forced a smile.

"Hello, Gilly."

Her voice had changed too, but she deliberately injected a Brummy accent and the old uncompromising hardness. Anyway, only she called him Gilly. To everyone else he was simply Gill.

"Good God Almighty!" He took a step back as if she'd hit him. "If it isn't . . . is it our Mon? God, it's our Mon! Where in the hell have you sprung from?"

Pleasure lightened his heavy features and he looked young again. But his eyes were smaller than she remembered. Everything was smaller than she remembered.

Her smile became slightly more natural; unexpectedly she felt sorry for him.

"London. The address I sent Mum."

"For Christ's sake. Come on in. You've got a bag. Give it here!"

He leaned forward and took it from her, and for an instant their shoulders touched. She imagined that through her dress and coat she could feel the heat of him. He had always been warm. In the war when there had been few blankets, and Mrs. Cook had thought hot-water bottles to be decadent and on the side of Hitler, Gilly had been so warm in bed. She had crept in with him when she was ten years old and shaking with fear as the enemy bombers went over. And then a year later, when her periods began, she had been given the boxroom to herself and Gilly came to her.

He hefted the bag into the front room which was kept tidy for visitors. "You've not come for long then, our Mon?"

"Was that why you took the bag? So you could tell how heavy it was?" She tried to make it jokey, but they were bitter words.

"Just wondered. I've got your room now, see." He glanced at her and she wondered whether he was about to throw his arms around her in welcome. He didn't. He cleared his throat and said heartily, "So. You've come to see us at last, little Sis. How are you then? How's it going?"

"Fine. And you?" She moved around the table and looked out of the window. This was terrible. Worse than she could have imagined.

"Fine. Doing double shifts when I can. With overtime I can bring home twenty quid a week."

He spoke without boastfulness and she wondered if he was telling her that he could support her now. That they could take Elizabeth back and make a home together.

Then he laughed. "Mind you, I can spend it too! I was always a good spender, weren't I, our Mon? That's mine out there. Getting new wheels for it, then I shall be off every Saturday night—you won't see me for dust."

She smiled blindly at the window. It really was amusing, the way she had fooled herself.

"Sounds fun," she said. "You haven't changed, Gilly. You were always fun."

He said eagerly, "That were it, weren't it, Sis? We had great laughs together. God, I missed that when you left. D'you remember Dad got me in at the munitions place so I wouldn't be called up, and we began practising my limp!"

He guffawed heartily, but she wondered now what had been so funny. Bob had fought in the war. She was suddenly proud of that fact.

She said quickly, trying to excuse Gilly, "You were only fourteen then."

"Yes, but like you said, the sooner I got used to having a limp the better. What between that and the munitions factory, they hardly looked at me when it came to the medical!"

"No." She remembered her relief. She had still thought he was her real brother then. She couldn't have lived without him. The guilt they shared each night had been a further bond. When he told her she was adopted, some of that guilt had gone; and perhaps some of the bond too.

He started to limp around the tiny sitting room, thrusting out one side of his body in imitation of Alfie Crump, the old snobbie who had a dislocated hip and rolled around Northfield like a wallowing boat; a local character.

"See? It's like riding a bike. You never forget. And the war's been over eight years!"

She turned to watch him and tried to laugh and he said quickly, "God, you're still beautiful, our Mon. I thought at first you'd changed for the worse, but I was wrong."

She knew she ought to treat that remark lightly. Maybe whip off her hat and show him her Hayworth hair-do had gone. Or dip a curtsey and say thank you, kind sir. But she did neither. She was turned to stone, looking at him. She forgot he was smaller and still immature and probably a coward. She remembered the warmth and security of his arms, his laughter in her ear, the feel of his mat of curls beneath her hand.

He said roughly, "Christ. Our Mon."

And still she said nothing.

It was only natural that he took her silence for acquiescence, because that was what it was. It was more than acquiescence, it was an invitation. His arms went round her and his face crushed hers, knocking off the hat, sending the coronet of hair tumbling to her shoulders. And although the walls behind which she had entrenched herself ever since her pregnancy were shoved aside so shockingly, she let the whole thing go on. She let him take possession of her as he had always done. As if she belonged to him by right. She waited for his left hand to hold the back of her head steady. And it did. She waited for the right hand to attempt to cup her breast through the thickness of winter clothing. And it did. She waited for the full mouth to part on hers and the tongue to demand an entrance. And both those things happened. He was so familiar, so much part of her past, there was nothing strange about it. She was dissolving into him as she had always done. This was why she had come to Birmingham.

And then, from the next room, came the bellow she had heard when she first rang the bell. Gilly withdrew his head and grinned at her without embarrassment. They were the same height so he must have shrunk.

"Gus," he said. "You'd better come and show yourself, otherwise he'll say something he shouldn't to Mum."

She stared at him dazedly, unable to pull away from that moment as he had done. He pecked at her parted lips.

"Come on, Mon. Pull yourself together."

And he laughed. And in that laugh there was a note of triumph.

He opened the door to the back room and announced her uproariously.

"Our Mon! Proper growed-up now, but just as gorgeous as ever!"

She hardly knew Gus. He was much older than Gilly and had always been "out at work" when she was home. Also, unlike his clever young brother, he had not escaped the war. When she went to the Albion he had been in Malaya.

She wouldn't have recognised him from the old snaps she had seen. He was fat and squat like a buddha, and his hairline had receded to a monkish fringe. She did some calculations as she held out a formal hand to him. He must be well over thirty. He looked much older.

"I'd have answered the door myself, girl. Thought it was one of Gill's mates to help with the car. Well. You have grown and no mistake. Just a little thing you was. Now you're almost as tall as that friend of yours."

"Carol Woodford," Gilly supplied. "She's away in France so you won't see her." He glanced at Monica as if checking her reaction to that piece of information. Did he guess about Elizabeth after all?

"Oh, I've lost touch with everyone," she replied airily. "I was never any good at writing letters, and I've been busy." She took a breath. "Actually, I'm thinking of going abroad. This is . . . might be . . . a farewell visit."

Gus said, "Abroad, eh? Good for you, girl. Doing well for yourself I reckon. Where you goin' exactly?"

"America. Actually."

Gilly mimicked, "Oh, jolly dee. Ackcherly."

Monica flushed, but Gus took the teasing at face value and nodded lugubriously. "Aye. Plain to see you're not one of us, girl. Tall and skinny for a start. And a few brains too."

"Speak for yourself, our Gus!" Gilly wasn't teasing now. "I'm doing all right, thanks very much. Take a look out of the window at the Vanguard. And I'm taller than you. And this is all muscle!" He pounded at his chest, Tarzan-style.

Monica felt a helplessness near to despair. He was awful; and she still loved him.

She said desperately, "I suppose I'd better go and have a word with Mum. Is she still at the caff?"

"Aye. Come on. We'll all go."

Gus went into the hall and opened the cupboard under the stairs. Clothes fell out on to the floor. He selected two overcoats and gave one to Gilly. They trooped into the street. Monica was painfully aware of her own clothes. She should have remembered her erstwhile family much better and worn higher heels, a short jacket, costume jewellery.

They crowded into the tiny steamy cafe on the Bristol Road where Mrs. Cook worked. If Monica had wanted to create a sensation she would have been well satisfied by her mother's range of emotions at the sight of her long-lost adopted daughter. Beginning with shock and amazement, she went quickly from tearful delight to recriminations.

"Why haven't you bin to see us before? Ingratitude is one fault I cannot forgive, Monica. I'm sorry, but that's the way I'm made. Charlie and me, we brought you up like our own—you wouldn't have known otherwise if that great lummock hadn't told you—" She flipped a dirty tea-towel across Gilly's curls, and he pretended to cower. "And how do you repay us? Immediately you start earning, you're off! What benefit is that to us? I ask you! Sixteen years I slave to bring you up nicely. Grammar school—yes, I know she got a scholarship, Gill, but there was the uniform and all the outings and trying to keep up with her snobby friends!" She collapsed in a chair and fumbled in her overall pocket for cigarettes. "When I see that Mrs. Woodford in town with that adopted kid of hers, I want to tell her a thing or two. No, I'm sorry, Gill, I've got to have my way. That's the way I am. I don't harbour grudges. I up and out with them." She lit up and drew ecstatically on her cigarette. Then she leaned back, opened her eyes and smiled at the three of them. "There. I've got it off my chest. We'll say no more about it, Mon. You're home again, and that's all that matters."

There was a little silence as the boys waited for Monica to confess that she was off to America. She said nothing.

Mrs. Cook's smile widened. "Listen. Sausage and chips on me. Okay? There's half my wages gone for the week, but I can't help it. And bread and butter. And a pot of tea." She stubbed out her cigarette and stood up, laughing. "My God, Cookie, stop it, you generous, crazy fool. Well . . ." She made for the kitchen. " 'Tisn't every day your long-lost daughter rolls up."

"She's cracked," Gilly said proudly. "Bet you'd forgotten how cracked she was, hadn't you, our Mon?"

"No wonder she's cracked, living with our dad," Gus said. He shook his head at Monica. "You won't get much out of him when you see him tonight, Mon. It's as much as he can do to open his mouth and shove in his food these days. Don't know how she puts up with it."

Gilly said, "He was always like that. You were in the army so you didn't know him like me and our Mon. When Mum was fire-watching and Dad just sat in front of the fire, looking, it was like being in a loony bin. Good job we had each other, eh Sis?"

He grinned conspiratorially, and after a second's hesitation she found herself grinning back. Then the sausages and chips arrived, and Mrs. Cook sat down again to watch them eat. It was so familiar: like sliding into a very old and threadbare pair of slippers. Gilly's arm around her; her mother talking non-stop as if frightened to let a silence gather around them; greasy food and greasy smells; Gilly smiling; and the addition of Gus who seemed now strangely avuncular.

She could slip into the pattern of it all so easily. Her voice, carefully controlled for school, could slide up a register and become nasal and Brummy. She could dip her bread into the sauce, blow on the tea, suck her fingers after picking up a chip. They would accept her again and find a place for her, and she and Gilly would take up where they had left off. No fuss, no big row. No wedding.

"Yowse looking solemn, our Mon," commented Mrs. Cook. "Penny for 'em."

"Just remembering old times." Monica forced a smile, then picked up a chip, ate it, and sucked her fingers.

"Ah. It's real nice having you back, love. I'll put up a bed in Gus' room, and Gilly can go back in there. You can 'ave your own room again."

Monica did not look at Gilly. The clock was slowly and inexorably being turned back.

Afterwards, Gus went to watch Aston Villa play at home, and Mrs. Cook disappeared into the kitchen.

Gilly said, "We'd better get back. Too cold to wander around, and if we run into the Bakers or the Dennings, that will be it."

Monica certainly did not want to see Liv or Myrtle, but she had half-planned to call on Mrs. Woodford. She knew it wasn't the time now. On the other hand she did not want to go back to the mean little house in Turves Green.

"Gilly. Did I ever take you to see the Haunted House?"

"Haunted what? Come off it, our Mon. You're a big girl now."

"No, really. I'll show you if you like."

He was easy about it, certain that very soon now they would

make love. So they wandered up through the old village, past the stocks and the ancient church, and kept going into West Heath road. Gilly did not take her hand, but when they came to the stile that led to the brook he swung her down and kept an arm around her waist.

"We waded along here. Liv Baker and Myrtle Denning and me." She did not want to mention Carol by name. "It was this time of year actually. Cold as charity. We were glad to find this old house."

"I remember Liv Baker. You and she hung around together a lot. Saturday afternoons window-shopping. Or were you shopping for something else?"

He made her sound like a street-walker. But wasn't that basically why she and Liv had tarted themselves up and paraded the shopping area. She'd had Gilly then, but she had still seemed to need the odd "conquest" to prove herself. Was that all Bob represented—the odd conquest?

It seemed to take a long time to reach the bend in the brook where the old labourer's cottage squatted among the willows and the wild uncultivated garden. It looked completely derelict now; the front door was gone and several slates were missing, while others hung drunkenly at odd angles. Gilly went first, curious but wary of rotten floorboards. They explored downstairs, holding their noses but still tasting the smell. Door frames and floorboards had been ripped away, presumably for firing. The sink was missing in the kitchen and there was no glass in any of the windows.

Monica retreated into the hall. The gaping space into the foundations was still a deterrent to anyone going upstairs. She giant-strode it as she'd always done, and looked up at the stair-lid. It was either raised or missing. She could see the familiar ceiling of the bedroom and that was intact. She took the stairs two at a time, crossed the landing, and went through the open door.

"It's the same!" She ran across to the stair-lid and looked down at Gilly. "It's just the same, Gilly. Just like it was on V.E. day when I came to tell Carol . . ." she broke off. Gilly was staring up at her and the truth was suddenly clear between them. He had turned away from it for nine years; pretended it hadn't happened. Now he knew. She waited, holding her breath, praying that he would take her in his arms, or tell her that they would go right away with Elizabeth and make a new life.

And then he laughed, that knowing laugh of his that she had

always thought was confident and happy. And he said, "So. It was a kid, was it? That's why you did a bunk. You told Carol Woodford and her old lady looked after you. I did wonder." He laughed again, this time with a ring of pride or triumph. "Well done, our kid. Well done. I might have guessed you would come out of it okay."

He started up the stairs and she gripped the edge of the lid and wondered if she might be sick.

He entered the room and she heard him collapse on to the bed. She turned to look at him. He was grinning broadly and expectantly.

He said, "Come on, our Mon. We've messed about enough. Come 'ere."

She did not move; she began, quite consciously, to marshal her strength.

"It's all right, our Mon," he said, sensing a withdrawal in her. "You're older now. You know what to do. There won't be any more babies to get rid of."

It was the last straw. She remembered now that there had been times in the past when she had hated him. Love and hate. Inseparable. She forced a laugh.

"Oh Gilly. You haven't changed either, have you? Just a few more slates missing perhaps!" She let the laugh begin to gurgle away. "Yes, I'm older. And just a bit wiser. And I know what to do."

She took off her hat and scooped her hair to the top of her head again. She stuck pins in her mouth and began to secure the hair, one pin at a time, talking through them, making it all sound very simple.

"If it *had* been my baby, d'you think I'd have let it come back to this dump?" She shook her head. "Oh Gilly, I wasn't the little innocent you thought I was. I knew what to do in those days too, and I did it. There was no baby, big brother. Just boredom. Complete and utter boredom." She stabbed the last pin into place as if she were driving it into him. Then she swung her hat casually from one hand. Protect Elizabeth. She had to protect Elizabeth.

"Why do you think I went to stay with Carol? To look after her, of course. Give her an alibi now and then. And to get away from number thirty-one!"

She sighed dramatically. "Gilly, I'd better confess. I'm getting married. To a rich American. That's why I'm off to the States. I wanted to say goodbye. And maybe have another fling!" She brushed past him. "But the old magic . . . it's gone, hasn't it? Even coming to this place hasn't resurrected it." She started down the stairs. "You're right, big brud, I am older. Older, and very much wiser. Come on. Let's get back to the house. I've got time for a cup of tea before my train goes."

He did not protest much. Oddly enough even that hurt. He caught her up when she reached the gate and walked half a pace behind her until they reached the road.

Then he said, "A rich American, eh? I might have guessed it."

She waited for the whiplash of scorn or petty jealousy. It did not come. They walked back to Turves Green in silence.

The Goslings, Gander and Dilly, came to the wedding, but Monica did not invite her parents nor Mrs. Woodford and Carol. Bob assumed there had been some big bust-up when she told her family of her marriage plans, and she did not enlighten him.

He said, "Listen honey, if you need a family, we'll cut our wrists and become blood brothers, like the Indians. How would that do? Huh?"

And she laughed and rubbed his nose with hers.

She said, "I'd like my own family, please Bob. How do you feel about children?"

She knew how he felt, but was surprised at his fervour.

"We can give them such a life, hon. We'll have an apartment in town and a place in the country—maybe near Hildie and George— you'll like Hildie and George. Our kids can ride and fish with the boys. Hildie and George have two boys. Oscar and Leo. Did I ever tell you about the time . . ."

She touched the back of his hand. He was at his most endearing when he talked about his sister. It made Monica feel guilty about what she was doing. Yet it opened the way to repay him for his overwhelming love.

"It sounds great, darling. But I'd like some girls as well. How about three girls and two boys?"

"I want more boys than girls, baby. I was the only boy in our family and it was hell. I want four boys and one girl."

She let herself be led into one of the silly arguments he enjoyed.

"I had two brothers, remember. I insist on three girls at least."

"Brazen hussy!" He kissed her and then kept kissing her.

Yes, she could repay him. She was good at sex and she would

be a wonderful mother too. She would forget all about Elizabeth. She would start again.

But on their wedding day there was a moment, as they stood before the registrar, when she knew she was wrong. It was only a moment, and when she recalled it later she had to smile to herself, because she of all people knew that you could make things work properly just by sticking at them.

3

*I*t was spring in Paris, and it was raining. Cass wondered whether you could call March spring. It was only four weeks until her mother and Bessie would be coming over for Easter, and that was most definitely spring in her calendar.

She smiled as she glanced out at the grey sky. Things were going so well now, she could barely remember her terrible distress of three years ago. Luck had been with her on that first assignment to Paris: she had handled it well, and when the firm had suggested opening a permanent office here, it had been assumed from the outset that the job was hers. She'd never have taken it if it hadn't been for Myrtle's cruel words. She had run away, no doubt about that. Not the best reason for taking a job. But it had worked out. It had worked out splendidly.

She glanced over to where Gaby sat, typing fiercely. Gaby was another stroke of luck. She had been the first applicant for the job, and though she was everything Carol was not—pert and pretty and an incurable clock-watcher—she suited Carol ideally. They came together at nine each morning and went their separate ways at five-thirty. Carol had no wish for any more close friendships.

Gaby's other advantage was that she was married to a journalist working for *La Planète* as a foreign correspondent. He specialised in French colonial affairs and had twice put Carol in touch with likely authors. It was a happy coincidence that augured well for the job.

The manuscript he was delivering that afternoon had been written by someone on Carol's own special list, however. She had met Clive Hubert at a dinner given by the British Council; he was on his way to the Shott Plateau of Algeria to teach the Arabs how to extend their animal husbandry into arable farming. Carol had suggested the book and Clive had very diffidently agreed to "give it a go." And he had done just that. Jean-Claude Durant, Gaby's reporter husband, was bringing it back some time today after a stint in Algiers.

He arrived at four o'clock when Carol was drinking her English tea. As usual, Gaby completely ignored his entrance into the office; they were an odd couple. He went to her desk and dropped a kiss on top of her gamine haircut, then turned immediately to Carol, smiling warmly.

"I have it here." He put his briefcase in front of her and extended his hand. As usual she held it as briefly as possible and did not quite meet his intelligent black eyes.

"It is not absolutely complete. He will bring the final chapter when he comes out next month."

Carol thanked him formally. If he had not been quite so good-looking perhaps she could have been more natural. Though with Gaby sitting in the window, hitting the typewriter keys with unnecessary force, perhaps not. Gaby had not seen her husband for a month; he had been on a potentially dangerous assignment reporting on Algeria's struggle for independence, yet she did not even look round at him.

He grinned suddenly at Carol as if guessing her thoughts, and crept up behind his wife.

She said laconically, "I know you are there." She returned the typewriter carriage with a crash. "I am busy. I will see you in just one hour from now. Please go home, light the oven, pour drinks, wait."

Gaby spoke in English because of Carol, but her accent was so

48

French it was almost comic. Jean-Claude had no accent. Apparently he spoke Arabic without an accent too. Also German and Italian.

He replied to his wife in very colloquial French which Carol did not try to understand. Then he turned back to her desk.

"You will enjoy the book. And be surprised too." He looked at her speculatively. "Though I am never entirely certain how much you understand of the Algerian situation."

"Only what I read in the papers." Carol slid the bulky parcel out of the case with care. When she handled a manuscript she was always conscious she was handling part of someone else's mind, besides a year's work. In this case, rather more than a year. She smiled quickly. "And you newspaper people tell us only what you want us to know."

He shrugged. "Or what we are commanded to tell you. It is not always the same."

"You spoke of Clive getting out of Algeria. Is there—might there be—some difficulty in leaving?"

"Possibly. The country is a powder keg. Someone like Clive Hubert could light the fuse."

Carol opened a drawer in her desk, pushed aside pencils and erasers and a S.C.N.F. timetable and laid the manuscript carefully down. She stared at it. Jean-Claude was already by the door.

She said, "He—Clive—went there to teach agricultural husbandry. I should have thought the Algerians would be grateful." She knew Jean-Claude's political opinions from his newspaper articles. He was still a colonialist; Algeria was another part of France to him. She meant nothing inflammatory; quite the opposite. But she knew by the way Gaby's typewriter roller suddenly squeaked a protest that she had probably put her foot in it.

Jean-Claude shrugged. "Of course. Clive will be all right. But feeling runs high out there. And after Indo-China, Africa . . . perhaps we are too sensitive about Algeria. If the conference can happen in Geneva then perhaps our national pride will be . . ." Uncharacteristically he searched for an apt word and came up with "appeased." He went through the door, then stuck his head back into the room. "It is just that . . . when Clive gets back here, dissuade him from returning to Algeria. If you can. For his own good."

Carol looked at the closed door. Gaby continued to type.

Carol said, "Gaby, I'm sorry."

"What for?" The girl did not stop her staccato stabbing. She underlined something and corrected herself. "I should say, for what?"

"Well . . . if I put my foot in it about Algeria." She smiled. "Made a faux pas."

Gaby whipped out the envelope, whirled her typist's chair and brought the letter to Carol's desk for signature all in one fluid movement. She was older than Carol but had the childish looks of Brigitte Bardot.

"Boulder Desh," she said emphatically. Carol correctly deciphered that as "balderdash" and smiled again. Gaby went on, "Jean-Claude is too much in the past." She struck an attitude. "The Free French Army, headquarters, Algiers." She made a very French sound of dismissal. "He should have been here through the war, in occupied Paris. It was not so bad. I am a realist. The word honour means nothing. To survive—that is what is important." She whirled her chair again and threw a crumpled waterproof cover over the typewriter. "But Jean-Claude is not so—so—fanatic—as you think. His writing in the newspapers has to be very . . ." she thumped her chest ". . . patriotic. But he is a realist like me in many ways." She went to the mirror and made a moue at her reflection. "He might think he married me to save me from certain death!" She rolled her eyes. "Ah yes, some people imagined I was a collaborator. Just because I was alive and well-fed! So Jean-Claude—who is the brave liberator, you remember—gave me his name and his protection!" She laughed. "But he was certainly a realist." Her reflected face became defiant. "I was nineteen and he wanted me."

She saw Carol's intense embarrassment and lifted her shoulders in a Gallic shrug of helplessness. "He wants Algérie for the French, but he knows it cannot be so. Eventually, everyone must be free to choose their own . . . damnation!"

She shrugged again and concentrated exclusively on her make-up, giving Carol time to collect herself, or rather to push the unwelcome images which Gaby had created right to the back of her mind.

At last Gaby was satisfied with her enchanting appearance. "Now I go and leave you in piss to read this manuscript from Monsieur Hubert." She shouldered her bag. "Do not picture the passionate reunion, please, Carol. Jean-Claude will not go to the flat. He will not light the gas. He will go to the Left Bank and sit in Montmartre with other journalists and they will talk for a long time." She turned with a smile of pleasure. "Which will give me time to cook his favourite coq-au-vin and soak in a bath, yes?"

"Yes. Of course, Gaby. You go. And thank you."

Cass watched the whirlwind departure of her secretary and then caught sight of her reflection as she sank back in her chair. She was as plain as Gaby was pretty. There was nothing to be done about her long face and lank hair, and she had ceased to make any efforts. Everyone wore their hair very short in Paris, and even back home she noticed most women had cut off their shoulder-length bobs. Rita Hayworth was out and Jean Simmons was in. Carol's concession to fashion was to roll her mouse-brown locks into a bun that missed being chic by a mile. She did not mind. She was quite astute enough to know that her dilapidated look removed any kind of threat from her appearance. Her face and thin figure were overtly intelligent, and could have put people off. Her hairstyle and the way she wore her clothes cancelled all that.

She smiled helplessly as her gaze swept on around the tiny office. It wasn't much, but it was in a good address just off the Avenue Foch; the building had an imposing foyer and a fatherly concierge. And it was hers. Her office. She had hired Gaby, and she could fire her tomorrow if she wanted to. Her smile inverted at that thought; being the person she was, she could not fire Gaby tomorrow however much she might want to. Unless she caught her setting fire to the place or forging cheques or something. But that wasn't the point. She, Carol Woodford, was twenty-six years old, and in spite of looking like nothing on earth, being over-diffident and unambitious, she had come this far. She represented Universal Publications in France. She was their sole representative. And she hardly knew how it had happened.

Another self-deception: of course she knew how it had happened. Even now she became hot, then very cold, at the thought of the scene at Myrtle's wedding. She had had to get away from Northfield even if it did seem like desertion in the face of the enemy. Her mother had known. She had said, "Take the job. Bessie and I are all right here—that rumour won't go any further unless we all move. If we stay put we shall outlive it. We can see you every holiday—you can come home weekends. Take the job."

And Ralph Morrish had been delighted when she obtained translation rights from such different authors as Sartre and de Beauvoir—there had never been any question that the job was hers.

She had precious "clout" now. And Bessie was almost ten. She'd be changing schools quite soon, no reason at all why she shouldn't change to one in France.

Carol smiled at her own secret plans. She was negotiating directly with her authors these days and many of them lived in the south of France. If she could persuade Universal to let her open another office in Marseilles, she was in a position to buy a villa inland. Maybe on the edge of Provence. Just where the Alps and the flowers began. There were convent schools there; she had visited several of them over the past few months. Most of them took children of other faiths and respected those faiths. Bessie had been with her one day and they had watched the sisters taking a group of children on a nature walk. "They look like butterflies," Bessie had commented delightedly. And she had been right. The wide coifs flapping among the flowers had indeed looked like cabbage butterflies on the wing.

Carol stood up and went to the window, unwilling to let her thoughts go further. She must open that drawer and begin to read Clive Hubert's manuscript. But not yet. It might be awful, and she couldn't bear that.

It was raining. So much for spring. However the rain partially obscured the view which was euphemistically described as *interne;* in fact the window looked out on a massive air shaft. She stared up. The cloud was like a cork on the top of the shaft. It reminded her of that day she and Liv and Myrtle and Monica had found the Haunted House. It hadn't been raining then, but winter had pressed all around them, making the heath private and very personal. How simple life had been. In spite of the war there had been an inner purpose which almost amounted to peace. She toyed with the thought that war might be a projection of personal battles, a kind of externalisation of emotions too much for one soul to bear. Like funerals. Like weddings. But then, she hadn't been involved in the war. She knew nothing of its miseries.

She turned impatiently from her own feeble ideas and went to the drawer. She hadn't matured since V.E. day when she had vainly tried to reconcile her father's death with physical science. Surely she knew better now. Surely she knew that her stupid mental ramblings were a guard against other thoughts: speculations on the kind of marriage Jean-Claude and Gaby had. Thoughts of Jean-Claude himself.

She sat down and opened the drawer with unnecessary force. The string around the parcel defied her attempts to unknot it; she rummaged at the back of the drawer for scissors, and cut it. The brown paper was stiff and awkward and infuriating; she did not dare rip it in case it took some precious pages with it. Eventually the pile of foolscap was before her. She remembered Clive saying doubtfully, "If ever I do get anything on paper, will this size do? I've got so much of it from teaching days." And she had responded instantly, "Of course. Anything will do." Though it was hard on poor Gaby when it came to typing it up. But Clive needed reassurance. He was a brilliant teacher and the British Council had sent him into Africa several times to advise on agriculture. But he had not written a book before.

She read his first words: "It was almost dark when we arrived. The tiny mud hovels were silhouetted individually in this vast, flat land. I was conscious that we were in the sky; it was no longer above us, it was all around." Her eyes opened wider and she sat back in her chair. This was going to be all right. Clive Hubert could write.

Some time later, when the reading lamp was making a pool of brightness in the gloom, the telephone rang. Carol reached for it without taking her eyes from the page before her. It would be her visiting femme du ménage, asking why she was not at home yet. But it was Jean-Claude Durant.

"You are still there! I thought you might be. You have started to read the book. It is good, yes?" "It is." Had Jean-Claude read Clive's manuscript? Or was it simply a polite surmise?

"Save the rest until tomorrow. Come to dinner."

She frowned. Did he really expect her to intrude on his reunion with Gaby?

He anticipated her refusal, his voice came urgent. "Please, Carol. I need to talk to you. It is important."

"But Gaby—"

"Gaby and I . . . we do not enter into this. This is about your work."

"Gaby and I work together," she said stubbornly. "Anything you have to say about our work, we can hear together."

He seemed to take this as acceptance. "I will be there in ten minutes to pick you up. Please lock the book away carefully. It is an important document."

Her heart thumped. She knew suddenly that Clive Hubert was in some danger. And it was connected with the book which she had asked him to write.

She said, "I think I should take it home and finish—"

The phone was humming emptily. She replaced it, frowning slightly. She did not want to spend an evening with Gaby and Jean-Claude. Gaby would be scented from her bath, she would lounge around, pouting adorably, not a bit interested in work. Jean-Claude might simply want to talk about de Gaulle and French imperialism.

She opened the pile of papers in various places and read at random. It was going to maintain its atmosphere; it was a description of another world. Clive was pro-Moslem; that much was evident although he did his best to be the anonymous observer. Instead of setting the people impossible goals he had made himself one of them, trekking miles with the goats each day, treating disease on the spot, explaining pasteurisation as he heated their milk over an open fire. A sentence stood out on its own: "To abandon old ways is wrong; we must adapt them, but keep their intrinsic harmony and rhythm." It was typical of the man; she had met Clive Hubert only half a dozen times before he left for Algeria, but she knew that those words were the basis of his philosophy. He had gone in for agriculture because he needed to find an intrinsic harmony and rhythm of his own.

With a sigh she slid the wodge of paper into its packing and put it into the drawer again. She knew she could never marry; the "physical side" of marriage was not for her. She had wanted a family, and Monica had given her that. But if she could ever consider the matrimonial state, then someone like Clive Hubert would be her choice. He was small, withdrawn to the point of secretiveness, but with a rich inner life.

She turned the key in the drawer, snapped out the light, and went into the corridor. The cage lift creaked as it climbed up the shaft, and creaked more loudly on the way down. She stepped out into the marble-tiled foyer. The concierge held the door for her and followed her through on to the wide steps above the Avenue. It was still raining.

"A taxi for madame?" He always gave her the courtesy title. "Ah.

Madame has no umbrella again." He made a moue of despair.

"I like the rain, Henri." She smiled at him. "Besides, Monsieur Durant will arrive at any moment."

He smiled back. French concierges were notoriously deadpan, but Henri could not resist Carol's English teeth. He waited with her beneath the awning until Jean-Claude's Renault squealed from the Avenue Foch and drew up much too suddenly beneath them. Carol ran down the steps and collected a large drip down the collar of her coat. She turned and waved to Henri. The last she saw of him was his Gallic shrug.

Jean-Claude turned in the road and made for the Place de la Concorde as if sheer speed could force him into the constant rotation of traffic there. It could. Cass gently closed her eyes so that she would not shame herself by screaming, and did not open them until much later. They were cruising down the Boulevard Saint-Germain between the acacia trees. It was almost dark and the rain had stopped.

Cass said, "Where are we going? We're past the Rue Dauphine, surely?"

"The Reine Blanche. I always go to the Reine Blanche on my first night home."

She caught a glimpse of his dark eyes as he turned his head momentarily. If only he were small and terribly diffident, like Clive Hubert. It was impossible to feel this sense of discomfort with Clive.

She said very calmly, "Will Gaby meet us there?"

"I do not know. Perhaps."

"She told me she was cooking coq-au-vin. At the flat."

"Ah. That is her favourite. Coq-au-vin. All I need is onion soup. Very clear. Very full of onions. No goat's milk."

She was forced to laugh but her discomfort did not go away.

"Jean-Claude. I thought you were inviting me to the flat. I really ought to have stayed at the office and finished reading. You said you needed to talk to me."

"And that is exactly why we do not go to the flat and eat coq-au-vin, English Caroline." He turned his quick smile on her for an instant. "Please do not retreat into your shell. It was very important that you should be with me tonight."

Her outward calm had gone. She hardly knew what to say. What would Monica reply to that sort of remark? She cleared her throat.

"I don't like it. It's not right. Gaby is a friend as well as a colleague."

He actually laughed at that, tipping his head so that she could see his Adam's apple silhouetted against the side window.

"Gaby is nobody's friend, Cass! Only her own. And you know that because you know people. Your blue English eyes see into them, inside them. That is why you are frightening. And endearing."

"Please, Jean-Claude," she said faintly.

"We are here." He swerved on to the pavement, slapped the car into reverse and backed into a side street. The rain-soaked acacias smelled of the coming spring and everything shone wetly in the lamplight. Cass was suddenly conscious that her perceptions had gone into top gear, probably because of reading Clive's book. Sight and scent were emphasised by the touch of the cool damp air on her face and hands. She pulled on her gloves quickly as if to ward off danger, but she could not veil her face and she did not wear a hat. And her ears could not be blocked off either. The sound of water dripping from trees struck her as special, unique. She could imagine the languorous journey of each droplet along the length of each leaf until it gathered tremblingly on the tip. She must be going mad. How could she distinguish such sounds amidst the clatter of iron tables and pernod glasses? How did she sense that the river was close and darkly flowing beneath the Pont Neuf? How did she know that Jean-Claude's sudden silence as he piloted her inside was deliberate, so that she could absorb such sensory information?

He put her into a chair at a corner table where they could see outside to the lamplight without being cold. The way he settled her, taking her coat, pulling the table slightly away so that she could put down her bag and gloves, was very French. That was the trouble with him, of course: besides his ridiculous good looks, he was French. She tried to think of Clive Hubert and could not. In England she might have fallen gently in love with Clive and even married him if he'd asked her. But not in France.

She said, "Seriously, Jean-Claude, this is not right. Gaby is expecting you."

"No." He shook his head firmly. "Gaby is always surprised to see me. She would have you think otherwise, of course. You noticed her sang-froid when I turned up this afternoon. But when I touched her shoulders they were rigid. She never expects me to return." He sat down and looked at her across the table. "She thinks that I will be killed. One day, yes. Not today."

He smiled, but she knew he was serious. He was an imperialist in a republic. Imperialists were outmoded. She thought sombrely of her own country and the difficulties surrounding Indian independence. But much more important than thoughts of international affairs was the fact that Jean-Claude had found Gaby's shoulders rigid.

Carol swallowed and looked away from the hypnotically dark eyes opposite her.

A waiter came and took Jean-Claude's order. He did not ask her opinion. She knew he had ordered six bowls of onion soup, and that this was not unusual. The waiter smiled and went away, and two glasses of pernod were brought. Cass did not like the drink, but she knew it had a high alcohol content and hoped it would deaden some of the peculiar sensations of the evening. She sipped it carefully.

Jean-Claude smiled again. "You take it like medicine, Carol. Not permitting it to touch your tongue. Is it so distasteful to you?"

She had to smile back. "I am not enamoured. But there is nothing I like better. However . . . this onion soup. I am not so sure about that."

For the first time, he looked dismayed. "I have ordered three bowls each!" he protested.

"I know. Perhaps you could manage five and I will—"

"No, no, no. You must choose something you would like. Carol, I apologise. I thought—I *felt* it—in my bones—that you were addicted to onion soup, as I am! Forgive me."

She restrained his hand as it signalled the waiter.

"Leave it. Please. I would like to try your onion soup."

At her touch he became very still. That stillness was more convincing than anything he had said or done. She removed her hand and felt up her sleeve for a handkerchief.

He said quietly, "I have never seen anyone so English as you, Carol. So contained and secure in yourself, in your Englishness. Yet you are also the most vulnerable person I know. It is a paradox. A complete paradox."

She flushed. She hated any limelight to fall on herself.

"And you are the most French. Though in fact you are cosmopolitan, multi-lingual. Another paradox." She laughed, blew her nose, returned the hanky to her sleeve. He watched each action.

"Please, Jean-Claude," she shook her head slightly. "All this analysis! Tell me what it is we are to talk about."

"You. Of course. You." He gestured widely. "Your Virginia Woolf face, your English skirt and jumper, the handkerchief in the sleeve, the scarf tucked into the neck, the blue eyes and the big mouth—"

"Jean-Claude!" She silenced him sternly. She was suddenly annoyed. And with herself. She should not have come; he was, after all, the archetypal philanderer and by allowing herself to be aware of him, she was entering into his kind of game. She half rose, but he restrained her this time, and his touch had an immediate effect. She subsided.

The waiter arrived with the soup and placed the six bowls carefully around the table. Sticks of bread overhung their basket.

"Ah. Now these—" Jean-Claude pushed a bowl towards her, "will be scalding. We drink carefully with lots of bread. The next one will be bearable. And the last will soothe the palate, tongue and throat, like balm."

The waiter laughed. Either he knew English, or he had seen this performance many times before. Cass dunked her bread and felt her anger dissipate. An awful loneliness took its place. Not for her—ever—the joyous flirtation; certainly not the physical union of man and woman. Fleetingly she thought of Clive and knew that between them there could never be more than friendship. Because of this fear. She was frigid. There was no other word for how she felt. It was not the first time she had had to face that fact. She had known it in the Haunted House. She had known it when Malcolm Lennox had assaulted her drunkenly; she had known it a dozen times when reading books or watching films. Something was lacking in her: more than that, something was completely revolted by the mechanics of sex. She could know deep love: for her mother and for Bessie. Probably that kind of love was stronger than sex. She would certainly steal, perhaps even kill, for Bessie. But that kind of love was no bolster against the loneliness of eternity. She imagined, indeed she knew from her reading, that the joining of man and woman accomplished that. One became two; two became one; loneliness was impossible.

Jean-Claude said, "I know, always I know, when you are . . . dissecting." He leaned over his bowl with the French lack of inhibition when eating; he bit into his dripping bread. "Please forget

58

everything except onion soup. There is you and there is onion soup. Nothing else for the moment."

Again she was forced to laugh. He continued to make nonsensical sounds through the mouthful of food, encouraging her to be silly. She forgot her fears, and the sense of desolation. Fleetingly she wondered if she were being inveigled into a flirtation. If so, it was painless.

"The next bowl, please Miss Woodford. No pause. No interval. The leisure, the savouring, the tête-à-tête comes with the third helping." Even so he was slowing down, his eyes flicking over her face when he thought she would not notice. "This is delicious." She straightened. "But I don't think I can manage the last bowl. Really."

"Try." His voice was no longer bantering. He sounded gentle and pleading. "Please try, Carol. I would so much like you to be . . . replete."

For some reason, she made an effort. Their spoons went back and forth. They ate no more bread.

She said, "You have something to say. What is it?"

Still he parried. "The soup first. Afterwards—"

"If you have something important to say, you had better be quick, Jean-Claude. I intend to return to the office when I have finished this. Now what is it?"

"You are offering me an ear—a shoulder? You write a column in the magazines for lonely hearts?"

She was in no mood for this stupid teasing. If it was nothing to do with Clive's book, it must be something to do with Gaby.

She pushed aside the bowl. "I have no advice to offer on personal problems. You have chosen your confidante wrongly."

"I don't think so." He proffered a packet of Gauloises and when she shook her head, put them away again. But he narrowed his eyes as if he were smoking. "Would you like coffee?"

"No, thank you. I would like to go back to the office."

"Now? But why?"

She said with exaggerated patience, "I wish to pick up Clive Hubert's manuscript, then take a taxi home."

"That is ridiculous. It is late. Do you not intend to sleep tonight?"

"Jean-Claude—" she pushed back her chair. "I am leaving. Thank you for the soup. Good night."

He rose and got behind her chair, easing her out of it and into her coat with the same fluidity as before. It was beginning to rain again.

"Walk as far as the Seine," he suggested, turning up his collar. "It is special when it rains. The reflections dance crazily like the dervishes."

She did not ask him whether he had actually seen dervishes in Algeria. All red herrings would be ignored, she decided.

"I haven't an umbrella and I don't wish to get wet to the skin," she said instead, tightly. "Will you drive me back or shall I get a taxi?"

"I will drive you, naturally. But please, Carol. Please walk to the river with me."

"I'm sorry. I do not want to hear about your marital troubles," she said straightly.

"It is not about Gaby. I promise you. I know about Gaby and Gaby knows about me. It is something else entirely." He hesitated. "It is something about your work. Nothing personal."

She started to ask him whether they could talk in the car, but already he was walking down the boulevard, past the statue of Diderot. She joined him. It was a cold evening, but he had been right, the onion soup still glowed comfortingly inside her.

It was a long walk, much further than she remembered. They passed his apartment in Rue Dauphine, and she looked up, wondering which of the lights was his, or whether Gaby had given up and gone out herself. When they came to the Pont Neuf, he paused at last. They were both out of breath. Her awareness of him was softened now by sheer anxiety.

He leaned on the parapet and looked into the water, breathing deeply. After a moment, she did the same. The rain machine-gunned the river and the floodlighting gilding the Tour Saint-Jacques reminded her of war-time searchlights.

He lifted his head at last. "Can you see the Palais de Justice?"

"No." She dried her streaming face with the sleeve of her coat. "Where is it?"

"Sainte Chapelle is rising out of it. There." He touched her shoulder momentarily, and again the contact was electrifying.

She said hoarsely, "You've brought me here to show me the heart of France? Remind me of its greatness? There is no need. I love France as you love her. I know Clive's book is pro independence. It will come anyway. There is no need for . . . protestations."

"I know that." His voice was low. "People come first. Always." He took a breath. "Are you in love with Clive Hubert?"

"No! Of course not! Why on earth do you ask me that?"

He turned her to face him. His hands on her shoulders were very hard.

"Because I need to know. Carol . . . English Carol . . . Clive Hubert is dead."

The shock of it quite literally froze her. She was already turning to wrench herself free of him, and she stood there, corkscrewed, twisting her head to look at him.

He nodded. "He handed the book to me. An hour later he was shot. And I smuggled the manuscript back inside my typewriter. My sympathies are known and it was quite safe."

"But . . . why?" The words came out with her breath, a wail of perplexed anguish.

"He made no secret of his feelings, Carol. He had become the European representative of F.L.N."

"I don't believe that. He was too . . . low key. He would never have taken an official stance with them."

"You have read enough of his book to know that he believed in their aims."

"He thought Algeria should belong to the Algerians—yes! He thought they should practise their own religion—he spoke of their harmonies, the harmonies of the soil . . . oh God!"

She put her hands to her face. The next instant she was in his arms, her head was cradled on his shoulder, he was whispering sympathy in her ear. She hardly knew why she was weeping. It was not entirely for Clive, but for the shocking waste of life, for struggling humanity, for everyone she had known who had suffered. She forgot about the intensity of physical feeling between herself and Jean-Claude. He was a fellow traveller, and for an instant in time they were united in a kind of universal grief. She clung to him; she felt his mouth against her wet neck and smelt the rain on his hair. When she tilted her head back to look at him, his face too was streaming, and she did not know whether it was rain or tears.

"Carol—" his voice choked. "I did not want it. I did not want any of it. The end justifies the means, they say. But it is not so. I liked Clive Hubert; he was a good man. And he thought a great deal of you. I was so afraid that you too . . ."

"I did think a lot of him. Oh Jean-Claude—"

She stopped speaking and stared at him. One of the lamps on the bridge struck shadows across his already dark face. She thought he might be the devil come to tempt her. "I must get back to the office and fetch the manuscript," she said on a high note.

"No!" His hands were spread across her back, unconsciously kneading comfort into her spine. They became still and hard. "No, Carol. You must not go back to Avenue Foch."

"But I have to. Surely you can see that now?"

"I love you, Carol. That is all I know. All I care about. I want you to stay with me. Please."

In spite of the awareness, which she had known he felt too, she was amazed at his declaration. Love. What had love to do with the kind of breathless attraction she had felt this evening? Love was friendship and loyalty and selflessness. What she had felt for Jean-Claude was based on their physical reactions to each other.

She stared up at him. The rain was still coursing down his face. She said, "This is complete selfishness. Clive is dead. Gaby is waiting for you. She was going to have a bath. Specially."

He barked a laugh and then brought his head down and kissed her. She had not been kissed since Malcolm Lennox had "tried it on" as her mother put it, at Myrtle's wedding. She felt a quiver of fear, but he made no attempt to force an entry to her mouth. His lips touched hers and went, touched again, then went to her eyes. Her body felt heavy and voluptuous. Warmth flooded her. She linked her gloved hands behind his back and leaned on him. He kept on kissing her face and neck until she turned her mouth towards him and returned the kisses. Then he paused and looked at her.

"Is it all right, Carol? Is this all right?"

He sounded untypically tentative. She had her chance to withdraw then without hurt pride for either of them; with dignity and integrity. But she did not withdraw.

"Yes, Jean-Claude. It is all right," she whispered.

After a long while they began to walk back down the Rue Dauphine, entwined like lovers. She could hardly believe what was happening. She had just heard of Clive Hubert's tragic death; she had long faced up to her own cold nature. Yet here she was walking in rain-soaked Paris, not knowing or caring where she was going, with a man she distrusted and disapproved of, who was married to a charming sex-kitten of a girl, a man who obviously had done this with many women before, who was . . . *practised* in the art of seduction.

They reached the Renault.

"We will drive for a while." He settled her inside, carefully. "Then we will go to the apartment."

Her heart jumped and skittered. He came around the bonnet and got in beside her. He turned and took her in his arms and kissed her passionately. They looked at each other in the light from the street lamps. His face was luminous but still so dark. He kissed her again, lightly, and started the car.

She said, "We cannot go to the apartment. Gaby will be there."

"She will wait till midnight. Then she will go. Surely you know about Gaby?"

"We cannot go to the apartment." She took a breath. "We will go to mine."

He glanced sideways and put a hand on hers.

"Thank you, my darling. But no." He drew into the Boulevard Saint Germain. "I love you, Carol Woodford. I love you and I am thankful for you."

He drove to the river again and crossed to pass the Louvre and the Pont des Arts. And then, without warning, the sky was lit beyond the Place de la Concorde. Carol jerked in her seat and then was flung forward as Jean-Claude braked violently, stalling the Renault. It was like one of the worst land-mines of the war, as if the bowels of the planet itself were erupting. The blast burst the doors of the car and flung them out of it, still joined. They lay, shocked and sick, in the gutter, while flames silhouetted the Arc de Triomphe and the huge mass of the Louvre. Carol could hear herself begin to cry, though she wondered why; Jean-Claude was holding her very tightly but uttered no sound. She wailed, "My God! My God! It's in the Avenue Foch. I have to get there!"

She tried to stand, and could not. Bells were ringing in her head. A police car screamed by, then an ambulance. Jean-Claude stood with obvious difficulty and pulled her up beside him.

"You are all right, Carol?" His voice was stern, cutting through her near-hysteria. "You are all right? Answer me!"

"Yes. Yes. It is in the Avenue Foch. We must go—"

"No. It is not safe."

"I must. Henri will be worried."

"Henri?"

"The concierge. I should have gone before. You should have let me—"

"Don't be a fool, Carol. We shall not be allowed anywhere near such a fire. I will take you to the Rue Dauphine."

She could not stop the tears. Where was his tenderness now?

He bundled her into the car and started it with some difficulty. The flames were leaping high and klaxons could be heard converging on the scene from all parts of the city. A gendarme appeared from the darkness and held up his hand. Jean-Claude muttered "Merde!" and leapt from the car. Carol translated what was said laboriously inside her head.

"Ask him about Henri. Ask him whether the concierge—"

An ambulance flashed by and the gendarme said something. Jean-Claude interrupted him, but not quickly enough.

"Oh God." She put her forehead against the windscreen and remembered how she had seen Henri last, shrugging acceptance of her mad Englishness. And the office, gone. The desk with the drawer containing Clive's manuscript. "Oh God!"

The car moved again and when it eventually stopped they were outside the flat in Rue Dauphine.

She said dully, "You knew. They were after the manuscript and you knew. I want to go home."

"Your flat is less safe than the office," he said brutally, and practically manhandled her upstairs.

She sat numbly where he had put her, drank the tea he handed to her later.

He said woodenly, "I heard that Hubert was dead. I knew they would want to destroy his book. If you were with the book, you too would be destroyed. I had to separate you from that manuscript."

"You could have stopped it. Henri . . . . he could be alive now."

"I couldn't be sure. I didn't know Henri would be there. I got you out. That was all I could do."

She stood up. "I need the bathroom."

He indicated a door and she walked stiffly towards it. Afterwards he shoved her into a small boxroom furnished with books and a bed. She crept into the bed. There was a hot-water bottle there, freshly made. Weeping, she held it to her and fell asleep.

■

She arrived in Northfield before the news of the bombing had reached the rest of the world. Bessie was at school. Her mother opened the door to her and knew immediately that something was wrong.

"You're ill," she said accusingly, taking the small holdall which had been packed for her by Jean-Claude.

"I've got one of my throats. Nothing much."

"No, it's more than that. You're really ill. Run down."

Mary backed into the living room where there was a fire and a low table laid for tea. Her eyes went over her daughter like twin probes. Carol tried to laugh.

"Honestly, Mother." She went to the fire; she was terribly cold. "Who is coming to tea?"

"Bessie, of course. It's cold enough for tea by the fire. And anyway she loves to be cosy." Mary put the holdall on the floor and came closer. "You're crying."

"It's just so lovely. You and Bessie, cosy. Having tea by the fire." The tears wouldn't stop, they dripped from her nose on to the hands which clung to the mantelpiece. "I mean—Easter is always cold, isn't it?"

"Not quite Easter yet, darling." Mary withdrew a hanky from her sleeve and put it into one of the clutching hands. "Have a good cry, then sit down and we'll have our tea before Bessie comes in. I'll go and fetch it."

She picked up the holdall again and went into the kitchen, wishing that she felt as briskly reassuring as she sounded. The kettle was simmering on the gas, and she put an extra spoonful of tea into the pot before making it. She hoped that just for once Bessie would be late home from school. She carried in the tray and set it on the table. Carol was sitting on the log box, staring into the fire. At least she was dry-eyed now.

Mary said, "Have they given you the sack?"

"No." Carol looked up with a fleeting smile. "I wish it were that." She spread her hands to the blaze. "It's just that I've made a complete fool of myself. And one of my authors has got himself killed out in Algeria. And the office has been blown up by a crazy nationalist movement." She smiled again at Mary's expression. "Yes. Quite. I'm glad I can tell you before Bessie gets in. Better not say anything in front of her."

"My God. Cass. My God. Were you anywhere near the place when this happened?"

"No. I saw it. Felt it. But there was no danger. But . . . an important book went. It was in my top drawer."

"Oh darling. I'm sorry. But thank God—thank God—you escaped."

"Yes." Carol's voice was flat. "Yes. I escaped."

"You're suffering from shock. When did it happen?"

"Last night. Half-past twelve."

"And you saw it?"

"I was out. I had dinner with Jean-Claude Durant. He brought this book out of Algeria." She took a cup of tea from her mother and it wobbled dangerously. "I'm all right. It's just that . . . I might have prevented it. Part of it. If only I'd taken the book and gone home straightaway." She shook her head. "They would still have killed Henri. You remember Henri, the concierge? He's gone."

"Oh, dear God."

"The thing is . . ." Carol looked up. "I think I've been used, Mother. I think I have to take the responsibility for some of this."

"Rubbish. I don't know what you're talking about, but I know that such an idea is rubbish."

"I took Gaby on as my secretary and thought it was a great stroke of luck that her husband was a foreign correspondent who was very co-operative. I think now it was planned a long time ago. After the book about Cambodia, when Universal had got a reputation for international hot potatoes—"

"When you got that reputation," Mary inserted.

"That was when Gaby appeared."

"You think she was foisted on you? To report back?"

"I don't know what to think."

There was a long pause. Some colour was returning to Carol's face.

Mary said, "This whole business is very frightening, but I rather think you're jumping to conclusions, darling."

"Possibly."

There was another long silence. Then voices were heard outside the window. Someone said, "Will you come to my house after Tina's party?" And Bessie replied, "I'm not going to the party. It's Easter Saturday." "It's not church. It's church on Good Friday and Easter Sunday. Not Saturday." Bessie said smugly, "Grannie and I go to Paris for Easter."

Carol looked at her mother.

"Not this year. I shall have to go back and sort out what I can, but you must stay at home this year, Mother."

"We'll see."

Carol's eyes widened in panic. "Mother. Promise me you won't bring Bessie to Paris. Promise. I mean it."

The gate clicked and feet were heard running round to the kitchen door.

"I promise," Mary said quickly, and put her hand over her daughter's before she went to let in her other daughter.

4

*M*yrtle looked on the move from Bournemouth to Cheltenham as a new beginning. The tall Regency house overlooking Imperial Gardens boasted a real nursery, and the ground floor provided a luxurious waiting room for Malcolm's patients and two treatment rooms behind.

"Once I've had junior, I'll be able to take the occasional patient myself," she said to Malcolm. "I'm still a member of the Society."

Malcolm glanced at her casually, making her immediately aware that her maternity smock was stained with milk from the baby's last bottle.

But all he said was, "I remember you suggested that when we were still in Bournemouth."

"Yes, but the babies came so quickly then. After this one we'll have a little pause, shall we darling? Then I can pull my weight in the practice."

"It's up to you," he said indifferently. "I didn't want to leave

Bournemouth particularly. But you seemed to think it was the answer to everything."

"Darling, Bournemouth was full of osteopaths! We never stood a chance there. When I think how well you were thought of in Wales when I knew you first—"

"That was before we were married," he said significantly.

"You mean when you could give your woman patients something a little more substantial in the manipulation department!" she snapped, diplomacy going to the winds. Then, when he merely smiled indulgently, she said quickly, "Darling, don't let's quarrel. Let's make this a new start for us. I know you feel I've held you back, but don't you see—a wife and family add respectability to a practice. Especially if the wife is a qualified osteopath too. Listen darling, I shall meet doctors and nurses at the ante-natal clinic. I can make contacts. We might be outside the medical profession, but there must be some doctors who will bend enough to make discreet recommendations."

He said, "*I* never quarrel, Myrtle. You quarrel. And you repeat yourself too. You said all this in Bournemouth." He chucked her under the chin. "Be honest, Myrtle. You wanted to come here because it's just as posh as Bournemouth, it included a very nice house, and it's less than an hour on the train from Northfield and your family."

She smiled roguishly. "You know me too well, darling. Just as I know you!" She reached up to kiss him, but he stepped back.

"Myrtle, for God's sake—I don't want to smell of sour milk for our first patient!"

"It's your fault I smell like sour milk, Malcolm Lennox!"

"Is it?" He held her gaze challengingly.

She was furious. "D'you think I've got time to mess around like you do! My God, I was pregnant before we came back from our honeymoon, and I've either been pregnant or breast-feeding ever since! Babies are a full-time job you know, Malcolm!"

"And you wanted them." Suddenly his bored indulgence was gone and he was angry. "I know I fathered them, Myrtle. But it was you who wanted them!" He assumed a high falsetto, nothing like her voice. "I want to be filled with babies, darling—I want twelve children—" he caught her hands as she struck at him. "You know damn well it's true!"

"I say those kind of things to please you!" She was panting, on the edge of tears.

He held her by the wrists at arms' length.

"And they do. Sometimes. But not all the time. There are times when those little speeches make me feel as if I'm wearing fetters. As if I'm chained to you."

She lowered her eyes. She usually made those "little speeches" after she had discovered one of his liaisons. It was her way of fettering him; he was quite right there.

His hands were very warm and she realised, from the change in his grip, that he wanted her. She smiled slightly and whispered, "I'm sorry, darling."

But the smell of sour milk was not so easily forgotten. He released her and said jovially, "Oh, it's working at home, baby. That's the trouble. If I were a nine-to-five man it would be different. We live in each other's pockets."

He turned to go out and she slid up behind him and put her hand in his trouser pocket. He stopped and laughed throatily and would have grabbed her—she was sure of it—if there hadn't been a terrific crash on the front door knocker.

"Mrs. Herron!" He pulled away and picked up his white coat from the chair. "She's bloody early!" He went into the hall to intercept the new maid. "Hang on Gilda—wait until I'm in the consulting room, for Christ's sake."

Myrtle pushed the sitting-room door almost shut and peered through the crack. She wanted to see this Mrs. Herron. And was Gilda going to be a threat too? Her skirt was fashionably long, but she had a tiny waist and a tiny, neat bust. Gilda indeed. Myrtle had to remind herself that Malcolm preferred big breasts.

Gilda opened the door as she had been instructed, backing away with it so that the patients had plenty of room for their walking sticks. Her white, pseudo-nurse's cap, sitting well back on her head, jerked with surprise. Obviously it was not Mrs. Herron.

The next moment Myrtle was in the hall, arms spread wide.

"Borrie! Little brother! How marvellous—come here and be hugged by your big sis!" She folded the fourteen-year-old into her smock and he did not recoil at any smells.

"Hiya, big cyst!" He grinned widely at his own joke. "Mother said someone had to come down and welcome you to your new abode . . . so I volunteered!"

"Oh, darling, I'm so glad to see you!"

And she was. Boris had been a nuisance when she was at home but she had been proud of him at the wedding, dancing with Bessie

Woodford, and he was improving all the time. It wasn't really fair that he took after handsome Daddy, while she was a replica of her mother. But he represented her life in the Midlands. And she hugged him again.

The door knocker thumped.

"That'll be Mrs. Herron. Come on upstairs and see your nephews, Borrie. They look a bit like you."

It was fun having Boris. He could tell her all the news from home and he was at that satisfactory in-between stage of development, young enough to want to please, yet mature enough to know how to please. Occasionally he would become the typical smart-alec schoolboy, but most of the time she treated him as she would have treated a close woman friend—if she had one now.

"Honestly, Borrie, you don't know how I miss Cass and Liv and Mon. We were inseparable. Absolutely inseparable."

"Don't I know it. You shouted at me if I just knocked on your door when you were all in your room." He grinned and ran his hand through his crisp curls till they stood on end. "I could have told you a thing or two if you'd let me in!"

"You were just a baby, for God's sake!"

"Well . . . you could have used me as an example of the male body!"

"Filthy little beast. You haven't changed." She surveyed him affectionately. His eyes were bigger than hers and much greener. And his mouth was gorgeous.

"Take care of your teeth, little brud. You'll go a long way with those teeth!"

He bared them and growled much too loudly. Next door the baby woke and bawled lustily.

"Now look what you've done!"

She rushed into the nursery and picked up her youngest. He was nine months old and had had to come off the breast when she found she was pregnant again. As a result, he did nothing but burp up curds and whey, usually down her maternity smock.

Boris, watching her jog him, said, "You ought to let him come down with Nicholas. They could play together."

"Ridiculous child. Martin isn't a year old yet."

"Well, Nicholas is only a year older than him—they'd amuse each other."

"Malcolm couldn't stand both of them at meal times. It's bad enough with Nicky. At least I can give him all my attention while Gilda feeds Martin."

"She just shoves a bottle in his mouth and reads the paper. I've seen her. No wonder he cries so much."

"You have a go at it then, clever dick."

"Okay."

He took the baby from her. "Go and have a bath and put on that silky kimono thing. Makes you look all Oriental."

She looked at him, startled. What with his previous remark and now this, she wondered if he might be rather precocious. Then he held Martin beneath the armpits and gazed into the screwed-up face.

"Hiya, nephew. You gonna behave yourself for Uncle Borrie?"

It was incredible. The screaming stopped to be replaced by hiccoughing sobs.

Myrtle made for the bathroom.

That night Boris had Martin on his knee during supper. At first Malcolm was silent and tight-lipped, but when Boris kept up a stream of chatter which diverted the baby and delighted Nicholas in his high chair, he relaxed.

"See your big brother eating his meat and carrots?" Boris let the baby find his feet and look down on the plate of food. Nicholas immediately shovelled in a spoonful. Martin laughed. Boris said, "There's a clever Nicky. Now shall we show him what we can do?" He took a spoonful of mashed potato from his own plate and popped it into Martin's mouth.

"Borrie, I really think he's too young—" Myrtle began.

Malcolm said, "Rubbish, Myrtle. Boris is doing a grand job." He winked broadly at the boy and gave his wife a warning look. "If it means you and I can eat our meal in peace . . ." He passed his plate for more of Myrtle's braised steak. "You're looking rather charming this evening, my dear. That mandarin collar frames your face perfectly."

Myrtle flushed and gave him more than his share. After all, meat was no longer rationed.

Malcolm approved of Boris not only because he was so good with the children, but because he kept Myrtle out of the treatment room. She had a bad habit of bringing in a cup of tea for his patient just when his sensitive fingers had discovered a knot of tight muscle in the base of the neck or across the shoulders. It was off-putting for all concerned. With Boris as a close companion, she tended to take the little ones out for walks.

Gilda felt the same way about the young visitor. Within two days of his arrival she was relieved of the boring chore of giving Baby Lennox his night-time bottle, and she no longer had to keep an eye on both children while Mrs. Lennox popped in and out of the treatment room like a yo-yo. Gilda very much liked the idea of being a receptionist; she had not bargained for all the extras that went with it.

And Boris seemed to be enjoying himself. Just as Myrtle had, he was already wondering how soon he could get right away from the family home where his father treated his mother like a doormat, there were never any decent meals and the char dropped cigarette ash in his darkroom . . . Boris was a keen photographer.

He saw this visit as the first of many temporary escapes. Cheltenham was only an hour on the train from Northfield, and the new house behind the promenade was much better situated than his own. Besides, he had plans for the future.

He started laying a trail towards these while they walked up to Montpelier to view the first of the snowdrops.

"Bet these park places are a picture by Easter," he commented as they passed the Queen's Hotel and had the first glimpse of the rotunda with King William guarding it. "Half-terms are never long enough to see anything much. Can I come down in April, Sis? For a bit longer? That is, if I'm not a bloody nuisance."

"Watch your language, young Borrie. I might put up with a lot, but pas devant les enfants, if you please. Dammitall you're only fourteen yourself!"

He looked at her and they both laughed. He said experimentally, "I'm almost bluggy-well fifteen."

"Bluggy?"

"A squashed up bloody and bugger."

"Borrie!"

"That's nothing. You should hear what some of the seniors say at school. In front of us juniors too."

"Not much, I bet."

They crossed the road and entered the gardens. A chill February wind swept the empty tennis courts and the emptier trees. Boris tugged his cap closer to his ears and Myrtle pulled the hood of the pram higher to protect Nicholas who was perched on a pram seat.

Boris said, "Monica Cook came home just before Christmas last year. I suppose she told you?"

Myrtle stopped fiddling with the hood and looked surprised.

"No. I've never heard from Mon. Not since she went to London for that hotel job. I wrote to her lots of times, but she didn't reply. I didn't think she'd come back to Northfield."

"Several people saw her. She came for the day. Had sausage and chips in that awful caff where Mrs. Cook works. Then went for a walk over the heath."

"Good God, you had your spies out!"

"I thought you'd be interested."

"I am. I am. A walk on the heath? I bet she met Cass at the Haunted House."

"Carol Woodford? She's in Paris. Monica was with her brother."

"Oh, was she? I thought she and Cass would be in touch. I thought Cass would have to tell her about the business at the wedding. Oh God, when I think of that! You were too young to understand, Borrie. I must have been mad! Fancy accusing Cass— of all people—anyway, as if it mattered! I've sent her a Christmas card every year."

"She hasn't sent any to you?"

"No. Nor to Mon. Liv writes reams to me, of course. I mean, Reggie and Malcolm were friends, so obviously we're still quite close. But Liv hears nothing from Cass or Mon either. So there's no news from that quarter." She pushed the pram ahead of him and kept her head turned away. "Can't expect you to understand, little brud."

"Well . . ." He hung back diplomatically. "What it amounts to is that the four of you are split into two and two. And you don't like it."

Myrtle did not answer immediately. Then she said merely, "Yes. That's it."

She wheeled the pram to a holly bush which provided a wind-break, unstrapped Nicholas and set him down on the damp path. He walked stiff-legged to the edge of the grass and tried to pick a snowdrop through his mittens. She made a groaning noise and Boris produced a tennis ball and rolled it along the path. The next minute the two of them were running exaggeratedly after the ball aiming mighty kicks at it, laughing like hyenas. Myrtle sank on to the damp seat next to the pram and joggled the handle as she stared glumly at her family. They were all male. All so horribly male. Sometimes she thought she'd give anything to talk to another woman. Of course there was her mother, besides dozens of sycophantic women who thought they might worm their way into Malcolm's affections via his unlikely wife. There was even Gilda. She wanted none of them. She wanted to be a girl again and squat on the floor of the Haunted House talking nonsense to the three girls who knew everything about her and accepted her faults with a scathing criticism that had nothing to do with unkindness or sadism. Yes, Malcolm was sadistic in his way.

"I say, Sis. You're not crying, are you?"

Boris was alarmed. He pushed the ball further up the path so that Nicholas would run after it.

Myrtle said crossly, "Of course I'm not crying. It's this bloody wind making my eyes water."

"Swearing!"

"Oh . . . sod it!"

He had succeeded in making her laugh. She reached up to him.

"Sit down a minute. Nicky will be all right for fifty-two seconds. Then we'll go home and have tea and pikelets. Your favourite."

He sat down and said brightly as if he'd just thought of it, "Listen, Myrt. You could write and ask Mrs. Woodford if Bessie can come and stay for a while. At Easter. She's crazy about babies apparently. Would that patch things up, d'you think?"

"Bessie? Bessie Woodford? But she was . . . I mean, it was about Bessie that we . . . what I mean is—"

"Sis, listen. If you said something horrid about Bessie, don't you see that to ask her to stay with you would show that you didn't mean it?"

"Yes. Yes, it would, wouldn't it? And she's a dear little soul— well, you know that. You danced with her that day."

"I see her in the park sometimes. And at church. Things like that."

"How old would she be now . . . nine or ten?"

"Nine. She'll be ten next December."

Myrtle looked at him sharply. He said sheepishly, "We talk. I didn't like to tell you because it sounds awful. I pump her about Carol. It was Bessie who told me that someone had seen Monica Cook."

"Well, for goodness' sake! Tell me about Carol!"

"Nothing really. Just that she is doing very well in Paris. She's supposed to be going to buy a house in the south of France somewhere. Mrs. Woodford and Bessie go out there a lot. If they go out there to live, you'll have lost your chance of patching things up."

Myrtle stared wide-eyed. After a while she said, "They'll be going to Paris at Easter then. She won't come here."

"They're not going at Easter."

"Why not?"

"Bessie doesn't know. Some trouble with Carol's work, I think." He shrugged. "Mrs. Woodford is worried."

"Might Carol have the sack?" Myrtle speculated. "Or is there some trouble with a man? She might have to come home to nurse a broken heart. *She* could come to stay with me then."

"Especially if you'd had Bessie here."

Myrtle was brightening by the minute. Bessie might be only nine, but she was female.

"I think I'll write and . . ." she slumped suddenly. "What am I talking about! They'll never let her come down here."

"They would if she pestered. She's quite good at pestering."

"Oh God, is she? But why should she want to come to see me? She doesn't know me—not as well as she knows Liv, for instance. Not that Liv would have a child within two miles of that house of hers."

"Let me ask her. If I say I'm coming down here for Easter, she might want to come."

Myrtle's look became very sharp indeed.

"Are you her hero or something, Borrie? What's going on? You're up to something. Like Daddy. Like Malcolm. My God, she's only nine!"

"Sis, calm down. What's the matter with you? I have a chat with Bessie Woodford in the park. For your sake. I'm suggesting she comes here. For your sake. And you jump down my neck."

Her stare faltered, and went past him to Nicky.

"Yes. Okay. It must be because I'm pregnant. You wouldn't understand. Nobody would. Maybe Cass of course . . ." She shook her head, annoyed at the way her thoughts had gone again. "Oh God. I don't know. It's too coincidental. But Cass, of all people!" Her eyes focused abruptly. "Oh Borrie. Why did you give him that ball? He's fallen over it and his coat will be filthy."

Boris leapt up and ran to give assistance. Nicky stopped crying and allowed himself to be dusted off. He didn't look too bad, Malcolm wouldn't be able to make any cracks about him coming from the wrong side of the tracks.

Myrtle let Boris plonk him back on the pram seat and strap him in. She smiled.

"I'll write to Mrs. Woodford. And next time you see Bessie in the park you can tell her that you'll be here too."

"Good old Sis. Cass won't be able to resist that." And Boris looked very well pleased with himself.

Malcolm wasn't quite so certain. Myrtle said nothing to him until she had received a reply from Mrs. Woodford. Then she broached it as "rather a good idea to have someone to keep Boris company."

Malcolm frowned. "I thought the whole idea of having Boris was to use him to amuse the boys. He won't want to do that if he's got a pal." Malcolm's practice had developed rapidly and it was all because of that first appointment with Mrs. Herron. He now had a reputation to keep up in more ways than one, and he needed Boris to take up Myrtle's slack.

"Oh, it's not a pal in that sense, darling." Myrtle put a hand beneath her enormous abdomen to support it. Unfortunately it also outlined it most unattractively. "You remember little Bessie Woodford at our wedding? She's much younger than Boris and has the tiniest crush on him." She giggled. "She'll be marvellous with the boys. She'll want to play mummies and daddies."

"Poor old Boris," Malcolm grunted. "I don't like the sound of it. Bit of a responsibility for us, isn't it? He's just at that age."

"He's fourteen, Malcolm. And anyway I'm around all the time to keep an eye on things."

"Oh well. That's different. Sorry baby."

He sat on the sofa by her and cupped the abdomen caressingly. Then he kissed her. Then he kissed her again very deeply, massaging her stomach as he did so. When she closed her eyes, he glanced up at the clock. He just about had time. He pulled up her smock.

Bessie said politely, "It's awfully kind of you to invite me to stay, Auntie Myrtle. It means Grannie can go to see Cass in France and not have to worry about me."

"Hello, darling." Myrtle kissed the girl with genuine affection. There was something about her that reminded Myrtle amazingly of her own childhood. It must be a spiritual likeness to Cass; it certainly wasn't a physical one. With her black hair and eyes she was like a little gypsy. "I've been longing to see you. What with having a family and a busy practice, it's been difficult. But we're nearer home now, and Boris is here to keep you company."

"That will be nice."

Bessie spoke with a kind of quiet satisfaction, as if Boris were an elderly uncle instead of a child.

Myrtle had determined not to fish for information, but she could not resist one question.

"Grandma tells me that you weren't keen on going to France this Easter, Bessie. I hope you haven't had a quarrel with dear Cass." She made her voice teasing, hoping to goodness Bessie knew nothing of the scene at the wedding reception.

She didn't. She spoke with the kind of flat honesty that Myrtle also remembered from her own girlhood.

"I had to say that, else Grannie would have been upset. I knew they wouldn't let me go, you see. It's dangerous. If I'd pestered about it, then Grannie wouldn't have gone either. And Cass would have been lonely."

"Dangerous?" Myrtle felt her heart beat hard in her throat. "How do you mean?"

"Didn't you see it in the newspaper? Boris and I read it together and we knew it was the place where Cass works. It was blown up." Bessie hung her matching coat and hat inside the wardrobe in the guest room. "Boris said never mind, I could come to Cheltenham with him. He said he'd fix it. And he did." She turned and smiled at Myrtle. "It really is so awfully kind of you to invite me."

Myrtle swallowed. Of course it didn't matter why the girl was here, but she'd certainly have a word with Borrie some time. Conniving little beast. Just like Daddy. Meanwhile this business of Cass' office was worrying, to say the least.

"There are so many dreadful things happening . . . must admit I didn't see . . ." she took a pile of navy-blue knickers and put them in a drawer. "Can't Cass come home?"

"Well, yes. I suppose so. But she wouldn't. It would be like deserting her post."

"Oh . . ." Myrtle just stopped herself from rapping out one of Malcolm's oaths. Really, Cass couldn't have grown up at all. She was as quixotic as ever. Myrtle knew she ought to let it rest there, but still she said, "Why on earth would anyone want to blow up

Cass' office, for goodness' sake? I thought she ran some little book agency. Translations or something."

Bessie stopped admiring the real grown-up dressing table laid with powder bowl, hair tidy, ring stand and lace mats by the dozen, and looked round again with a different expression.

"Cass is a very important person, Aunt Myrtle. She works for the biggest publishers in—in—the whole world! And she runs the French office on her own—which shows they think she is very—very trusty. And good. And people like her. Even the French like her. Even the Germans. Everyone likes Cass."

Myrtle realised she had made a mistake. And Bessie was right, Cass was eminently "trusty."

She shifted ground.

"Yes. But books . . . why blow up books?"

That had evidently floored Bessie too. She tugged at one of her socks.

"Grandma says that the pen is mightier than the sword," she suggested. "Anyway, ackcherly it was the whole building that was blown up. Not just Cass' office. So it was a sort of accident."

"Ah, I see."

Myrtle felt impelled to give the small girl a sudden hug. They were both a bit embarrassed by it.

Myrtle laughed. "I'm so glad you've come, Bessie. You make me feel I'm living my childhood over again. That must sound completely potty to you, darling."

"Oh no." Bessie smiled forgivingly. "Cass talks about the four of you. And Boris can remember you having secret meetings in your bedroom. I feel as if I know what it was like."

Myrtle wasn't one hundred per cent certain she approved of such empathy. After all she was now the mother of almost three children and the wife of a very successful medical man. She wondered if Borrie had got his ear close enough to the keyhole to hear some of the things they had talked about in those days.

"Well, my love. You come to the nursery when you've finished putting all your things away. I'm going to get the boys ready for their walk. We can go and look at the shops if you like."

Bessie watched her honorary aunt close the door. The stomach really was very big indeed, and Bessie wondered how on earth whatever was inside would manage to come out next month. Or even why it hadn't fallen out a long time ago. But Auntie Myrtle was nice. Grannie said she had been Cass' special companion when the two of them had gone on their country rambles. Bessie liked that thought. She had just read *Girl of the Limberlost* and the idea of exploring untamed country pleased her very much. She went to the window and squeezed behind the cheval mirror of the dressing table to lift the net curtain and look out.

She loved the smell of curtains and nets and the sort of flaky paint you always had on elderly windows. They smelled of all the suns that had shone on them and all the Jack Frosts that had painted them. She sniffed luxuriously as she surveyed the view. That was good too. There were railings around a sunken area, then the wide flagged pavement—that was a nice word, "pavement"— then the road with its graceful trees, then Imperial Gardens. She repeated the words "Imperial Gardens" aloud. They had a Russian sound. Not like the Russia the grown-ups meant when they moaned about the "veto," but the Russia of sleighs and big fur coats and winter palaces. How lovely to have a winter palace and a summer palace. She decided that Cheltenham was very Russian.

At the moment, Imperial Gardens were full of daffodils in carved formal beds. Stabbing them at intervals were heavy tulips, and around the fountain were wallflowers. The grass was close cut. Bessie could not see one daisy or buttercup. She looked hard. If she concentrated on interesting words and views and looking for buttercups and daisies, she did not think of Grannie going over to France all on her own, and Cass being brave about the bombing.

Myrtle watched the children walking ahead of the pram down the length of Cheltenham's famous Promenade. Even Nicholas enjoyed window-shopping in the Prom. The pavement was so wide and the trees enabled a constant running game of his version of hide-and-seek, and the grown-ups never seemed to hurry. His new auntie called Bessie chased him satisfyingly; in other words, she never actually caught him unless he stumbled into someone's legs or someone's dog, or just went sprawling on an uneven paving stone. Then she would gather him up and give him to Borrie who was almost a man. And in her matching blue coat and hat she was very pretty.

Myrtle, reading her son's thoughts as if they were blazoned on his own small cap, smiled smugly. She had done the right thing in inviting Cass' daughter to stay with her. Fleetingly she recalled that it had been Borrie's idea; even more fleetingly she acknowledged that if the bomb had not precluded Bessie spending Easter in France, Mrs. Woodford would have turned down the invitation. Already she was well on the way to believing that she had arranged the whole thing; healed the terrible breach between herself and Cass. Her baby was due next month. If only—if only—if only it was a girl, she would call it Carol. That would do it. Anyway she wanted to call her daughter Carol, it was a beautiful name, reminding her of Christmas and candles and . . . Bessie's voice floated back to her.

"Boris. Let's pretend we're Nicky's mother and father, shall we?"

And to her amazement Boris, who should have cringed with embarrassment at such whimsy, said, "Okey-dokey. You'd better take my arm. Or shall we swing Nicky in between us?"

Bessie put on a voice. "Oh, the latter, darling. Definitely the latter!"

They both doubled up with laughter and after a startled second, Myrtle leaned over the pram to hide her own giggles.

"Have we got a future match there, Martin?" she whispered. She kissed his adorable face. "That would be one in the eye for Cass and her mother!" she murmured.

They got back when the wonderful spring afternoon had turned damp and chilly. Myrtle wanted a cup of tea and a welcoming fire so badly she was almost in tears. The last patient was just being driven away from the front door in a taxi, which meant Gilda wouldn't have to be a receptionist any more. With luck, the kettle would be on, and the fire lit in the sitting room. She dug Martin out of his wrappings and gave him to Boris. Nicky was clinging to "Mummy's" hand.

"Be angels and take them up to the nursery," she said. "I'm absolutely dead on my feet."

"We'll look after them, Sis." Boris was far more sentient than she'd realised. Presumably that was why he could form a friendship with a small girl like Bessie. "Go and put your feet up till dinner time."

"You're a darling." She blew a kiss at him. "You too, Bessie," she blew another one.

She tucked the pram into the large hall cupboard and made for the kitchen. It was empty. Of course. She filled the kettle and lit the gas. Gilda was doing less and less these days. Didn't the blasted girl remember she'd been taken on first as mother's help and second—very much second—as part-time receptionist? She had ideas above her station, that much was obvious.

Myrtle made tea and stirred it vigorously to hasten the brewing, then poured herself a cup and carried it to the sitting room. No fire. Not even laid. She felt the tears bubble up her nose. It was too bad. She'd had a lovely afternoon and everything was going so well. You would have thought that a fire wasn't too much to ask.

She put her cup on the mantelpiece with some force and it slopped tea into the saucer. Making little moaning sounds of self-pity, she got to her knees and began to place paper and sticks in the usual wigwam. She had to get up again to find a match, then down again to light the wigwam and feed in small coal. Then up again to reach her cup. Then down again to crouch like Cinderella over the first flickering flames. Thank God for Boris and Bessie. They at least helped and supported her. Where the *hell* was Gilda?

She began to feel better and to remember Malcolm clearing up in the treatment room. She would take him a cup of tea; that would please him. She glanced at herself in the mirror. She'd leave that smudge of coal dust on her nose, it looked rather sweet and might provoke him into having a word with Gilda. She went back into the kitchen and poured more tea. It was not steaming any more. She sipped experimentally. Malcolm did not like tea unless it was scalding. She poured it into the milk saucepan and boiled it over the gas. More washing-up for Gilda. Serve her right.

In the wide, thickly carpeted hall, the children's voices came pleasantly down the stairs. Malcolm would think she was with them, of course. He would be pleased and surprised to see that her idea for inviting Boris and Bessie together was working out so well.

She turned the handle and went into the all-white room. Then she stopped. The light inside the room was unusually dim; the heavy velvet curtains had been pulled over the thick white nets, though at half-past-five on a fine April day it would be light for some time. Even so she had no difficulty in discerning the main event. On the treatment table Malcolm lay supine, fully clothed in white coat and serge trousers. However, his flies must have been opened because above him straddled Gilda and it was quite obvious that although she too was still dressed in black and white, even to her cap, she was without her knickers.

It took them all of two seconds to realise from the light that the door had been opened. Even then they were quite unable to disconnect for another two seconds. Perhaps it would have been longer, but the force of a cup and saucer hitting Gilda's shoulder, and the sudden shock of the scalding tea on bare thighs, hands, faces and other parts, accelerated their actions dramatically. Gilda screamed and fell to the floor. Malcolm sat up, clutching his revealed penis with one hand, his left cheek and eye with the other.

"Christ al*mighty*, woman! What the *hell* do you think you're doing?" he roared furiously.

Myrtle felt her self-control leave her. She rushed around the table and kicked Gilda as hard as she was able.

"Get out!" she panted. "Get out of this house now! D'you hear me?" And she went on kicking as Gilda scrambled up, grabbed her knickers, which were hardly worth calling knickers, and made sobbingly for the door. Myrtle then slammed it hard and leaned against it, knees slightly bent, the back of her wrist to her forehead.

"I hate you," she said fiercely. "I hate you with all my soul! The patients—oh I suppose half of them expect it and pay for it! But Gilda! The maid!"

Malcolm swung his legs down and dealt with his flies. He was as upset as she was.

"Damned woman," he kept repeating in varying registers. "Damanblasted woman! Interfering. Things she knows nothing about." He glanced up. "Christ, you look like someone from the silent movies except that you don't know what the word silent means."

"Good mind to throw you out after her."

"Don't seem to realise that when a girl like that keeps pestering, the easiest way to shut her up—"

"Lock stock and barrel. The new electro-massager. The lot."

"She's been asking for it ever since she arrived. And you went off without a word this afternoon, taking everyone with you."

"Once too often. That's what you've done, Malcolm Lennox. You've done it once too often."

"Trying to scald me into celibacy! Christ, I've heard some stories about what women do to their men. But trying to scald the balls off me—"

They both stopped speaking as noises were heard outside. Myrtle looked a warning and turned the door handle. Boris' voice came loud and clear.

"Where do you think you're going, Gilda?"

"Leaving." Gilda did not sound regretful. There was a small ring of triumph to her voice. Boris on the other hand sounded suddenly mature, and Myrtle realised his voice had completely broken.

"Not with my sister's fur coat, you're not!"

Blustering noises were suddenly cut off as Malcolm took the door handle from Myrtle and closed the latch by the simple expedient of leaning against her.

She looked up at him. He was laughing.

"Malcolm. We really should go and sort things out," she whispered.

"Boris can do it. Good for him." He rested his forehead on hers and looked at her. "Did you want to castrate me? Really?"

"Yes. If it stops you making love to other women."

"I don't make love to them. I"—

"Don't you dare use that word to me, Malcolm Lennox!"

"No. Not to you. Because I make love to you, Myrtle Lennox. That's what we do. Together. We make love. And we make babies."

"There! You said it to me!" She glowed with triumph. "It's not me who says it to you. Not always."

"No." He was breathing into her mouth. She was reminded of Cass telling her that you made friends with a horse by breathing into its nostrils. "No. Not always." He tilted his head so that he could kiss her. She moved slightly to free her mouth.

"It's all very well. But I don't like you doing—what you do—to every other woman in sight. Especially the maid!"

"Oh, bunny rabbit. She did it to me. Honestly."

"I know. I saw." She tried to sound frigid. She tried to stiffen her body against his. But then she remembered throwing the tea at him and a little giggle shook the baby. He felt it.

"Myrtle. Myrtle. Myrtle. Myrtle . . ."

Each time he said her name he kissed her. Each kiss was different. Better. Or worse, depending on your point of view.

Boris called, "Myrtle. Are you all right? What the hell is happening?"

Malcolm lifted his head.

"We've fired the maid, old man. And Myrtle and I are just clearing up in here. Can you cope for ten minutes?"

A slight pause, then Boris said, "Yes. Is that okay with you, Sis?"

She was nearly swooning against the door, but she forced herself to sound natural as she called reassurances.

Then she was lying on the treatment table, wriggling her pants down beneath her smock.

"Are you sure you can manage?" She eyed him with sudden concern. He really was very red.

"Ask me in ten minutes."

Thoughts crossed her mind hazily during that time. Firstly that though he was over-sexed she really wouldn't have him any other way. Secondly that it was almost worth catching him out each time, because it brought him so close to her for a few days; even sometimes a whole week. And thirdly . . .

She whispered to him afterwards, "You know what Gilda . . . did . . . to you?"

"Baby-bunny-darling, I'm sorry. Forgive me. I adore you—you must know that—"

"Sweetheart, I'm not angry. But I thought . . . I wondered . . . shall *I* do it to you next time?"

"Oh . . . *baby* . . ." He was almost on his knees. She sat up and smiled at him as if he were a small boy. Perhaps that was the answer. To be Gilda as well as Myrtle. She took his face in her hands and was a long time kissing him, breathing into his mouth gently all the time. Yes, she must remember that. And something else too. Malcolm did not mind if she hurt him. It seemed to raise his passion to fresh heights.

She started to laugh quietly.

"What are you laughing at, naughty girl?" he asked.

"Just thinking. I could do with a nice hot cup of tea. Right now. Couldn't you?"

Clutching each other, almost helpless with laughter, they went into the kitchen where Bessie was tying on bibs while Boris laid the table. Myrtle was on top of the world.

"Darlings, you're absolutely marvellous. If you ever need references—"

Nicholas chanted, "Gilda gone. Gilda gone."

Bessie said indignantly, "D'you know, she was going to take your fur coat, Auntie Myrt!"

"No! Was she really?"

"Yes. And she said you were a—"

Boris interrupted. "She said some pretty insulting things, Sis. I bundled her out fast."

"Well done, old man!" Malcolm took Martin on to his knee, an

85

unprecedented action. "Good job you were around."

Boris said straightly, "Yes, it was."

Bessie put milk in four saucerless cups. "She wasn't really insulting, Borrie, was she? She was on about Auntie Myrt being on heat or something."

Boris looked apprehensively at his sister and brother-in-law. They could no longer contain themselves. They leaned over Martin, almost weeping with laughter.

After a while, with Bessie and Martin joining in, Boris said in the same stern voice, "You shouldn't keep laughing like that, Sis. It's not good for the baby."

Myrtle wailed anew. "Not good for the baby! Did you hear that, lover man? Not good for the baby!"

Boris had had enough for one day.

"Better get the tea, Sis. Before your strength runs out completely!" he snapped.

Somehow, between them, they produced a scrap meal. It was like a party. Except that Boris was so glum. Even he cheered up when Bessie said contentedly, "Gosh. I'd rather be here than anywhere else if I can't be with Grannie and Cass."

That night, as if to justify Boris' gloom, Myrtle went into labour. It was her fourth pregnancy; she had had a miscarriage six months after her wedding. The first pain woke her with a jerk. It was bad, but she smiled into the darkness, glad it was early, glad it had been brought on by Malcolm's love-making, because it would be a future weapon in their constant duel. But when the pain did not stop her smile disappeared, and she held the edges of her mattress in sudden fear. She was stoical where pain was concerned and had been able to put up with the ripping convulsions of childbirth in the knowledge that each one had an ending. This went on and on. She had barely enough breath to call Malcolm, and wished—not for the first time—that he hadn't insisted on single beds for health reasons. He took so long to rouse, which wasn't surprising after his exertions that afternoon. She pulled the mattress upwards. It was a firm orthopaedic one, but by the time Malcolm had struggled out of his bed she had almost wrapped it around herself.

"It can't be yet!" He snicked on the light and narrowed his eyes at her. "God. Myrt. Something must be wrong. You've never been like this before."

She managed to croak the word "doctor," then "hospital," then she went into the private world of pain where there was just herself and this monster twisting her insides to bits. She knew she mustn't scream. For one thing it would take some of her concentration away from the enemy pain, for another it would wake Nicky and Martin. And Bessie. Oh God. She thought suddenly of Cass having Bessie, alone and sixteen years old, stuck somewhere godawful, going through this. They should all have helped, all stuck together . . . they'd had something, something precious, and they'd let it go.

After that she could not put her thoughts together properly. Two things protruded like iceberg tips in the sea of frightfulness; one was that this time it must be a girl, because everything was so different; the other was that she and Liv and Cass and Mon must get together again. For Bessie's sake. One big family. For Bessie's sake.

Malcolm woke Boris when the ambulance arrived. He was by this time crazed with terror.

"She's going to die! It's never been like this before—I tell you she's going to die, Boris!"

Boris bundled out of bed and across the landing in time to look at his sister's face at one end of the stretcher. He turned with sudden venom on his brother-in-law.

"If she does, it's your fault! I know what went on in that room this afternoon! I've seen it at home! It's nothing more than rape—d'you hear me?"

Malcolm heard but barely comprehended. He shook his head as he trailed down the stairs with the pre-packed suitcase.

"You don't understand," he muttered. "I love her. I really love her." He looked up from the hall and his face was running with tears. "Take care of things, old man. I'll be back. As soon as poss."

Boris stared after them. The front door closed and there were noises that diminished as the ambulance drove around the square and into Oriel Road. He tried to stay with his sister inside his head. He conjured up a picture of her distorted face and silent writhing body. Behind the picture he could see the scene of degradation that he imagined had taken place in the treatment room hours before. He had witnessed other scenes between his own parents and had no way of knowing that every seduction is different. His mother's was instigated by pleading: "Please Ivan. I love you. I've said I forgive you. Please darling." The ensuing copulation was abject on her part, impatient on his father's. Boris was certain that his father's acts of infidelity were his way of announcing his innate supremacy over his wife. In fact, a complicated system of rape.

Boris put his head on the newel post. He could not very well murder his own father. But Malcolm was a different case altogether.

He felt a touch on his shoulder and looked up with a spine-aching jolt. It was Bessie.

"What is it?" she whispered. "You look terrible. Awful."

She was just a kid. In her sprigged cotton nightie with her black curls wild, she looked younger than ever.

He whispered back, "Myrtle's started having the new baby. She's gone to hospital with Malcolm. She looked very ill."

"Oh, poor Borrie. You're anxious. You're so sweet."

He said, "No. You're sweet, Bessie. You're sweet and innocent and good. You're the only truly good person I know."

Her eyes were round and very black.

"Borrie. Are you crying?"

"No." He swallowed. "Promise me you'll stay the same. Promise me you won't ever do anything . . . horrible."

"I'm always doing horrible things, Borrie. I forget to say my prayers, and I put salt in Cass' tea last time she was home."

"You what?"

"It was a joke. But when she started being sick, I felt terrible."

He spluttered. "Oh, Bessie."

"Listen." She put on a busy voice that he recognised as Mrs. Woodford's. "Just stop worrying about Myrtle, and go back to bed. I'll read you a story. And when you wake up everything will be all right. You're going to be an uncle again."

She sat on the end of his bed and read from *Girl of the Limberlost.* He watched her avidly. She *was* good. She had been the only good thing about Myrtle's wedding, and since then he'd met her often outside her school and in the park, and each time she carried this air of purity with her.

He stopped thinking of Myrtle's tortured face, and drifted off to sleep. And Bessie crept back to her room and wished very much she was with Grannie and Cass.

■

At eight o'clock Myrtle was wheeled to the operating theatre and given a Caesarean section. After eight hours of agony she no longer remembered that she was in labour, and when she surfaced weakly for a few minutes she wondered why Malcolm kept talking and weeping.

It wasn't until another day and night had passed that she knew she had another son. And two days after that they told her the boy was a mongol.

5

Monica paid off the cab and stood outside the apartment block in Beekman Place, staring at it without her usual pleasure. The doorman came forward with an umbrella although the rain wasn't worth mentioning, and ushered her inside.

"Almost June," he grumbled sympathetically. "Wouldn't you think President Eisenhower would do something about it?"

Monica smiled obediently at the sally. Everyone in the block knew that Donaghue was an ardent Democrat and had actually wept real tears when Republican Eisenhower took over.

"It wouldn't have happened in Truman's time," she said automatically as she went through to the elevator.

She had become adept at what dear old Gander had called the "relevant rejoinder" in her days at the Albion. She eased the damp fur of her collar away from her neck and smiled briefly again and with cynicism.

The apartment was magnificent. In spite of her terrible ennui it hit her again as she went inside. Beekman Place housed the elite of New York and was opulently discreet—Bob called it downbeat. But in spite of his scoffing he shared her taste—her yearning—for "quality." They could have had a house on Long Island, a complex with fountains and a heated pool. But to reside in Beekman Place was to have made it in New York. The residents were nearly all connected with the Boston Five Hundred, and Bob had secured a lease solely because he had married an English lady who might well be the daughter of a duke.

She smiled again; at least she could be proud of that. At least she had brought something to the marriage. And perhaps this latest doctor was wrong. Perhaps this time next year she would have the baby she and Bob wanted so much. No-one could say definitely that she was unable to have children, it was impossible to predict such a thing.

But at the back of her mind she remembered Dr. Martin talking to her all those years ago. Telling her seriously that the infection in her Fallopian tubes might well have damaged them.

She had been uncaring then.

"It doesn't matter. I'd never go through that again anyway."

Her smile died and her whole body seemed to droop despairingly. She tried to recapture the stupid consoling thought of a moment ago: she might not be able to give Bob children, but she had given him a certain status. She trailed into her bedroom and kicked off her shoes. It was ironic: if she had gone ahead and married the first rich American she could find, she would have arrived here as a tart. By giving away her child and working for Dilly and Gander Gosling, she had come as a lady. That would tickle Gilly.

Nancy tapped on the door and came in. Monica surrendered her coat and lay back on the bed, exhausted. It was soothing to watch the tiny Korean girl hang up the coat, put away the shoes, ease the damp gloves on to stretchers.

"Tea please, Nancy. Plenty of hot water."

If only she could go into the kitchen and make it herself. She desperately needed to be doing something. If Nancy was the sort of maid in whom she could confide, it would help. But Nancy, a refugee from Inchon, was a little short on colloquial English. Besides, brought up in a Japanese household, she served Monica solely because she happened to be married to Bob.

The tea arrived. Nancy made a great to-do of lighting the spirit lamp beneath the pot.

"No sugar, Nancy?" Monica queried. She did not take sugar, but somehow she had to make someone else feel a little of the total inadequacy that engulfed her.

"Pliss?"

"There is no sugar on the tea tray," Monica enunciated.

"I t'ink Madam not take sugar."

"Madam needs some sugar today, Nancy. And, for the future, kindly note that a tea tray needs sugar as a woman needs children."

"Pliss?"

"Go and fetch sugar, Nancy."

Nancy disappeared and Monica lay back and looked at the corniced ceiling. For a moment she felt ashamed at taking out her despair on someone like Nancy who had run from war. Then she said aloud, "Who cares? I'm just as much a refugee as she is. And she can trot along to the South Korean Club and hobnob with fellow refugees. Where can I go?"

And then, with the honesty that gave her her integrity, she added, "Self-pity, Mon. Be careful."

Nancy returned with the sugar, and she said, "Are you going out this evening, Nancy?"

"Maybe." The girl gave her a wary look from those gorgeous almond eyes. "If Mister Bob not want me."

Monica squashed her irritation. Different culture, different language . . . She said, "Look in my scarf drawer, Nancy. Choose one. Whichever you like."

Of course the girl would have to choose the pure silk one that Bob had given her for her un-birthday present four years ago. She could hardly retract her generosity now.

"Fine," she said. "The colour is good on you."

Nancy draped it over her shoulders and smiled prettily.

"Very nice I t'ink." She glanced over one shoulder into the mirror. Her smugness grated unbearably on Monica—she had to keep reminding herself that the girl was a refugee.

"That will be all," she said sharply. "Go as soon as you are ready."

They had worked out the dinner menu this morning. Monica had thought it would be a celebration meal: tête-à-tête in the kitchen with coffee in proper big cups instead of the demi-tasses, and a steak for Bob that filled his plate.

Nancy disappeared again and Monica sat up slowly and swung her legs to the floor. She did not really want the tea. She wanted the comfort it could give, the sense of normalcy. She removed the lid of the teapot and inhaled the steam with closed eyes. She had felt twinges of homesickness before, but never like this. It had been enough to be Bob's wife, to be as rich as Croesus with a whole new world to explore. She reminded herself of her two sisters-in-law who had welcomed her into the family with overflowing American generosity. She had found herself saying, "This is wonderful, Hildie. Leone. Wonderful. Has Bob told you I was adopted? I've never felt I had a family. Until now."

It had been ridiculously sentimental; and untrue. She might have had unsatisfactory parents, but she had always had a brother. Oh God.

The steam made her eyes water, and she blinked angrily. How could she hanker after Gilly and that grotty little council house in Northfield when she had all this?

She said aloud again, and very calmly, "I don't think I can bear it." Then she poured her tea and drank it sedately.

Bob arrived home earlier than usual. She heard him talking to Nancy and Nancy's high-pitched giggle. Then he tapped and opened the door. No Englishman would tap on his own bedroom door; she was so damned lucky and she must remember that.

"Honey . . ." he came over and kissed her with great tenderness. "How did it go? You're exhausted. Hell, I could kill that gynecologist. Is it worth it, baby? Is it?"

She did not answer that.

"I'm a bit tired, I must admit. Has Nancy gone?"

"Yeah. Just wished her a good evening. What d'you suppose they get up to at that club of hers?"

"The usual. Music. Dancing. Flirting."

He laughed and kissed her again. "What do you know about it, miss? Is that the kind of thing you did when you were her age?"

"God, I'm not twenty-nine yet, Bob!"

"She's seventeen, hon. Can you remember that far back?"

She had to remind herself he was only teasing.

"Just about. Liv and I used to walk along Bristol Road eyeing up the boys. Nothing much changes."

"What about the other two? Myrtle and Carol?"

"They tried to make things happen."

"Huh?"

"Never mind. Let's go to the kitchen and I'll put the steaks on."

"Hang on. I want to hear about your afternoon. And I've got something for you."

Her heart sank. He'd bought her another present for this special occasion. And she had to tell him there was no occasion. Yet again.

To put off the moment, she reached up and took his velvet-soft ear lobe in gentle fingers.

"Come here, man," she said, and drew him to her.

He came willingly and they made love in their usual profligate fashion. The detached part of her mind that always stood sentinel on such occasions thought how very useful sex was. The other half thought that she would tell him everything: about Gilly, about Elizabeth. Everything. She owed it to him, but more than anything she owed it to herself. Dammit, she'd had a baby, she couldn't be barren. She couldn't be.

They lay side by side, sated. He continued to caress her and she closed her eyes.

"Was it all right, baby?" he whispered.

"It still is."

"Oh honey. Was there ever another woman like you?"

"Lots. Don't stop. Kiss me."

He did so and continued to do so.

"God. Monica. You know you drive me wild."

"Yes."

"I'm so bloody jealous! Just the thought of that doctor seeing you like this . . . being here . . . I can't stand it, honey!"

That meant she could never tell him about Gilly, of course. She held his head against her navel and opened her eyes to the same old ceiling, the same old cornices.

"You're crazy," she whispered.

"Yeah. I just said so. Crazy about you."

He moved and her body responded automatically. Yes. Sex was useful. Very useful indeed.

She had forgotten that she had stipulated oysters, and Nancy had gone to the market for them. Bob made jokes about their aphrodisiac properties and she pretended to be affronted. "Who needs aphrodisiacs?" she said pertly.

"Not me, hon. And not you either." He looked at her. "I take it everything was okay?"

94

"I'm not pregnant, Bob," she said bluntly, not meeting his eyes. "Sorry."

"Christ, hon. Early days."

"You're taking it better than me."

"I guessed it was negative when you went overboard in bed just now. I mean, when there's a positive result, we'll have to be careful."

"Rubbish." She rather resented the implication that their recent session had been all her doing. "You don't know the meaning of the word anyway!"

He reached for her hand. "Honey, when you tell me we are having a child, I'll be the most careful man in the world."

She took avoiding action and stood up to see to the steaks. She should have said there would never be any need for him to be careful where she was concerned. But she didn't.

He waited in silence while she dished up the steaks and put salad on the table. Then he said, "Okay, Monica. What's wrong?"

She kept her eyes on his plate while her heart jumped. He was too sentient. He knew.

"Nothing. Is there? It's practically raw. Just as you like it?"

"Idiot child. Your periods. Why did they stop? If there's something wrong for God's sake tell me, Monica. I'm your husband, remember?"

She laughed, surprised at her own relief.

"Oh that. Nerves. Apparently I was wishing pregnancy on myself. Did you know that bodies can do that sort of thing? It's okay, I'm not going funny or anything. It's quite common apparently."

"Oh . . . shoot!" He leaned back in his chair, grinning again. He was so easily fooled. So easily.

She said, "That's an Americanism I don't understand, darling. Shoot. What does it mean?"

"I'm not going to tell you. You'd be shocked. Oh baby, I thought—just for a moment—"

"Well, don't."

"Okay. But in that case, why not? Something's wrong. Is it my fault? There are tests for men, surely? Look, I don't mind going for a test if it would make you happy. You're all screwed up about this baby business—"

"Not so." She cut into her meat and thought that back home it would have been a month's ration a few years ago. "Everything is okay. I don't need you to take any test, my darling. I know you'd pass with flying colours. It's just a question of time and patience."

There. The lie was said. Everything okay. Hunky-dory.

He looked as smug as Nancy had.

"Yeah. I reckon I would," he said.

For a split second she hated him. Then she thought with the objective half of her mind: what the hell, sex is useful. So it's just as well he's good at it.

Much later, he produced a letter from his jacket pocket.

"I forgot. Told you I had something for you, didn't I?"

It was a letter addressed to his office. She looked inside the envelope. It was from Dilly Gosling.

"Why addressed to your office?"

"She says you didn't leave an address, honey."

"We had no address for ages. We went to Hildie's."

"Yeah, sure. But we've been here over a year. I should have thought you would have found time to write to her. I kinda look on her as your family."

Monica nodded. "She was more my family than the Cooks, that's for certain. You've read it?"

"I told you I was jealous. I wondered who was writing to Mrs. Gallagher at Mr. Gallagher's office address."

"Bob!" She was surprised. "It has an English stamp."

"Quite. You might have had a lover I didn't know about."

She didn't like it. Just supposing . . . Gilly had written to her. She said tightly, "Letters are private in my country, Bob."

"Not from husbands, honey."

She looked at him. His grey eyes were unfathomable.

"What about the other way round? May I open your mail?"

He laughed. "Not on your pretty little ass, you may not!"

She was suddenly angry. "Don't be so bloody patronising! Not on my pretty little ass, indeed! Typical. One law for men, another for women! Absolutely typical!"

He enveloped her in his arms and kissed her. "God, I love you when you're angry," he quipped. Then he tightened his grip against her struggles. "Listen. Mon. There's some bad news in it. I guessed there would be and I wanted to prepare you. If you'd been pregnant . . . you know." He kissed her again and she lifted her head and said, "Is it Gilly? Is it my brother?"

"No. It's poor old Gander. He died last winter. Bronchitis. I'm sorry, Mon."

She started to weep. Not for Gander Gosling. At least not only for Gander Gosling. But for Dilly and the Albion. And for Carol and Mrs. Woodford. And for Elizabeth her baby. Hers and Gilly's. Once started, she could not stop. Eventually Bob lifted her in his arms and carried her bodily into the bedroom. There he cradled her in one arm and stroked her hair and face with his free hand.

She sobbed, "I made lemon meringue pie. Hildie said it was your favourite, and Leone sent me the special recipe your mother always used, and I got the meringue to rise up like the Alps—"

"Oh baby." He combed her hair with his fingers. "Listen, how about if I bring it in here with a big pot of coffee and we plan a holiday for next month? Huh? I wondered about Yellowstone. We could hire a camper. What do you say?"

"Yes," she said simply.

She knew how it would be. He came to the bedroom door half a dozen times to ask where was the pie. And where did she keep the dessert plates. And no, they weren't there.

"Nancy has moved them again. Try the dresser."

"She's only seventeen," he said inconsequentially.

"It's the oldest age there is." She got off the bed and picked up Dilly's letter.

"What?" he yelled.

"Nothing. I'm going to the bathroom!"

It had been the only room in the house at Turves Green where she could get privacy. Nothing changed. She sat on the lavatory and spread the single page carefully.

Dilly wrote: "My dear girl . . . do you remember how Gander called you his dear girl? For seven years you were our dear girl, Monica, and you are still mine. Yes, I am writing to tell you that Gander died on Monday, and nothing will ever be the same again. I keep telling myself that I lived forty years before I met him, but I cannot remember how I managed. Perhaps I shall feel better after the funeral. Well dear, the funeral was yesterday and I do not feel better. Just empty. The church was quite full because he was captain of the bowls and a sidesman as well. I wish now we had not sold the old Albion after you got married to your nice American.

It would have done me good to work again. I am not seventy yet, it is nothing these days. Gander was seventy-five. Some people live until they are ninety. I wish you would write to me, Monica. You promised to send me your address and you didn't. But at least I know where your nice American works, so can get in touch with you there. It is a week later now, dear girl, and I have to tell you that Mrs. Woodford came over from France last Wednesday and stayed with me for three days. She read about Gander in *The Times* and came as soon as she could. She is a good woman. She wants me to go and have a holiday with them in France. I might do that, but I don't expect I shall really. Please write to me, Monica. This letter has taken me a fortnight. I must close now. God bless you, dear girl. From your old friend, Dilly Gosling."

Monica folded the letter slowly and gazed before her. Poor Dilly. Why hadn't she met her Gander much sooner and had a few more years with him? How we all waste time.

Bob called, "You all right, honey? Why have you locked the door?"

She said very clearly, "Because I can't go unless I do."

"Okay. But I've got everything together in the bedroom. Don't be long."

Monica sighed and pulled the flush. Sex was useful and invalidism was useful. But there were limits to both.

She stayed in bed for a week. It wasn't all put on, she felt really groggy and sometimes when she went to the bathroom it was like walking on the deck of a rolling ship. But she knew at the back of her mind that if she had a purpose in life, she would be instantly better. She and Bob planned to "do" Yellowstone in the fall; Hildie came in from Connecticut with grapes and tickets for a concert. Nancy ate the grapes and although Monica got up and went to the concert, she fell asleep halfway through.

Hildie said, "You come back with me to the farm, honey. Leonard will fill you up with good fresh eggs and butter."

"You're sweet, Hildie," Monica said sincerely. "But I couldn't expect your husband to look after me."

"Monica! Leonard is the hired help for godsakes! Surely you remember the name of my *husband!*"

"Oh lord. I'm sorry, Hildie. Of course I do." But it had completely slipped her mind. She wondered if she were going mad.

"Wait till I tell George that! And he thought he made such a great impression on his English sister-in-law! Oh my dear! You always make me laugh! What a girl!"

Hildie did not often come to New York, so they had to do a lot of things in the two days she was with them. They shopped in Fifth Avenue, and they trailed around Macy's until Monica wanted to scream with boredom. She remembered how she and Liv had endlessly window-shopped during the war and wondered why. Perhaps it was only enjoyable when you couldn't afford to buy anything. Now there was no need to shop. You saw a model you liked, you ordered it, it was delivered.

The weather was suddenly glorious. "Dwight might be getting the hang of things," Donaghue said grudgingly. They went for lunch at Saks and Hildie talked. She loved talking and George was not a good listener. She was mad about the British Royal Family. She had actually met the Duke of Windsor back in '38 on board a yacht in the Mediterranean.

"I could understand why he fell for Wallis Simpson, my dear. She wasn't strictly beautiful but she had a sort of chic."

Monica thought of Cass. She did not have chic, but she had the long nose and face of the Duchess.

"George always said I reminded him of Wallis," Hildie confessed archly. "Maybe that was why he fell for me!"

"Maybe." Monica tried to make an effort. "Did Bob tell you how we sat up all night along the Mall for the Coronation?"

"He sure did." Hildie smiled. "Leone and I knew you were right for each other after that. I mean—if you saw Lillibet and Phil-up getting crowned, well, what else could you do?"

Monica laughed at last, and let Hildie pat her hand.

Later, when the coffee arrived, Hildie was a little less reassuring. "Listen, honey. I'm going to talk to you like a Dutch uncle now. You're good for Bob. You know that as well as I do. He hasn't looked at another woman since he set eyes on you. And that's something. I'm telling you, Monica, that is something."

Monica murmured, "We're very close."

"I'm glad to hear it, honey. And make sure you clinch it. As soon as possible now, d'you hear me?" Her tone became teasingly hectoring. "You give him a baby just as soon as you can, and he'll never look at another woman. That's what Bob wants . . . needs. A family of his own.'

Monica swallowed. "Me too."

Hildie looked partially reassured. "Of course you do, honey. I said to George you were the maternal sort. But . . . well, you know . . . with your face and figure a lot of women would want to give child-bearing a miss. Like Tansy. I said to George, history doesn't repeat itself and Monica isn't a bit like Tansy—"

"Bob's first wife?" Monica said faintly.

"Sure. Hasn't he mentioned her? Well, maybe it's all for the best. He was very bitter. She wouldn't have children, you see. She conceived—of course—and she had an abortion. Didn't bother to mention it to Bob. That was when he divorced her."

"Oh, my God."

"Maybe I shouldn't have told you."

"No, I'm glad you did." She was. But it made things worse.

Hildie said, "You're looking peaky again, honey. D'you want to get back to Beekman Place?"

"If you're sure you're all through shopping." Monica used the American phrase deliberately. She liked Hildie. She thought how marvellous it would have been to tell Hildie that she was pregnant and to live out here with these people for always.

When Hildie went back, Monica felt so tired she hardly knew how to dress in the mornings and undress at night. Invalidism had well and truly taken the place of sex now, and Bob even offered to sleep in the spare room until she was well again. She shook her head at him, but she was usually asleep when he came to bed anyway.

One evening at the end of June, he tried to talk to her about Indo-China.

"It's Korea all over again," he said. "De Gaulle had to give them independence, but the Communists won't be satisfied with a partition."

She tried hard to be interested. "I suppose if you believe in an ideology enough, it's natural to want to spread the message. Look at missionaries."

"For chrissakes, Monica, what have missionaries got to do with Ho Chi Minh? Do missionaries kill people if they won't go along with Christianity?"

"Of course not. But I guess we thought God was on our side in the war. We killed for His sake."

"Honey, you're unable to follow a logical train of thought. You'll be bringing in the Saracens and Crusaders next."

"I'm sorry, Bob. It's a long way off. And there is no personal connection. It's difficult to . . . to identify."

100

"Think of Nancy. Is that personal enough for you?"

"She's Korean."

"You weren't listening. I said to you it's like Korea all over again. Nancy was a servant in a Japanese household in Korea. When the Japs left, the Commies came down from the north and she had to leave fast. Think of all the Nancies that will have to leave fast if Ho Chi Minh has his way."

She did not want to think of Nancy. She suspected that the girl had been more than a servant in that Japanese family.

"Yes. Well. What can we do about it?"

Bob looked moody. "At least think about it. The United Nations should take a hand, of course. But after Korea . . . ."

Bob had had a desk job in the army and had been too old for Korea. She knew that part of him longed for action. Typically American, he had too much energy which sometimes festered into dissatisfaction.

She said, "Let's go to bed, darling."

He raised his eyebrows. "Are you up to it, honey? I'd rather wait until you're strong again."

"I'm up to it. I'm strong enough."

"What about the dishes?"

"Nancy will do them when she gets in from her club."

He hesitated. "Tell you what. I'll scribble a note telling her to leave them till tomorrow."

"She'll never be able to read it. Leave it, darling."

"Go and get ready. I'll be with you in a minute."

She crossed the hall to the bedroom, her good intentions already dissipating in dragging exhaustion. Her suspenders almost defeated her; tears pricked her eyes. Why hadn't Bob offered to undress her?

She heard Nancy's key in the lock and Bob's voice telling her about the dishes. Then nothing.

There was no point in putting on a nightdress; she slid between the sheets naked and lay on her side, waiting. Half an hour later, when Bob came to bed, he found her fast asleep with the light still on. Carefully he switched it off.

She woke with a start. She felt she had been asleep for two minutes, but when she looked at the clock it was three in the morning. Bob was not there. He must be in the spare room. Thankfully she closed her eyes again.

∎

The next morning she could hear him singing in the bathroom. She pushed back the bedclothes and swung her legs to the floor, feeling weaker than usual. Also ridiculous without any clothes. Strange, if Bob had been with her last night her morning nakedness would have felt voluptuous. She drew on the satin dressing-gown that reminded her of Ginger Rogers, and went to the window. The view of the river never failed to give her pleasure, but this morning it was already shimmering with heat and she knew she would not be able to go out. Her heart sank. Another day to get through.

Bob breezed in smelling of cologne.

"Hi there, honey! How d'you sleep?"

"Like a log. Why didn't you come to bed?"

He sat on a chair and fiddled with a shoehorn.

"I did. You were dead to the world." His feet clicked into his shoes and he stood up, marking time experimentally on the thick carpet. "Honey. Why did you give that scarf to Nancy?"

"Scarf?" Her head throbbed as she thought back. It was almost two months since she'd tried to be nice to Nancy by giving her the scarf. "Oh. Yes. Darling, I'm sorry. I told her to pick herself a scarf one day. She would have to take that one." She went towards him. "You don't mind too much, do you?"

His pumping legs took him past her to the window.

"You shouldn't open this, honey. It defeats the object of the air conditioning." He closed the window. "I don't mind about the scarf, baby. It was yours to give. Suits Nancy a lot."

He pecked her briefly and was gone. And when Nancy brought her breakfast, she could tell from the girl's secret smile exactly what had happened.

She looked listlessly at the letter propped on the silver teapot, and sat up straight when she recognised Dilly's spidery scrawl. Eagerly she tore at the envelope.

"Dear girl," it began, as before. "Your letter was balm to me. Absolute balm. Yes, I can still sew a fine seam, Monica, and I took your advice and started straightaway. I've just finished a lovely wedding dress for the daughter of a friend. I wish you could see it, dear girl. You would be proud of me. The other thing you asked about was not so easy, as it was difficult to write to Mrs. Woodford about that particular matter. I did drop a note enquiring for Elizabeth's health and well-being, but have heard nothing to date. However, life is strange, dear girl. On Sunday last, the young lady mentioned above came for a fitting and enquired whether I would accompany her to Cheltenham to match up the headdress. I went with her and who should I see there but your friend, Myrtle Denning that was. My dear girl, what a change there! So ill-looking. It seems she has a little boy of two who is Not Quite the Thing. He is obviously wearing her out. But in the course of conversation she told me she would never be able to manage if it weren't for Bessie. Bessie Woodford no less. Bessie comes to stay with her quite often and has a way with the little boy. He will do anything for her it seems. So you see, Monica, Elizabeth must be a very special child. I hope that answers your question. And now, dear girl, for mine. When are you coming home for a visit? You and your husband can stay with me at any time. It would give me so much pleasure . . ."

Monica read on to the sentimental end, her eyes filling with tears. Then she found a handkerchief, dried her eyes, blew her nose and picked up the phone. She dialled Hildie's number.

"It's me. Monica. Listen, Hildie. I'm leaving. For England. Can you tell Bob? Make it sound . . . okay?"

There were noises in the background. The farm was a busy place. Hildie said, "What's that, honey? Tell Bob what? You sound better, honey. Why don't you come out to the far—"

Monica said firmly, "I'm going home, Hildie. I might not come back. You see, I can't have children and I can't seem to tell him. And when I thought that one day . . . I mean I could put up with him . . . you know. But he slept with our Korean maid last night."

"Oh my God. Oh Monica, honey. Are you sure?"

"Yes."

"Fire her. Now. Put her on the line. I'll fire her."

"There'd be someone else. You tried to warn me. Remember?"

"Honey. Don't take any notice of me. Bob loves you. He has told me often, you're the most exciting girl he's ever met."

Monica said firmly, "Hildie, sex is only exciting up to a point. It must have a meaning, an end result. Can you tell him—try to explain—make it easy for him—"

"Monica, wait. Listen. Don't you love him? You must love him else you wouldn't be talking like this. You have to fight for him. You have to—you have to—"

Very carefully, Monica replaced the phone. Then lifted it and laid it on the bedside table. She went to the bathroom and showered, then came back and dressed without too much difficulty. And then she began to pack. In a funny kind of way she was grateful to Bob for sleeping with Nancy. It made her feel less guilty.

She thought of Elizabeth, and a surge of excitement swept through her.

6

iv had been close to Myrtle since that fateful wedding
day back in '51. It was then she had met her own
husband, and as he and Malcolm Lennox had been at
school together, it was natural that the four of them
should feel a strong bond. Besides, Liv and Myrtle felt
they were the only survivors from the schoolgirl foursome of the
war years. But they had never shared a roof before, and as Liv
ushered Myrtle and her brood inside her four-bedroomed detached des. res. in Barnt Green, she knew a moment of pure terror.
The hall and stairs were carpeted in grey and pink velvet, the
woodwork pristine white. The lounge suite was pale leaf green
with curtains and wallpaper to tone. The only room that would
absorb fingermarks was the dining room which was pseudo-oak-
panelled with parquet block floor and a refectory table to match.
She led the way quickly to that room and held the door wide until
they were all inside, then shut it firmly and stood against it.
   "How absolutely lovely to see you all," she said faintly, surveying them through the blue-tinted glasses that made her eyes look

bigger than ever. "We thought Malcolm would drive you up, Myrt. Reggie was looking forward to seeing him at dinner."

Myrtle pulled out a dining chair which must have weighed a ton, and sat down, dragging Mally on to her lap. He turned in against her and put his fingers in her mouth.

She spoke with difficulty through the tiny fist.

"He had appointmentsh all day. He put ush on the train. Ghashly journey. Got a taxshi okay though."

Mally started to laugh, so of course Nicky and Martin had to join in. They egged each other on until they were screaming hysterically. Myrtle made it worse by pretending to eat Mally's fingers. They weren't even clean fingers.

Liv said loudly, "Would you like a cup of tea before dinner, Myrtle?"

"Absholuly adore one!"

Nicky mimicked screechingly, "Absholuly, shertainly!" And Martin clapped his hand over his mouth as if to hold his innards in place and immediately blew a huge bubble from one nostril.

Myrtle removed Mally's hand, and used a handkerchief on her middle child.

"Let me come and help you, Liv. My goodness, what a noise. I think they might be pleased to be here, Auntie Liv, don't you?"

"Yes. No. It's quite all right. Stay here and rest for a few minutes, Myrt. I'll bring the tea in, then we can take your stuff upstairs."

She went into the hall again, sliding through the door as if frightened one of them might escape. Myrtle's luggage lay about where the taxi driver had dumped it. Refugees' luggage. Lots of soft leather bags bulging odd shapes, a basket overflowing with nappies and baby bottles, and a towel covering what was obviously a potty.

She felt completely helpless. She went into the kitchen and plugged in the kettle. The tea trolley was laid ready with biscuits for the children and scones for Myrtle and herself. As she put the pot on the brass stand, there was a flash of colour outside the window. She looked out. Nicky and Martin were running around the garden like puppies, jumping the flower beds, rolling down the grassed slope to the sunken garden, jumping for the apples on the laden tree. She went to the door and opened it, intending to call to them to come in at once, but she saw that Myrtle had somehow managed to open the French doors from the dining room and was helping Mally down the single step to join his brothers.

Liv withdrew and wheeled the trolley through the hall.

"Darling, how delightful!" Myrtle tapped Mally on the bottom to send him off, and came back to the table. "And I'd forgotten how marvellous your garden is. If only the weather holds, we won't see much of the children. Look at them! They're like prisoners let loose! That train was so full, my dear. I just can't tell you how awful it was." She sat down without grace and pulled up her dress. "D'you mind if I take off my stockings, Liv?" She pulled at her suspenders and revealed unsavoury underwear.

Liv put a cup of tea on the table and went to fasten the French doors back.

"These haven't been opened for years. I wonder you managed it." She stared anxiously. 'They won't trample the flowers, will they?'

"Relax, Liv. Make the most of their absence." Myrtle smiled over her shoulder with real affection. "Oh Liv . . . it's so good of you to have us like this. You don't know how I longed to get away. Having to keep them quiet when the patients come . . . well, you can imagine."

"Yes. It must be difficult." Liv smiled back, forgetting for a moment the furniture and flower beds. "You're marvellous, Myrt. Everyone is full of admiration about the way you're coping. How do you feel these days?"

"Oh. About a hundred and eight. Mally's not easy, of course. And Malcolm is as demanding as ever." But she laughed comfortably at this last.

"I wouldn't have that if I were you," Liv said definitely. "Malcolm should help you, pull his weight. When Reggie told me you were pregnant again, I couldn't believe it. Men are utterly selfish of course, but really—"

"Liv, it was me who wanted this baby!" Myrtle said frankly. Then she drooped. "But I must admit I really do feel about a hundred and eight. And when Borrie said he was going on this camera course, I nearly died. He's such a *help*, Liv. You wouldn't believe it. He and Bessie Woodford between them take the boys off my hands entirely. The thought of the whole of August without them—ugh!"

"He's certainly healed the breach with Cass. I had a birthday card from her last month. Must remember to send her one next winter. Goodness, d'you remember my fourteenth when we had one of our après-midis in the Haunted House?"

"I can remember you playing that blasted violin of yours. And Mon and me pelting you with ink pellets, and Cass saying she thought you had talent. Just in case your feelings were hurt!"

"Cass was so—so kind." Liv sipped her tea and tried not to notice the veins in Myrtle's bare feet and legs. "I suppose that was why she got into trouble."

"Yes. Oh God. I shouldn't have said anything to her, should I? I was just so mad to think she'd caught Malcolm off-balance on our wedding day! Suddenly, just for a moment, she looked like some femme fatale. Oh, I hated her!"

"No you didn't. You hated Malcolm. But you couldn't do much about that, so you hit out at Cass." Liv gave her worldly-wise smile which had so irritated Myrtle once, but now seemed justified. "What surprises me, looking back, is why Cass took it so to heart. Running off to France like that. Rather extreme."

"Yes. But Cass . . ."

"Quite."

There were sounds in the hall and Reggie came in, smiling broadly. "Have the evacuees arrived, Mother?" he asked, pretending not to see Myrtle. Then, with a double take, "It's them! All one and a half of them!" He scooped Myrtle up and hugged her soundly. "Where are the other displaced persons?"

Liv thought he was going much too far, but Myrtle didn't mind. "In the garden, trampling your flowers, Reggie dear," she said sweetly.

But he didn't seem to mind that either. He went through the French doors and started chasing the boys all over the place. Little Mally screamed and dribbled and the next minute Martin screamed louder still as Mally went into the fishpond.

"Oh . . . *Christ!*" Liv practically sobbed.

Myrtle shook her head. "Oh, Liv. You'll never go to heaven. Swearing like that!"

"It's not funny, Myrt. The hall carpet . . ."

Myrtle looked at her pityingly. Sometimes she had the feeling that Liv didn't know what life was all about. She took the squalling Mally from Reggie and airlifted him over the precious floors and up to the bathroom. Reggie followed with the bags. Martin and Nicky sat up at the refectory table with Liv standing sentinel at the door.

"This is what family life is all about," Reggie said enthusiastically from the bathroom door. "May I come in and sponge my trousers, Myrtle?"

"It's your bathroom!" Myrtle finished stripping off Mally and stood him in the bath. She turned the taps on and stirred the water vigorously. "Is Liv going to be able to put up with family life for a whole week, d'you think, Reggie?"

"Oh, she'll get to love it. That's why I suggested to Malcolm . . ." he sponged away, leaning away from Myrtle so that she couldn't see his face. "Thing is, old girl, life is a bit monotonous for Liv and me. It'll be like Christmas, having you and the kids. I just wish Malcolm could have come."

Myrtle said nothing for a long time. Eventually she turned off the taps and sat Mally in the tepid water. He tried to put his muddy arms around her neck again, and she disengaged herself and reached for the soap. As she began to lather him, Mally went into what his father called his vegetarian state. She looked at him with the infinite sadness that came to her now and then since the birth and had replaced the anxiety and discontent of before. His body was stunted and squashed, rather like his flat mongolian head, his hair rigidly straight, but his tiny hands and feet were perfect. The doctors had said that the chance of it happening again was a million to one, and it would be good for them to have another baby. Malcolm had shaken his head decisively, but she had worked on him. She needed another baby to prove . . . something.

She let Mally lie back in his dream state, and straightened her spine. Reggie had his back to her still, and was rubbing at the damp patches with a beautiful, pristine huckaback towel.

She said quietly, "You're an idiot, Reggie. I thought it was just Liv who didn't know anything about anything. But you're both as bad as one another."

He said defensively, "I don't know what you're on about, Myrt. Just because we haven't had to go through the hoop like you and Malcolm, doesn't mean we don't sympathise."

"Oh my dear. Of course you sympathise. Which is very good and noble of you in the circs. Because you don't understand." She sighed. "Reggie, let me get this straight. Malcolm rang you to tell you about the new baby. You suggested that we have a holiday with you. Firstly because you care about us and want to help. Secondly because you find your life empty, you'd like children, and you thought that given a taste of family life, so would Liv. Am I right so far?"

Reggie wasn't used to this clear-thinking Myrtle. The girl he knew as his wife's friend and his friend's wife, was scatty, passionate and very laissez-faire.

He sat on the lavatory seat and looked at her. She was thinner than she'd been on her wedding day and her eyes were lined from lack of sleep. She had disguised her incipient bump with a dirndl skirt which did nothing for her short figure, and the knitted top above it emphasised her enormous bust, but she had a definite earthy attraction and Reggie could feel it. He took a breath and looked away.

"Well . . . perhaps. Not quite so . . . but on the whole, yes. I suppose so."

She sighed sharply. "That's why you're an idiot, Reggie dear. Why do you think Malcolm jumped at your invitation and then didn't come? Because he'll have a clear field with his female patients, that's why. Don't get me wrong—he loves me and I know it. But . . . he still wants that clear field, and it's difficult when his pregnant wife and three children are swarming all over the place." She laughed without a trace of bitterness and leaned over to pat his knee. "It's all right, Reggie. Don't look like that. I could have refused to come, and I'm here, aren't I?"

She sat back on her heels and looked again at her supine child.

"The other thing is, Reggie, surely you know Liv by now? Having us here will put her off a family for life. Can't you see that?"

He was on firmer ground there.

"Rubbish. Oh I know there will be hiccups, especially at first." He laughed determinedly and brushed at his trouser legs. "I mean—it wasn't clever of me to chase the boys so that Mally fell in the pond, was it? I admit that. But give me credit for some sense, Myrt. Please. Liv and I . . . we go deep now. We've been married almost as long as you and Malcolm. Nearly six years. My God, hasn't time flown! Liv wanted a detached house near Northfield, membership of the golf club . . . all that. She's got it. Now she wants something else."

Myrtle stood up and took the towel from him, then scooped Mally into it.

"All right, Reggie," she said. "All right. We'll see what we can do. I promise. Okay?"

"You're a good egg, Myrt." Reggie stood up and put a hand on her shoulder.

A voice floated up the stairs.

"What on earth are you doing up there, Reggie? I need some help with these boys and their tea!"

"Coming, darling." He smiled at Myrtle. "See what I mean?"

He shut the bathroom door carefully on the woman and her child, and went downstairs.

By the end of the second day, Liv and Myrtle were both making secret plans to cut the holiday short. Myrtle was far more tired than she would have been at home where Tom and Doris, the married couple who had taken Gilda's place, would have kept an eye on Nicky and Martin and left her free to give all her time to Mally. The boys went to a select kindergarten each morning, where they were encouraged to "explore their environment." Suddenly that was not such a good idea; Liv's stipulation was that they should not explore.

On the phone to Malcolm, Myrtle said brightly, "Fine, darling. Really fine. Liv and I are having such lovely natters." And then, looking over her shoulder at the empty hall, she said in a low voice, "It's dreadful, Malcolm. The boys don't know what to do with themselves and Nicky has broken two glasses . . . well, she gives them glasses of water at lunch time . . . yes, two of them . . . he simply bites pieces off them, darling. Of course it's dangerous. I nearly had a fit both times. I'm surprised I'm still carrying this baby . . . Mally? You know Mally. He loves everyone. Yes, even Liv!" She listened and gave a low laugh, then said hastily, "Don't you dare say anything like that to Reggie! Seriously now, Malcolm! He's a nice man—a good man—and he's got a tough life here." She listened again, lips thinning with exasperation. Then she said, "You! You have an easy time of it, my lad, and don't you forget it! I wish you could try coping with Liv like Reggie has to! You might appreciate me a bit more then. What? Oh . . . yes, of course I love you too. But you're wicked. Yes, all right, I do . . . I do . . . very much."

Liv appeared in the hall from the kitchen. She was wearing pale green linen slacks which looked wet.

"Myrtle! That son of yours has got into the fishpond again! I've left him to drip on the grass, but the other two will talk him into trying it again if you don't come quickly!"

Myrtle gabbled, "Must go, darling. Mally. Bye." She clapped down the phone and went quickly.

Liv did not follow her. She stood on her beautiful grey and pink carpet and stared down at the dark water-stain on her beautiful pale green trousers. A tear dropped from her eye. The phone rang.

"You're through, caller," sang the exchange. And Malcolm Lennox's voice said, "What has happened to Mally?"

"Oh, Malcolm, it's you again." Liv's voice lightened and her tears dried instantly. She had always been aware of Malcolm's attraction ever since that wedding day six years ago. "Sorry to grab Myrtle away like that. My fishpond has a fatal attraction for your son, my dear! He simply has to get in it! He did it immediately on arrival last Monday. He did it yesterday morning. He did it yesterday afternoon. He did it this morning. And now, this afternoon—"

He said tersely, "Is he all right? Can't you fence the bloody thing off?"

She tinkled an offended laugh. "Hardly, my dear. This isn't a zoo, you know. At least, it's not supposed to be."

He ignored that. "Listen, Liv. Is Mally all right?"

She thought of the squat, ugly child who would climb on to her lap a dozen times a day if she didn't stand up quickly. How could he be described as "all right"?

"Yes. Of course he's all right." Malcolm's concern for his son made him endearing again. She decided to forgive his ridiculous question. "He doesn't fall in, my dear. He goes in. He enjoys it."

"Oh, Liv. What an affected little devil you are." Malcolm's laugh was an explosion of relief. "D'you know what I'd like to do to you at times?"

"No. What?" Liv felt suddenly breathless.

"I'd like to put you across my knee and whack that pretty little backside of yours until you couldn't sit down for a week!"

She gasped, "Malcolm! Stop messing about!"

"I haven't started yet! Listen, little Livvie Baker. If you want to avoid that tanning, here's what to do. Look after Mally. Cuddle him as often as he'll let you. He needs plenty of cuddles. It's his way of talking. Got that?"

"Tanning indeed. You wouldn't dare!"

"Wouldn't I? D'you want to come down and find out?"

"Reggie would kill you!"

"Reggie wouldn't know."

"I'd tell him."

"Oh no you wouldn't."

He started to laugh. Then so did she. When she stopped it was to hear an empty buzzing in her ear. He had hung up. She looked at the receiver, her eyes bright and smiling. "I bet you don't talk to your patients like that," she said tartly. But she guessed he did, and she guessed they loved it.

Of course Reggie was highly tickled by Mally's fifth immersion. Liv wondered if the child was more intelligent than he seemed and was doing it just to amuse this new uncle. Powdered, pyjama'd and acceptably milky from his supper, he sat on Reggie's lap and rocked monotonously, making cooing noises.

Myrtle was upstairs putting the other two to bed. Liv poured sherry and thought about the casseroled chicken they were having for supper. This time of day was the best part of Myrtle's visit. The boys almost gone for the night, Reggie all soppy and sentimental about them, the supper perfectly organised as only she could organise things, and a blessed return to civilisation. Tonight something extra was added. She did not analyse what it was. She felt excited: very conscious of her small neat bust, her small firm buttocks, her perfect complexion, her long nylon-clad legs, her short curly hair-do. She felt beautiful and proud of her beauty. She wasn't thirty yet, there was a lot more life to live, she had got what she wanted which was an adoring husband and a modern home full of nice things; now she wanted something else. She did not know what it was but it seemed to be hovering on the horizon.

Reggie said, "He really likes me, Liv. Have you noticed how he runs to me as soon as I arrive each afternoon? Funny, I was damned sorry for Malcolm and Myrtle when I heard they'd got a retarded kid. But they're both daft about him, and I can understand why. He's so full of love, isn't he?"

"Mmm."

Liv sipped her sherry delicately and looked across at Mally. He was dribbling again. Yet he could swallow food all right so there was nothing wrong with his throat muscles.

She leaned over him. "Swallow please, Mally," she said firmly. "Go on. Swallow."

To her surprise he looked up at her and swallowed obediently. She took out her wispy hanky and wiped his mouth.

"Good boy."

He seized the hanky and for a second there was a tug of war between them. Then she surrendered it.

"All right. You can keep Aunt Liv's hanky, if you'll remember to keep swallowing and wipe your mouth with it afterwards."

He immediately shoved the scrap of cambric into his mouth and before they could do a thing began to choke.

"Oh my God! Oh—Myrtle—oh—Reggie—" Liv hit Mally fruitlessly on the back. He turned a nasty shade of purple-puce.

Reggie turned him face down across his knees, put his hands around the small body and pressed hard. With a gush of vomit the handkerchief landed on the carpet. He gurgled and turned his head to give them both his big, formless smile.

"You little . . . look at my carpet—just look! You're a very naughty boy!" Liv was beside herself with relief and horror. Mally's blue winceyette bottom was just beneath her hand. She smacked it. He began to cry. Myrtle entered the room at the double.

"What the hell—?" Myrtle took in the sick and the fact that Liv had just smacked her son, and she put the wrong two together. "You . . . *bitch*, Liv! And you're no better, Reggie! Holding him down like that so that she could . . . there, there, baby. Come to Mummy. I could kill you, Liv. Bloody carpets. Who cares about them? Mally never cries. Never. And we're here for two bloody days and what happens?"

Liv made the mistake of trying to answer the rhetorical question.

"He was choking on the handkerchief, Myrt. We had to do something. Reggie saved his life—he was *choking* I tell you!"

"I saw what happened, thank you very much, Liv. If Reggie . . . it sounds as if I should thank you, Reggie. But what you did, Liv, was unforgivable. He's completely innocent. He—"

"Is he? He seemed to understand when I told him to swallow. And when I told him he could have my hanky if he kept swallowing, he put it straight into his mouth."

"You mean you *told* him to swallow your hanky? Are you mad?"

"Don't be ridiculous, Myrt. Of course I didn't . . . oh, can't you shut him *up?*"

Reggie tried to take a hand.

"Listen Myrt, it wasn't like that—you're taking it the wrong way. The child *responded* to Liv. Honestly. It was amazing. He—"

"So she hit him, did she?" Myrtle said with abrasive bitterness.

"And he was supposed to respond to that too, was he?" She hoisted the heavy load further up her shoulder and turned. "I'm going upstairs. I won't want supper. I'll feed Mally. That always soothes him."

"You'll feed him?" Liv bleated. "You mean—?"

Myrtle said deliberately, "Yes. Breastfeed him. Does that disgust you too, Liv?"

"He's three years old!"

"African women breastfeed much later than that."

"But you're English. And you're pregnant!"

Myrtle said a very rude word indeed, and left the room. Liv began to cry. Reggie put his arms around her.

"It's just a storm in a teacup, darling. Natural, in the circumstances. Myrtle is under strain—"

"What about me?" Liv wailed, trying to keep her spouting eyes away from the shoulder of his suit. "I'm under far more strain than she is! All she has to do is sit around all day and eat the meals I get for her! I have to put up with those children—clean up after them every five minutes. You should see the bath after they've used it—go on up and look at it now—go on!"

"Yes, but you shouldn't have smacked Mally. It would have been bad enough if it had been Nicky or Martin. But Mally."

"He did it deliberately! I know he did! He deserved that smack. Anyway, whose side are you on?"

"Nobody's. You can't have sides in a case like this. Look darling, go up and make your peace. Please."

"I have to dish up supper."

"She won't come down if you don't go up and ask her."

"You go up. Tell her what happened. She'll listen to you. And while you're about it—" she disengaged herself and made for the door ahead of him—"have a look at the bath." She glanced back and remembered the sick. "Oh my God. If I don't get some water on that, it'll be stained for ever!" She rushed away and Reggie said to thin air, "I've never heard you call on God so often before, darling." Perhaps it was as well she didn't hear, he reflected as he went upstairs; that sort of bantering never made her laugh.

The door to the bedroom which Myrtle was sharing with the boys was ajar, and Nicky's and Martin's voices could be heard within, arguing more or less amicably. Reggie put his head inside and saw them on one of the single beds, conducting a fight between two toy soldiers. In a pale gold Lloyd Loom chair by the window, Myrtle sat with open blouse, Mally—looking bigger than ever—at her breast.

Reggie would have withdrawn very quickly indeed, except that Myrtle looked up, saw him and smiled a wan welcome.

"Come on in, Reggie. I'm sorry about all that. Have you come to tell me what an unreasonable cow I am?"

In the circumstances the appellation was almost too apt. Reggie felt his face become explosively hot; he stood fidgeting in the doorway.

"Not at all. She—Liv—just wanted me to say that she's sorry and won't you please come down for supper?"

Myrtle's smile became less wan. "I bet she didn't apologise! But of course I'm coming down. As soon as I've got this little lot settled." She shook her head gently at all their foolishness. "I'm sorry, Reggie. It's not much fun for you, is it? But you know, my dear, this is what family life is like. Are you still as keen as ever?"

He had to stay and reassure her; he couldn't very well leave after she'd come full way to meet Liv.

"Of course I am. Let me put the boys to bed. May I?"

"Help yourself." She sounded very tired. He knew Liv was right, she shouldn't be breastfeeding a two-year-old child, especially when she was pregnant again.

He went over to the single bed and took another soldier from the box. The boys welcomed him as an "umpire" and allowed him to pronounce a draw fairly speedily. He put the lid on the box and stowed it out of reach on top of the wardrobe. Then he tucked the boys into their beds and told them an edited version of Jack and the Beanstalk. He tried to feel paternal, or at least avuncular. All he could feel was desperately lascivious. He was sideways on to Myrtle and when Mally's head dropped back in sleep, he could see quite clearly the huge bell of her breast with its shining wet nipple. When she stood up carefully to carry the boy to his bed, he had to clench his hands in Nicky's bed cover; she was not wearing a brassiere and made no attempt to button her blouse. Both breasts were fully and shockingly visible. His palms ached to hold them.

"What if the giant wasn't really dead at all, Uncle Reggie?" asked Nicky. "What if he jumped up and began to chase Jack? What if—" Martin wailed and put his head under the bedclothes.

"Oh, he was definitely dead," Reggie said, swallowing frantically. "He never moved again, you see."

Nicky looked at the writhing shape of his small brother and said scornfully, "Anyone can shut their eyes and pretend to be dead."

"But his eyes weren't closed. That was how Jack knew he was properly dead. When your eyes are closed, you're asleep. But when they're open and you can't move, then you're dead."

"Oh." Nicky had no more shots in his locker and Martin was convinced that the giant was dead. Reggie tucked them up and drew the curtains, then turned to face Myrtle. She had buttoned her blouse and was combing her wiry hair.

"Bless you, Reggie," she whispered. "I'll be with you in a minute."

The only trouble was that now he knew what was under the blouse, she might just as well leave it off.

He whispered back, "Okay," moved swiftly into the bathroom and locked the door. There he stared at his reflection in the cabinet mirror and breathed very deeply. Then he looked at the ringed bath and got down on his knees to begin cleaning it.

Later that evening when the two girls were chattering away as if nothing had happened, he told them he would take the next day off.

"I'll drive you over the Lickeys. We'll take a picnic. What do you say? The boys would love it and I think it would do both of you good to get out of the house for a bit."

"Oh, Reggie, you are sweet," Myrtle said unguardedly.

"Quixotic is the word, Myrt," Liv said, smiling indulgently at her husband. "D'you know, when there was all that Hungarian business last year, he wanted to take in a family of refugees!"

Myrtle knew she was being firmly put in her place, but a sudden empathy with Reggie carried her past discretion.

"Oh, I wanted to do something too," she said to him. "But of course, Malcolm . . . the practice . . . it wouldn't have done it much good."

"I should think not." Liv helped herself to more potatoes though she was cutting down on carbohydrates. "And where on earth would you have put them, darling?"

Myrtle shrugged diplomatically, recognising the endearment as a sign of Liv's extreme annoyance.

Reggie altered the subject smoothly. "Last year was grim all round. Suez—what a fiasco. Eden should never have withdrawn. My God, France and Britain built the bloody canal and have maintained it all these years—"

"Language, Reggie," Liv interrupted lightly.

"And this Khrushchev chappie. All smiles and Father Christmas on the outside, but it's his deStalinisation business that started the Hungarian troubles. Not to mention Poland."

They were getting back to refugees again. Myrtle said hurriedly, "When Malcolm and I went out to dinner last week, one of the men was saying that Russia would be putting some kind of capsule into space before this year is out."

"Rubbish." Liv took another spoonful of gravy to go with her potatoes. The thought of Myrtle and Malcolm going to dinner parties together was not welcome. She had imagined she could bring a little glamour into Malcolm's life. Surely Myrtle spent all her time being pregnant and washing up? She knew for a fact they did not have an automatic dishwasher. "Surely you remember your physics lessons, Myrt? Miss Edgeworth told us that if anything ever did get out of the earth's atmosphere, it would explode instantly."

"Mm. She was wrong about the atom though, wasn't she?" Myrtle smiled at Reggie. "She said that if one atom was split in two, the energy released would split the next and the next and the next and the next and the next . . ."

They were both giggling helplessly and foolishly. Liv spooned the remainder of her gravy into her mouth in the way Mrs. Cook's customers fed themselves at the cafe; as if they were starving.

"Right. Has everyone had enough? I think you've had too much, Reggie darling. You're overflowing. There's potato on your chin and is that some chicken on your tie? Really, Reggie."

She'd made an apple pie for pudding. Myrtle spent the rest of supper time extolling the shortness of the pastry and the delicate flavouring of cloves with the apples. Mollified, Liv fetched her recipe book and offered to copy out the particular recipe. They took their coffee into the pristine lounge, and Reggie opened the doors of the television and they watched a programme called "Little-known Talents."

"That name is familiar." Myrtle leaned forward, frowning. "Clive Hubert. Good lord. He was one of Cass' authors."

Liv, interrupted in mid-flow, also frowned.

"Cass and her very important career! She's just a middleman. Or woman. Isn't she? Like a shopkeeper."

Myrtle did not reply; she was listening to the broadcaster with untypical concentration. When he went on to something else, she sat back and looked at Liv with wide eyes.

"I say. Did you get all that? They thought this Clive Hubert's book was blown up in Paris a couple of years ago. Now it turns out there was another copy or something."

"Fascinating," Liv said.

"No, but don't you remember the Paris explosion? It was in Cass' office. The book must have been in Cass' office. My God, no wonder she didn't want Bessie over there that Easter. They could have been after Cass herself. I mean, if she knew what was in the book."

There was a little silence. Liv said slowly, "Clive Hubert. I've never heard of him. Is he famous?"

"He's dead, Liv. That's what they've just been saying. He was killed, then his book was destroyed."

Liv made a downward moue. "Melodrama. Who would have thought it of our Cass? No wonder she moved to the South. I imagined it was for the weather, but obviously there were other reasons." She sipped her coffee. "Was there anything in it? With this Clive wotsit I mean."

"That doesn't matter now. What does matter is that they've found another copy of the bloody book!"

Reggie took a tentative hand in the conversation. "Surely that's good for your friend? The book can be published—it's saving something from catastrophe, I should have thought."

"But if someone thought it worthwhile to kill because of it . . ." Myrtle put her cup on the table without its saucer and Liv leaned forward with her handkerchief at the ready ". . . Mrs. Woodford and Carol will send Bessie home. Mrs. Woodford won't leave Cass. I'm certain of that. But they won't risk Bessie's safety. She can come to me." Her face lit up at the thought. "Boris has gone off on this camera course, but she will be all right with me."

Liv stopped polishing and said dryly, "And she's so good with the boys, isn't she?"

Myrtle nodded, unoffended. "And she adores Mally. And they all adore her." She smiled at Liv. "She is quite special, Liv. Rather like Cass when she was a kid. She seems to understand things. Instinctively. I mean, she's much too young to work things out. But she knows about people."

"I have met her. I knew her quite well until your wedding, Myrt. She didn't seem a bit like Cass to me. Much too dark and pretty."

"I didn't mean she looked like Cass. But she's got all her mannerisms. Gosh, I hope Cass will be all right. I loved that girl—really loved her."

Liv tucked her handkerchief away and looked back into the past. "We had something special then, didn't we? Me and Mon were so different from you and Cass, but there was a very strong link."

Myrtle stood up.

"I'm going to write to her tonight. Suggesting it." She smiled. "I'll go upstairs now. Liv . . . I'm sorry about Mally and the fishpond. I really will try to impress on him—"

Reggie said heartily, "Don't bother, Myrtle. We're out all day tomorrow—give them all a chance to run wild."

Myrtle started to tell him again how sweet he was, then stopped herself and left them to it.

Liv said, "Reggie dear. If Cass isn't that keen on sending her daughter to Myrtle's—where it's quite obvious she is some kind of skivvy—we could have her here if you like."

Reggie realised his plan was working. He stood up and pulled his wife to her feet.

"Oh, darling. I love you."

He began to kiss her; her eyes, her nose, then down her face to her neck.

She said, "Just let me stack this stuff in the dishwasher, and we'll have an early night, Reggie."

"Bugger the dishwasher," he said.

"Language," she replied. But she met his mouth with her own when he came around her chin, and allowed him to come inside, thankful that she had already cleaned her teeth. He would have done it then and there on the carpet, but she couldn't go that far. Laughing breathlessly, she let him pretend to chase her up the stairs and into the bedroom, and even to unzip the placket of her slacks, but after that she had to draw a line. The thought of going to bed without creaming her face and hands was impossible for Liv. She was lucky that her hair was naturally curly and needed no pinning. When she came out of the bathroom slippery with cream and a new satin nightgown, he was already on the bed, stark naked, holding out his arms to her.

"Why on earth did you bother with a nightie?" He laughed at her as he practically tore it off. "You're mad, Olive Bradbury. Mad. D'you hear me?"

There was no time to answer, because the kissing began again, but she hadn't liked him using her full name. She had been eight years old when she truncated it, and apart from at her wedding, it had been rarely heard since. She pursed her lips against his.

It was then that the screaming began.

At first she thought one of the children had wandered into the room and seen their two bodies entwined on the bed. There was a split second when she imagined what it must be like, the horror of it, the damage done to the innocent child for the future. Then she realised that the screams came from the room down the passage and must indeed be piercing to penetrate two walls so clearly.

Reggie would have run to investigate as he was, but she threw his dressing-gown at him even as she dug her arms into her own. They burst into Myrtle's room neck and neck.

Myrtle already had Martin in her arms and was rocking him soothingly. His screams threatened to burst their eardrums, so she merely shook her head uncomprehendingly above his. Incredibly, Mally and Nicky did not move in their beds. Reggie crouched opposite Myrtle and touched the child's face, and as if by magic, the screams stopped. The boy turned tear-swollen eyes towards him and hiccuped, "He closed his eyes, Uncle Reggie. He weren't dead at all. He closed his eyes."

Myrtle whispered, "Oh God. The giant in Jack and the Beanstalk. You little idiot. I'll give you dead tomorrow morning!"

Reggie felt in his pocket and found a handkerchief; he dried Martin's face.

"Listen, old man. It's just a story. But the giant was dead all right. They closed his eyes before the funeral. But he was dead. No doubt about it."

Liv watched it all in astonishment. Not only was Reggie crouching there with his dressing-gown doubtless flapping open, but it was obvious, in spite of the cradled child, that Myrtle slept in the buff. She could hardly believe it. Reggie must see . . . what she could see. It was indecent. Myrtle was as brown as a berry, too. Did she also sunbathe in the buff?

She said bracingly, "All right now, then? Can we get back to bed?"

"Sorry." Myrtle surrendered Martin to Reggie who carried him back to bed. At last she seemed to realise her own nakedness and with what seemed like brazen slowness, she reached for a sort of shawl and draped it inadequately around herself. "Very occasionally he gets nightmares. I should have warned you."

Reggie finished tucking Martin in and whispered, "No more

dreams, old man. Sleep tight. All right?" And Martin giggled sleepily at the rhyme and closed his eyes immediately.

Reggie stood up.

"I should be apologising. I'm sorry, Myrtle. I'll be more careful about stories in future."

They both laughed. Everyone said goodnight. Liv led the way back down the landing.

"Poor Malcolm. That's all I can say." She spoke tightly, not removing her dressing-gown, sitting on the edge of the bed with ramrod back. "She's gone to pot, hasn't she? Her bust . . . and those stretch marks. Poor Malcolm." She saw in the mirror that Reggie had taken off his dressing-gown and was very aroused. "And poor you, too. Quite a shock."

He reached over the bed and slid his hands over the silk.

"Mmmm, nice." He grinned. "Not really. She was feeding Mally earlier, if you remember."

She did remember now. And she had sent him up to see that! And no doubt all this rampant passion was a direct result of what he had seen.

She said, "Darling. I'm sorry. But not now. I simply couldn't. It was too disgusting. Put me right off."

She stood up, picked up her nightgown and made for the bathroom. And Reggie, astonished, rolled on to his back. Then thought of Myrtle.

The next day Liv told them she had had a telephone call from a friend in Worcester who was ill. She did not want them to postpone the picnic, in fact she had packed a hamper that would have fed an army, but she felt she must visit this friend. Someone she had known in her Civil Service days. And she did not need the car because she would take the train. She kissed the boys and Mally, then Myrtle.

"Have a wonderful day," she instructed. "And look after my husband for me!"

Myrtle held her warmly for a moment and would have asked more, but Liv broke away. Reggie said nothing at all. He seemed relieved when a taxi arrived and whisked her to the station.

"Right. Let's get packed up. Ready boys?"

Myrtle said, "Look, Reggie. If you'd rather not . . . honestly we shall be quite all right here. Nicky adores the television and I'll take them down to Northfield this afternoon to see Mummy and Daddy—"

"You've planned to do that tomorrow, Myrtle. Today we're going on an expedition to them thar hills! Aren't we boys? We're going to make a camp fire and cook sausages—"

"Liv has done a huge picnic!" Myrtle protested through vociferous approval from her brood.

"Bugger the picnic!" Reggie declared, and Nicky echoed, "Yeah. Bugger the picnic." And Martin said, "Let's bugger the picnic." Mally snorted his laugh, and Myrtle threw everything to the winds. "Okay. I'll bugger it out to the car. Then you can bugger it to the camp site. How's that?" She picked up the hamper and marched outside. Reggie shouldered Mally, laughing like a drain. They looked like a gaggle of gypsies as they loaded up with fishing rods and frying pans. It was what family life was all about. On a sudden crazy impulse, Reggie leaned over Martin's head and planted a kiss on Myrtle's mouth.

"We're going to have a lovely day," he said.

She looked at him, amazed. Then returned the kiss.

"We are," she agreed.

They did. Reggie put his heart and soul into everything. The fire was one hundred per cent successful: crackling flames that they could war-whoop around at first, then a long-lasting glow over which sausages spat and sizzled satisfyingly. Then, while Mally slept and Myrtle read the newspaper, there was French cricket and tree-climbing and finally fishing in the reservoir.

Myrtle knew now that he wanted her. It made her feel proud and special, guilty and conscience-stricken. They must have had a row, the two of them, and it might even have been over her. She couldn't think why. Compared with Liv she was downright ugly; besides, she was mother of three and pregnant again. Men didn't lust after the likes of her. But he was lusting. She knew it and felt a response in her own fertile body.

Of course she would let nothing come of it. Liv would be home when they got back and she would make sure the two of them had the rest of the evening together. She did not want anything to come of it. She loved Malcolm. And even more importantly, she loved Liv. Her loyalty was flawed where Malcolm was concerned because of his own constant infidelities. But it was strong for Liv.

Meanwhile each time Reggie's shoulder brushed hers, she deliberately enjoyed the thrill. It could harm no-one.

They got back to the house at seven o'clock to hear the phone ringing. Myrtle hopped out of the car and answered it. It was Liv. She wasn't going to be able to get back home that night. Could Myrtle possibly manage supper on her own? There were chops in the fridge and veg in the crisper. Reggie needed fresh greens each day, so Myrtle must not open a tin under any circumstances. And she was to let Reggie load the dishwasher.

Myrtle said, "Never mind all that. Of course I can manage—how do you think I cope at home with five mouths to feed? But listen. Liv. *Listen.* What has happened with you and Reggie? You *are* coming back, are you? I mean, this is ridiculous. Reggie adores you—you must know that—"

"I've told you, Myrt. My friend *needs* me! Surely you don't mind looking after things for another day? Good lord, I've done everything all this week, I shouldn't have thought it was too much to ask you to hold the fort for one day!"

Myrtle said wearily, "Of course it's not. What's your number in case of emergencies?"

But the phone was dead in her hand.

Reggie got the supper while she put the boys to bed. When she went downstairs she wondered how they would get through the evening. Maybe she could ask him to baby-sit while she borrowed the car and went into Northfield. It was a frightful cheek. But then he would probably understand her motives. She knew, even as she planned it, that she would not do that. She was tense as a spring. She wanted to be with him.

In the same state of mind as a drowning man reaching for a lifebelt, she grabbed the phone at the bottom of the stairs and dialled the operator.

"Cheltenham, please. Five, four, seven, four." She cleared her throat and repeated the number. Malcolm would save her. He would talk to her over the line, stake his claim as he always did. Reggie would become just Reggie again. Liv's husband.

"You're through, caller," said the disembodied voice of the operator. And then someone said, "Hello?"

Myrtle was transfixed. She gripped the receiver frantically and stared at the virgin-white newel post as if it had sprouted wings.

"Is that Cheltenham five, four, seven, four?" she asked tremblingly.

The line went dead.

"What is it?" Reggie was in the kitchen doorway, apron on towel over one arm à la waiter, even a makeshift chef's hat atop his fair hair. "My God. What has happened, Myrt? Tell me. Quickly."

She began to weep, and he leapt forward and gathered her into his arms. She held on to him desperately. His hat fell to the floor. He kicked it away and pressed their bodies together.

"It's Liv—" she sobbed into his neck. "Oh, Reggie. Liv is with Malcolm. Liv is with Malcolm. What shall I do?"

His mouth came over her open one. He kissed her fiercely as if he could drive out physically the horrific pictures that formed and re-formed in her head. It was answer enough. She continued to cry for a while, but already she was conscious of him against her; already she responded to his kiss; already her hands slid into the nape of his neck and behind his ears. She knew so well the mechanics of sex. After a very short interval in the hall, they found themselves in the lounge where the brand-new television was switched on low. Before Cliff Michelmore's eyes, they undressed each other with indecent haste and took to the carpet. The chops congealed in the kitchen as their love-making continued and the evening darkened. Myrtle's passion now had something vengeful about it. When Reggie would have finished, she put his hands on her breasts and leaned over him as she had seen Gilda lean over Malcolm. Reggie groaned, "Oh, darling . . . I worship you . . . I worship you . . ." And it was balm on an open wound.

When it was completely dark and a man in a dog collar appeared on the screen and talked about eternity, she rose at last and they went into the kitchen to eat. They sat naked in front of the cooker, tearing at the cold meat like animals. Occasionally they would laugh, almost hysterically.

After the meat, Reggie shovelled the fresh vegetables into the waste disposal and looked at her.

"Upstairs or downstairs?" he asked.

She baulked at using Liv's bed.

"Downstairs."

She led the way into the lounge again. The screen was dark and emitted a high-pitched whine. She switched off the set and they continued where they had left off.

Liv arrived at the house in Imperial Square at eleven o'clock that morning. She told herself she was going to talk to Malcolm about Myrtle's health. There was a residential nursery school for mentally subnormal infants in a remote corner of the Cotswolds between Broadway and Evesham. Her women's club had entertained a speaker from there not long ago. It would be the ideal place for Mally. With the other two boys in kindergarten, Myrtle could rest during the day. It was so obvious.

The door was opened by Tom, a prematurely elderly man, who usually did the outdoor work. His wife, Doris, had taken the opportunity of Myrtle's absence to visit her sister for a few days, and Tom was doubling as receptionist. He knew nothing of appointment systems, and assuming Liv was another patient, showed her into the waiting room. Mercifully it was empty. Perhaps Malcolm was not as busy as Myrtle made out. Even so she waited nearly an hour before he appeared. When he did, he was minus white coat and his thick hair was almost standing on end. The woman he ushered out was in her fifties, maybe even older. In spite of the heat she wore a fur cape over a black crepe de chine dress. She had a walking stick over one arm, but she must be almost cured now as she walked without trace of a handicap. Malcolm was bending over her deferentially and did not immediately spot Liv.

"Let's make your next appointment right away, shall we?" he was saying. He laughed in his throat. "How long do you think you can wait?"

But she had seen Liv. She said haughtily, "I did not realise anyone else was waiting, Mr. Lennox. I'll telephone you." And she swept into the hall and out of the front door without waiting for Tom's assistance.

Malcolm looked round.

"What the hell are you doing here?" he asked unwelcomingly.

Liv felt like a schoolgirl. She stammered, "I wanted to talk to you about Myrtle. I'm worried about her."

"Why? Is she ill?" he asked urgently.

"No, of course not. She's tired, that's all. She's doing too much." She paused, then burst out suddenly, "Do you know she still breastfeeds Mally?"

He laughed at that. "Of course I know, you idiot. There's nothing there. She does it to comfort him. She does it for me sometimes."

He intended to embarrass her and he succeeded. She turned bright red and gasped as if he had struck her. He laughed and ran his fingers through his hair, returning it to its usual Brylcreemed splendour as if by magic. Then he laughed again and reached for a clean white coat behind the door.

"My midday appointment will be here soon. Was that all you wanted to say?" he asked, leaving the coat unbuttoned and digging his hands in its pockets.

"I . . . yes. I suppose it was. Perhaps I'd better go."

"Oh no you don't. You came here for your punishment and you're going to get it. Meanwhile I can make use of you. Come with me."

He walked out of the room and after a split second of token and silent rebellion when she told herself she was going to leave that minute, she followed him meekly to the kitchen.

It was a total wreck. The sink was piled high with dirty dishes, more were on the big scrubbed table in the middle of the floor, a heap of unwashed laundry was pushing open a door at the far end, and an unpleasant smell told of unemptied bins. A bluebottle droned around the light flex.

"Right!" he said briskly. "I want this lot cleared and a meal cooked. Something light. Scrambled eggs, you know the sort of thing. Myrt tells me you're an angel in the kitchen. Can you prove it?"

He smiled at her and she felt again the unexpected charm of the man. He was all the things she loathed, yet . . . yet . . .

"I can prove it," she said, holding his stare somehow.

He came very close to her. "Good girl."

Her breathing went to pieces as she waited for his kiss. It did not come. When she opened her eyes he had gone.

She had worn a new dress, green cotton to go with her oddly flecked eyes. The skirt was too tight for comfort, her heels too high. And the weather was very hot. She had not worked so hard for a long time. Myrtle's housekeeping concentrated on essentials, and little luxuries like clean sinks and store cupboards were left out of her timetable. Liv could not cook a meal until she had clean crockery, and she could not wash up until the sink was scoured and disinfected. She thought longingly of her dishwasher and the new electric cooker. She eyed the ancient gas stove beneath its huge hood, filled the sink again and began to take it to pieces. By the time Malcolm returned to the kitchen there was a cloth over the table, flowers in the centre, a rack full of toast and a covered dish full of the fluffiest scrambled eggs she had ever made. But she was red and shiny-faced and she had a nasty feeling her deodorant was not working.

He surveyed everything with a smile.

"Congratulations." He sat down. "Sauce? And where is Albert?"

"Albert?" she asked faintly.

"The bluebottle. I haven't eaten without the company of Albert for many moons."

"Oh, Malcolm!" She laughed and collapsed on to a chair.

"That's better. You looked like a coiled spring."

"I'm fine. But how on earth Myrtle lives in these conditions I do not know."

"I'll show you in a minute." He spread butter on toast and scooped the ethereal egg on to it. She was having trouble with her breathing again. He cut off a wedge of toast and crammed it into his mouth, then pushed the plate across to her.

"Go on, get on with that," he ordered through his food. "I can't stand it without sauce." He got up and fetched the bottle from the dresser. "God. You've scrubbed the shelves too, haven't you? No wonder you look so hot and bothered."

She said, "I can't eat anything. Honestly."

"Get on with it, woman." He swallowed and grinned companionably. "I really am a good osteopath, Liv. Myrt lives and thrives with me for a lot of reasons, and that is one of them. When she gets wound up I make her eat, then I give her a massage. So . . . eat."

She took a forkful of egg, then another. He ate greedily and massively. She had made eight pieces of toast, never dreaming it would all go. It did.

He sat back.

"It's not going well at home? Mally upsetting you?"

"Oh, it's not that." She took the plates to the sink and ran water on them. "Though as you've mentioned Mally, I was going to tell you about a little nursery school I've heard of. Near Broadway. Very beautiful."

"And very remote. Is that so no-one will hear them yelling, d'you think?"

"Oh, Malcolm, Mally doesn't yell."

"No, he's a good kid." He stood abruptly and picked up a grubby tea towel. "I don't think Myrt and I could face life without him now."

She said, "I haven't washed up properly, only rinsed."

He ignored her and rubbed at the plates busily.

"Funny. When he was born I was horrified. Horrified for Myrt and horrified for myself. But I'd heard mongol children were very lovable. It's true."

"He's always on Reggie's lap. Reggie loves him."

"And you?"

She said, "Malcolm, have you got a washing machine? The little scullery place is full of laundry."

"I'll show you. Come and have that massage first." He flung the towel at the drying rack and it missed. "We'll have to do it in two parts. I've got another appointment at two."

She did not know whether she was coming or going. She could not have a massage if she was smelling. But if she had a massage she would have the strength—surely—to go for the train and get back home before Myrtle and Reggie returned from their picnic. But was he really intending to give her a massage? Or was he going to rape her? And would he have to rape her?

That was the most difficult question of all.

Still, she went with Malcolm into the treatment room.

He did not rape her. She took off her unsuitable shoes and her nylons, her dress and petticoat, and lay face down on the high table. There was a hole for her face and her arms hung over the edge. It was amazingly comfortable. He sponged her with tepid water, lifting the top of her pants to go around her waist, holding up each arm. Amazingly there was no embarrassment, he was so professional, so clinical. When he put his hands on her spine she knew without doubt that he was good. She felt so relaxed it was as if she were melting and would end up a small pool on the floor. His thumbs went into her lumbar region and undid knots she hadn't known were there. She closed her eyes and surrendered to him. She hoped quite desperately that he would kiss her. He did not.

"That's all for now, little Liv," he said. "Get dressed and go out of the other door, will you? I'll finish you off before dinner, never fear."

The doorbell rang while she was putting on her stockings and she heard Malcolm go into the waiting room and greet his next patient. It was an exquisite relief to hear it was a man. She crept into the hall holding her shoes in one hand. No-one was about. She went into the kitchen and picked up the fallen towel. In the scullery, beneath the mountain of dirty washing, she found a machine and began to sort the clothes. When the first load was pounding away she searched the fridge for food. There was nothing worth mentioning. In the cupboard were tins of salmon. She began on a salmon mousse.

At five o'clock Malcolm came in and drank a cup of tea. He was sweating profusely, which was something she hated normally. Now it struck her as excitingly physical, proof of his strength, his male-ness. He opened the fridge and eyed the mousse and salad.

"God, I'm hungry. We'll eat at six and go straight to bed." He looked at her. "You are staying?" The shock of his words was almost too much for her. She did all the movie star things: gasped, clutched her throat, felt for a chair and sank into it.

"They . . . they've gone for a picnic. They're expecting me to be there when they get back."

"When will they get back?"

"I don't know. In time to put the boys to bed, I suppose. Half-past six."

"You can phone then. Let's finish your massage." He was gone again.

She was slightly more assured this time. If he thought she was staying the night he wouldn't do anything now. And afterwards she could catch the seven twenty-eight back home and feel that she'd struck some sort of blow for herself. Yes. She didn't need a host of children to prove that she was a complete woman. She had herself.

So she went into the treatment room and took off her dress and stockings again and lay on the couch. But she had forgotten the magic of his hands. In ten minutes she was enslaved again. All thought of the seven twenty-eight left her mind. It was the most sensual experience of her life and she longed to conclude it with a kiss, but, as before, he walked away from her to the wash basin and she went behind the curtain and dressed hurriedly.

He was in a jocular mood now.

"Food, Liv. D'you know, I haven't lived so well since I married Myrtle! Salmon mousse. And fruit salad. And then . . . your punish-ment." He glinted at her. "I'm looking forward to that. It's what you came for, isn't it?"

"Oh. Really, Malcolm! I don't know what you're talking about! What about the old man who answered the door? Is he going to eat with us?"

"Tom? He's gone now. The house is ours. No-one to hear your cries."

"Stop it, Malcolm. I have to go home. I must go home."

He shrugged. "Another time then. If there is another time."

It had the inevitability of a dream. She washed up and took coffee into the sitting room. He indicated the telephone and she rang the Barnt Green number and got Myrtle and told her about Marion Lonsdale being ill. When she replaced the receiver he started to laugh, then he got up and moved menacingly towards her. She shrieked and ran and he chased her through the kitchen and hall and upstairs where he cornered her in the nursery and got her across his knee. He gave her a token beating which occasionally hurt even through her clothes, then he stood them both up and kissed her. She had waited all day for that kiss. She was exhausted with work and anticipation and almost collapsed in his arms. He wasn't mad for her as Reggie had been last night; he lingered over her mouth as if it were a glass of wine to be savoured. His hands outlined her body like a sculptor's, discovering her shape and glorying in it. Every move was calculated, and she didn't mind. After a long time, he lifted her bodily and carried her downstairs. It crossed her mind that she must be a very light weight after Myrtle; that was the first time she had thought of Myrtle all day. She banished the thought quickly. He put her down in the hall.

"Go into my room, Liv. I'll get a bottle of wine. We'll do the thing properly."

She was lost when he went. His voice said the wrong things: shocking, brutal things. His hands were sweet and sensitive. She needed his hands. The heat of the day was going and she shivered convulsively.

The phone rang.

She waited, thinking he would answer from the sitting room, but he didn't. Perhaps the house had a proper cellar and that was where he was. The phone rang again. She lifted the receiver and was connected with a long-distance caller.

"Hello?" she said faintly.

There was a pause, then Myrtle's voice asked, "Is that Cheltenham five, four, seven, four?"

Liv replaced the receiver very carefully and Malcolm came through the kitchen door.

"Where are you, woman? Don't hang about there."

Liv went slowly into the treatment room again and accepted a glass of wine. She drank it quickly and passed it back to be refilled.

"Dutch courage?" He grinned and gave her the bottle. She

stood there, drooping, hearing again the incredulity in Myrtle's voice.

She whimpered, "I can't, Malcolm. I'm sorry. I can't."

He didn't believe her. He removed the bottle and began to kiss her again and undo the buttons of her dress. She kept repeating no, no, but he completely ignored her and at last she found the energy to push him away and run for the door. Her shoes had gone and her dress flapped around her waist. She ran down the hall weeping, wanting to get away, yet at the same time desperate for him to run after her and make her go back.

She opened the front door knowing she couldn't possibly go down the steps to respectable Imperial Square. But there was no need. Standing on the top step, hand raised to the bell, was a woman. She was not tall, very dark, her long hair pleated neatly around her head to form a coronet. Her make-up was the most perfect Liv had seen and her clothes the most expensive.

Behind Liv, Malcolm started to laugh. She looked round at him, startled. He couldn't possibly know who it was.

Then she turned back to the picture of elegant simplicity before her.

"Mon. What the hell are you doing here?"

And Monica smiled. "You've changed, Liv. You never used to swear." She looked down the hall. "And you must be Malcolm. I expect Myrtle is seeing to the children, is she?" She leaned forward and touched her sweet-smelling cheek to Liv's. "D'you think I could come in? I'll help you with your dress, my dear. It seems to be undone."

7

Cass opened her eyes on a perfect August morning and listened for the single tolling of the bell at the tiny église further up the mountain. The sun was already over the cypresses which provided a windbreak for the Bergerie in the winter, but the air coming from the High Alps was still cold and clean and she relished the goosefeather quilt on the four-poster.

She thought luxuriously, "Sunday. Church with Mother and Bessie. Lunch. Siesta. Walk. Oh . . . oh . . . bliss."

The door opened a quarter of an inch, and Bessie's voice hissed, "Can I come in?"

Carol groaned theatrically, and Bessie took this for assent and came giggling into the bedroom. She wore no slippers and her pyjama trousers ended just below the knee. She would be thirteen this winter and she was tall for her age.

"If you get a splinter in your foot, don't blame me," Carol said, not very seriously. The bare boards of the Bergerie were polished into a diamond-hard surface. The furniture was old and heavy and they enjoyed moving it about; it never scratched the floors.

"Never mind that." Bessie galloped over to the bed and got beneath the quilt. "Can you smell the flowers?"

"Yes." Carol sniffed. "Yes. Those little roses. And honeysuckle, and that bed of godetia—"

"I saved the seed from last year. And the nicotiana seeds. All the flowers from Northfield too—forget-me-nots and marigolds and stocks. Gardening is much more interesting here, even Gran's salad garden really *grows.*"

"Where is Gran?"

"Gone to early Mass."

As if in agreement, the bell began to toll. It sounded tinny but very commanding.

Carol rolled out of bed.

"Come on. Let's go and cook her a real breakfast." She dragged a skirt under her nightie and turned her back to fasten her brassiere. Bessie, who stayed with uninhibited Myrtle fairly often, made a wry face at the narrow back and went off to her room to dress.

They met in the big kitchen which had been a barn in the days when the Bergerie really was used by shepherds. Mary Woodford had already opened the damper on the range and filled the kettle; Carol lifted down the big iron frying pan and fetched bacon from the cold slab in the larder. Bessie darted about like a fly, laying the table, rushing out to pick flowers and arrange them as a centrepiece.

It was often like this on a Sunday when the maid, Sylvie, did not come. The Woodfords had a talent for making an occasion out of everyday happenings. For just over two years they had lived in the converted bergerie. Carol had an office in Marseilles, but she worked a great deal from home, and most of her writers preferred to see her there.

In the village further down the mountain the English-women were known affectionately as "les trois" and were dealt with almost protectively. Their foibles were indulged—newspapers and post delivered before nine in the morning, fish and liver twice weekly . . . for the cat if you please! But they were proud of young Bessie who could sing like a bird and draw every flower which grew on the mountain; and if they could not afford a visit to the doctor, Mrs. Woodford offered excellent medical advice.

As for Carol, she could pen a better letter than the notary himself, and if there were any local disputes she could often sort them out with her quiet diplomacy.

When Mary came back from church they ate bacon and eggs and drank a great deal of tea, and discussed the week that had gone and the one to come. Bessie's school had closed for the summer and she wanted Carol to take her holiday too so that they could go on one of their treks up the mountain.

"It's going to get hotter and hotter, Cass," she pointed out. "We could take the tent and live like gypsies wherever we chose. You always say that August is the silly season for your job anyway. Nothing happens."

"I thought you'd want to go and stay with Aunt Myrt. You did last year and the one before." Carol helped herself liberally to marmalade. "I thought we might all go home for a couple of weeks. It's about time I took an interest in my godson." She looked over at her mother. "Perhaps Dilly would come back with us, if we really pressed her?"

"I don't think so." Mary poured more tea. Provence suited her so well, she felt younger and more alive than she had for years. She sipped blissfully. "Why don't you and Bessie go and stay with Myrtle? She asks you every time she writes. I think she'd like to feel the old breach was well and truly healed."

Carol glanced at Bessie expecting her to ask "What breach?" but she was wrinkling her nose in disapprobation.

"Don't let's split up. Let's all stay here. It's no fun at Aunt Myrt's unless Boris is there, and he's gone on a camera course with his school."

Carol shrugged helplessly. "Fine with me. I thought you'd like to go back home before winter comes." She smiled warmly. "I'm delighted you want to stay at the Bergerie. When I remember how worried we were about moving out here . . ."

"It was the best thing we ever did," Mary Woodford said definitely, remembering Carol's distress three years ago. "This place has given us so much."

"Let's go camping," Bessie urged again. "Follow the river up to its source. We could swim in it. We could—"

Just then Sylvie's husband, Pierre, arrived with milk and post and rolled newspapers. Carol looked idly through half a dozen envelopes, froze for a moment on one then passed casually on.

Bessie was chattering to Pierre about the flower festival which preceded harvest, and featured a battle of flowers. Mary was clearing the crockery into the big stone sink; her French was not up to Bessie's and she smiled at Pierre, but made no comment. Carol said quietly, "I must go to the bathroom, Mother. Will you come to church again with Bessie and me?"

"Certainly." Mary glanced at her daughter. "Is something the matter?"

"No. Nothing. I'll be with you in a moment. Leave that."

She did not wait for a reply. The corkscrew stairs had never seemed so inconvenient. She closed her bedroom door carefully and went to the window. The letter was heavy in the pocket of her gathered skirt, though it was only a thin airmail sheet. Even so she left it there while she stared out at the distant peak of their special mountain, the view which had become so dear to them all over the past three years. She had fought quite consciously to make this life all in all, to blot out the memory of that night in Paris when she had so nearly lost her very soul to Jean-Claude Durant. And she had succeeded. He had never attempted to get in touch with her which had been a help in one way, but a terrible blow to her damaged pride in another. Now, suddenly to see his name on the back of this air letter, to see the address "Algérie," had, quite literally, taken her wits. She needed to orientate herself again. She was Carol Woodford of the Bergerie, near Aix-en-Durance. She could no longer be manipulated or used by . . . anyone.

She took a deep breath of the clear air. Below her, Pierre and Bessie emerged from the house, and Bessie—still chattering—took Pierre to see *les haricots blancs,* also transported from Northfield. Carol reminded herself that she had Bessie too. She had wanted children, and Monica had given her Bessie. She looked beyond the garden to the terraced fields which belonged to her farmer neighbour, Monsieur Lassevour. His sheep had gone further up the mountain for the summer, and he was growing crops of flowers for the parfumeries at Grasse. The French rarely grew anything for mere ornamentation. He had thrown up his hands when she told him that their flower garden was not destined for the scent factories.

She smiled at the thought and drew the letter calmly from her pocket, walked to the chest of drawers for scissors, and cut carefully around the glued edge. She glanced at the signature and read

"Ever yours, Jean-Claude" and sat down on the edge of the un-made bed very suddenly.

Just for a moment she closed her eyes, then began to read determinedly.

"My dear Carol . . ."

Not even his writing looked French. Instead of the typical slanting, spidery spikes which she was used to from all her French contacts, his script was upright and bold.

Please do not throw this letter away until you have read it—I beg you. It is of great importance, not only to yourself, but to your family. As you see I am in Algeria again and have managed to spend some time on the plateau; in fact last week I travelled with Berbers who knew of Clive Hubert. I cannot explain my anxiety to walk the ground he walked. It is not for his sake of course, but for yours. I will not enter into a one-sided dialogue about that night, Carol. Please believe that I had no idea your regard for Hubert was so deep. You must have realised my feelings for you, and I know your solution was the right one. I have always respected your wish to cut yourself off from Paris and me, until now.

Carol, the Berbers took me to a Sufi mystic. Did you know that Hubert had been converted to Islam and especially Sufism? I talked with the mystic for some time. Eventually he handed me a tin box which he said had belonged to the pasha. Inside was the original of Hubert's book, handwritten, almost illegible after all this time, but certainly substantially the same as I handed to you in Paris. I wanted to bring it to you. I wanted to impress you, Carol! You see, I am still love-sick and ridiculous! But also I thought it would dispel any suspicions that you might harbour against me. Though surely you must have known I could not have had anything to do with the explosion? I would never have given you the manuscript had I realised its potential danger. It was only later, when I talked with friends, that I learned of the plot, and even then it was so rumour-laden I could not be certain.

I soon realised that to send you Hubert's book was to put you under threat again, so I resisted that temptation. Instead, I posted it immediately to your publishers in London, and asked them to hold it until the trouble over here is settled . . . which I think will not be long now. There is talk of asking de Gaulle to come out of retirement and put an end to the war. However, Carol, as you will see from the newspapers, someone has told the press that the book has turned up. Frankly, my dear, I think the risk is very small, but it is there.

Please will you leave your cottage for a while? Could you go to England for a holiday? At any rate, do not stay there, where I understand you are very vulnerable.

When I leave here I fly to London to see what is to happen next. I shall stay at a small hotel near Paddington station called the Albion. If you wish to contact me, that is where I shall be. Gaby and I were never together after the night of the explosion. Ever yours, Jean-Claude Durant.

Carol folded the single sheet of paper and smoothed the creases to knife sharpness. Her heart was hammering and she was breathing quickly. She controlled herself with an effort of will and opened the letter again. She tried to read between the lines: Algeria was war-torn, the Front de Libération Nationale, composed mainly of Arabs, were inflicting savageries which had shocked decent French people into acts of retaliation as bad if not worse in many cases. After Clive's death in 1955 there had been a clamp-down on foreign journalists travelling in the country, but this was probably relaxed now. She knew that Jean-Claude had been in Egypt reporting on the new President Nasser and his nationalisation of the Suez Canal. During *that* ill-fated war she had followed the casualty lists with a trepidation she never consciously admitted to herself. He must have badgered his paper to let him re-enter Algeria as soon as he returned from Egypt.

And Gaby . . . Gaby whom she had suspected of being in collusion with him . . . Gaby and he "were not together." Exactly what did he mean by that? She closed her eyes again. She wished he had not discovered Clive's original manuscript. She wanted to forget the whole terrible episode.

She went downstairs and the three women left for church. Theirs was a strangely sedate way of life in the Bergerie, not unlike that of three ladies in the English countryside fifty or sixty years ago. There was more freedom of course; but Bessie's schooling at the convent, their attendance at the village festivals, the enormous interest in the garden and growing things, all gave a structure to their lives that was slow and rhythmical and very pleasant to them. It was not surprising that Carol and her mother appreciated it, but it was unusual for a twelve-year-old girl to feel the same way. Perhaps Bessie's regular visits to Myrtle's chaotic household provided the necessary comparison. Even so she was glad when the service was over and they could walk through the village square in the sunshine and talk to the people they knew. Solange and Brigitte Metier from her class were trailing behind their parents, and Bessie caught them up and asked what they were doing for the vacances.

Brigitte made a face. "Grandmère is coming. It will be sewing and prayers."

"All the time?" Bessie asked, wide-eyed.

"Oh no," Solange grinned wickedly. "Sometimes it is prayers and then sewing."

The three of them giggled, then Solange asked, "You go to England as usual, I suppose? You are so lucky, Bessie."

It was Bessie's turn to make a face. "I am not sure. I would rather stay here and go camping. I don't know what Cass has decided." She added quickly, "Listen. If we go, could you come with us? Would your parents agree?"

The French girls raised their brows expressively, registering doubt and hope at the same time. Bessie ran back to Carol who was staring aimlessly at the slightly different view of the mountain peak, and put her request. Carol seemed to have some difficulty in understanding.

"Solange and Brigitte . . . where, Bessie? Ah yes. Of course. We could go tomorrow, couldn't we? This afternoon is rather soon, but I think we had better leave tomorrow."

Bessie stared at her big "sister" who she knew must really be an aunt, and who made the plans for the little family.

"I thought . . ." she changed her mind, and nodded vigorously. "Yes. We had better leave tomorrow. Can you talk to Madame Metier?"

So it was arranged.

They took a tent as usual but there was an ancient shepherd's hut six miles up the side of the Victoire mountain, which provided a more permanent shelter for the nights and a fireplace for cooking. They could see as far as the Camargue one way and Nice the other. But the real attraction was the profusion of wild flowers. It was as if the tiny hut had been dropped from the sky into a carpet of aquilegia, gentians, giant saxifrage, moon daisies and a myriad tiny flowers which Bessie and Mary would spend hours identifying and pressing.

On the day they arrived they felt it was sacrilege to track through them with their haversacks, and they did so in single file and on tiptoe. When Carol lifted the wooden latch of the hut and everyone crowded beneath its overhanging eaves, Solange, looking back, immediately exclaimed, "But they grow again after us!" And Bessie said, awed, "It's like the Red Sea."

Mary laughed. "Not quite. And I don't think Sister Michael would be exactly delighted with the comparison. Come and help me open the shutters." She went inside and found Carol standing by the fireplace. "Is everything all right, darling? I can't see a thing. Don't tell me it's full of dead birds!"

Carol seemed to pull herself together. She laughed.

"No, Mother. I don't think anyone has used it since we were here before. Bessie stacked fresh logs in a criss-cross pattern, and here they are, untouched."

"Good." Mary knocked up the retaining beams of the shutters and began to lift them down. The one-roomed hut was flooded with sunlight. "What is it, Carol? Aren't you well?"

"Sorry. I'm dreaming." Carol smiled quickly and went to the table where five haversacks were piled anyhow. "What are the girls up to?"

Mary said accurately, "They are running and screaming."

Carol managed a laugh, then she walked around the table peering into the rough bunks which had been mangers when the shepherds lived with their flocks. She said, "I'm glad we came. It—it's so normal!"

Mary laughed too. "Two Englishwomen with three small girls alone on a mountain plateau with the minimum of provisions—normal? You must be mad!"

"Normal for us!" Carol began to unwind sleeping bags. "If that clothes line is still at the back, I'll hang these out to air. Then we can send the girls for fresh hay. They need a task!" She paused by the door. "We must be fairly normal, Mother. Otherwise the Metiers would not have entrusted us with their daughters."

Mary cocked an ironic ear. "Don't you think they might well have been thankful to be rid of them? With Grandmère arriving too?"

Carol laughed again and went out to deploy her forces. Pierre had arrived with a laden mule and the rest of the luggage. Mary spent some time reassuring him that they would be quite all right, the farmhouse was only a mile away and walkers used this route frequently. Then he went away and the wonderful peace of the high place descended on them. Mary knew that Carol had had some bad news, and this was a kind of escape for her. She watched her daughter sweeping out the bunks and the hut as if her life depended on it. And she closed her eyes momentarily and said inside her head, "Please John, let her be happy. Always."

It was a halcyon time for all of them. After the heavy heat of summer by the river, the mountain air gave them a new energy. They spent all day out of doors making forays up their special peak to discover new vistas, a waterfall, a bubbling spring, different flowers. They would eat their supper beneath the eaves of the hut, watching wonderful sunsets night after night; then they would spread fresh newspaper over the straw in the bunks and climb into their bags with much crackling and laughter. For the first two nights if one of them turned over the others would wake at the sound, but after that, the air did its work and they slept through, Mary rising at six with the dawn, to light the fire and make tea.

The three girls declared they were "going native," but after an hour of walking barefoot, they took to their sandals again, and the joy of bathing in the stream kept them all very clean. It was Monday when they arrived. On Thursday Pierre came again with fresh food and letters. One of the letters was from the London office telling Carol what she already knew and suggesting that as she had seen the final draft of the Hubert book, she might like to help sort out the jumbled script which was now safely with them. She handed the letter to her mother as soon as they were alone, and Mary read it and pulled her mouth down.

"I knew it was too good to last. When?"

"No hurry. They know I'm on holiday. I could be in Timbuctu for all they know." She smiled at her mother. "We'll have another week. It's doing us all good. And then . . . darling, I want you and Bessie to come with me. I know you're not keen on going again so soon after your visit to Dilly Gosling, but . . ." her voice petered out and she coughed. "If I'm going to see Myrtle again, I'd like you there."

"Not me. Bessie is your ambassador in Cheltenham." Mary laughed, then stopped. "Cass, what is it? Really?"

"Jean-Claude is in London. Incredibly enough he is staying at the old Albion. Can you believe it? Life is so strange. No word from Monica for years, but the links cannot be cut."

"Of course they cannot. Bessie will always be the link."

Carol was silent for some time. Then she said, "You will come with me?"

Mary smiled. "Yes. Yes, of course."

That night they heard cowbells. It was an unusual sound during the hours of darkness, and Carol opened the door and peered in its direction. She was suddenly terrified. If they had been "vulnerable" at the Bergerie, they were doubly so here. The safety of the hut depended entirely on its secrecy, and they had not asked the Metiers to keep silent about their daughters. And Pierre was coming up every fourth day . . .

Lights flickered at the far edge of the plateau. Carol's heart was hammering suffocatingly. She reached behind the door for one of the stout pieces of wood which barred the shutters. Should she wake the girls and send them scurrying into the night to the farm?

Then Bessie's head bounced under her arm.

"Cass! Oh, joy everlasting! Angélique is having her calf! Solly! Gitte! Wake up, *mes petites!* Quick. Coats—socks—where *are* they?" Mary was lighting the lamp, her eyes flashing around in wild surmise. Bessie babbled, "Gran, didn't we tell you? One of the cows is having her accouchement! Isn't it wonderful? Old Beppo—the cowman—he said we could go. D'you want to come? Cass, what about you?"

They were gone without waiting for an answer. Now that her eyes were used to the darkness, she could recognise Beppo's burly silhouette holding the cow by the horns while Mrs. Beppo and the little Beppos crowded around the operational end.

She relaxed tremblingly against the door jamb and closed her eyes.

Mary said, "All right, darling?"

Carol did not want to mention the word *danger* to any of them. She did not let it enter her mind. But it was there. She remembered that night when the building off the Avenue Foch had gone up like a torch, killing Henri so needlessly. Somehow that had been partly her doing. She must not let it happen again.

"Fine, Mother. But I imagine we shall have more peace in England!" She tried to make it sound funny, but Mary did not laugh. "As Professor Joad would say," she commented, "it depends on what you mean by peace."

■

They called the calf Bluebell, and Bessie pronounced it like the French girls: Bleu-beel. Beppo fenced it off with its mother who was neurotically possessive except where the three girls were concerned. She would actually nudge Bluebell to the fence so that they could stroke her and tell her how beautiful she was. Mary took a lot of photographs of them, and Bessie made sketches of the animals with elongated Disney eyes and smiling mouths.

"Your flower drawings are far more accurate," Mary commented.

"Oh I know, Grannie. But these are *fun!*" Bessie explained.

On their last full day, the girls roamed further than usual. They were playing at mountaineers and scrambled up a long chute of scree to another very small and unexpected plateau. It was a hard climb and they were breathless and gasping when they reached the top.

Then Gitte saw the hut.

"It's another shepherd's hut!" she exclaimed. "But why here? There is no grazing—not even for goats."

The girls approached the tumbledown hovel curiously. Inside, the single room was much smaller than "their" hut and there were no mangers nor a fireplace.

Solange said knowledgeably, "It's a climber's hut. Yes? Perhaps halfway up the Victoire?"

Bessie said, "I claim it in the name of S.B.B."

"S.B.B.?" the other two asked in unison.

"Solange. Brigitte. And Bessie!"

They all laughed, but then Solange said seriously, "Yes. Let it be ours. And let us meet here every summer until we are *ancien!*"

Bessie said, "Oh, joy everlasting! A secret tryst!"

"Where we share our secrets?" asked Brigitte.

"If you like." Bessie frowned. "I have no secrets."

Brigitte giggled. "We have. Shall we say, Sollie?"

Solange shrugged, embarrassed. "It is just our parents. We saw them. You understand. Bouncing on the bed." She shrugged again. "Anyway, you have the biggest secret of all, *chérie.* You are adopted."

Bessie, still puzzled regarding the Metier secret, raised her brows. "That is a secret, *polichinelle!* I am—" she struck an attitude—"a chosen child!"

Brigitte giggled. "Yes, but the secret is . . . who bounced up and down on a bed before you were born?" She sighed with impatience at Bessie's incomprehension and her sister's red face. "Who were your parents—your real parents?" she enlarged.

"Does it matter?"

"*Naturellement* it is of great import. And . . . Maman says she thinks that Carol is your true mother. She thinks that Carol had a wonderful *affaire de coeur* when she was very young, and when you were born, Mrs. Woodford adopted you!" She spread her hands. "Is it not very romantic?" Bessie was stunned.

When at last she got her breath, she said slowly, "Cass . . . my mother? She is too young, I think." She did some calculations in her head. "She would have been sixteen when I was born."

Solange shrugged expressively. "It is possible."

There was another silence, then Bessie said, "But why would she not tell me? It would be wonderful!"

"Ah . . ." Gitte rolled her eyes. "It would also be a disgrace!"

She and her sister started to laugh at the ridiculousness of adults, and after a while Bessie joined in. But she was laughing with sudden excitement. She had never thought about her parentage before; Grannie and Cass had shared their family anecdotes and made them hers as a gift. But if Cass was her real mother, then they were also hers as a right. She felt a great upsurge of joy. She stood on the lip of the plateau where it disintegrated into the long slide of scree, and she shouted at the top of her voice, "You belong to me! My plateau! My secret hut! My mountain!" Her voice bounced back off the sides of the chute, and before the echoes died she turned to her two friends and said exultantly, "And I have a boyfriend! There! Another secret which you must tell no-one. I have a boyfriend who thinks I am the absolute bee's knees!"

She spoke in English and very quickly. They could not translate it and before they could ask what she had said, she squatted on her heels and took off down the scree. The back of her cotton skirt was in tatters when she got to the bottom, but she was still laughing.

Carol walked down by herself to tell Pierre to bring the mules unloaded next week, so that their things could be carried back down the mountain. She arrived at the Bergerie without anyone knowing she was there. From the flower terraces of M. Lassevour she surveyed the house and garden carefully. It was exactly as they had left it ten days ago. No broken windows, no ravaged plants. Pierre had obviously been watering the night before, but other than that she could have sworn no-one had crossed the grass to the door.

She slipped her key into the lock as quietly as she could, swung the door wide and stood listening while she counted sixty. Then she went from room to room doing all the things she'd read about in crime books, even to sniffing the air and looking under the beds. Nothing.

Smiling with relief, she left the house again and went down to the village. She met Pierre en route and gave him her message. When she told him they would soon be off to England on business, he threw up his hands.

"The little one will miss the flower festival!" he mourned.

Cass had forgotten that. She hoped they would not have trouble with Bessie.

"Has anyone called at the Bergerie while we have been away, Pierre?" she asked casually as she turned.

"No-one, *madame*." Like poor Henri, he invariably gave her the courtesy title of madame.

She smiled. "Of course, I should not enquire. How could you know. You are there infrequently for the watering of the plants."

He spread his hands. "I would know, madame. There is only one way to the Bergerie and someone would always tell me if anyone took it."

"Naturally." She nodded, well satisfied. "Thank you, Pierre. Thank you very much." He looked surprised, and she went on quickly, "So, we will see you on Thursday. Early, yes? I will begin to pack our things now, but we shall need to clean up and sort the laundry. So . . . early."

"*Certainement, madame.*" He took off his cap and held it across his midriff respectfully while she turned and went back up the track to the Bergerie again. He was a comfort and a support, and at that moment she loved all the villagers who kept an eye on the Bergerie, even if they probably did it from sheer curiosity.

She pulled out cases and opened them wide on her bed. The first was easily filled with underwear and night clothes. The second with blouses, skirts and summer dresses. The third was for her files. She went to the desk in the corner, and stopped. The second drawer was not closed.

She stared at it, mesmerised by it, trying to remember whether in her lightning check an hour earlier she might have given it a careless push which hadn't quite closed it. That must be the explanation. No-one could have come to the villa in that hour; she would have passed them on the track; Pierre would have seen them. Nevertheless however carelessly she pushed at drawers, she always waited for them to click into place. She would have shut that drawer properly.

She swallowed and forced herself to walk forward normally in case she was under some kind of surveillance. Her heart hammered frantically, just as it had done two nights ago. She was terrified. She glanced over her shoulder at the dressing-table mirror which invariably tipped forward. It reflected the base of the bed. No-one was beneath it. With a sob of sheer relief she reached the desk and looked carefully around the drawer for a telltale wire. There was nothing. She left it and went downstairs again for a broom. On the cooking range was Mary's enormous iron frying pan. She picked that up too.

Once more she searched the house, catching glimpses of herself in the mirrors, frying pan held high: a ludicrous sight that could not raise even a smile. At last she was back in her own room, allowing her breathing to be very audible now. Crouching low, her pillow held in front of her face, she inserted the broom head into the open drawer and pulled. She jumped and screamed a little as the drawer clattered on to the polished boards, scattering its contents everywhere. Nothing else happened. After a long time she removed the pillow and gazed at the empty drawer. She knew she should laugh. First the calving, and now this. But she, who was usually good at laughing at herself, could not do so now. She only just stopped herself from weeping.

With forced calm, she replaced the pillow on her bed and knelt down to clear up the mess on the floor. It must have been her own doing; it must have. But she knew it wasn't.

Everything went according to plan. It had been a wonderful holiday and though the French girls wished it could have lasted longer, they accepted without question that Carol's work was taking her to London and that Bessie and Mrs. Woodford must go with her. Carol knew that her mother would be a willing companion once her first reluctance had been overcome, but she had expected objections from Bessie. After all, Boris Denning was away. But Bessie was strangely elated about everything. She said, "Families stick together, don't they? Through thick and thin!" And although it was the sort of clarion call Bessie often made, this time it was different. Carol couldn't put her finger on the difference, but it was there.

She was like a cat on hot bricks. Moving slowly down the mountain in the wake of the loaded mules, she constantly glanced around her, and when they reached the neighbouring farm she ran ahead and was there to welcome them at the door when they arrived.

"Everything is fine," she panted. "And a letter from Liv by the look of it—" She brandished an envelope.

"Of course everything is fine," Mary said rather tartly. "You were here only a few days ago."

Bessie called, "I'll go on down with Sollie and Gitte, Cass. See you for *déjeuner*."

"We have a great deal to do if we're to be off tomorrow, Bessie," Mary objected. But Carol seemed relieved.

"It'll give us a chance to get cracking," she explained to her mother.

By the oddest coincidence, the letter from Liv was to ask them all to come and stay for as long as they liked. Carol couldn't get over it.

"Myrtle is staying with Liv too. She's expecting again—how marvellous. Oh, it will be much easier if we're all there. How very sweet of Liv!"

They flew out the next day, landing at Stansted without mishap. It was tea time when their taxi drew up outside the Albion. The August day had turned brassy and breathless; thunder was on the way and the smell of sulphur from Paddington station made Carol feel sick.

The new owners had filled the foyer with flowers and each doorway was striped with multi-coloured plastic strips. It was a jumble of such contradictions: Irish linen curtains and bedspreads, paper towels in the cloakrooms. But the welcoming atmosphere was still prevalent. Mary said to Bessie, "Your Aunt Monica was the manageress here. She had this room built on to the back of the house. Isn't it nice?"

Bessie, who had never met Aunt Monica, though she knew her from the many apocryphal stories told by Carol and Mary, glanced around without much interest.

"It's all right. But I don't like the place very much. Right in the middle of all these streets—"

"The park isn't far," Carol said quickly. "And anyway, you and Grannie will be going to Northfield tomorrow. You'll see all your old friends."

Bessie shrugged, withholding co-operation, her esprit de corps a thing of the past. "They'll have gone away for their summer *hols*. And Boris isn't back yet. And Aunt Liv doesn't live in Northfield."

Mary glanced at Carol and said, "You could have stayed with Solange and Brigitte, Bessie. You chose to come with us."

"S'ppose so." Bessie shrugged again, clinging to her Frenchness. She added, "Anyway, I came so that the three of us could stay together. I didn't know you were going to stay in London, Cass."

"A few days. A week at the most." Carol was ill at ease. She had not seen this new room before. Big French doors opened into the small sooty garden, and a handful of people sat outside, swatting at the gnats. She checked them over with a quick glance and saw no-one she knew, but she was anxious to get out of this public place to their rooms. They need not have come here. Some sense of fairness had made her force a meeting with Jean-Claude; she knew now that decision had been a mistake.

For at least the third time she explained the arrangements to Bessie. "I have to check a special manuscript that has turned up out of the blue, darling. That's all. It won't take long." She looked helplessly at their luggage. "I thought Mrs. Arlen had gone for someone to help with the bags."

Mary said soothingly, "She has, darling. You and Bessie are so impatient. Look, I'll see to the luggage and settling us in our rooms. You two go outside and sit quietly."

Carol said eagerly, "No. You go, Mother. Please. I'm fidgety." She blinked. "It's this place. We shouldn't have come here, perhaps."

"Why on earth not? It seems entirely appropriate to me. And you need to be here to *liaise* with your Monsieur Durant." Mary watched her daughter closely. That had been Carol's excuse for staying at the Albion; Mary thought it was probably her way of facing her own particular weakness.

Bessie said impatiently, "Oh come on, Grannie. I'm fed up with standing about like a potted palm in a *patisserie.*"

Carol and Mary laughed as Bessie had intended, and Carol left them and went into the hall in search of Mrs. Arlen.

There was no sign of Jean-Claude, either that evening or at breakfast the next day. Carol felt her nerves were as taut as violin strings; every time a door opened she jumped. Finally, just before she took her mother and Bessie to Paddington, she enquired at the desk for him.

"Ah, Mr. Durant. He has gone to Paris for the rest of this week, Miss Woodford. To see his wife apparently." Mrs. Arlen smiled. "You know the gentleman?"

Carol swallowed. The sense of anti-climax was appalling.

"We are colleagues," she said. "Publishing. Books."

The smile became roguish. "I wondered if he was a film star. So handsome."

Carol forced an answering smile. "Yes." She wished it were not so. His classic Latin good looks somehow denigrated everything she had felt that night two years ago. Had it been just a schoolgirl crush for a handsome man? She turned away, sickened by her own thoughts. "I won't be in for lunch, Mrs. Arlen. I'll go straight to my office from Paddington and work through until this evening." It was the obvious thing to do; she would need to take her mind off from Bessie and her mother, and she ought to start work as soon as possible.

It was agony saying goodbye. They were often apart, and in any case she would be joining them at Liv's in two or three days; nevertheless this parting was particularly painful. Carol took a taxi to Blackfriars, trying not to think of Jean-Claude and his return to Gaby. He had lied to her in his letter, but that should not surprise her. Nothing should surprise her about human nature. And she was lucky; she had Bessie. She had wanted a child, not a husband. She surely had the best of both worlds.

Ralph Morrish greeted her in the tiny foyer of the offices. People coming here for the first time had difficulty in realising that this old Dickensian building housed the most important publishers in Europe, but Carol was always delighted that the two brothers who still held the reins refused to consider major modernisations. She shook Ralph's hand warmly; he had created the French post and made sure it went to her six years ago, and it was he who had made it easy for her to move to Marseilles after the fire.

"Carol. We did not expect you so soon. Monsieur Durant has taken a couple of days off to see his family. He particularly wants to collaborate with you on this book." He drew her closer and kissed her cheek. "It is good to see you, my dear. Are you alone? Is Bessie with you? Your mother?" Ralph had met them both and was a firm favourite.

"Yes and no. We arrived yesterday, but they have gone to see friends at home. I hope to join them as soon as I have finished here." Carol smiled. "They send their love of course. How are you, Ralph?"

"Very well. And it is obvious you are, too. You are so brown, Carol."

She could accept compliments from him without suspicion.

"We've been camping—living outside for nearly a fortnight. It suited us all." She asked after his family and colleagues. Someone brought coffee and they went up the first flight of stairs to his office and settled themselves in chairs by a window looking out on the river.

Ralph leaned forward. "This book, Carol. Quite a find. Wonderful from the point of view of the firm. I understand, however, it could be dangerous for you. Monsieur Durant is most anxious to dissociate you from it. But we need you to look through it, verify it, if you like. You read the finished copy, didn't you?"

"Not all of it. About half. I don't see it as dangerous now, Ralph. You have it and will publish it whatever part I play. I should think Monsieur Durant is in an invidious position, however. His newspaper will not like him giving the manuscript to you. And he represents the imperialists' views. Clive Hubert's book is pro Algerian independence. Very much so."

"You are not worried for yourself, then?"

"No. I am a very small cog in a very large wheel."

"I can't agree there. But I am inclined to agree that you are in no personal danger. Otherwise we would not have asked you to come over. As you say, it is different for Monsieur Durant. But he chose to come—he was adamant actually."

"Really?" Carol thought of her panic on the plateau; the half-hour of sheer terror in the Bergerie. Had Jean-Claude deliberately planted that fear in an effort to drive her into his company again? Or was that her schoolgirl wishful thinking?

She took a deep breath. "Anyway I'll work on it in the office,

Ralph, if I may. Then obviously I shall be perfectly safe." She put her cup down. "In fact, I'll start now. Have you got the manuscript here?"

He stood up and went to a safe in the wall.

"Durant has frightened us into locking it away!" He laughed wryly as he took out a bulky package and put it on his desk.

She did not respond. The sight of it reminded her of the first time she had seen it; how free she had been then. She stood up. Of course she had been free since then. The Bergerie had offered solace and a new life. Coming here like this had been her choice. There had been no coercion at all.

"I'll read it in two or three days, Ralph."

He shook his head, still smiling. "I don't think so, my dear. Wait until you open it." He drew out a chair. "Come on. Sit here where you can still see the bend in the river. Do you need the fan? No? Then I'll send up more coffee and collect you at one o'clock sharp for lunch."

He was as good as his word, and by that time Carol knew that to do Clive's work justice, she would have to give at least a week to her reading. She sipped her coffee and closed her eyes against the almost illegible script and the wide sweep of the Thames, as she tried to remember again the small, self-effacing man with the enormous sense of justice. It was necessary to hold him in her mind and to forget the other man who was so different.

She worked through the weekend and by the following Thursday the end was in sight. Jean-Claude's continued absence made it easier by the minute to forget him. Clive's enormous word canvas of a country still living in the eighteenth century was breathtaking. At times she could smell the gunpowder from the cannon of deys, at others the French war-time government seemed little different. She worked chapter by chapter; reading, typing some of the more illegible passages and making notes. Sometimes there were insertions, then deletions. But she was gradually pulling the book into some kind of order so that the typist could begin to make a finished copy.

The weather was still sulphurically hot. Ralph wanted her to go to his home in Maidenhead where it was comparatively cool by the river, but something took her back to the Albion each night. She was living in a curious limbo peopled by the Arabs from Clive's book, and the sultry weather made it more real. After dinner in the front of the house, she would sit in the new extension with her coffee and respond to desultory remarks from the other guests. Nobody remembered Mon, certainly no-one had heard of the Goslings.

She telephoned Liv's number twice a day and spoke to Bessie and her mother. They seemed odd; distant, even evasive. She put it down to her own peculiar state of mind. On Thursday evening she told them that one more day would see an end to her work. She could join them at the weekend.

"Oh, joy everlasting," Bessie responded in a flat voice. "Can we go to the baths or something? It's stifling here."

"Well, of course. Anything you like."

"You might change your mind. You haven't had an all-girls-together meeting since you were sixteen, Auntie Liv says. You might want to do that."

"Don't be silly, Bessie. Auntie Myrt will be much too busy with the children for us to go off together. We shall have our chats when you're in bed." There was a silence and Carol frowned at the receiver. "Let me talk to Grannie, darling."

But her mother did not sound quite right either.

"Of course everything is all right, Cass. Why on earth wouldn't it be?"

"I simply wondered whether there was an atmosphere or something. So many of you in Liv's house at one time. She's rather house-proud, isn't she? Is it awkward for you to talk? Just say yes or no."

"No."

"Is Myrtle behaving badly?"

"No."

"What about Liv?"

"Same answer."

"Well, all right then. Listen, I'll see you on Saturday definitely. And if it's too much of a good thing, we'll go to an hotel. How's that?"

"Fine. Just fine. Take care of yourself. And be prepared."

"For what?"

There were muffled voices on the line, then her mother said quickly, "Anything. Goodbye, darling." And the line went dead.

She went back to the office that evening and worked until she had finished. It was quite dark; the desk lamp made a pool of light around the typewriter and scattered papers. Outside the glitter of the river was just discernible beneath a murky moon; the heat made the air feel thick and tangible. Carol tipped her chair back and stretched enormously. Her eyes felt gritty yet damp. Clive had died for this book and she had done her best to ensure that his death had not been in vain. She should feel relief; she had done the entire backbreaking job without Jean-Claude's doubtful help. She could leave earlier than she had planned and thereby avoid seeing him. And she could surprise Bessie and her mother.

But there was no relief. She wondered now why she had returned this evening to finish off. She had effectively scuppered her reasons for staying and seeing Jean-Claude, if that was what she had really wanted all the time.

She closed her eyes and put her hands over them. Tears oozed between her fingers. She did not know what she wanted any more. Poor Clive. At least he had known. Beneath that diffident surface he had been a great man.

Wearily she found a handkerchief and dried her face, then tidied the papers into a pile and locked everything away in the safe. She scribbled a note for Ralph and propped it on the typewriter. She would call into the office before she went back to France, but she left Liv's telephone number in case there were any queries. Then she rang for a taxi.

It was two o'clock when she let herself into the Albion. Mrs. Arlen had given her a key and told her to make herself a hot drink if she felt like it, but her one thought was to go to bed and find oblivion in sleep. The plastic door strips stirred momentarily as she closed the door behind her, then subsided into the stillness of the breathless night. She crept upstairs and went to the bathroom, then unlocked her door.

At first it did not register that the light was on. She leaned down to unbuckle her sandals, and then froze in an awkward stoop. Even without the light she should have known she was not alone in the room, and her immediate thought was that the intruders who had visited the Bergerie had found her here in London. And then she saw a pair of feet in very feminine high-heeled sandals; she let her eyes travel up a pair of very beautiful nylon-clad legs, until she could see a whole person sitting in her bedside chair. A woman, hair as black as a raven's wing, a book face down on her lap, a strange, twisted sort of smile on her beautiful face; it was Monica.

Carol gave a gasping sob and straightened, arms already extended in welcome.

"Mon! Dear God . . . it's you! Oh my dear girl—where have you come from? Oh Mon—"

She cast herself on the unresponsive figure, her previous state of mind forgotten in a mixture of relief and joy. After a hiatus of perhaps two seconds, Monica too gave a sob and scrambled her arms around Carol's neck. The book fell to the floor; somehow Monica stood up and the girls did a kind of dance, clutching each other convulsively, speaking single-word sentences, laughing meaninglessly.

"How—?"

"Surprise—"

"Where?"

"Liv's. Over a week now."

"See you."

"Mother."

"Nearly gave the game away."

"Oh . . . Mon!" Carol drew off slightly to look into the familiar face. It was eleven years. The brown skin was smoother, almost enamelled; the plucked eyebrows were thicker but just as definitive; the pouting mouth was firmer, the eyes as guarded as before. "You . . . you're beautiful! Like a film star! Oh, Mon!"

"And you haven't changed either."

"Worse luck."

"Stupid woman. You're lovely and you don't know it. Hasn't anyone told you that?"

"Stop it, Mon. Sit down. Tell me. Everything."

"How can I? You're punch-drunk. Get to bed. I've got a room down the hall. I'll see you tomorrow. Midday."

"No. Mon, stay. I can't sleep, I'm too wound up. This is absolutely right, you coming—being here—now. At this moment. I'm in a state. I need you. Don't go."

"Okay." Mon opened her hands in a gesture typically American. She turned to the bed table. "There's coffee here in a Thermos. I've been drinking it to keep me awake. D'you want some?"

"Yes. Please. You shouldn't have waited up. But I'm glad you did."

"I nearly didn't. Then I got damned worried. I was going to give you another hour then ring the police."

"You could have rung the office."

"Yes. But I still wanted to surprise you."

"You did. Oh God, you did." She took the proffered cup and laughed hysterically. "I thought you were the terrorists again. Oh God."

"I heard. From your mother and from Myrtle. You shouldn't be caught up in this F.L.N. business, Cass. For Christ's sake. There's Bessie to consider."

"I know. I'm out of it now. The whole thing is finished and done with." Carol sipped, eyes closed. Then she sat on the bed and after another pause, Monica sat by her. Carol opened her eyes and smiled. "You being here . . . you've changed things. You've sort of taken hold of fate . . ." she giggled. "You're a kind of deus ex machina."

"You mean I've thrown a spanner in the works?" Monica said, not smiling.

"I don't know. Just banished the nightmares, I think. Done away with the uncertainty."

"You're bushed."

Carol nodded. "I'm bushed." She drank the coffee and put the cup from her. "Mon. I'm so pleased to see you. Of course." She looked into the black eyes, so like Bessie's. "How long are you here?"

"I don't know. It sort of depends on you."

"What about your husband? Bob."

"I don't know about him either. He's got someone else."

"Mon. I'm so sorry. So sorry." She looked at her friend. There was no expression on the carefully made-up face. She said, "Come back with us. To the Bergerie. You'll love it."

"I've got my own place, Cass. And—with Elizabeth—it could be a home." There was a pause, then she added very calmly, "And I want Elizabeth. I want to make a home for my daughter, Cass. I'm in a position to do that, you see. And you always said if ever I wanted her back, I could have her." She stood up, picked up her handbag and went to the door. "I wanted to tell you immediately even though you're so tired. I've met Elizabeth. We've been together a great deal over the past few days. We get on well." She opened the door. "Sorry. I always believed in dropping my bombshells quickly, if you remember. Get to bed now and we'll talk about it in the morning. Good night."

Incredibly, she was gone. Carol made no attempt to stop her. She felt frozen to the bed, literally frozen solid in spite of the heat. She might have told herself the whole interview had not happened, except that the bedside table held two empty coffee cups.

After a long while she took off her dress and slid into her old-fashioned nightdress. Then she lay on top of the bed and closed her eyes.

8

*C*arol fell into a fitful sleep just before the early dawn. She was conscious of the hotel coming to life with the sound of bathrooms and breakfast, but she did not have the will to struggle out of her murky half-world and face reality. Even when she forced herself to roll over and look at the clock, she played a kind of gruesome mental game. Just out of sight where she knew her hairbrush lay on the dressing table, were some unpleasant facts. She couldn't quite see them though she knew they were there. She registered the time, nine-thirty, and closed her eyes quickly in case her gaze should stray to the hairbrush. Then she forced herself to think of the Bergerie and the little shepherd's hut halfway up the Victoire, where they had been only a few days ago.

After five minutes tears oozed from her closed eyes and ran saltily into her mouth, and she sat up, angry with herself.

"Maudlin," she said aloud and very calmly. And then, "Whether you had stayed there or come here, it would have been the same. Mother and I always knew that we had Bessie on loan. We've had her for nearly twelve years. Wouldn't you think we could be grateful for that?" She closed her eyes again and took a long trembling breath. Then she whispered, "Monica is my best friend. My best friend."

She swung her legs out of bed and sat for a moment, holding her head. Fleetingly she remembered the fuss about Clive's book; her palpitations about whether she might meet Jean-Claude again. That all seemed petty now. Her ridiculous fear on the mountain and in her bedroom at the Bergerie had been practically self-delusion. She had wanted to run into Jean-Claude's arms, so she had fabricated reasons for so doing. And all the time, fate had this in store. A blow more terrible than any explosion.

Her head throbbed and she felt very sick. She had eaten dinner last night before going back to the office—she recalled all that with difficulty—but perhaps she needed food. As if in reply to the thought there was a knock on the door and Mrs. Arlen appeared with a tray.

"Are you all right, Miss Woodford?"

Curious eyes glanced at the ravaged bed and carelessly discarded clothes. Already the hotel owner knew that this guest was normally very neat.

"Your friend Mrs. Gallagher said you weren't very well last night after all that work. She asked me to bring you your breakfast at ten o'clock if you hadn't come down. And give you this letter from her."

Carol switched her eyes from Mrs. Arlen's face to the tray. Her head throbbed alarmingly.

"Come on now. Sit back on the bed." Mrs. Arlen put the tray down and tried to lift Carol's legs. Carol flapped her away feebly.

"I'm better up. A touch of migraine. That's all." She forced a sickly smile. "I didn't realise Mrs. Gallagher was leaving. She *is* leaving?"

"Oh, she's gone, my dear. She wanted to leave before the traffic got bad. It will all be explained in her letter. Here, let me pour you a nice cup of tea and you'll feel better. Do you need an aspirin?"

"No. Fine. Honestly." Carol took the tea and gulped too quickly. The roof of her mouth burned agonisingly.

"I'll leave you then." Mrs. Arlen made for the door, excusing herself at some length. Thankfully Carol closed her eyes again and let the steam from the cup soothe the front of her face. She wondered if she really was ill. She put the cup down and fumbled in her handbag for aspirin. She would have some after all and lie still until she felt better. She couldn't face Monica's letter yet.

An hour later, with her head still thumping as thoughts milled inside her brain, she opened it. Words hopped about on the single page; she picked out "sorry" and "barren" and then blinked hard and brought the whole thing into focus. Monica's writing had always been atrocious. Carol had to concentrate.

Cass. I cannot face you so am leaving early. I'm not exactly running again, but almost. I'm sorry, my dear. I did not realise how hard it would hit you. But Cass, she is my daughter, and the doctors in New York say I cannot have any more. Can you imagine what it is like to be barren when you already have a child? My marriage is over. Elizabeth is all I have. Can you understand? I shall say nothing, but please help me. Join us as soon as you can and suggest Elizabeth and I have a holiday together. Or something. Anything, Cass. Please. Forgive me. Mon. P.S. You still have your mother.

Carol closed her eyes again and lay very still. Unbidden mental pictures of Monica flashed by like flipped pages in a photograph album. Monica clouting Liv with her satchel; Monica telling them brutally that she had "lost her virginity"; Monica announcing she was pregnant. There was something ruthless about the girl; when she felt she had to do something she did it as quickly as she could. Like ripping off a bandage. Like grasping a nettle.

With heart-stopping suddenness, the telephone rang. Carol snatched at it, convinced it was Bessie full of questions, full of . . . anger? It was Ralph.

"I can see you have finished, Carol. But are we not to see you again?"

"I should not be here now, Ralph. I want to join my family as soon as I can."

"You worked all night and overslept," he guessed.

"Yes. More or less."

"Listen, Carol. You've been wonderful. I will send the proofs to the Bergerie. And if there is anything—not only with work. I like to think we're friends."

"Thank you, Ralph. I do too." She could so easily have wept again; she must be sickening for something.

"This whole thing has been a strain, Carol. Are you going to be all right? Marion keeps asking me to get you to come down to

Maidenhead for a break. Bessie and your mother too, of course."

"No. Really. Thanks, Ralph, but . . ." For a moment she almost told him then and there. "Actually there are a few domestic problems. I need to go to Birmingham. But thanks again."

"Bear it in mind. Any time."

She replaced the receiver carefully and nibbled at some cold toast. Then she got up and began to tidy her room. There was a train at two something. She would catch that. She needed to be in Birmingham. Monica might say something to Bessie. And why had Bessie sounded odd on the phone? Her mother too. She must get up there as soon as she could.

She put her case near the door for Mr. Arlen to collect, shouldered her bag and pushed her hat down to meet the knot of hair at her nape. Then with a final checking glance around the room, she opened the door. Jean-Claude stood there, hand raised to knock.

For a long moment they stared at each other. She saw that he had changed physically. His black, crisp hair was blotched with grey, and his dark eyes were no longer knowing and confident, they were wise and rather tired. His shoulders were slightly bent. It was only three years since they had shared that night together, but he was different.

Seeming to become aware of his lifted hand, he made a small apologetic sound and put it in his jacket pocket. He still did not look French. His jacket was leather-patched, his flannels would be out of place on the Champs Elysées. He wore an open-necked shirt. After Ralph's formal office suits, he looked as if he'd just returned from a conventional seaside holiday.

She said, "It's you."

The small apologetic sound came again. "Yes. I wanted . . . I'm sorry . . . you were leaving. I should have let you . . . go."

"The book is read and I have to go to Birmingham."

"Ah yes. Your mother. And your small sister. I understand." He seemed to droop, as if surrendering to something, or someone, much stronger. But neither of them moved from the doorway.

She said, "Gaby? Was Gaby all right?"

"Yes. She will not divorce. We do not go to church, we had a civil marriage at the *mairie*. But she claims she does not believe in divorce."

"I did not know. I mean that you wished for . . . wanted . . ."

"It is you I love. You know that."

"No!" It was a protest rather than a negation. She blurted, "You don't know about me! There's Bessie—"

"Of course I know. She is your child. I always knew that. Perhaps it was one of the reasons . . . not so, I always loved you."

Carol cried out again, "No!" And then she put her hands to her face. "Bessie belongs to my friend. My schoolfriend. And now she wants her back. And I cannot stop her—we always agreed—she was a trust—Mother and I had her on trust—she was a kind of honour for us. And Monica cannot have any more children and she wants Bessie back!"

Tears spouted between her fingers. One hand was gloved and she tried frantically to wipe at the tears with the soft kid.

He said, "A-a-ah," as only a Frenchman could say it, and she noted fleetingly that his origins were still there somewhere. Then she was in his arms and his cheek was against hers and he murmured in her ear, *"Repose. Ma pauvre . . ."* and the tears ran between them, into his neck and hers. She could no longer control herself; the silent weeping escalated into tearing sobs. He lifted her feet clear of the floor and moved inside the room, closed the door with a kick, sat her on the bed.

"Now. Now, *chérie."* He found a handkerchief and mopped. "Don't speak. It is nothing. An eruption of the heart, of the soul. It is good. It is good." His hand beneath the handkerchief cradled her face. "That night after the fire . . . this should have happened then. So much control is not good."

Her hat was hanging from a hairpin. She tore it off.

"I look a mess," she wailed. "I wanted so much to see you yet I was determined it should not happen. And now—now—this!"

"Carol. Darling girl. Darling woman. You are beautiful to me always. So un-un-obvious. You know?"

Her sob hiccoughed into a laugh. "Of course. So unobvious no-one can see it!"

"Always you must laugh at yourself. Listen, my Carol. You are a special human being. Such a special human being cannot be kept in an obvious body. Obvious hair. Obvious face. It has to be . . . encased . . . in something very special. A kind of asceticism. A kind of strength."

She had to stop him. She looked up, eyes and nose liquid. "Oh . . . Jean-Claude." And she kissed him.

It was a circumspect English kiss, but it stunned him into silence. Words, conventional gestures, solace, concern, all went out of the window. He let the handkerchief fall and stared at her again, one hand on her shoulder, the other lying against her neck.

After a long time when she too neither moved nor seemed to breathe, he whispered, "So be it." And then he cupped her face and bent his head to hers.

At first his kisses alarmed her and she had to hold herself still against an urge to run. Then she sensed a reverence about them which was infinitely reassuring. He touched her mouth with his over and over again, as if sipping wine, and very tentatively she began to relax. Her eyes closed; she let his hands take the weight of her head. She moved her own hands to his neck and held him to her longer. The ungloved hand felt his ears, the rough short hair at the base of his skull. She remembered them from before. She remembered that it was not like Malcolm Lennox at the wedding party. It was not an invasion, a demand. It was not like that. Together they tasted the wine.

At some moment, he unpinned her hair so that it fell around her shoulders, still in sun-bleached stripes from her mountain holiday. It gave her confidence; she knew it was ample and deeply waved. Incredibly, beneath his touch, she did indeed begin to feel beautiful.

"Carol." He traced the contours of her face with his thumbs. "I would like—so much—to consummate this love. But I cannot offer . . . respectability."

She began to laugh. His Frenchness had come to the fore just in time to sabotage any hint of a sordid seduction scene.

She sat back, seeing his uncertainty, remembering the suave Parisian of two years ago who had been so sure of himself.

"A-a-ah," she deliberately mimicked his accent. "A-a-ah, Jean-Claude. You can offer me the whole world. What would I want with respectability?"

He smiled wryly. "Shall I ever really know you, Carol? Will you always surprise me completely?" He slid out of his jacket then touched the back of her hand. "Are you certain, my darling? I cannot lose you now."

She stood up and with calm deliberation unbuttoned her blouse and took it off. She unzipped her skirt and let it fall to the floor. As his hand touched her shoulders she was conscious of his warmth melting her cold and knew that this could not have happened if Monica hadn't turned up when she did and claimed Bessie. Somehow this blinding happiness now lightened that awful event. She saw, in its clarity, that Bessie could never be taken from them; she could live elsewhere perhaps, be happy elsewhere, but she belonged to the Woodfords. Everything seemed inevitable and leading to this moment. The horrors were woven into the good things to make a whole: the tragedy of her father's death had led relentlessly into the adoption of Bessie. The terror of the explosion at the Avenue Foch had seemed pointless. Now she saw that it had enabled Jean-Claude to go back to Algeria and find Clive's manuscript, so that she knew without doubt that he loved her.

Her thoughts described a full circle in that protracted moment of awareness between them, and then, gently, they came together like travellers at the end of a long journey.

He wanted to come with her to Birmingham, but she could not agree to that.

"I have committed myself to you, my dearest. But it would be unfair to expect Mother .... Bessie ... the others—no, I cannot present them with a fait accompli just yet. Forgive me. I am not ashamed of our union. You know that."

He nodded. "I am being selfish, Carol. I do not want to be away from you ever again. Also, I am frightened. That you will change." He was propped on one elbow, looking at her. She lay, totally relaxed, her arms above her head. He touched the pale, blue-veined underside of her elbow, then the swell of her breast, then the concave curve at the top of her hip. "I cannot believe it, my darling. You have been inside my head for so long. And now, you are here." He laughed. "I thought always you would run. But you are . . . here!" He put his face into her neck and held her close, and she cradled his head and smiled blindly at the ceiling. There was a word game she and Mother played with Bessie on journeys: word collections, Bessie called it. She started now with happiness . . . not enough. Happiness. Joy. Ecstasy. She said aloud, "Deliriosity."

He lifted his face, dark eyes wide. "Deliree what?"

"That's what I'm suffering from. Deliriosity."

"Oh, my Carol. You are so English. So mad."

"And you . . . you are so very dear to me."

They were lost again in laughter and tears and their special kind of communion. But at last it was settled that she would go to Birmingham that evening and he would stay in London, see Ralph, check her work on the manuscript and wait until she could join him. Then they would make more decisions.

"Will you be all right, *chérie?* This Monica, will she really take your Bessie?"

She said soberly, "I don't know. Monica is—used to be—a very determined person."

"She will have to take into account Bessie's wishes. I do not think the child will want to leave you and your mother." He spread his hands. "And yet . . . how will she take me, Carol? Might my sudden arrival in your life drive her away?"

"I don't know that either."

"Carol, I will not interfere with your life in Provence. I will visit you sometimes . . . whenever you tell me I may do so."

She smiled. "A clandestine affaire? I am hopeless at intrigue, Jean-Claude."

"I know that. But if—I want you to know that you may tell me always when to go. I will understand."

She almost wept again. She kissed his eyes and nose and then his mouth. And then she laughed. "When did I take off my glove?"

He laughed too. Like all lovers they firmly believed that tomorrow would take care of itself.

Liv thought she might die: either of sheer exhaustion or terrible, soul-shaking loneliness. Two weeks ago she had returned home with Monica. Inexplicably—because after all she had not been going to succumb to Malcolm's undeniable charms—she was disgraced. She had explained everything to Monica, and Monica had accepted her explanations and smiled into Malcolm's eyes and he had smiled back.

Monica had said to Liv as if humouring her, "We'll go back to Northfield together, shall we darling? Perhaps I can help to keep Mallie out of your fishpond. I shouldn't worry too much about Myrtle. I think she is probably coping very well in her own way."

Malcolm had actually laughed aloud at this, all through Liv saying defensively, "It's all very well, taking it so lightly. She's expecting again at any minute. It's just too much for her. I thought Malcolm might listen to my suggestion about a residential school for Mallie. But he's as bad as Myrtle—"

"Mallie's best at home," Malcolm had said defensively, closing the subject for good and all. "But it was good of you to come down to see me, Liv." He turned that glinting smile on her. "I appreciated it. No regrets?"

She flushed dark red again. She had grabbed at a coat in the hall and told Monica she was going upstairs for a bath, but she was aware that Monica did not believe her. She wanted to say, "Yes, I'm full of regrets. I've made an idiot of myself. Acted like a bitch on heat one minute and a frigid schoolgirl the next. I wish I'd never come."

But she didn't say that.

"Not at all, Malcolm." She turned to Monica, though she did not meet her amused gaze. "The four of us have been friends for years. We're like one big happy family."

Monica nodded. "So I gathered. Sorry to barge in. I've been staying with Dilly Gosling and she told me that Cass and Elizabeth might be here. So I turned up on the off-chance."

"Not this year. Myrtle was rabbiting on about some book or other which might bring Carol to London—to see her publishers, you know." Liv began to feel in control again. "Anyway, I shall have to get back home. Reggie is expecting me. Have you booked into a Cheltenham hotel, Mon?"

"No."

"Why don't you come with me then? We've got heaps of room and we three girls have got a lot of talking to do!" She attempted a laugh. It sounded slightly hysterical.

Monica said, "Actually, I've hired a car. It's outside. Perhaps we could drive up together? Could we make it tomorrow though—I'm bushed. I'd love it, Liv. If you're sure . . ." She had lost some of her veneer; she wanted to come. Liv straightened her back. It was all so ridiculous. Of course everything was going to be all right.

But back home it was quite obviously not all right. She had done nothing, but Reggie acted as if she had. And Myrtle too, was curiously distant. They both kissed Monica with surprise, but not amazement. They were in a world of their own. Not that night, because she was so tired, but the next night, she put her arms around Reggie and asked if she should take off her nightie.

"No thanks, darling," he said as if she'd offered him a biscuit. "I'm rather tired. Heavy day at the office."

"And I bet Myrtle had you running after the kids every minute on Tuesday, didn't she?" She wanted him to criticise Myrtle. To reassure her that he would prefer to be without children.

He said coldly, "We both ran after them, Liv. That's how it is with children. I enjoyed it and it didn't tire me at all."

The trouble was, it did tire Liv. It was lovely for the three girls to be together again, and at Mon's suggestion Liv wrote to Cass and asked her to join them. Mon had lots to tell them and she had gifts for them too. Lingerie such as they'd never seen before, and make-up by the sackful. She talked about Fifth Avenue and Macy's, and the wonderful apartment she had in Beekman Place. She hardly mentioned her husband. Liv felt that she and Mon still had a great deal in common; funny, it had always been the two of them pairing off in the old days. She would have liked a tête-à-tête with Mon, but the opportunity could not arise just yet. There was so much to organise, so much to do. Meals were endless, so were bath times, play times, reading-aloud times.

Then came the phone call from Carol. It was incredible that Myrtle had been proved right; it was all something to do with this wretched book she kept on about. Anyway whatever it was, Carol and Bessie and Mrs. Woodford were coming home, and Carol chose to stay with Liv.

Liv thought this might give her an edge over Myrtle. Myrtle was the one who had Bessie and wrote to Carol. Yet Carol had accepted Liv's invitation.

Myrtle said, "It'll be nice for Mrs. Woodford to be able to pop into Northfield and see all her old friends."

"Yes." Liv could afford to be generous about it. She smiled. "Perhaps we could get along to the Haunted House one afternoon. That would make the reunion absolute, wouldn't it?"

Mon said quickly, "Don't tell Carol I'm here. Let it be a surprise."

"Okay." Myrtle hugged Mallie to her shoulder and spoke over his head. "She'll be so pleased to see you, Mon. You two were always close, weren't you?"

And Liv felt lonely again.

Mrs. Woodford looked different. Not really younger, but more relaxed, more free-and-easy. She had been a mother, a matronly figure, respected by everyone who knew her in Northfield. Now she was not matronly. Her grey hair could look ash blonde in sunlight, and it was very short and brushed upward like Ingrid Bergman's, and the lines in her face shot upwards too when she smiled, which was often. But as far as Liv was concerned, the real shock was Bessie.

Liv had not seen Bessie for some time, probably since Myrtle's wedding. She had always thought of her as "belonging to the Woodfords." She was convinced that Bessie was the result of some ghastly experience Carol had suffered as a teenager. Now she had to reverse her ideas: turn them inside-out. Because with Monica and Bessie side by side under one roof, it was quite obvious who belonged to whom.

Monica watched the child with a kind of avid curiosity; she listened to every word she said even when she was telling one of the boys, "*Ferme ta bouche!*" She laughed inordinately at her jokes, then stopped herself as if she were afraid she might miss another gem. And as the days went by and she gradually used less make-up and let her black hair fall straight to her shoulders, she looked so like Bessie it was incredible.

Myrtle couldn't—or wouldn't—see it.

"It's a coincidence. Matter of fact I don't think Bessie belongs to anyone local. It was just like Cass told us at the time—her mother needed something to fill the gap, especially when Cass was at Bristol, so she decided to adopt a baby."

"You're just saying that because you want to forget what an idiot you made of yourself at your wedding!" Liv snapped unguardedly.

Myrtle did not get angry. She looked at Liv consideringly and then said—as if she were actually sorry for Liv—"Yes, maybe you're right."

Somehow they prevailed on Mrs. Woodford and Bessie to keep Carol ignorant of Mon's presence, though neither of them seemed to see any point in it, and Mrs. Woodford obviously did not like it. Whether she spoke to Mon privately, Liv never knew, but on the Thursday after their arrival, Mon suddenly announced she had some people to see in London, and swung out of the house, into her hired car, and was off before anyone could say a word. Liv, perspiring as genteelly as possible in the kitchen, felt again the sense of isolation, almost desertion. None of the children really liked her, not even Bessie; Myrtle and Malcolm were completely absorbed in a world of fecundity which Malcolm might well have extended to her if she'd had the nerve to enter it. Now Monica had simply up and gone, and if Bessie was her child, then she was not the special friend Liv had thought she was.

There was a yell from the garden; Bessie went sprinting by the kitchen window; five minutes later she appeared at the door holding a dripping Mallie.

"I suppose your Aunt Myrt is sunning herself somewhere!" Liv said acidly as she took the wet clothes and dumped them in the washing machine.

Bessie looked up from the grinning child and grinned herself. "She's reading that book by Iris Murdoch," she said. "You know, the one where all the husbands and wives change over."

Liv looked at the dark, gypsy face that was so full of life.

"You shouldn't know about books like that!" she said.

Bessie laughed. "I don't. But I've heard Cass talking about it with one of her authors. It's funny—they were both laughing."

"Yes. Well. In books maybe it is." Liv pursed her lips. The child had stayed in Myrtle's house three or four times. She must have seen Malcolm getting . . . up to things. "It's not in the least funny in real life," she finished austerely.

Bessie did not reply. She took Mallie up to the bathroom and brought him down to lunch looking angelic. Liv wondered what went on in a thirteen-year-old mind. She herself had deliberately gone to see Malcolm in the hope of being seduced . . . hadn't she? So wasn't that funny? Or was it just fun? And what was the difference?

Liv wasn't used to such introspection. Her perspiration turned sweaty and she wanted to cry.

Mrs. Woodford said, "Bessie and I are going to the village today, girls. Shall we take the boys? Then you two could have a nap."

Mrs. Woodford was an angel. Both Liv and Myrtle told her so unreservedly. And the boys—even Mallie—raised a cheer.

Liv slept the sleep of the exhausted. Around six o'clock she heard Reggie's car draw up . . . or perhaps Monica's . . . semi-conscious, she waited for a cup of tea to arrive. She would have a cool bath and suggest that she and Reggie went out for dinner. Myrtle could then take over the kitchen and cook up one of her revolting high teas: beans on toast with curdled scrambled egg, or something similar. She stretched luxuriously on the bed. A little breeze stirred the curtains. She wondered how they would manage when Cass arrived. It was rather a coup that they should all decide to meet at her house, but it was also a great strain. She smiled; she would put it to Reggie that they move out and let everyone else get on as best they could. No, she wouldn't. Reggie wouldn't realise it was a joke, and he'd start talking about the joys of a big family again.

The tea did not arrive. It was too bad. Her tongue was cleaving to the roof of her mouth. She rolled her head on the pillow and looked at the bedside table. Last night's glass of water sat there, but it had air bubbles in it and looked as tired as she felt. Sighing gustily, she sat up. She'd have to get her own tea. As per usual.

She wandered on to the landing. There was a sound from Myrtle's room: as if she were having a bad dream. Liv thought it served her jolly well right, then she softened. Poor old Myrt, misshapen with yet another child, burdened with little Mallie, plagued by Nicky and Martin—she probably didn't get much cosseting from Malcolm. Liv knocked on her door.

"Wakey wakey!" she called like Billy Cotton. "How about a cup of tea, Myrt?"

There was no reply save for a ghastly snuffling sound. Suddenly alarmed, Liv opened the door just in time to see Reggie scrambling off the bed. In his birthday suit. She closed the door quickly and went on downstairs. Reggie joined her three minutes later, clothed if not in his right mind, and started babbling something. She glanced at him wide-eyed.

"Are you all right, darling? I didn't realise you were home yet. I'm just making some tea for Myrtle and me. Would you like some?" He didn't say anything, just stared at her with his mouth open. She giggled insanely. "Did you hear that? I'm a poet and don't know it. I'm just making some tea for Myrtle and me."

She marshalled a tray and cups, poured boiling water into an empty pot, and carried the lot upstairs. And still he did not move or speak.

She didn't go in to Myrtle. In the shattered security of her own room she poured herself a cup of hot water and milk and sipped it, little finger cocked automatically. It hadn't happened. It had been a dream.

But that was when she thought she might die from soul-shaking loneliness.

Monica found herself applying her make-up again when she came back from her overnight visit to London. Her blood seemed to stop flowing in the middle of her neck and her sun-tanned skin looked like rather ancient dough. Every morning she smiled fiercely at herself in the mirror and applied rouge to the cushions of her cheeks, then powdered and blotted in the required fashion until the necessary sheen was achieved. She was at once thankful and aghast when Carol did not turn up that afternoon. Thankful because to face her after their interview and her subsequent note was a frightening prospect. Aghast, because Carol might have done anything. Or she might be ill. Monica recalled her face that Thursday night and felt physically sick at what she had done. And what she must still do. She must stiffen her spine, and do it. After all, Carol had always known Elizabeth wasn't her child. She'd always known that.

Monica tried to avoid Mrs. Woodford. In the unnaturally large household, it was not difficult. Sometimes she caught Mrs. Woodford regarding her and knew that the older woman would like to talk privately. Probably she only wanted to ask about Mrs. Gosling, or to say "D'you remember how we played Monopoly when we were at Rhyl?" Or to ask Monica about Bob . . . or . . . anything. But Monica could not risk a direct question. Carol would explain it all to her mother. She would know best how to do it. After all, it might be quite a relief to Mrs. Woodford. She wasn't getting any younger and she probably worried herself sick about Elizabeth's schooling and . . . things.

Monica told herself now that she had not run away from Bob at all. She had always known that Bob's ideas of fidelity were his own; and he had many good qualities to offset his . . . wandering eye. No, she had run from herself. She had run because she had failed to produce children and failed to tell him she could not produce them. And if . . . when . . . Cass and Mrs. Woodford honoured the promise they had made thirteen years ago, then at least one of those failures could be redeemed. She would go back to Bob with a child.

But she had to win Bessie first.

She thought about the problem until her head ached. The solution was simple, of course. If she took Bessie back to the States, the child would be a long way from old associations. She would have a new world to explore and new people to meet. She would charm Bob and when he had got thoroughly used to her, Monica would tell him and she would be his daughter too. Bessie would love America and she would love Bob, and Hildie, and everyone. In fact they could go to Hildie's first. She would talk it all over with Hildie.

But she had to win Bessie first.

She found reasons for taking the girl to America. Carol's involvement with the F.L.N. was irresponsible to say the least. And the entirely female household was not good. Then surely France could not offer the same educational and social opportunities as

America. Also she did not like the way they had renamed Elizabeth. Bessie was an unfashionable diminutive, reminiscent of comfortable old housekeepers or faithful dogs. So far she had avoided calling the child anything but "honey," but she intended asking her whether she wouldn't prefer Liz or Ellie. Once they were back in the States she'd be able to increase the closeness of their relationship so that it would dawn on the girl gradually and naturally that she was Monica's daughter.

It would all work so well if only Bessie would agree to come with her. She could make it work. In a year's time they could be a proper family.

Just before lunch on Friday, a taxi crunched over Liv's immaculate gravel and Bessie shrieked, "It's Cass!" and dashed down the hall to rip open the door before it could be knocked on.

Even Cass herself seemed surprised at her welcome. Bessie hugged her so passionately her hat was knocked askew and a glove pulled off.

"Oh, Cass—Cass—oh, I've missed you so much!"

"Darling—you've been here just a week without me! When you're at the convent I'm often—"

"Oh, it seemed like forever! Besides, it's different now! I mean, we're family and when we're in a strange country we should stick together!"

"A strange country! Bessie, what are you saying?" Cass was laughing and hugging and paying off the taxi and gathering up her cases, all at the same time. Monica could have sworn she was happy; really happy. She felt a sense of anti-climax. After the way she'd worried and fretted, consumed with guilt, here was Cass taking the whole thing on the chin.

Mary Woodford encircled them both.

"Well, anyway. So everything is all right. Really all right."

It was a sort of question. Monica noticed that Cass didn't answer it. Or maybe she did because as soon as she was able, she kissed Monica. Monica saw Mrs. Woodford's eyes widen and felt she was being identified by Carol as the traitor in their midst. A Judas kiss.

"Well. So what's happening?" she asked, sounding like Bob arriving at the apartment and finding her once again in bed. It was a meaningless question and should have been answered accordingly. Carol could have said, "Ghastly journey" or "It's still as hot as London." Or Myrtle could have started on about little Mallie. Or Liv could have ordered Reggie to collect the luggage.

Instead, everyone looked at her oddly, and after a pause Carol said hesitantly, "Well. Let me see. Tentative plans only, of course. But I did wonder . . . if you'd like to take Bessie for a holiday in the States, Mon." She flashed a smile at the girl. "Auntie Mon and I met up in London, did she tell you or is it a surprise? We talked and talked. And I told her you were at rather a loose end for the rest of the vacances, and she suggested—"

"I'd rather not," Bessie said flatly.

"Darling, why ever not?"

Monica said swiftly, "I'd simply love it, Eliz . . . Bessie. You'd be doing me a great favour actually."

And Liv said, "Good idea. Get to know each other."

Bessie said, "But we could go back up the Victoire." She looked at Mrs. Woodford who appeared to swallow and then said enthusiastically, "It's the chance of a lifetime, Bessie. New York! Who will be able to say they've been to New York in the summer holidays?"

Bessie stared at her, then Carol, as if they had stabbed her. Monica said quietly, "Not if you don't want to. Of course."

There was a strange silence. Then came a screech from the garden and Nicky's triumphant yell of "Mallie's in the pool again!"

Bessie said, "I'd love to, Aunt Monica. But I have to be back for the end of September."

Monica took a long slow breath. "Yes. That will be okay, honey. I'll see to Mallie. You have a chat with Cass." And she made her escape into the garden.

She booked a call to Hildie and asked whether she could bring Elizabeth to the farm for a week or so. Hildie was delighted. "Bob is mad to see you, honey! If you'll see him, everything will be okay. Believe me!" Monica began to feel hopeful; so far so good. Bob had continued to pay her allowance into her account, and had written to her twice, care of Dilly Gosling, saying that he "understood." It might be possible to pretend everything was all right. Elizabeth would then have a father as well as almost limitless wealth. Monica told herself firmly that the child would be getting a very good bargain indeed.

Carol spoke to her mother and Bessie that night in the privacy of their communal bedroom.

She said quietly and directly, "I've met someone, my darlings. A Frenchman. I knew him . . . before, and wondered then if we loved each other. Now I am certain." She looked at them in turn. "I love you more than ever, because of him. Can you understand that?"

Mary Woodford's eyes filled with tears. She reached for Bessie with one hand and Carol with the other.

"I can understand. You are loving for two people now, Carol, not one. I love you and Bessie in the same way, for myself and for Daddy."

"Oh, Mother . . . ."

Bessie said, "Is that why you want me to go to America with Auntie Monica?"

The two women turned to her, shocked.

Bessie said defensively, "You want to send me away. So that you can be by yourself with this—man!"

Carol began to protest, but Mary stopped her.

"In a way she's right, Cass. You're not sending anyone away. Naturally not. But you need to be by yourself for a while. It is important for you." She pressed Carol's hand meaningfully and smiled at Bessie. "You're going on this really special holiday with Aunt Mon. And I think I'll stay on in Northfield for two or three weeks and look up all the old friends."

Carol did not know how to respond to this. She said lamely, "There's no need. Jean-Claude and I cannot marry, Mother. We shall simply be friends."

Bessie said pressingly, "He won't live with us? He won't be proper family?"

"He won't live with us. No."

Mary said, "Ah. Jean-Claude."

"Yes. Jean-Claude Durant. He is the foreign correspondent for *La Planète*. It was he who rescued Clive Hubert's book from Algeria."

Bessie looked a little less defensive. "An adventurer?" she queried.

"I hope not." Carol walked to the window and looked out. Liv was standing by the fishpond, gazing into its depths. "He has to go to places that are often dangerous."

"Does he take photographs?" Bessie asked unexpectedly.

Carol said, "He usually has a photographer with him. Why do you ask that, darling?"

"I might know a good photographer. Who could help him out," Bessie said. She joined Carol at the window. "I'm sorry I was horrid about Aunt Mon. I'll be a sort of foreign correspondent in America, won't I?"

"You certainly will."

Carol smiled again, determined not to think about the possible consequences of Bessie's visit to New York. Tomorrow she would be with Jean-Claude again. If her mother stayed in Northfield, she could be with Jean-Claude at the Bergerie. She understood fully the selfishness of lovers.

Bessie said, "What on earth is Auntie Liv doing?"

They stared through the window in disbelief. Liv was wading into the fishpond. Even as they looked she slipped on the slime at the bottom and fell forward on all fours.

Mary said, "Oh my God—" and was gone through the bedroom door. But it didn't seem all that serious, and Carol and Bessie continued to watch as Mary appeared at the kitchen door and dashed down the garden.

And then Bessie was in Carol's arms and they were transfixed with horror. Liv had staggered to her feet holding something. She began to pull. Mary joined her and they pulled together. And with a sudden jerk, the lily roots gave up their dead, and Mallie's small muddy body was beached on the crazy paving that edged the pool.

9

The funeral seemed to last all week. There was an inquest; there was Malcolm clinging to Myrtle, bent, a pathetic ex-Lothario; there were thrice-daily phone calls for Carol from London; there was Liv repeating, "If only I'd seen him before—I'd been standing there for ages—if only—"; there was Myrtle stunned and white-faced with guilt; there were Carol and Mrs. Woodford reading endless stories to Nicky and Martin in an effort to divert their bewildered grief; there were Monica and Bessie cooking and washing and "seeing to things"; there was Reggie inexplicably saying, "I'm sorry, Myrtle, so terribly sorry."

Neighbours called and were kind to their faces and condemning behind their backs. Bessie, standing in a queue for liver, heard someone say "too busy with Mrs. Bradbury's husband I daresay." She wondered if she should spring to Aunt Myrt's defence, but wasn't entirely sure the remark was derogatory.

Aunt Mon, waiting outside with Mallie's pushchair full of vegetables, frowned slightly when Bessie told her what had been said. Then she sighed deeply.

"I suppose everyone will think poor Myrtle should have known he wasn't in his bed. But she couldn't keep an eye on him all the time, and he did love that bloody pond." She looked at Bessie, her huge black eyes suddenly swimming. "The four of us were there, darling. In a way we share all you children. So in a way we were all responsible for Mallie."

Bessie liked that. Sometimes the small family unit of Grannie, Cass and herself seemed somehow beleaguered. Monica extended it threefold with her words.

Bessie put the liver on top of the kidney beans, and said briskly, "That's good then. No-one is to blame. Come on, let's get back and tell Aunt Myrt what you said."

Monica blinked hard, then smiled. "My God. You're like your mother, Elizabeth."

That pleased Bessie still more. She grinned and relaxed fully towards this American aunt.

"I wish you'd call me by my proper name," she remarked.

"Oh . . . shoot." Monica laughed. "Okay. Bessie."

Monica's words, reported faithfully by Bessie, had little effect on the sombre company at the Barnt Green house. Liv had completely lost interest in her grey carpets and pale furniture and already the place looked far less than pristine. The people in it looked the worse for wear too. Liv's naturally curly hair was limp and flat, and Monica's sophisticated veneer had rubbed away. Only Carol retained the shine she had acquired so recently; it was subdued, but it was still there.

She knelt before Myrtle, repeating what Bessie had said.

"You see, Myrt? It must have been a pure accident, mustn't it? The four of us here . . ."

Myrtle said suddenly, "Cass. I don't want this new baby. I don't want it. If I can't have Mallie, I don't want any other children at all. Nicky—Martin—" her voice began to rise hysterically. Carol leaned forward and encircled the heaving shoulders with her long arms. Malcolm, hunched up by his wife, put his big manipulative hands to his face, and started to cry.

Carol said over her shoulder, "Mother. Bessie. Take the boys into the garden for a while, will you?" She stroked Myrtle's frizzy hair and made soothing sounds. "Listen. Both of you, listen. This is going to get better. Just hang on to that fact and take the present as best you can. It's going to get better. Honestly."

She continued to stroke Myrtle. Reggie crossed the room and clapped a manly hand on Malcolm's shoulder. Liv and Monica exchanged glances.

Monica said, "Shall we go for a walk? I think you should get out of this house for five minutes, Myrtle. Come on. Let's go down to the heath."

Malcolm blubbered, "I can't come. Can't face it again. After that court business and the funeral . . . can't face anyone again."

Reggie tightened his grip. "We'll let the girls go by themselves, old man. Shall we? Perhaps at opening time we could go down to the Swan for a swift one. Break the ice as it were." He looked meaningfully at Liv. "Don't hurry back, girls. Find somewhere for tea. Take it easy."

For the first time in two weeks, Liv met his eyes and gave a slight answering smile. Somehow they got Myrtle on her feet and draped a cardigan over her awful misshapen floral frock. Monica waited with her in the hall while the other two went to the bathroom; she squared Myrtle's shoulders and moved her to the mirror. Myrtle looked at her reflection as if she'd never seen it before. Monica picked up the clothes brush and brushed out the wire-wool hair and smiled encouragingly.

"It's like Cass says, darling. You'll heal. Gradually."

Myrtle whispered, "No. I'll adapt. A man who loses a leg has to adapt. But it doesn't heal. And it doesn't grow back."

"Okay. Then you'll adapt."

"I still don't want this baby. It'll come between me and Mallie. I don't want it."

Monica said lightly, "Then give it to me. I want it."

Myrtle's dead, haunted eyes focused for an instant on Monica's film-star face.

She whispered, "Like your mother gave you away? Like you gave Bessie to Cass?"

Monica stiffened into alertness, and gradually Myrtle subsided into her private hell again.

"It's all right," she said dully. "Liv saw it first. I've told her she's talking rubbish. I won't say anything. No-one will say anything."

Monica continued to stare into the mirror for a long moment, then she put her forehead on Myrtle's shoulder.

"Oh my God," she whispered.

"I don't think He wants to help us," Myrtle commented with unusual bitterness, and made for the door.

They walked for over an hour in almost complete silence. It was not as hot as the previous week, but Myrtle soon removed the cardigan from her shoulders and trailed it along the footpath like a disconsolate child. They left the road as soon as they could and clambered over a stile to skirt the golf course and eventually drop down to the heath. On one of the small country roads they had to cross there was a black and white cottage advertising teas. Remembering Reggie's words, Liv led the way through the gate to one of the small iron tables in the front garden. They sat themselves down, suddenly tired.

"God. We've got all that way to get back home," Myrtle said mournfully. "Look at my feet."

They looked as she stuck a leg ungracefully above table level. Her bare foot bulged over the straps of her sandals.

"Well, it's not for want of rest," Liv said with a sudden return to her old self. "You had them up all morning on the sofa. I don't understand it."

Monica said, "It's fluid. What does the doctor say?"

"Haven't been to the doctor yet."

"You damned fool."

Carol intervened. "Tell you what. We'll ring for a taxi back. It's been marvellous getting out, but probably we've done enough. Let's have boiled eggs and loads of bread and butter and go home when the gnats come out."

"Sounds lovely." Myrtle managed a smile. "You're right. It is good to get out. My feet don't bother me actually." She leaned forward. "Girls . . . thank you."

Everyone looked embarrassed. Monica saved the day by using one of her American phrases again. "Oh shoot," she said.

She gave the order to the matronly figure who emerged from the front door, and then went on talking, suddenly enthusiastic.

"Honeys. I think I've been this way before. If we strike across country we shall get to our part of the heath. If Myrt is up to it, we could look for our house again, then get a taxi from Northfield. What do you think?"

Liv said cautiously, "How far is it? I mean, Myrtle's feet do look bad."

178

"A mile? Maybe two? I'll ask the woman when she brings the tea. I went to the Haunted House three or four years ago and when I left I didn't want to return the same way as I'd come. So I struck away from the brook. And I came out on this road."

"You were here before? You didn't contact any of us." Liv regarded Mon wide-eyed. "You simply disappeared off the face of the earth. Why didn't you get in touch?"

Monica flushed. "I had to see the Cooks. Before I married Bob. Just to tell them. That was all. I was here for about six hours."

Carol intervened. "It would be rather special to find the house again, wouldn't it? I mean, it's thirteen years since we were there together."

"Since we were anywhere together," Liv said.

The woman came out with a tray of tea and bread and butter and Monica asked if they could get across the fields to the West Heath road. The woman was almost certain they could.

"Hubby's got an ordnance survey map in the cottage. I'll bring it with your eggs. Three minutes each?"

They looked at her uncomprehendingly then Carol said, "Oh, the eggs. Yes. Fine." And they all laughed almost normally.

The map arrived with the eggs. All the footpaths were marked and they pinpointed where they were with some excitement. Suddenly the afternoon had an objective, and with the objective, perhaps a meaning which might be revealed later. It became of paramount importance to find the Haunted House again.

"How long d'you think it'll take?" Myrtle asked.

"Not sure. Depends on the state of the footpaths I guess." Monica rummaged in her pocket and found a pencil. "Anyone got any paper? I'll copy this bit of the map. See, we have to go through this little wood . . . . I don't think it's far actually."

Liv had tissue in her pocket, always kept there against the possibility of a public lavatory minus toilet roll. Somehow Monica managed to transfer the relevant details. The woman came out again with a bottle of lemonade.

"Best take this. It's warm weather for hiking."

"We can drink a toast when we get there!" Carol hugged Myrtle's arm. "D'you remember that night we slept there?"

Liv said, "D'you remember the time I pinned up Mon's hair and she whipped it all out?"

Mon said, "What about when we found it first of all? We were soaked to the skin and I was certain I was covered in leeches."

Myrtle said, "We were happy then. The four of us. No-one else. Just the four of us."

They started off again and located the footpath immediately. It was a good omen. They trudged single file along the edge of a field of acid-yellow rape, over another stile, and down a steep sheep-bitten slope of a stream.

"There was a bridge marked on the map," Monica said, squinting at her tissue copy. "Right here."

"Well, it's not here now." Myrtle sat down and negotiated the stream's bank on her bottom. She put her feet, sandals and all, into the crystal-clear water. "Oh, this is good. Better than wading up the mini-Orinoco that time in midwinter."

They splashed across and ploughed soggily up the other bank. It was all so reminiscent of that time when they had been twelve. The intervening years might never have happened. Myrtle said, "This is better than looking for boys along the Bristol Road, isn't it Cass?"

Carol thought of poor Malcolm back home with Reggie, then of Jean-Claude waiting for her in London; she said nothing.

Unexpectedly, Liv, who had notched up her conquests like the Battle of Britain fighter pilots, said, "Oh yes. Much better." And Monica agreed fervently, "I'd rather be here with you three than anywhere else."

They crossed another two fields, climbed another two stiles. The sun was perceptibly lower in the sky.

Mon said triumphantly, "The map is right. There's the wood. And the other side of that will be our heath."

With renewed energy they plunged into the wood. It wasn't much bigger than a coppice: a suddenly different environment. Shadowed and breathing a life of its own, it silenced the girls again. They slowed and walked two abreast, smiling and pointing out wood anemones and strange lethally red berries in fleshy green sheaths. Monica, walking behind Carol, noticed again the still-awkward length of her body, the striped brown and beige hair knotted into a bun slightly higher on her head than usual in small deference to fashion. Liv watched Myrtle's large hips swaying from side to side beneath her multi-coloured frock, and tried not to remember that awful afternoon before Mallie had died. Myrtle looked up and caught Carol's wide grey gaze and smiled a question. She needed Carol now more than ever; it was no longer a game. She needed her more than she needed her parents or Malcolm. It was so ridiculous, that awful row. Bessie had turned out to be Monica's anyway.

She whispered, "I'm sorry, Cass. Forgive me."

Carol smiled back. Her own shining happiness had had to be tucked away in the face of the tragedy of little Mallie, but it was there.

"Nothing to forgive," she murmured, and pulled Myrtle's hand through her arm.

They emerged quite suddenly on the other side of the trees. There was a fence, and they leaned on it surveying the landscape with complete bewilderment. Gone were the undulating fields with their hedges and stiles; a strip of muddy green grass protected the coppice, then the land was gouged into baked mud-heaps; mounds of bricks and topsoil rose from the desert, metal skeletons of buildings lined the horizon, tunnels of sewage pipes lay waiting burial.

"My God. It's all being developed," Liv said blankly.

"Daddy was talking about it, wasn't he?" Myrtle remembered. "Slum clearance from the middle of Brum. Or something."

Monica wailed, "It's gone. Our house. It's been razed to the ground!"

They stared again, unable to find any familiar landmark until Carol pointed to the long cleft below them.

"There's the brook. They've left one of the willows. It might be the one by the house."

"Let's go and see." Myrtle was already clambering over the fence. "I just can't bear it. Perhaps there will be something left. Just something."

It was hard going, crossing the building site. The hot weather had fired the mud into ragged, rigid shapes, razor sharp at times. Carol and Monica got either side of Myrtle and half carried her down towards the brook. There was no-one around; no workmen climbed the scaffolding or operated the apparently abandoned machinery.

"Must be late." Liv was panting. "About seven o'clock. When does it get dark?"

"Soon. And we don't want to be caught here." Monica edged around a pothole and reached back for Myrtle. "They must have brought a road in, though. We're going in the right direction."

The banks of the brook were blessedly untouched. They walked to the willow and tried to work out where the Haunted House would have been. It was Liv who found the raked remains of wood and broken glass that appeared to be all that was left of the tumble-down building.

"There was a dresser in the kitchen with wood like that . . . and here are some tiles from the roof."

Myrtle gave a sudden screech.

"Look what I've found! Girls, look!"

She held aloft a flattened paint can. They crowded around her, unimpressed. She turned it over to show, faintly, an old war-time utility mark.

"It's the can we pinched from school, Cass! You know. We buried it in the garden and the digger thing has turned it up! Don't you remember, we painted the post office wall—"

"Of course—of course!" Carol was ecstatic. "The paint pot! The incriminating evidence! Oh God—this was it then—where we hid. Where we saw . . . things. Where we talked and did our work and you played the violin, Liv, and—"

Monica produced the lemonade bottle.

"Come on. I'll pass it round. Phoenix from the ashes and all that!"

"Phoenix from the ashes," they intoned in turn, tipping the bottle back so that it foamed and glinted in the dying sun.

"Who has the can?" Myrtle looked at Carol. "You have it. Tell Bessie about it. Give it to her."

Carol took the can and leaned down from her great height to kiss the top of Myrtle's head.

"Thanks, Myrt," she said.

Bessie was completely captivated by the story of the paint pot. She said, "Funny, Cass, but I don't mind going off with Aunt Mon half so much now."

Carol quickly squashed a feeling of foreboding.

"Why? Because of an old paint pot?"

"No. Though yes. Somehow. Oh, I don't know, she seems like our family."

"Yes."

Bessie said, "Besides, it will be lovely to get away from here. This place . . . it's awful, Cass."

"Because of poor little Mallie."

"I didn't like it before that happened. Everyone was so un-happy." Bessie ran her fingers through her thick black hair. "I guess Auntie Myrt won't want me to go to Cheltenham any more. She only had me because of Mallie."

"Oh, Bessie. She didn't. She had you for all sorts of reasons, and it was a bonus to her that you and Mallie got on. Really. Really and truly." Carol smiled rallyingly, determined not to notice Bessie's unconscious Americanism which she must have picked up from Mon.

Bessie's reaction was unexpected. She cast herself bodily on Carol and hugged her suffocatingly.

She whispered in her ear, "Listen. I'm going to try to like this newspaper man. I really am, Cass. I know everything now, you see. Everything."

Carol held the child's waist to steady her. She said carefully, "I see. Who told you, darling?"

"No-one. Well, in a way Solange told me. It made all the diff. All the diff in the world."

"What are you talking about?"

"You and me. It's why I'm jealous of your boyfriend."

"He's not my boyfriend."

"Don't go all prudy-rudy, Cass. If you can't get married to him then he'll have to be your boyfriend, won't he?" She sighed sharply. "And I shall have to learn to like him. And I will. I just . . . will."

She drew away. "What I mean is, don't worry about me in Connecticut. Aunt Mon being family-ish makes all the diff. I think I'll pack the paint pot. If that's okay with you."

"It's okay with me."

Carol watched Bessie "make a hole" in her suitcase and push down the paint pot. The child was such a pragmatist. Like her mother. Strangely, Bessie's obscure words reassured her. There was no sense of imminent loss any more. Maybe she would come back with an American accent, calling Monica "Mom." It would make no "diff." Carol smiled.

"May I tell Jean-Claude what you said?" she asked.

Bessie hesitated, then nodded. "Okay." She added grimly, "I just hope he'll try as hard to like me!"

Carol joined Jean-Claude two days later. They stayed at the Albion overnight, making love with an insatiable passion that secretly shocked Carol. She had not known such feeling existed in the world, let alone in herself. Jean-Claude had only to touch her for her body to flame into a life of its own. Suddenly and miraculously she could understand Malcolm Lennox and Myrtle, Monica and her adopted brother Giles, even perhaps her own parents. Sexual love was not an isolated emotion between one man and one woman: it encompassed the universe because it was universal.

Carol wanted Jean-Claude to see the Bergerie; she thought of this time together as a honeymoon, and knew that it might have to last them for a very long time.

"If we can live together for just a few days in the Bergerie, it will make it our home. So that afterwards, when we only see each other at intervals, your presence will be there."

Tears filled her eyes at the mere thought of his absence. He kissed her and held her to him.

"*Chérie*, it will not be for long. Bessie will grow up and leave home and your mother would always understand. She *would* understand?"

"Yes. Of course." Carol smiled tremulously. "It will work out, I know it will. It is just a stupid feeling I have. I never expected— never knew about—this kind of happiness, my darling. It seems too precious, too ephemeral, to last. Forgive me."

"There is no more danger, Carol. The book will be published. No-one can stop it now."

"There may well be recriminations, Jean. And you are so vulnerable. Travelling the world, always where there is fighting."

"Carol. I was not a member of the reactionaries. Nor the F.L.N. I was over there to report on what was happening and my newspaper had a nationalistic bias. Perhaps I also was biased that way at the time—remember the only thing I had to hang on to during the years of the war was my love for France. But neither one side nor the other can see me as a threat."

"If anyone finds out that you collected that original manuscript from the Sufi—"

"How could anyone find out?"

"If you could discover the manuscript, Jean, then so could others."

"I had a very important reason for discovering it." He smiled into her eyes. "Listen. Carol. The political climate is changing all the time. De Gaulle has been recalled to deal with the problem. I still have strong connections with him. I am safe. I promise you, *chérie*. I am safe."

■

They flew to Nice and took a train to Marseilles where she had left her Renault. They drove slowly north to Aix-en-Durance, bought groceries and paraffin and took the track which led to the base of the Victoire. The flower harvest, which started in April and went on until October, was evident in the baskets of flowers awaiting collection at every gate. The few south-facing vineyards were being picked; already there was a sense of summer's end. "The happiest summer of my whole life," Carol murmured, then turned to face Jean-Claude with a stricken face. "How can I say that when Mallie died right under our very noses? And Monica is going to claim Bessie?"

Jean-Claude turned his mouth down. "That is why it is so precious. It has flowered from fear and tragedy. Don't question it, Carol. Accept it. Be glad."

She could do nothing else, the whole thing was out of her hands. As she unlocked the door she glanced on the kitchen floor for a telegram or letter, and when there were neither, the outside world retreated for her; future and past were shadowy and irrelevant and her tiny span of life here with Jean-Claude was the only reality.

It was a time of deliriosity indeed. For the sake of her mother and Bessie she did not want to advertise Jean-Claude's presence in the Bergerie, though she was sure that the sharp eyes of Pierre would miss very little. However, for the time being she declined Sylvie's offers of help and delighted in lighting the fire in the range and doing her own cooking. Jean-Claude proved unexpectedly adept domestically. He scrubbed the huge table bleach-white and rolled out pastry that melted in the mouth. He dealt with the overgrown crop of haricots from Northfield, cutting them up and salting them down in the big stone jars beloved by Mary. And in the darkening evenings he would light the candles and wind up the ancient gramophone and they would dance around the uneven flagstones while the onions were cooking for his favourite soup. Choice of music was limited for dancing: Mary favoured Offenbach which was too sprightly, Bessie liked Tommy Steele. Half a dozen scratched records from schooldays sufficed. There were some Cole Porters and "Dancing in the Dark." When Carol rested her chin on Jean-Claude's shoulder and swayed slowly to that haunting melody, she knew it would always evoke this time.

"Like the paint pot," she murmured.

"Is that one of your significant non sequiturs, *chérie?*" he asked.

"A symbol. The paint pot is a symbol. You see it and immediately a whole era comes to mind. Now, when I hear "Dancing in the Dark," I shall be here. The candles flickering, the shadows, the scent of burning apple logs and . . . and you." She closed her eyes on the present which would so terribly soon become a memory.

"Carol, I know what you are still thinking. Ephemeral. Yes? It cannot be so. I would feel it too. And I do not feel it. I see us growing old. Perhaps quite soon Gaby will change her mind and divorce me. And we will be an old married pair. How do you say it in England—Darby and Joan?"

"Yes." She opened her eyes and tipped back her head. "We will not talk about the future. I forgot to tell you. Bessie is quite determined to like you. And she is hoping that you will try to like her."

He laughed. "It sounds as if she intends to come back here fairly soon then? Even though she knows that Monica Gallagher is her mother?"

Carol sighed. "I don't know, Jean. I really don't know. I haven't talked about any of it with Mother, but *she* seemed quite content with the situation. But then she is a very special woman." She shook her head slowly. "When I look back I see that she takes the awful things that happen and makes something good from them. Daddy's death and Monica's pregnancy. The bombing in Paris . . . the way she made this place into a home . . . it's amazing."

She moved away from him and carried the pot of soup to the table and they re-enacted the first meal they had shared in the Reine Blanche. She told him about Liv and her chapel background, her sharp little mother and rather nice father. She spoke of her own father and his long illness; the grandparents she could only just remember. And about Mon and the Cook family.

"That is sad," he murmured. "How did she bring herself to give away little Bessie?"

"She wouldn't look at her. It was as if she had internal bleeding: there was a raw look on her face. You see, I don't think she ever stopped loving Giles. She told us last week that she went back to Northfield just before she married Bob. It must have been to see Giles. It sounds as if she took him to the Haunted House."

"This house was important to you girls?"

"Just another symbol. The paint pot will do."

They both laughed.

Jean-Claude told her of his family and his rigid upbringing.

"My brother and I were destined for the Church. It never occurred to me to rebel. I was actually in the seminary when France fell."

He grinned boyishly. "I was sixteen. It sounds like the *Boys' Own Paper*, Carol. Yes? I left the seminary that very day and made my way to the coast. I joined the Free French Army as soon as de Gaulle arrived in London. It probably broke my father's heart. I do not know. Both my parents were shot for harbouring Jews. My brother is on the Vatican staff. They would be proud of him."

"They would be proud of you too, my dear." Carol touched the back of his hand. "I do not believe there were any broken hearts on your behalf. You did what you believed to be right. To do anything else *would* have been wrong. They knew that, I am sure."

"Perhaps. I am not so sure of my own motives. For me it was a great adventure. Just as my work since the war has been a series of adventures. Until I met you nothing seemed very important. Gaby began working with you and I came into the office—do you remember? I was covering the Indo-China business and had met that other reporter who wished to write a book. I told him about you. Do you remember?"

"I remember." She smiled. She had fought against admitting any attraction. His good looks and easy charm had worked against him.

"Gaby had spoken about you, of course. For the first time since I knew her, she was interested in something beyond her hair and make-up and clothes. So I knew you were special. I thought at first—the English blue-stocking. An academic. But you did not go into any mould, Cass. You would look up when I came into the office, and I felt I was looking into another human soul. I questioned Gaby. I learned that you were indeed a blue-stocking. And you were kind and very loving to your family. But I did not know I loved you until I heard that night that you might be in danger. And then I knew." His smile widened. "They talk about falling in love. It truly was like that. I had a physical sensation of falling all that evening. Until the explosion. And then we both landed. Hard, I think."

She looked at him for a long time without speaking. He was holding both her hands in his and she realised she was gripping his fingers as if he were physically pulling her through the experiences of the past few years.

He said at last, tentatively, "And you, Carol? Did you feel . . . anything . . . for me in that time?"

She relaxed and laughed, throwing back her head and showing the classic line of her throat.

"Jean-Claude! You are fishing! You know very well how I felt—you knew before I knew myself! How could I dare to admit any feelings for you! The plain, gawky English-woman—you said yourself, a typical blue-stocking! And you—you were the Rudolf Valentino of Paris!"

He silenced her with a kiss, and they were serious again.

She said at last, breathlessly, "Remember, my love, I compared myself always with Gaby. She was pretty and vivacious and all the things I was not. And when I thought you had organised the job for her so that she could tell you what kind of manuscripts were coming in—"

"You did not think that? Not seriously?"

"Of course I thought it! I thought everything! Everything underhand and cunning and—"

He stopped her again with a kiss.

And then he said in a low voice, "I am sorry, my love. My only love. If I had explained about Gaby right at the start, perhaps you could have looked on me separately. Seen me in my own right. But it is not done . . . to talk of one's wife so. Even now—"

"It's all right, Jean. She said something herself—that very evening. But, after all, you were still together. She was still cooking your meals and—and—"

He said steadily, "The room you slept in on the night of the explosion, Cass. That was my room. We did not sleep together. Whatever she told you, she did not cook for me. It was a marriage of convenience, *chérie,* and that was all. Until you, there was no reason to move out of the apartment. It cut down on expenses—she would not divorce me. Perhaps she was still frightened that some of the patriots had long memories and would seek revenge. I do not know."

They came together again; there were no barriers, no more shadows between them. But just before they slept that night, Carol wondered what the future might hold. What would happen if her mother did not like him. Or if Bessie could not overcome the jealousy she had spoken of.

It was the next day that Pierre brought a telegram from Ralph saying simply "Please phone." She stayed only long enough to find Jean-Claude in the small room next to Bessie's which he had been using as a study, and tell him what had happened. She was certain it was something to do with Bessie or her mother. She reversed the

Renault into a bank of pansies outside the kitchen door and roared down the track, passing Pierre on his bicycle long before he reached the road.

The telephone was in the post office which also sold everything else, and was always full of customers. At least none of them spoke English. While she waited to be connected with London, she half heard the topic of conversation. It was about the English lady and her amour. So much for all their discretion.

Ralph's voice was blessedly reassuring, if indistinct.

"It's not for you at all, Carol. The *Planète* office assumed that Durant was still working here. He told me he was holidaying in Provence and might drop in on you. If he does, tell him he's needed back in Paris. Pronto."

Her heart contracted painfully. She wanted to cry a protest. They had had only five days together. But all she said was, "Thank you, Ralph. Is everything else all right? What about the book?"

"Publicity are formulating a strategy. What about you?"

"Bessie has gone to America with my friend. Mother is staying in Birmingham doing the rounds. I'm taking it easy here."

"Feel like contacting Demetier again?"

Maurice Demetier was a playwright who summered in Antibes. He was one of Carol's less popular coups.

"Yes. Perhaps. All right." Carol wondered whether Ralph knew that Jean was here. Was he giving her a job to fill her hours when *Planète* wanted Jean to fly off somewhere?

"No hurry. Take the rest of the summer off if you feel like it. You've already done your stint over here with Clive's book."

She said her goodbyes, then asked to be put through to the *Planète* office. She told the girl on the other end that she could forward any messages to Monsieur Durant. A silence fell in the tiny shop.

A male voice came on the line, speaking English.

"Madame Woodford?" She did not correct him. "Durant is to cover the Civil Rights march in Washington next week. We have air tickets—everything—here."

Carol took a deep breath. This was it: the end of their time together. The future was here, now.

"I will tell him. Thank you."

She replaced the receiver carefully, and prepared to leave the shop with head held high. To her surprise everyone smiled at her as if in congratulation. She went into the sunshine and slid into the hot leather seat of the car. The French were . . . different. She could be proud to be the *chère amie* of Jean-Claude Durant. Her mood lifted.

Monica wondered why she did not feel happier. She had achieved her aim; Bessie was with her, and what was more they were already very good friends. And this end had not been achieved by Mallie's death—Bessie had agreed to come to America before that awful event. And it had not been achieved at Carol's expense either. Carol had been pathetically honest before they left Barnt Green: she had fallen in love. Monica had been pleased—personally pleased—about that. It explained Carol's enormous strength all through the inquest and funeral.

But it still did not seem to make everything "all right." Monica told herself it was because the hurdle of Bob had to be jumped. Once he knew Bessie, he would accept her. The child was delightful, unspoilt, beautiful, and with a sense of humour that would win Bob's heart immediately.

The trip over had been perfect: Bessie appeared to put her old life behind her almost physically; she was the ideal travelling companion, excited one minute, peaceably happy the next. They landed at Gander for refuelling and after that she slept until Idlewild and the customs. It was only six weeks since Monica had left the country, but now she saw it through Bessie's eyes, and the sheer efficiency of the place impressed her anew. Besides, she had left New York a failure. And she was returning a success. She should be on top of the world.

George met them, driving the enormous Oldsmobile that was so ideal for the boys and the dogs. Bessie was entranced.

"They're *gorgeous*," she said, referring to the dogs. "And their names are so right!"

Douglas and Fairbanks gazed at her from their drooping eyes and drooled thanks. They were bloodhounds, supposed to protect Hildie and the boys when George was away from the farm, but apart from barking loudly at strangers, they were harmless. Bessie sat in the back and reached through the dog guard to stroke them. They whined ecstatically.

George was apologetic.

"Hildie would have been here except she might be . . . not too good in the mornings. Guess you two just want your beds and a cup of coffee, anyway."

"Sounds heaven, George. Is this all right, really? We could have stayed at an hotel, but I wanted Bessie to see the farm. And I wanted to talk to you two before I contacted Bob."

George took his eyes off the road long enough to swivel them questioningly at Bessie.

"Bessie understands." Monica had said nothing at all to the child about Bob, and amazingly no-one had asked her about him. She recalled saying something to Carol about her marriage being over; probably Carol's tact had kept everyone else silent on the subject.

Monica turned to face her daughter.

"You'll like Bob, darling. And he'll like you, I'm certain. We had a bit of a bust-up before I left, so I want to phone him first." She smiled easily. "As it happens it worked out for the best." She turned to George again. "It's been a strange six weeks. Did Hildie tell you? Not all tragic. But I was very, very glad to be there when it happened."

"Sure. We understood that." George grinned in the mirror. "We're just glad you've come home. And brought this young lady with you. Say, you didn't warn us she was a budding Jane Russell!"

Bessie giggled. Jane Russell was considered very daring at the convent. She couldn't wait to tell Solange that she looked like Jane Russell. She leaned back so that the dogs could breathe in her ear. She was still very tired. She thought about Carol and Grannie. Her mother, and her grandmother. It was good, so good, to belong to them properly. She mustn't be jealous of this French newspaperman. Carol wouldn't let it make any difference. And, in an odd way, it was good to get away from everything just now; poor little Mallie. And poor Aunt Myrt. If only Boris had been there. If only . . . She slept.

America was *"fantastique."* Bessie loved everything about it. The Connecticut farm was like no farm she'd seen before; it wasn't all mud and manure. Aunt Hildie and Uncle George weren't real farmers at all; their "help" had originally owned the house—which was called a salt-box though it was hard to see why—and had sold it with the proviso that they stay on and work it. Uncle George did something with real estate and had an office in New York. Aunt Hildie and Aggie ran the house and looked after Aunt Hildie's two children between them. Aggie's husband saw to the farm and showed George's visitors around when they came. Aggie and Jim lived in a flat over the garage which had its own bathroom. Everyone else lived in the salt-box which had six bedrooms and three bathrooms and a basement which was called a rumpus room. They weren't quite rich enough yet to have their own swimming pool, but they shared one with their neighbours who lived in the next "lot."

Bessie loved Aunt Hildie. Aunt Monica told Bessie that Aunt Hildie was a bit scatty, a bit pretty, a bit clever, and very wise. She pretended to find her nine-year-old twins, Leo and Ossie, distasteful, but when they went to summer camp, she phoned them every day and spent a long time cleaning up their room for the fall. Bessie missed them too, though she had only known them a week before they went off. They weren't like her convent friends who liked talking and giggling. And they weren't a bit like Boris who understood everything even when you couldn't explain it. They woke each day with a "program." Usually the program started with a swim in the pool, then it might take in an inspection of the farm animals with Jim. Then there would be a run before lunch. They literally took to their heels and ran until they could run no more. "Just like the dogs," Uncle George commented in disgust, rumpling their heads fondly as he said it. When Leo brought home an injured pigeon and it died, they ran as if their very lives depended on it. Bessie gave up and went to her room where she hung out of the window and watched their distant stick-shapes tearing around a field of stubble. "They'll sweat it all out," said Aunt Hildie, turning her mouth down wryly. Aunt Monica said, "That's all very well, but where do they get their energy?" "From good American steaks," Aunt Hildie replied. "And it looks as if the two of you could do with a course of them, too."

Aunt Hildie did not want them to go to New York.

"Bessie is used to the countryside," she told Aunt Mon repeatedly. "Sidewalks and stores aren't for her this weather. Let's wait till it breaks, huh?"

Aunt Mon waited until Bessie was watching "The Beverly Hillbillies" on the giant television set, then said quietly, "Why don't you want us to see Bob? Is he still with Nancy?"

"No. I told you he wasn't, honey. My God, he went crazy when you left. Sacked her on the spot. He's written you, surely?"

"Yes. And I didn't exactly *leave*. I had to see Bessie. She was in some danger . . . too long to explain."

Hildie spoke quietly but with emphasis. "You left. When you phoned me that morning, you were leaving. At least be honest with yourself."

Aunt Mon was quiet for some time, then Bessie saw her dim reflection shrug in the television screen and she said, "Oh shoot!" Then they both laughed. Then Aunt Mon went back to the beginning and said, "Why don't you want us to see Bob?"

"I want *you* to see Bob. I think a certain person might be rather a shock for him."

There was another pause, then Aunt Hildie sighed sharply and said in an exasperated voice, "Surely you can see that, honey?"

"Yes. But if he loves me . . . listen Hildie, if it comes to a choice I have to choose . . . her."

"Honey. For Pete's sake. She's already got a family. You could end up with nothing. And Bob might—if the worst came to the worst—get away with zero alimony. In the circumstances."

Aunt Mon got up and walked to the window. She called, "Bessie! Jim is taking the tractor up to the high field to plough in the stubble. D'you want to go with him?"

Bessie did not take her eyes off Ellie May.

"In a minute," she droned, concentration obviously otherwise engaged.

Aunt Mon came back to where Aunt Hildie sat in a chair doing her nails.

"I have to do it this way. Or not at all. And I want to get it over and done with. Will you come, Hildie? Please?"

Hildie laughed. "I wouldn't miss it for anything," she said. As if it were a bullfight. Or Wimbledon.

They went in with Uncle George. Bessie wore her cotton frock with daisies all over it. It had pockets in the side seams of the skirt and she liked pushing her hands into them and making it stick out at the sides. The last time she had worn this frock had been when they came over to England at the beginning of August. Maybe it would be lucky. Maybe they would decide to go back to France today. Maybe it was a travelling frock.

But she was still loving America.

Fifth Avenue was amazing. She had expected the buildings to reach into the sky and make all the streets into tunnels, but she hadn't expected trees. Nor the street vendors, nor the politeness of the girls in the shops, nor the expensive women with little dogs, nor the screaming traffic. They bought presents for each other; Aunt Hildie bought earrings for Auntie Mon, and Aunt Mon bought an expanding gold bracelet for Bessie.

"Shall we have them sent to Beekman Place?" Aunt Hildie asked half-teasingly. Aunt Mon shook her head.

"Stop making a big thing out of this," she chided. "Bob was perfectly all right on the phone. He's looking forward to meeting Bessie. We don't have to lay claim to the place by having stuff delivered there! Besides, I'd like to wear my earrings if that is okay by you."

"Sure. How about you, Bessie?"

So Bessie wore the bracelet and they took Aunt Hildie to buy things for the new baby which she seemed to be concealing more successfully than Aunt Myrt concealed hers. Then they went out to lunch.

Aunt Hildie said, "You don't know what a treat this is for me. No kids, no husband . . . do you realise, Aggie and me—we're the only women on the farm? Apart from the cows of course."

They all giggled and people looked round at them and Bessie put one hand over the back of her chair so that everyone could see the bracelet.

"Having a good time, honey?" It was strange how Auntie Mon seemed to be talking American now.

Bessie grinned. "I sure am!"

They laughed again.

Central Park was like a very big Cannon Hill in Birmingham. On the paths there were people running for no reason, like Leo and Ossie, but then there were huge areas of grass and trees and bushes and emptiness.

They took a horse and carriage and meandered slowly down a wide driveway lined with drooping aspen trees. The driver was a coloured man with a beautiful white smile; he told them they had better leave the park by four P.M. at the latest.

"There's a rally today, ladies. It's running at the same time as the big Washington march. It's going to be mighty crowded in an hour or two."

Bessie said, "Why are they marching? Is it like the changing of the Guard?"

"No." Aunt Mon glanced at the driver's broad back. "It's a freedom march."

"I thought America was free already?"

The driver looked round. He was still smiling.

"Not everyone isn't free, little lady. Down in the south, people like me can't go to the same places as people like you. And white children can't go to school with coloured children."

Bessie was mildly surprised. "We have coloured girls at the convent. They come from Morocco mostly."

Aunt Hildie said quickly, "It's different in France, honey."

People were already arriving when they left the park. They were carrying flags and big notices on poles which said starkly, "human rights." For some reason they made Bessie remember again the dark and terrible two weeks at Barnt Green after Mallie's death. She forgot her pretty dress and new bracelet and took Aunt Mon's hand.

"All right, baby?" asked Aunt Mon.

"I was just wondering what Carol was doing now," Bessie said in a small voice.

"She and Grannie are getting the French house cleaned up for the winter, I expect," Aunt Mon suggested.

Bessie wondered whether Aunt Mon knew about Jean-Claude Durant.

"Have you ever heard of a newspaper called *La Planète*, Auntie Monica?" she asked.

"Vaguely. One of the Paris newspapers, isn't it?"

Aunt Hildie said, "They have offices in New York."

She hailed a taxi and they all got in and Aunt Mon gave the Beekman Place address. They both seemed suddenly nervous and preoccupied and no-one asked Bessie any more about *La Planète*. She sat back in the slippery leather seat and put her hands in her pockets.

The apartments were more like a big London house than anything she'd seen in New York. There was an awning over the pavement at the front door and a concierge like in Paris who seemed delighted to see Aunt Mon.

"Say, Mrs. Gallagher! I've missed you. What about the marches? Comes of having a Republican in office, that's what I say. My old lady's sister says they're bringing in the troops in Arkansas. The army! Can you believe it?"

"Is Mr. Gallagher at home yet, Donaghue?"

"Sure is, Mrs. Gallagher. And he went up that elevator with the biggest bunch of roses you ever did see. And a grin from ear to ear!"

"Thank you, Donaghue," said Auntie Monica, and Auntie Hildie said very clearly, "Familiarity."

They took the lift for miles. Bessie didn't look at the indicator because it made her feel worse. She, who had climbed the Victoire, could not stand lifts. When the doors opened, a man was waiting on the sumptuous landing. It must be Uncle Bob. He carried flowers and he was grinning. Maybe Donaghue had telephoned him.

"Hello. Hello. Hello. Hello. Say, is this wonderful, or just wonderful? Hello, Sis. Hello, Honey. I thought I might never . . . hello. Gee, you look wonderful. How was the trip? How is George? And the boys?"

He couldn't seem to stop talking. He didn't give Auntie Monica a chance to say anything about Bessie. They all moved—shuffled—to a big carved door with an enormous brass door knob and letter box. Uncle Bob, still half hidden by the flowers, let them go in first, then he followed, shut the door and stood with his back against it in case anyone tried to escape.

Auntie Mon said, "It looks great, Bob. You've had help, obviously."

Bob said, "Listen, honey. She's about eighty-four and she goes home at nights. Honest to God. Her name is Mrs. Bergdorf, and I got her from an agency. Hildie will bear me out."

Aunt Monica said, *"Pas devant l'enfant,* please Bob." Then caught Bessie's eye and grinned. "I was forgetting you speak the language like a native, honey. Come here and meet your Uncle Bob. Bob, you've heard me talk of my friend, Carol Woodford. This is her small sister, Bessie Woodford. She came back with me for a holiday. I have to take her home at the end of September." She closed one eye, reminding Bessie of her own words. Bessie felt a surge of thankfulness. Even if she was enjoying America, even if Carol did have a man friend, even if Uncle Bob was as nice as Aunt Hildie said, she still wanted to know she was going home in two weeks' time.

"How do you do," she said politely, extending the hand with the bracelet.

He dumped the flowers at last, and took the hand.

"Say, that's some bracelet. And some wrist it's on."

She explained about the bracelet and he said, "Mon's got an eye for jewellery." He kept her hand and led them all through to an enormous sitting room with windows looking out over a river. The sense of space was amazing. Bessie wanted to be thoroughly child-ish and run about and even jump on the huge squashy sofas that were everywhere.

Hildie said, "Can we have some tea, please Bob? We've done the town all day and we're exhausted."

He twirled Bessie round and sat her down.

"Tea. I'll get it." He had hardly looked at Auntie Mon since they came into the room. Now he glanced at her. "Give me a hand, hon?"

"Only too pleased."

They left.

"Well," Aunt Hildie said. "Well, well, *well.*"

Bessie said, "They've made up the quarrel, haven't they?"

"Temporarily, at any rate." Aunt Hildie looked at the open door speculatively. "She chickened out. Temporarily at any rate."

"Chickened out?"

"Yes. She ducked out of telling him something important."

Aunt Hildie transferred the speculative gaze to Bessie.

"Hope it's not temporary." She seemed to shake her shoulders. "My motto is, least said soonest mended, Bessie Woodford. What d'you think?"

Bessie thought of Carol having to keep her secret all these years. She nodded.

Aunt Mon and Uncle Bob were gone ages. Aunt Hildie asked if she wanted to see the apartment, then took her into the bathroom and a bedroom and another bedroom. She slid back some doors.

"Your Aunt Mon's clothes," she said, as if introducing another person. The cupboard went along the whole length of a wall and was full of clothes. Aunt Hildie grinned. "Go on, try some on. Monica won't mind. I have to go to the bathroom."

Bessie didn't think she wanted to try on any clothes, but after a very few minutes she found herself pushing at the hangers to get a better look at the dresses, skirts, suits, blouses—everything. There was a long satin dance dress in pale cream. It had a boned top. Bessie had never seen anything like it before. She unbuttoned her daisy dress and pulled it over her head. The dance dress slid into its place. She looked at herself in the mirror. The boned top did not touch her body at all. She opened a drawer and found handkerchiefs, and stuffed them into the gaps. That was better. She giggled. She went to the dressing table where lipsticks and rouge were laid out on a glass tray and began to apply make-up with a liberal hand. A blue scarf hung over a chair and she pulled that through her bracelet. She looked gorgeous. Like Jane Russell. Sultry. She half-closed her eyes and pouted at herself. If only Solange could see her now. Or Boris. But Aunt Mon would appreciate her too. She fluffed out her hair with spread fingers, and made for the kitchen.

At first it was just embarrassing. Aunt Mon was engulfed by Uncle Bob's enormous shoulders and arms, it was as if he had wrapped himself around her. She had seen Aunt Myrt and Uncle Malcolm having a cuddle, but Aunt Myrt was bigger than Aunt Mon and she didn't practically disappear into Uncle Malcolm. Even so, it was Aunt Mon who caught sight of Bessie first. Sideways and almost upside down, her wide-open eyes dilated then narrowed with amusement as if sharing a joke with Bessie. She put a hand to Uncle Bob's neck and moved her face sideways.

"Darling. Bessie is here."

It was when Bob surfaced and registered her appearance that embarrassment became bewilderment and then alarm.

He obviously didn't remember who she was. He lifted his head and stared at her as if she were a ghost. Auntie Mon looked up at him and gave a nervous laugh. "It's Bessie, honey. In my dress." But he went on staring and staring and Bessie started to stammer in apology, and Aunt Mon moved to her and said, "It's all right, darling. I don't mind a bit. You look gorgeous." And Uncle Bob blurted, "Christ, she's yours. Don't deny it. She's your kid! Christ—" And Aunt Mon said, "Go and get changed, Bessie. We'll have some tea in just a moment." And as Bessie fled, it was as if Uncle Bob exploded with a final *"Christ!"* And then the door slammed on them as Aunt Mon said, "Shut *up*, Bob!" And she was in the thick, silent hall again by herself.

She did not let herself recall any of those two minutes. Like an automaton she went back into the bedroom, stripped off the gown and let it lie on the floor with its tumble of handkerchief-paddings. She put on her daisy dress and smoothed her hair with the palms of hands that were trembling slightly. She found her handkerchief in one of the skirt pockets and scrubbed at her face. Then she walked across the hall once more, through the heavy door, on to the landing. She pressed the button by the side of the lift and a moment later it arrived and the doors opened silently. She squeezed her hands inside her pockets and closed her eyes. It was worse going down, but she didn't care.

The nice concierge asked her how she was doing and she said, "Fine." And he said, "Say, where are you off to, little lady?" And she said, "Going for a walk." And she was gone.

It was so easy. The pavement was wide and small trees grew in tubs along its edge. She thought she would go as far as the first tub, and when she got there she decided to go to the second. The concierge shouted something behind her, so she ran to the third and fourth, then there was a corner and she went around it and did not hear him any more.

She had to get to Carol. Or to Grannie. Yes, Grannie would know and tell her the truth about everything.

IO

*A*fter the first overwhelming impulse to get away had been satisfied, Bessie did not know what to do. Her day of shopping and sight-seeing in New York had not prepared her for using its transport facilities. She knew nothing about the mysterious subway, and the yellow taxis that cruised along the kerbs of the hotels cost money; she had no money. She kept walking because someone might speak to her if she stopped, and she had not made up her mind what to say to the inevitable question, "Have you lost your way, little girl?"

The streets around Beekman Place looked the same; she needed to see some shops, though she had no idea why. She kept walking. When she saw it, she would know what it was she wanted.

It was a policeman. He was talking to a lady with a white poodle dog. He had his truncheon swinging from his wrist, and he pushed his hat to the back of his head and said something about the weather. As Bessie drew near, she heard the woman say, "I always go north for the summer, but this year I decided to stay put. I sure have regretted it. What a summer!" She turned and saw Bessie coming towards them. She smiled. Bessie in her daisy frock was unmistakably a nice little girl.

"Hi there, honey. You're new around here, aren't you?"

Bessie leaned down and stroked the poodle.

"I'm visiting."

Her accent caused ecstasy.

"Say! You're English!" The poodle lady turned to the policeman. "Officer, did you hear that? She's all the way from England. Visiting New York!"

The policeman grinned amiably. No trouble here.

"Welcome to the city, little lady. But you shouldn't really wander around on your own."

Bessie straightened and looked at the policeman, and knew what she had to do. It wasn't a welcome decision, but the alternative of going back to Beekman Place was worse.

"Actually, I'm looking for my uncle. We were going back to his office, and he was talking to someone, and I went round the corner, and—and I seem to have lost him." Somehow it was better to have lost her mythical uncle than be lost herself.

They were concerned.

"Hey. That's not good in a big city like New York." The poodle lady picked up her dog as if she expected him to dash off and get himself lost. "Maybe you'd better come back to my apartment, honey, while this officer puts out a call for your uncle."

Bessie said, "There's no need for that. If you can direct me to his office, I'll be fine. I can meet him there. Or they will phone him. Or something."

"Do you know the name of his company?" The policeman looked less relaxed.

"Oh yes. He works for *La Planète*. The French newspaper, you know."

"I ain't heard of that one."

"They share an office with an American paper. I can't remember the name . . ." She began to feel really frightened. She had to get back to Cass, and *La Planète* was the only link she had.

"Listen, honey. I'll take you along the block and phone in for a car. They'll drive you to your uncle's office. They know every inch of the city. Relax, honey. We'll take care of you."

"I'm not a bit worried," Bessie lied. "My grandmother told me when I was a little girl that if I was in any difficulty I only had to ask a policeman for help."

The policeman looked gratified, and the poodle lady said, "Isn't that cute? Isn't there some little old English song about asking a policeman? And you've really done that. Just that!" She trilled a laugh. "What's your name, baby? I just have to tell my ladies' group that I've met a little English girl."

Bessie swallowed. "Elizabeth . . . Durant," she said. "I am English, but my uncle is French."

It didn't make much sense, but they accepted the name instantly. Bessie said goodbye to the poodle lady and walked alongside the policeman to a phone booth, where he made his call. In less than a minute a car drew up at the kerb and Bessie sat inside it while the driver spoke on a radio to someone called Frank who was given the task of finding out where the offices of *La Planète* were. Then they were driving through the evening traffic on the wrong side of the road, sirens screaming, the driver shouting remarks back to her about taking more care next time. Nobody seemed to realise she was running away from danger, not into it.

La Planète had an office in the enormous Herald building in Thirty-Second Street. The revolving doors did not stop. The policeman took Bessie's hand and ran to catch them up and held on to her tightly as they were ejected the other side. It was blessedly cool in the big foyer.

Bessie said, "I'm all right now. Thank you very much."

"I'm not letting you go till I can hand you over to a responsible citizen," the policeman said, only half humorously.

He went to the desk and found the floor occupied by *La Planète*, then led her into the elevator. "My chief would have my badge if I reported half the story!" he grinned. "Took us ten minutes to get you here—it'll take half an hour to write it up!"

"I'm sorry," she said in a small voice. She wondered how much longer it would take when the people in the *Planète* office disclaimed all knowledge of her.

There was just one person in the small room at the end of the corridor. He had round owl eyes behind glasses, and when he stood up behind the large desk where he was tapping at a typewriter, he was still very short indeed.

"How can I help you, officer?" He held out his hand, and Bessie knew that in spite of his American accent he was French.

The policeman said, "Picked up this little lady on the East side by the river. She says she is meeting her uncle here. Name of Durant."

Bessie took a step forward. "Jean-Claude Durant. I am Elizabeth Durant." Deliberately she closed one eye. Then she waited without hope.

The little man was momentarily silent, then he beamed.

"Jean-Claude. One of our best foreign correspondents. He is covering the Washington march." He came around the desk. "I am the New York representative, officer." He removed some papers and revealed a name board. "Louis Gotthard. I cannot sufficiently thank you for bringing in Elizabeth."

"Washington?" The officer frowned. "He is in Washington?"

"Was in Washington," Monsieur Gotthard said smoothly. "You became lost, *chérie?*" He looked at her questioningly and in spite of her astonishment at this turn of events, she took up his cue.

She spoke in French. "He was showing me the city and stopped to talk to someone and I went on for a few metres, then I could not see him."

The policeman said sharply, "What did she say?"

"She was explaining how she came to be lost. Of course, Jean-Claude has such a short time in New York, he would want to show her the sights." He turned back to Bessie. "Will you wait here for him? He will surely arrive very soon and be very worried."

"I will wait. Please." She went to the window and closed her eyes on the view. In her head she began to pray very hard.

"Okay. I'll have to report this to the Juvenile Department. They will want to check it out." The officer produced a notebook and Monsieur Gotthard had to sign it as if she were a parcel being delivered. And then at last the door closed.

She said in a very small voice, "Thank you, monsieur. Perhaps . . . could I stay here tonight?"

"You really know Jean-Claude?"

"Yes. Sort of. He knows my . . . mother."

"Ah. I see."

There were sounds. Bessie turned her bowed head and looked beneath her arm. Monsieur Gotthard was filling a kettle and plugging it in. He turned quickly and forced her to meet his glinting spectacles.

He said, "I went along with you because I thought there might be a story for the paper. I am wrong?"

She swallowed. Was he still going to give her up?

"Yes. I mean, I can't explain anything. But I have to get home to France somehow. And I remembered that Jean-Claude's paper . . . is he really in America?"

"Yes. Washington. He is covering the Washington march."

"I know about that. There was another one in Central Park."

"You're a bright child." He stared at her for a long moment, then made up his mind. "Come, we will drink tea and you can tell me what you would like to tell me."

She looked out at the view. They were so far up she could not see the street below. "Thank you, God," she said in her head. Then she went to the chair Monsieur Gotthard indicated and sat down. Her legs were trembling.

Bob said for the umpteenth time, "You choose. The kid or me. My God, when I think that all the time you had this on your mind . . . no wonder you were ill. No wonder you were bloody ill!"

Monica quelled a flutter of panic. She said, "Bob, I have to go to her. She didn't know a thing till you spoke. She'll be upset—"

But he wouldn't move from the door and he was very large.

"You stay here until you've made up your mind. I mean it, Monica. You've twisted me round your finger till I can't see straight, but I know this isn't right. If you want me for my own sake, then you'll have no trouble making up your mind. But if you've come looking for a father for your bastard kid, then I'll know it, won't I? What's the big idea? For Christ's sake, what goes on in that mind of yours?"

"Bob. You keep asking me questions then you don't let me answer. Just listen." She couldn't stop thinking of Bessie, stripping off her finery, bewildered and perhaps frightened. With difficulty she brought her mind back to Bob. "Listen. It was when I was a child. Sixteen. It was my brother—my adopted brother. I was farmed out when I was born then . . . then . . . oh God . . . I had to do it to my baby!" She sobbed suddenly and she hadn't meant to do that. She mustn't get upset, for Bessie's sake. She gulped. "The doctor said—back in the summer—he said I couldn't have children. But I've got a child. I've got a daughter. Can't you understand—I had to find her and get to know her—"

"And then palm her off on me. Was that it? Someone else's kid? The child of your *brother* for Christ's sake! Incest!"

"He was my adopted brother—I just told you that—"

"Moral incest then! That makes it all right, does it? Did you love me in the first place, Monica? Or were you planning even then to foist your daughter on to me? When I think of you—the way you practically seduced me—night after night—"

It could have been hilarious. But it wasn't.

She said, "Bob. Stop it. We'll talk about this another day. When we're both calmer. I have to go to that child."

But he wouldn't move. He started again. "You'll stay here until you've made up your mind. The kid or me. That's the offer, Monica. The kid or me."

Behind him came a knocking. It was Hildie. He turned and pulled open the door.

"We've got some trading to do, Sis. Get lost for half an hour. Take the kid with you."

Hildie said, "Never mind that. Where *is* Bessie? I've looked in the bedroom and the sitting room and—"

Monica made an animal sound. "Oh no—!"

Bob said, "Go find her, Hildie. Bring her back here and keep her in the living room—"

"She's run off!" Monica's nails tore on the door. She thrust herself past Bob and Hildie and ran into the bedroom. "Bessie—darling—where are you? It's okay—it's me, Auntie Mon. Bessie—where are you?"

It was obvious that Bessie had gone. Hildie was wide-eyed and as frantic as Monica herself.

"How long ago? Where—? Ring Donaghue—Bob, *do* something!"

He rang downstairs and heard that Bessie had "just stepped out five minutes ago." He looked at Monica.

She said, "She's in this city. Alone. Oh God."

Hildie said, "What happened? Why has she gone?"

Monica did not look at her. Her eyes never left Bob's.

"You said we were doing some trading." Her voice rose until it was a scream. "I will trade you for my daughter!" She lifted her head and shrieked at the ceiling. "Do you hear me, God? Give me back my daughter and I'll never go near this man again in my life!"

Bob caught her as she fell.

Immediately she saw him, Bessie knew why Cass loved Jean-Claude. And quite soon after that, she knew too that he was her father. It was suddenly so obvious. Cass would not have loved twice, it was not in her nature. She had fallen in love with this man, then he had gone away and Cass had had a baby. Then she had found him again. It was simple. He had dark hair like Bessie herself had, he had black eyes like she had. And he was somehow oddly familiar. Her body and bones knew him already.

He arrived late that evening in response to a telephone call from Monsieur Gotthard and they met him at the airport. He had cameras with him because the message had been so obscure he thought the New York rally had exploded into unprecedented violence, and he was to cover that angle for the newspaper.

Confronted by Bessie, he was still uncomprehending. When Louis introduced "Miss Elizabeth Durant" he began to wonder. Then she blurted, "I'm sorry. I'm Cass' daughter, Bessie. Bessie Woodford. I didn't know how to contact you. I have to get back to Cass. I must. I didn't know how . . ." An enormous tear of sheer exhaustion blurred her vision, and she blinked hard.

He unloaded his bags and sat down so that he was on a level with her. He did not ask a lot of questions. Obviously the child was terribly confused about her true parentage. It did not matter to Jean-Claude. He knew that Cass loved Bessie and Bessie loved Cass. That was all that mattered.

He held out his hand.

"Bessie. I have wanted to see you very much. I am very honoured that you too wanted to see me."

She took his hand, intending to shake it politely. It was warm and dry and infinitely reassuring. The tear ran down her face and was followed by others. He drew her on to his knee and she hid her face in his shirt and behaved like a baby. And it was then she knew he must be her father.

He took her to a drugstore and bought her a soda and some food and she told him what had happened. She kept talking about Mallie's death and Boris, and how unhappy Aunt Liv was, and he held her and rocked her and finally said, "The sooner we get you back to the Bergerie, the better. Do you agree with that?"

"Oh *yes, monsieur.*"

"And you had better call me by name. Jean will do. Could you manage that?"

"Oh *yes.* Oh, Jean, Grannie and Cass will be disappointed that I ran away. Can you explain to them? Monica's husband did not recognise me when I was dressed up, and I felt so ashamed and . . . sort of . . . frightened." She looked up, tears already drying. "I don't know why. Not now. It was just—after Mallie— and Boris not being at home—"

"And Cass telling you about me, perhaps?"

She flushed darkly.

He said quietly, "It is nothing to be ashamed of, *chérie*. Cass belongs to you and you thought I would take her away. Yes?" He did not wait for an answer. "It is not so, Bessie. Can you try to think of all love and concern and friendship being pooled—a lake of it—a sea of it—" He stopped and smiled at her. She was only thirteen, he would probably drown her in his sea of concepts. But she smiled back at him.

"Like Mallie. Always wading into the fishpond at Aunt Liv's. Perhaps that was why he did it."

He thought about it, then nodded. "Perhaps it is so," he agreed.

He telephoned the Connecticut farm and spoke to Aggie. He told her that Bessie had become lost and had asked a policeman to take her to the office of *La Planète*. He would bring her back to the farm himself. Bessie watched him, wide-eyed, aghast that he was betraying her.

"You understand this is best, *chérie?*" He replaced the telephone. "This Aggie—she will now telephone Monica and by the time we all meet at the Connecticut farm, everyone will be calm. I will introduce myself as a colleague of Cass' and suggest that you come home with me at the end of the week. So we all avoid unpleasantness— perhaps a rift between Monica and Carol—you understand?"

"Yes. Of course. You are . . . good. But—" she breathed deeply. "You see, Jean, Aunt Mon won't agree to it. She will want me to stay with her and Uncle Bob."

"I do not think so, Bessie. Trust me. If she asks you to stay, simply tell her that you think it would be best to go home now. Then I will talk to her. Trust me."

Bessie trusted him. She would have told him that she knew he was her father, but innate good manners insisted that she must wait for him to mention it. She nodded and sat back on the high stool. She felt suddenly very tired and relaxed. Jean was telephoning about hiring a car. He was so competent. He would look after them all. He would train Boris to use a camera. He might even make it all right for Auntie Liv and Auntie Myrt.

Monica did not know what to think or do. She had never fainted in her life before and by doing so now, she had lost them all valuable time. She sat with her head still between her knees; her tears dried; she stared at the carpet. Unexpectedly she thought of

Myrtle and the new baby. No wonder Myrtle did not want it any more; Monica would give up anything—anything in the world—to see Bessie walk through the door.

Hildie was crouched by her side.

"Listen, honey. I'll go and look. Right now. You and Bob get on to the Juvenile Department. When I get back—if I haven't found her—Bob can wait here for calls and we'll get a cab and scour the area. Okay?" She stood up. "She can't have got far—I'll find her. Okay Bob?"

Monica heard him mumble something; he sounded like a sulky schoolboy. Hildie said sharply, "I don't know what you said to scare away that kid, but you'd better pull yourself together now. She's thirteen years old dammit, and New York is a big place."

She left, and Monica stood up and made for the phone much too quickly; the pale walls of the apartment swam around her.

"Sit down. I'll do it." But he went to the kitchen first and returned with a whisky. She could have wept at the delay. "Drink this." He thrust the glass at her, and at last went to the phone. It was a long business. First of all they put him through to something called Missing Persons, and after he'd told the story and made it sound almost unimportant, he was put through to the Juvenile Department.

"Description? Well . . . she's kind of tall for her age, and she has dark hair and eyes. Dress?" He looked over his shoulder. "What dress was she wearing, Mon?"

Monica put the glass down on the floor and made for the phone. He surrendered it without argument.

"She was wearing a blue dress. Covered in white daisies. And white sandals. Yes, socks. And a gold bracelet. No, no other jewellery." She began to shiver. "She hasn't got a coat or anything, and when the sun goes down . . . yes, I know it's been less than an hour. No, there was no argument. Not exactly. Yes, she might have been upset. No, she wouldn't be hiding in the apartment—we've looked. Searched? No, not really, but yes, we will search. And the elevators. Yes. Yes, of course." She put the receiver down and looked at Bob. "They think she's playing us up. Hiding. To worry us. Sort of . . . punish us."

"Well, that's what she's doing, isn't it? She didn't like me yelling at her—she didn't like me, period."

Monica said wearily, "Bob. She heard what you said. And she doesn't want to be my child. She wants to belong to Cass and Mary

Woodford. Like I wanted to belong to Gilly. Belonging. That's what it's about, Bob."

"Weren't you going to tell her? Were you going to trick the pair of us? For the rest of our lives?" He was still rigid with anger.

"Bob. Please. You wanted me back. I couldn't have come back without Bessie. If you'd accepted her, then I would have stayed and told her one day. She might have just come by the knowledge gradually. Herself." She gave a dry sob. "Oh, I don't know. It sounds crazy now. I didn't work it out. It just happened. I was miserable—you'd rejected me—I wanted to see Bessie and Cass— and the others. And when I saw them, I just wanted to—to— borrow Bessie. First of all for my—my self-esteem. And then because I loved her. And I told myself that she was in danger with Cass and that I was doing her a favour taking her right away from Europe. And then Myrtle's child was drowned in the garden pool and it was so awful, I wanted to get back here myself. I thought we might make ourselves into a family. A proper family. If Myrtle can put up with Malcolm playing around with every woman in sight and still make something good out of it, I thought I could too." Monica stopped speaking, listened, and said, "Is that the elevator? Hildie might have her—"

"No, it's not the elevator. It's the fridge." Bob came and stood by her. "Listen, Mon. Nancy threw herself at me. She was nothing to me and I was nothing to her. It was just that . . . nothing. I've never played around, as you put it."

"Hildie told me how much you wanted children. I can't have them."

"You're enough for me. I thought I was enough for you."

She bowed her head. She knew he wanted to take her into his arms and comfort her. And she knew if she let him she could eventually make him agree to keep Bessie. But she had cheated enough.

She said in a low voice, "I can't think about that now, Bob. I can't think about us."

"All right, honey. All right. Listen, finish that whisky and Hildie will be back with the kid."

"With Bessie."

"Yeah. Okay. With Bessie."

She downed the whisky and as if on cue the elevator whined. They met it, the doors slid back, Hildie was alone.

The cab driver was almost too keen on his mission: he became Philip Marlowe and did unnecessary U turns every time he glimpsed a child on the sidewalk. They went back to Central Park but there was no hope of seeing any one individual in the ordered crowds marching solemnly with banners and placards. "She wouldn't have come back here," Hildie declared. The cab driver agreed. "The Empire State. That's where she'd go. That's where they all go." Monica was silent. Bessie had thought the march might be something like the Changing of the Guard; might she have joined it? Either for its ritual ceremony, or in a bid for her own freedom of choice? Monica dropped her head for a moment, fighting off nausea again, then raised it quickly in case she missed a glimpse of that slim schoolgirl figure in her blue and white dress.

After an hour they drove back to Beekman Place to see whether there was any news from the Police Department. Bob had heard nothing. He met them at the elevator doors; he was smoking fiercely. The hour had given him a lot of time to think, but his thinking had got him nowhere. He wanted to yell a disgusted "Women!" and leave for the nearest bar. He couldn't do that.

Hildie rang the Juvenile people. She was incisive, almost hectoring.

"There's only so much we can do." She looked at Monica then quickly away—it was like staring at a recent wound. "Where would a twelve-year-old go in a strange city? We've tried all the drugstores round about. We've been back to Central Park . . . yeah, we were there earlier . . . no, hopeless, the place is packed with marchers. We can't cover every angle and you've got the manpower. Sure I realise she's not your only problem, but we're asking for action now. It could actually save time in the end." She held the receiver, breathing hard while she listened. "Go back home? Home is France or England for this kid." She nodded. "Okay. She just might have tried to get back to Connecticut. We'll cover that angle." She replaced the receiver without saying goodbye, and immediately picked it up to dial another number. "George," she explained over the mouthpiece.

Bob said, "Monica, honey, come into the kitchen and have some food. Another drink."

She was going to shake her head, then thought that anything was better than sitting on the chair in the hall. She went through to the kitchen and automatically filled the kettle at the faucet. She thought of Nancy. Then by an incomprehensible link, of her adoptive mother, Nelly Cook.

"We'll have some tea," she said as if it were a line in a play. She looked round at Bob and realised that he was at a complete loss. She said, "I'm sorry, Bob. I really am. You were so good, oh, better than good—you were wonderful. Lots of men had tried to get through my barrier in the old Albion days. You just didn't see there was a barrier there." She laughed shakily. "You battered it down."

He made an enormous effort. "Like Sleeping Beauty I guess. Huh?"

"I suppose so. Maybe." She poured hot water into the teapot to warm it and swilled it gently around as Liv did in her immaculate kitchen. "I didn't want to cheat you in any way, Bob. I loved you. I went back home and saw my brother. If there'd been anything there . . . anything left . . . I would have called off our wedding." She measured tea carefully. "But he didn't love me. He didn't understand about love. It was just fun . . . all those nights . . . just fun. He thought he knew about Bessie, but he wasn't going to try to find out in case it made things difficult for him. I couldn't love a man like that. So I came back to London and married you."

He swallowed. He did not like her references to Gilly. But still he said, "And it was wonderful, hon. Wasn't it?"

There was no tea cosy, the silver teapot was vacuum sealed, but she fetched a clean tea towel from the drawer and wrapped it around the teapot as best she could. Then she put three bone china cups on a tray without their saucers, and went for milk from the refrigerator.

"Yes, it was." She remembered the desperation with which she had made love with Bob. As if by sheer exertion she could shut out memories of Gilly and Bessie.

"Then it could be wonderful again." He shook his head as she started to speak. "I know. You can't talk about the future with this hanging over your head. But . . . there is a future, honey. I want you to know that it could be wonderful again. It's up to you."

She did not ask him whether his ultimatum still held. She poured tea almost steadily, and let him carry the tray to the kitchen table. Hildie joined them.

"I've rung George. I've rung home. I've rung George again." She sat down heavily. Monica remembered she was pregnant. She put a hand on her shoulder, and Hildie covered it with hers. It was as if Hildie was standing in for Cass. Or Myrt. Or Liv.

An hour later the Juvenile Department came through. A woman spoke to Hildie at some length, and for once Hildie listened intently.

She put a hand over the mouthpiece.

"Listen. A girl in a blue dress was picked up earlier by a cop car. She was taken to the offices of the *Herald*—she wanted to talk to some reporter in a French newspaper office, called *La Planète*, which hangs out in the same building. The guy who vouched for her was called Louis Gotthard, and she gave a name—Elizabeth Durant. D'you think it's Bessie? Didn't she ask about *La Planète* earlier?"

Monica was completely thrown. The name Durant meant nothing to her. She vaguely remembered hearing the name of the newspaper. She looked wildly at Bob.

He said, "Get the address. We'll go straight there."

Hildie returned to the telephone. She spoke, then listened again, then lifted her head.

"They say they will follow it up and be through again in a few minutes." She avoided Monica's eye. "There's no answer from this newspaper office. The reception desk says the Gotthard man left with a child half an hour ago. He says Gotthard is completely trustworthy."

"What can they do, then?" Monica asked wildly.

"Go into the office. Look for notes . . . something."

So again they waited. It was dark. The lights of the city seemed to twinkle heartlessly. They drank more tea and Bob switched on the television to get the news. No bodies had been found that day.

George rang through. There was no sign of Bessie at the farm. Someone from the Juvenile Department was with him and they had searched the buildings.

Half an hour later another call came through. An officer was waiting outside Gotthard's apartment in Brooklyn. He had not arrived home yet. As soon as he could be interviewed they would come back with more news.

At half-past ten, Monsieur Gotthard returned home and the crucial information filtered back to Beekman Place. The child, Elizabeth Durant, had indeed been wearing a gold bracelet and a blue and white dress. She had wanted to contact her uncle Jean-Claude Durant. Monsieur Gotthard had telephoned him in Washington. He had then taken the child to the airport to meet the plane. When he had seen them installed in a nearby drugstore, he had left. Gotthard was a reputable newspaperman, so was Durant. There was no reason to worry; but it might be as well if Mr. and Mrs. Gallagher reported to headquarters now. It would be necessary to find out why the child had run away from them, and exactly to whom she belonged.

Ten minutes after replacing the receiver, when they were still affronted and baffled, the phone rang again. This time it was George speaking from the farm. Bessie and her uncle were on their way.

They were all exhausted. Bob shook Jean-Claude's hand, but his jaw was clamped hard and the muscle under his ear twitched rhythmically throughout the garbled explanations.

Jean-Claude provided most of these.

"It seems that Bessie was reminded of my assignment in America. The march in Central Park and—er—so on. She took a walk—got lost and decided to find her way to the newspaper office."

Monica said faintly, "I'm sorry. Who are you? Bessie has not mentioned an uncle at all . . ."

"I am a very old friend of Carol's. We have worked together—I was with her last month when she edited a book in London. Perhaps she mentioned it."

"I know about the book. Yes."

"But she did not speak of me?" He smiled with all the charm he could muster. Cass had said Monica was beautiful, but this gaunt creature with sallow face and staring eyes looked menacing to him. He wondered how soon he would be able to extricate Bessie from this situation. It wasn't good for the child. The sister-in-law was normal enough, but the Gallaghers seemed on the brink of a furious marital break-up. If Bessie had triggered it, there was nothing to be done except spirit her away.

He said, "Probably there was much to talk about. I heard that the four of you met for the first time in twelve years. Also I heard of the tragedy of the small boy. It was most kind of you to bring Bessie away for this holiday."

He stared into Monica's eyes and she stared back. She told herself this was another reason why Bessie should stay in America. First the danger from the publication of this mysterious book; and now the presence of Cass' lover.

There was a long pause. Everyone seemed to be looking at

Monica. She felt a physical pressure from these looks. She blinked hard and turned her own gaze on Bessie. The child was strained and white, her dress crumpled, her hair like rats' tails. She seemed to be holding her breath and Monica knew what she wanted to do. What she wanted to do more than anything else in the world.

Monica blinked again and turned to the Frenchman.

"I'll have to talk to Bessie's mother on the telephone. You understand that? And if she is agreeable, I see no reason why Bessie shouldn't return with you."

She felt Bob's arm across her shoulders; she saw Bessie's smile. She could have been referring to Mrs. Woodford when she said "Bessie's mother," but everyone knew who she meant.

Hildie, the only person beside herself who was not smiling, said, "Are you sure that's for the best, honey?"

"I think so." Monica let Bob take some of her weight. "If it's what Bessie wants."

"There's so much to do before school, Aunt Mon," Bessie began diplomatically.

Hildie cut across the careful words.

"Let's have milk and cookies then. And go to bed."

Of course Bob thought she'd "chosen" him. He knew the kind of sacrifice she'd made, and he wept that night, holding her like a child and whispering in her ear, "Thank you, honey. I love you— you know that. I'll never look at another woman."

Monica, lying on her back, wide-eyed in the milky darkness, wished she'd done it for Bob. She wished she could turn into his shoulder and whisper, "I love you too, darling." But she couldn't. Giving Bessie back to Cass this time was worse than it had been thirteen years ago. Then she hadn't looked at the baby's face; it had been an anonymous creature. Now it was Bessie. Had she done it for Bessie's sake? Or for Carol's? She did not know.

Long after Bob was asleep, she went on staring. Around four o'clock she heard Jim go across the yard to the cowsheds to start the milking machine. The whole ethos of the farm emphasised her own barrenness; she felt herself shrivelling and drying. Surely there was supposed to be some sort of satisfaction gained from making a sacrifice? She searched her soul for an atom of satisfaction, and could find none.

■

Carol met them both at Marseilles. Monica's phone call had been enigmatic to say the least, and until she saw them walking across the tarmac together she did not let herself believe that they were both all right, that they were both being returned to her.

It was obvious they knew each other intuitively. On the long double flight back to France they had not talked of their pasts at all; it seemed from Bessie's usual insouciant chatter that she had questioned Jean-Claude in detail about the techniques of his job.

"Boris wants to be a photographer, you see," she explained to them both.

She had chosen to sit in the back of the Renault, and Jean-Claude then chose to sit by her. There was no embarrassment or awkwardness between them; Carol could hardly believe it. If it had been anyone else, she might even have felt excluded. But Bessie hung over the passenger seat, explaining, turning to Jean-Claude for corroboration now and then, making the events of the last two days sound almost normal.

Carol drove out of the city and followed the north bank of the Rhône into the country. She glanced in the mirror and saw Jean-Claude sitting relaxed and smiling, directly behind her. That was incredible in itself. She had said goodbye to him only a week ago, trying to blot out the insidious feeling that she would never see him again. Her mother had returned home, and in the relief of having her back at the Bergerie, Carol had wept and said, "I know he will be killed, Mother. I feel it. I'm not meant to have a normal life with him. I'm sorry . . . I can't help it . . ."

And here he was. And with Bessie. The impossible had happened. When she was a child herself, she might have prayed for this. "Please God let Bessie and Jean be friends. Let them meet in America and come home together safely." As an adult, it would have seemed a ridiculous request. Yet it had happened.

Jean-Claude said, "Why are you smiling, Cass? Do you think Bessie is exaggerating? I can assure you that Providence had a hand in what happened. It is as she says—the march in Central Park reminded her of me—the friendly policeman talking to the woman with the dog—"

"Oh, I agree!" Carol shifted her head so that her reflected smile could include both of them. "Actually I was just thinking that God must have read my mind. I didn't like to bother Him with such a big thing. But He knew what I wanted and . . . here you are!"

They all laughed. It was, after all, nothing short of miraculous.

At the Bergerie, Mary Woodford waited for them. If she had any qualms about the direction their lives were taking, she hid them well. When Jean-Claude shook her hand solemnly, Bessie sprang between them and hugged her with her usual thoroughness. And as she did so, she whispered in her ear, "Give him a kiss, Grannie. He wants so much for you to love him."

For a startled moment, Mary stared at the child. Like Cass, she could hardly believe that this instant relationship was real. Bessie, for all her good intentions, had been guarded about the advent of Carol's "friend." She had been ripe for a good old-fashioned bout of jealousy. What had happened in America?

But Mary could not refuse the urgent request.

She looked at the clever dark eyes of the man who had swept Cass completely off her feet, and gave a rueful laugh.

"Oh . . . come here!" She held his face in her hands and felt the strong jawbone, tense beneath her fingers. "I've never had a son," she said with a little break in her voice. "I think we should do more than shake hands though."

He was overwhelmed. Mary knew all about the strong sexual attraction that could batter down all barriers, and she had been terrified that Carol had been "smitten" by such an attraction. But in his delighted smile and the sudden release of the tension in him, she saw the likeableness of the man.

Carol lugged in the last case and said disgustedly, "Thank you for all your help."

And again, everyone laughed.

II

At the end of January, Myrtle went into a nursing home near Pittsville pump rooms, and gave birth to another boy on February 1st.

It was an easy birth; the baby was perfect, a carbon copy of Nicholas and Martin, who had both been ridiculously like Malcolm. Myrtle looked at him lying in the webbed canvas cot, and felt nothing at all.

But Malcolm was thrilled.

"What shall we call him, darling?"

He was always thrilled by babies, it was one of his endearing qualities. He seemed to have forgotten Mallie. He hung over the monkey-like scrap dotingly, offering his finger and searching the crumpled features for likenesses to himself.

"I don't know. Not Malcolm."

"Of course not, baby. We can't replace Mallie. But this . . . . this is a chance to start again, Myrt. Can't we start again now?" He looked up at her from where he knelt by the cot. His eyes pleaded.

He wanted the excitement again: the running battle of marriage which had been so sadly absent since last August. Myrtle never brought tea into the treatment room any more; she couldn't care less if he made love to every patient he had, male or female.

She said, "I suppose we've got to." She tried to smile at him. "It's just that I'm so tired, Malcolm. That's all."

"We'll take a holiday this summer, honey. Look up our old friends in Bournemouth. Good hotel. Sit on the beach."

"We haven't got any friends in Bournemouth any more, Malcolm. I never had time to write . . . keep in touch. Anyway there was no-one we wanted to keep in touch with."

"Well, we'll have a holiday somewhere, darling. You deserve a rest."

"A rest? With Nicky and Martin and this new baby?"

"Just the two of us, then. We could get a nanny. How about going to France to see Cass?"

She said half-heartedly, "Perhaps I'd be better going somewhere alone. I'm not good company at the moment."

He looked at her steadily in a way that in the old days would have made her melt. "You'd trust me with a nanny? Those white overalls? Those caps? You know what I'm like."

She couldn't make more of an effort. "In any case, Malcolm, Cass is fully occupied at the moment. She doesn't want us barging in on her little love-nest."

There was a deadening effect in her complete lack of interest; he wished he could generate one of their old-style rows. But the doctor had bandied words like "post-natal depression," and he knew he had to be very, very gentle with her.

He said pacifically, "All right. We'll see, this summer." He returned to the baby. "God, he's lovely, Myrt. You're a bloody clever girl. In fact we're a bloody clever pair, aren't we?"

Her eyes clouded. She was thinking of Mallie.

He went on quickly, "Come on. Let's think of a name. What about Ivan after your father? Or Chester after mine?"

"Whichever you like."

"Well, Chester is my name too of course. And he's the spitting image of me." He smiled. "Christ, Myrt. This is what immortality is all about. All these boys. God, it makes me feel randy. I love you, Myrt."

She said definitely, "I'm not having any more. That's final, Malcolm. I mean it."

"All right, bunny rabbit. All right." He smiled. She'd change her mind. It had always been Myrtle who wanted the babies. Always.

The nurses thought Chester was simply hilarious for such a tiny baby, and they simply shortened their own "Baby Lennox" to "Lennie." And Lennie he became.

Myrtle called him nothing. She knew there was something wrong with her, but she did not know what to do about it. She told herself that when she got home everything would start to be all right again. But she dreaded going home. The tall house in Imperial Gardens was so empty without Mallie. When they'd returned from Barnt Green last August it had looked messy and old after Liv's suburban luxury; the kitchen was so dark, her bedroom—where she spent a lot of time—was so cold. She couldn't go back to Liv's because of Reggie; Monica was trying to get her marriage back on its feet in far-away New York; Carol had, of course, made a newly structured and blissful family with the addition of the boyfriend. Myrtle was completely and utterly alone.

On bonfire night she stood in the long narrow garden with the boys and watched while Malcolm and Tom let off the fireworks, and in an effort to feel something, she took a burnt-out sparkler from Nicky and held it in her bare hand where the end still glowed redly. She dropped it very quickly, but she did not scream and it was much later that Malcolm discovered the blistered hand and dressed it.

She had hoped that after the shock of Mallie's death, she would miscarry. The thought had been in her mind during the long walk with the girls to find the Haunted House. But her short sturdy body had a strength of its own beyond her will. She continued to expand; her legs continued to swell; she even had obsessive eating fads. She craved Worcester sauce on everything, but when Doris brought some from the Maypole Dairy, she no longer wanted it.

She never complained, but Malcolm still said, "It'll be all right once the baby is born, bunny rabbit. Don't worry, it'll be all right." Whether he was comforting her or himself was a moot point. One night when again she turned from him, he asked sadly, "Don't you love me any more, Myrtle?"

She replied automatically, "Of course I love you. I'm just so tired, that's all."

But how could she know whether she loved him when she had no feelings left?

She would have liked to have seen the girls; she knew that much. When they'd been together on that walk, just the four of them, she had almost forgotten Mallie. She had felt normal; she had been a human being with her feet on Mother Earth.

Carol wrote to her:

Have you heard from Monica? Bessie's visit to New York was cut short and she came back to France with Jean-Claude. I think you will like Jean, Myrt. In fact I pray you will like him, because if he can get a divorce we shall be married. Has that shocked you?

It did shock Myrtle. It removed Cass in some way: she was no longer the property of the girls. If Cass was going to marry a man, it meant she was wholeheartedly in love with him. And it was obvious that Liv, Mon, and Myrtle herself, were no longer wholeheartedly in love with their husbands.

She sat on the edge of her bed and tore the letter up into postage-stamp pieces. They stayed on the floor until Doris vacuumed a week later.

The day she went home with Baby Lennox, it was snowing. She sat in the big front room and watched Doris taking the boys across the pristine expanse of the Gardens to a birthday party at the Queens Hotel. It was going to be a posh affair and Doris had bought them minuscule suits and white shirts with attached bow ties. They had come into the front room where she sat by Lennie's cot, and showed themselves off smirkingly. Nicky had grown up suddenly; he no longer bedevilled Martin, they were quite good friends.

"You look beautiful," she said as if by rote.

Nicky made a terrible face. "Boys don't look beautiful, Mummy. We look handsome."

"All right. Handsome." Before last summer she would have grinned at that.

"Say goodbye to Mummy and Lennie," Doris prompted. "Goodbye Mummy. Goodbye Lennie," parroted Martin.

Nicky dragged him over to the cot and insisted they went through the usual performance.

"Bye bye then, baby," Nicky cooed in perfect imitation of his father. "Be a good boy while we're gone."

Martin said more naturally, "I'll teach you to play football next week, Lennie."

They planted dry boy-kisses on Myrtle's cheeks and went into the hall to be booted and capped. Myrtle whispered, "They're lovely kids. I love them. I must love them."

They pretended to skate on the slushy snow, then turned and waved at the window, though they did not know whether she was there or not.

Malcolm's head came round the door.

"Did you see the boys? I waved a towel from the treatment room and they must have seen me and waved back. We've been doing that while you were away. I'm going to teach them semaphore."

He was gone. She almost smiled. The boys hadn't been waving at her, or clowning for her. They could live without her just as she could live without them. Which was good.

Malcolm reappeared with tea and told her he had a long appointment so wouldn't see her for a while.

"Will you be all right, bunny rabbit?"

"Of course."

He crouched before her chair. "Why don't you try to feed Lennie yourself, Myrtle? You had so much milk for the others, there must be something there. And it would help you to begin to feel like a . . . mother."

"I'd rather not."

He sighed. "All right." He went on giving her one of his looks. Her eyes slid away from his. He said, "Not long ago it would have been you bringing *me* tea. Right into the treatment room. Keeping your predatory eye on me, bunny rabbit!"

She said nothing. He whispered, "Aren't you worried about what I might be getting up to in the next hour?"

There was a pause. Then she said, "No."

The monosyllable was objective, passionless. She did not mean that she trusted him for the next hour. Simply that she did not care. He almost recoiled. He wanted to shout at her, call her names, tell her that it was Mrs. Herron he was seeing. But it would make no difference.

He stood up, and, like the boys, gave her a chaste kiss on her cheek. Then he left.

After a while the baby started to whimper. She unwrapped the bottle from its clean nappy and shoved the teat in his mouth. He sucked until the teat turned inside-out, then started to cry again.

She pulled out the teat, put the bottle back, moved closer to the fire. Ten minutes later, the crying began again. She let it go on for a while then looked into the cot. The bottle was empty, the baby had wind. If it went on crying, Malcolm would come to investigate. But she did not want to pick it up to wind it. Instead, she picked up the discarded nappy and folded it into a thick six-inch pad. Carefully she put it over the baby's face and went to the window. The cries went on, but they were muffled.

A car drew up outside the front door right behind Mrs. Herron's. She looked at it incuriously. It was vaguely familiar. It drove away again, chugged slowly up the road as if looking for an address, then turned at the top to go down the back lane where the mews had been turned into garages.

The baby's cries grew louder. It had turned its head away from the nappy. She went back and looked down on it. It was not a bit like Mallie. She wondered who was looking after Mallie now. She didn't want to replace Mallie. She took the nappy pad and put it on the baby's face, and pressed gently.

The door opened. Someone came in, tentatively at first then with a rush. Myrtle was pulled backwards, the nappy fell to the floor. The baby cried in earnest. Myrtle flailed her arms against the sort of thick camel coat beloved by all auctioneers, and then said in amazement, "Reggie!" And Reggie, almost weeping, said, "Oh, my darling. My darling girl. What has happened to you?" and held her to him in a hug that could not be resisted; a hug that was as cold as the snow outside and as warm as that summer's day when they had first made love.

He did not know she was dead inside. He kissed her repeatedly, her eyes, her ears, her mouth. He smoothed her rough, frizzy hair, and buried his face in her neck.

She said, "Reggie. Reggie . . ." but it was not a protest, more a murmur of continuing surprise.

He said, "I saw you standing by the window. I thought you knew it was me. I went round the back so that Malcolm wouldn't see me. Oh, my darling. I couldn't keep away. I love you so much. I've missed you so much. I think of you all the time. I think of Mallie. I blame myself, darling. It was my fault. If we hadn't been together that afternoon, you would have been with Mallie. I've tried to keep away, but . . ." he broke down and sobbed tearingly.

She heard herself telling him it wasn't his fault. She felt her arms pushing him into a chair and cradling his heaving shoulders. She actually kissed the top of his head and smelled the familiar smell of his hair. She was transported back to that time, that wonderful time, when she had managed to free herself from Malcolm and love someone else. When Mallie had been alive.

She whispered, "Perhaps we were both to blame, my dearest. Perhaps we're both guilty." And she began to cry.

It was Reggie who eventually dealt with the baby. The cries were filtering through the house and he knew someone must come soon. He lowered the crumpled Myrtle to the hearthrug and let her rest her head on the chair; now she had started to weep she could not stop. He picked up the child and hung it over his shoulder. Immediately it gave an almighty burp and a trickle of milk went down his overcoat. He cradled it in his big hands. The sudden silence was bliss. Myrtle breathed sobbingly and closed her eyes.

"He's lovely, Myrt. What's his name?"

She did not answer immediately, then she remembered.

"Chester."

"Ah. Malcolm's family name."

"Yes." She opened her eyes and looked at him. "He's Malcolm's. Nicky and Martin are Malcolm's too. Mallie was mine."

"Malcolm loved Mallie. He's terribly grieved . . . that day at home . . . I didn't know what to do with him."

"He's got the others. And his women."

"Oh, Myrtle."

"I don't mind. I'm glad in a way." She went on looking at him. She hadn't really looked at anyone for a long time. She said, "I haven't been with him since . . . then."

He swallowed visibly. Then he stood up and put Lennie back in his cot. He said, "I haven't been with Liv either."

She said with some of her old realistic cheerfulness, "We shall get over it, Reggie. We shall have to."

"We don't have to." He sat down again and looked at her sitting on the floor, her arms on the chair. She was looking so ill, white as a ghost, her body beneath the awful jumper and skirt was flabby and loose. "Myrtle. Why were you trying to suffocate Chester just now?"

"I don't know. Perhaps I'm going mad."

"You're not going mad. You're the sanest person I know. Don't you love him?"

"No. I didn't want him after Mallie died." She puffed a laugh. "I tried to get Mon to take him. I tried to have a miss."

"Why?" he asked again.

"Don't know. Because after Mallie, everything is different. And this baby is forcing me to go back to how I was. And I'm different. But now I've got to stay and look after it. I've got to sleep with Malcolm. I've got to take Nicky and Martin to school, and give dinner parties, and . . ." She stopped and looked at the cot. The baby was asleep. "I suppose I thought that without him I could go away. Stay with Cass. Or Mon. I don't know, Reggie. I don't know."

He said in a low voice, "Will you come away with me, Myrtle?"

That really did shock her. Her head came up and her grey eyes were wide.

"With you? What about Liv? What about having a family? I don't want any more children, Reggie."

"Liv and I—we're nothing any more. I'd have to tell her, of course. But I'd go. Whatever she said."

She went on staring, not moving.

"You fell for me first because of the kids. Because I was pregnant. You know you did."

"Okay. I admit it. But now . . . I can't think of anything else. Anyone else." He put out a hand. "Come with me, darling. I'll get a job somewhere else. We won't have much but we'll be together."

"Oh, Reggie." She drooped. "I can't. I haven't got the energy to feed the baby, let alone pack up and leave my husband. And I couldn't do it to Liv."

"You did it to Liv before when you realised she was here with Malcolm. Nothing has changed."

"I can't, Reggie. I *can't!*" She started to cry again with a new kind of despair.

He knelt and took her in his arms again. She thought he would "do a Malcolm" and try to seduce her with repeated kisses and his hands on her body. But he did none of those things. He cradled her as he had cradled the baby, making soothing noises into her hair and rocking her gently. When she was still again, he put her in the chair, found a rug and tucked it under her knees. He looked at the untouched tea tray on the table.

"I'm going to make some fresh tea, my love. Then I'll announce my arrival, in the treatment room. Everything is all right. Perfectly all right. What I have said is what I mean—what I want. But I'll not say it again. You can put it away from you. We will be friends. I am your friend, Myrtle. Remember that."

He did not wait for a reply. When the door closed behind him, she looked at it and knew that he was a good man. He was the sort of man she needed—and before her, her mother had needed. She put her hands to her face and wept again. But this time her tears were not for Mallie.

Perhaps nothing would have come of it if Liv hadn't forced the issue. The winter had seemed unbearably long to her and her old routine did not fill her days. The golf course had been under snow most of the time and anyway she wasn't that keen on the game, it was really the social life and the status she went for. She spent a lot of time with her parents, but the constant round of bazaars, whist drives, and jumble sales, which were bound up with chapel life, no longer appealed. Her parents still had rigid standards of behaviour which at times had little to do with Christianity and more with keeping up with the Joneses. Mrs. Baker noted religiously how often the minister's wife washed her curtain nets, and Mr. Baker kept his front lawn shaven and knife-edged like a bowling green for the sake of his public image. Laundry and lawn-cutting gave neither of them any personal pleasure.

Her mother was appalled at what Myrtle's children had done to the carpets at the Barnt Green house.

"You should have them steam-cleaned properly, Liv," she said, down on her hands and knees shifting the pile with a manicured finger. She looked up suddenly, a smile dawning. "Or you are planning to get new carpets out of Reggie?"

Liv, who would indeed have planned just that at one time, stared down at the revealed stain without interest.

"Of course not, Mother. That was a top quality carpet. It'll last out my marriage."

Mrs. Baker was seriously shocked. She sat up on the armchair, wide-eyed.

"My dear girl, no carpet is intended to last out a lifetime!"

Liv nearly said, "Who's talking about a lifetime?" But she stopped herself in time; she had no wish to deal with a fit of hysterics from her mother.

"I don't want new carpets, Mother," she said definitely, closing the subject.

So the house wasn't using up her slack as it always had in the past. As for Reggie, he might as well have moved out of his body. The body came home, was fed and watered, clothed and cleaned, but the man himself was somewhere else. He replied to her questions, he poured drinks for guests, he worked in the garden at weekends, he even accompanied her to chapel on Sunday evenings, but beyond smiling vaguely, he did not respond to her on a personal level at all. She tried to break through to him by what she considered cheap, erotic methods. In other words she bought one of the new shortie see-through nighties and dabbed Chanel No. 5 behind her ears before she went to bed.

Perhaps she did get a response, though it was not the one she wanted: two days later Reggie complained of a sore throat and suggested he should move into the spare room. It was the room where Myrtle and the boys had slept. Liv could not obliterate that particular memory any more. She had not contacted Myrtle since last summer, and when the news of Lennie's birth had come through she had sent her flowers and a card but no message. Somehow she had managed to hold on to the memory of Myrtle on the walk: the old Myrtle, pregnant and scruffy and down-to-earth with no pretensions at all. But when she took Reggie's clean shirts into that room, she saw again the fertile naked Myrtle. And then her own husband scrambling off the bed.

One Wednesday afternoon in May when an icy wind blew across the Lickeys and boredom hung tangibly in the shining house, the phone rang. Liv dived for it, delighted that someone was disturbing her "afternoon rest." If it was her mother she'd suggest coming down to Northfield and going to the cinema. They were showing an old film of John Wayne's called *Red River.* Liv felt like fantasising.

It was Ron Jameson, one of the clerks at the office.

"Just ringing to see if Mr. Bradley could cover a farm sale tomorrow, Mrs. Bradley. Copse Elms out at Bitton."

Obviously Reggie must be out at a sale. Liv had asked him what he was doing that day, and he had mumbled a reply which she hadn't heard.

"I should think so. You'll see him before I do though. I'm going to the cinema so I won't be around when he gets home."

"Oh, sorry. But he won't be coming into the office tonight as it's his golfing day. Perhaps you could leave him a message."

Liv was rocked back on her heels. Reggie's golfing day? Did he have a regular golfing day? Her pride would not let her enquire further.

"Of course," she said.

She did not go to the cinema. She waited for him to come home, planning what she would say, discarding plans then remaking them. Sometimes she hated him with a fierce hatred because he was hurting her pride so much. At other times she felt something much deeper, a keen sense of loss, of aloneness, of standing on the edge of eternity. It did not really matter where he went on Wednesdays. What mattered was that he had a life which did not include her. She was going to scream at him, shake him if necessary, make him see her again.

But when he came in at seven o'clock, he did not look like a man who had had a good day out. His face was grey with tiredness and she saw suddenly how much he had aged in the past year. She was concerned enough to feed him first and wait for the explosive row that would make or break their marriage.

But apparently not even her cooking was good enough now. She had poached a Severn salmon and scraped a pound of tiny new potatoes. He ate perhaps half a dozen mouthfuls and pushed his plate to one side.

"Delicious," he murmured. "Shall we go in the other room and see if there's anything on the box?"

"I've done rhubarb fool," she commented without emphasis.

He said in the same tone, "Jolly good." And made for the door.

She followed him into the lounge, went to the socket in the wall, and removed the television plug. Then she faced him.

"I want to know where you've been, Reggie. Shall we sit down or stand?"

Her action and words got through. He looked startled for a moment, then almost relieved. He took a deep breath.

"Let's sit down, Liv. Let's sit down."

They both sat. He leaned forward, elbows on knees; she sat determinedly back as if she was relaxed, fidgeting slightly with a cushion, then forcing herself to be still.

He said slowly, "Liv, I can't go on like this." He glanced up at her then looked again at the floor. "And I imagine neither can you. Shall we call it a day?"

Now that it had come—and from him, not her—she was appalled. She could have gone on; she was quite good at blotting out unpleasant thoughts. She'd had practice.

She left her first question and asked another. "What was wrong with supper, I'd like to know? That was fresh salmon. I got it from Prewett's."

"I had chips, Liv. With Nicky and Martin."

"Chips? D'you call that a meal?" Her mouth was dry; she tried to swallow and nearly choked.

"There were a lot of them. We had salt and vinegar and bread and butter, and a great deal of tomato sauce."

When she said nothing he looked up again. She was so pretty with her curly hair and big eyes.

He said in a low voice, "That's where I go every Wednesday, Liv. To see Myrtle. She's ill and I know you won't go to see her, so I go."

It was something to hang on to. "You go in my place, d'you mean? Well, I didn't know she was ill, did I? You've never said. I'll go next week if you like. I thought she'd had enough of us. After Mallie."

He nodded. "Perhaps she has. But I can't keep away. You must know I love her, Liv. She is the only thing that matters in my life now. I'm sorry. I can't do anything about it. I tried. I didn't go to see her until after the baby. Then Malcolm told me how ill she was, and I was terrified she might die, and I'd never see her again. So I started—"

She said sharply, "Shut *up!* Can't you see you're making it worse? She's married to Malcolm and they have three sons! You're married to me. For better or worse—remember? We've got to put up with it and you're making the worse worse!" The odd syntax gave her words a biblical sound. She tried to get out of the chair so that she could switch on the television and pour a drink, but her strength had gone. She sobbed suddenly, "We'll have a baby if that's what you want! All this ridiculous nonsense just because you want a family—"

He interrupted sternly. "It might have been that at one time. It's not any longer. Myrtle does not want any more children, but if she'd come away with me I would look after her for the rest of my life and ask nothing more!"

She cried out with the pain of such complete rejection. Then, at last, bitter anger came to her rescue.

"You swine!" she yelled. "You filthy swine! Under our own

roof! Don't think I don't know what went on! Here—in my lovely house . . . oh my God . . . when I think—" She sprang up and paced the floor like an animal.

He said, "I'm glad. Glad you can talk about it at last, Liv. Because now I can tell you why it happened. Oh, I'm not trying to shift any blame—Myrtle and I were fully responsible for our own actions. But she wouldn't have let it go further . . . she knew how I felt that day and she would have stopped it for your sake. But then she rang Malcolm and heard your voice. And that was that."

She wailed aloud again with a new pain.

"I didn't do anything—you must believe me! Nothing happened that day! Ask Monica—she arrived—she will tell you . . ." She collapsed into the chair again and bowed her head to the arm. "I knew something was wrong when I came home. I knew you were angry with me—"

"I was not angry, Liv."

"I admit that I intended to—to—flirt with him a little. That was all. He's got a reputation and I was curious and fed up with Myrtle and the kids . . . but when he got serious, I couldn't bear it. I ran off and Monica came . . . ask her. Ask Monica if you don't believe me!"

He watched her for a long moment, then said tiredly, "Liv, of course I believe you. All I can say is . . . I'm sorry."

"Sorry I wasn't seduced by your best friend, d'you mean?"

"No. Sorry Myrtle got the wrong end of the stick." He sighed. "Oh, Liv. If we're being really truthful, then that was a lie. I'm not sorry. I want to belong to Myrtle. How that was brought about does not matter."

She lifted a tearstained face.

"But Myrtle belongs to Malcolm!"

"No. She did. Even when we made love she belonged to Malcolm. But she doesn't now. She is in a no-man's-land now, belonging to no-one, not even herself. When she comes out of that land, I want to be there."

"But nothing can come of it, Reggie! Don't you see? Myrtle has three children—you can't take them away from Malcolm, and she won't leave them!"

"Maybe not. I'm not so certain. Myrtle has never been her own woman. She could be that with me."

"Reggie, you can't do this! Deliberately lure away your best friend's wife! It's not in you to do such a terrible thing."

"You don't know me. I did not know myself until I began to love Myrtle. I would do anything for her. If she doesn't want me, then I will never see her again. But if she does . . ." he looked at her directly. "Liv. When I went to see her first—after the baby was born last February—I quite seriously considered killing Malcolm. If there had been a way—"

"Be quiet!" She put a hand over her eyes. "I don't want to hear this!"

He obeyed her and for a long two minutes there was silence in the room, broken by Liv's breathing.

Then slowly she put a hand on each of the chair arms and levered herself back until her head was supported. She kept her eyes closed.

"So. What do we do?"

"I don't know. I know what I do. I don't know what we do."

"All right then. What are you going to do?"

"I'm going to keep on visiting Myrtle. Until she's better. Then I'm going to try to persuade her to come away with me."

"Have you had any thoughts about me?" Her voice was suddenly bitingly sarcastic, and in spite of his professed indifference he flushed.

"Of course. We've been married for seven years. I shall sell my share of the business. You'll have half. And the house of course."

"Of course. Of course. Of course." She was trembling on the edge of hysteria again and made a visible effort to control herself. "Perhaps I should go and live with Malcolm. Do a complete changeover."

"Is that what you want?"

She thought of the culmination of that ridiculous day in Cheltenham last summer, and shuddered. "No."

"You'll have enough money to stay on here. Nothing need change for you. You'll marry again."

"Stay on here? Mummy and Daddy would die of shame! I'd have to leave the golf club! I couldn't face anyone in the village!"

"Perhaps you could have a holiday with Carol."

"Play gooseberry, you mean? Thank you again."

"Liv, we're finished. Before Myrtle we didn't have much. Be honest. But if Myrtle sends me away and you want what is left—"

"Oh my *God!*" She leapt from the chair and threw herself at him.

Her nails scored red blood down his face. "You condescending, patronising . . . !" she screamed. "D'you think I'll stay here another minute now?" He held her off, at last thrown from the single track that he had made for himself all these months. She shouted and spat in his face. Words emerged somehow. ". . . hate you . . . hate Myrtle . . . we were friends . . . we had something—loyalty—you've taken that . . . she's a bitch . . . permanent heat . . ." He removed his right hand from her flailing arm and hit her across the face. They both collapsed on to the maltreated carpet.

"Liv, I'm sorry. I'm sorry."

But he had cured the hysteria, and she said almost sadly, "This is the end then. This really is the end."

Monica was delighted to see her. Hildie had had her new baby and did not go far from the Connecticut farm these days. Monica and Bob had joined a select club which offered everything from riding to poker, with people who had either money or breeding. Bob loved it. He loved some of the women he played tennis with, and he loved to see Monica attracting the men she swam with. Monica hated it.

Somehow she was in a worse position than she'd been before she left for England. Bob was treating her like a prized possession, or—which was worse—as if she might have a nervous breakdown at any minute. She had given Bessie back to Cass and she was missing her friends and what she privately thought of as a "real life." Mallie's tragic death had cut through so much superficial rubbish: they had all shared Myrtle's grief, and from this distance and in retrospect her two months back home seemed like the real ale beneath the froth. It might have been bitter, but it had some kind of meaning, some kind of purpose.

She did not write letters, but she heard from Carol occasionally and sent Myrtle a card when the new baby was born. Liv's request was like a shaft of light. She cabled back "Come. Stay long time." She got Mrs. Warren, the latest in helps, hopeless and helpless, to prettify the guest room with flowers and a new lace bedcover and bows on the pillows. It was sentimental and sickening but, remembering the house at Barnt Green, it would please Liv.

It became immediately obvious that Liv was not going to notice flowers or bows. She was like a coiled spring, tense yet on the point of collapse. The exclusiveness of Beekman Place was lost on her. They did the usual sightseeing trips and as she gazed up at the tops of the canyon buildings, she murmured, "It's a foreign country. I hadn't realised that. It's a foreign country, and I'm a foreigner."

Monica said, "The Americans don't want you to feel that, Liv. Bob's family and friends made me one of them immediately. I don't think I've ever felt a foreigner." She purposely did not recall last year when she had been ill; nor the month after Bessie's departure.

But Liv shook her head. "I don't mean America. I just mean . . . it brought it home to me."

"Brought what home, Liv?" Monica felt a sharp concern for her friend. The big baby eyes were not just tired any more, they were frightened.

"Oh. Nothing." Liv laughed suddenly. "Actually, I've got quite a lot of money. Shall we go and buy something?"

"Darling. Why not? There's a pink cocktail dress in a little place down here. It's ballerina length—and pink was always your colour. If you like it, I'll give a party especially for you to show it off."

It was hard to know whether Liv liked the dress or not, but she bought it and Monica hired caterers and gave a select little dinner party and got tickets for a concert featuring the Russian violinist who had recently defected. Hildie and George came; one of Bob's colleagues who was divorced; a couple from the club called Rosa and Jerry Palmer. Bob asked them. Bob admitted he was "making a play for" Rosa. It sounded so innocent: making a play. And in a way it was just a game to Bob. But Monica knew what he meant; she knew they would end up in bed together.

But that evening at any rate, the Palmers were still a happily married couple. They hardly left Liv's side. And they couldn't stop touching her; first they kissed her in turn, then they escorted her to the window so that she could show them the view. They both put their arms across her shoulders and kept their heads close to hers. The pink dress made her feel like a stick of candy floss, and she wondered whether they might take a bite out of her at any minute.

Jerry Palmer said, "And what do you think of our little city, Liv?"

She said truthfully, "It's what I've dreamed of all my life." And she should have added, "And I'm still dreaming it because it can't be real."

She was very popular with everyone. Her girlish prettiness captivated the women as well as the men. Hildie thought she was innocent and charming. Danny Connell, the divorced man, sat next to her in the theatre box and took her hand. It didn't worry her too much, she was wearing gloves.

"You're making me feel alive again," he said when the orchestra were tuning up. "Ever since Margaret left me, I've been half dead. No-one has wanted to listen. You've listened."

She felt a twinge of surprise. Had she listened? She certainly had not heard. But this attention was good for her damaged pride. She smiled into the darkness and allowed her hand to be kept while the young Russian bowed deeply and took his place close to the conductor. Monica whispered, "He looks so bewildered, poor man." Liv nodded.

Reggie took a room in the Bath Road, drove to Cheltenham after work, and visited Myrtle every evening. Malcolm's ego took this as a personal compliment.

"It's good of you, old man. Oh, I know with Liv in America you're at a loose end, but to come down and keep an eye on us . . . it's what friendship is all about."

Reggie's concern for Myrtle did not allow guilt feelings. He said, "I think she's getting better. Don't you?"

"She's not ill, old man. Just a bit twitchy after all that's happened. She should have fed Lennie. It's taking a long time for her to feel maternal again."

"I don't think she wants Lennie."

"Not want her own baby? You don't know anything about mothers, Reggie!" Malcolm tried to laugh. "What would you suggest? We drown the poor little devil?"

Reggie said, "She could do with getting away from the children. Haven't you noticed how she avoids them if she can?"

Malcolm, who had just picked up Nicky and Martin from school, helped them to change into cricketing gear, then driven them out to Dean Close for a match, downed his early drink violently.

"Of course I've bloody well noticed!"

He coughed explosively and grabbed his decent handkerchief from his breast pocket. Reggie beat his back.

"Sorry, old man." Malcolm looked up, eyes streaming. "It's just that there's nothing to be done. I've tried. Don't think I haven't tried. I wanted her to come up to you and Liv. She wouldn't have that at any price." He wiped his eyes. "Have they had a row or something?"

"Not that I know of. But come on, old man. Barnt Green is where Mallie died."

Malcolm flinched visibly.

"Yes. But I suggested she and Liv went away together. Bournemouth. Or somewhere. Anyway, now Liv's in Yankeeland. And Carol is too occupied with lover-boy apparently. I don't know. Her mother would go with her. Or Boris. But no."

Reggie said, "If I could persuade her to go away, would you agree to it?"

"Haven't I just been saying—"

"With me."

"With *you?*" Malcolm stopped pouring himself another drink and turned. "With you? What the hell's going on, Reggie, for Christ's sake?"

"You've heard the Royals are giving one of their places on the north-east coast to the National Trust? Hardfanger Castle? We requested permission to catalogue the books—the firm, I mean. They've got original stuff from Lindisfarne stored there. It's a big job. Four firms are involved."

"Well. Congratulations, old man. What the hell has that got to do with Myrtle?"

"It's a wonderful castle, for God's sake. No-one has seen its treasures. She could come with me whenever she felt like it. Other days she could explore the country—my car will be there."

"Well . . ." Malcolm finished pouring the drink. "Sorry, old man, but all I can say is, big deal. The north-east coast even in the summer doesn't sound exactly the kind of thing I had in mind for my wife!"

"It's within an hour's drive of Alnwick. Berwick-on-Tweed. Holy Island. Hadrian's Wall. We're taking over most of a hotel at Alnmouth."

"Okay, okay." Malcolm took his drink more slowly this time. "I've got to get back into the treatment room. Two evening patients." He sighed. "Look Reggie, I don't want to hurt your feelings. It's a great thought. But she needs another woman. You know how they are. Symptoms. Knitting. Babies."

"May I put it to her while you're working?"

"Well, if you . . . Sure. Okay. I suppose. But don't push her, old man. I'm not having her pushed."

"I won't push her."

But he had to talk to her for a long time. She laughed at him at first. Sometimes he could make her laugh.

"Don't be silly, Reggie. I can't walk out on Nicky and Martin. Malcolm wouldn't let me go anyway."

"He says he will. And Nicky and Martin don't need you. They've got Doris." Neither of them mentioned Lennie.

"Darling Reggie. You're so kind. But it's no good. Can't you see that? I'm not the Myrtle you fell for. I'm completely changed. I couldn't sleep with you."

He wanted desperately to pick her up and hold her again, but since that visit in February he had not touched her.

He said, "I told you ages ago we would be friends—just friends. I meant that, Myrtle." He stood up and began to pick up the newspapers littering the chairs and floor. "You need a holiday away from the family. You need not see me in the day at all. The beach at Alnmouth is wonderful, the sand is white and the waves churn in like trains." He began to tell her about Hardfanger and the Farne Islands and the glories of Hadrian's Wall. When he paused and looked at her she was smiling.

"You're very like Liv," she said. "A place for everything, and everything in its place."

He felt a terrible pang of disappointment; she hadn't heard a word he'd said.

But then she said, "I'd like to come with you very much, Reggie. Thank you for asking me."

He was so happy he almost cried. All right, it was just a holiday for her, but it was also the thin edge of the wedge. He would make her well again. Then he would woo her. He almost ran across the room to kiss her. But he managed to hold back.

"Thank *you*, Myrtle. I'm sure you won't regret it."

He would have been very surprised if he could have seen the letter she posted to Monica, care of Dilly Gosling, the next day. It was brief.

My dear Mon, d'you remember I said you could have my new baby. Do you want him? He weighs sixteen pounds, which is really

235

too heavy, but he is bottle-fed and that puts on weight. He is very healthy and Doris looks after him most of the time. I am going away with Reggie. It is just for a holiday until I get better, but I don't think I shall come back. I don't love Malcolm any more, and Nicky and Martin are like him. I don't know how you can work it, Mon dear, but you've not done too badly up till now. Love, Myrtle.

12

*B*oris was eighteen that summer. His National Service papers arrived the day before he left for his trek up the Victoire with Bessie. He had to report at Corsham in Wiltshire on 10th September.

His mother chose to take it as another tragedy.

"First Myrtle, now you," she wailed. "Just as you got that place at the art school! Everything is ruined!"

"Myrtle is having a holiday, Mother. That is all. And my art school place is being saved for me." He looked again at the railway pass. "I'm glad they've given me such long notice. I would have hated missing out on France again this year."

"You've always had a thing about Bessie Woodford. I hope it's natural, Boris. I've not got over last year when you wanted to become a monk. You are all *right,* I suppose?"

He said steadily, "It depends what you mean by all right. I hope I'm not like Father. Or Malcolm Lennox." The fact that he had not been with his sister or Bessie during the tragedy of Mallie's death had weighed heavily. He had been convinced during that winter that Myrtle was either dying or going mad, and Bessie's obvious happiness with the new situation in France had seemed like a rejection. His natural inclination to celibacy had persuaded him that the monastic life was for him.

Then at Christmas Bessie outlined one of her famous "plans." She told him that they might be able to get jobs together one day, he with his camera, and she with her drawing, and he had dropped the monastery idea like a stone. Bessie had said, "My favourite things at school are botany and art." Boris had dismissed the first. "Bots is boring. But art . . . and travelling the world together looking for unusual plants would be marvellous. But who would pay us?" "I'm working on that," she'd assured him.

He smiled at his mother, to take the sting out of his words. "Anyway, Bessie Woodford isn't on her own over there, you know. I thought you wanted me to bring you back news of the others?"

Mrs. Denning nodded. "Especially how Mary is coping with that very *vairy* tricky situation."

Boris had no intention of reporting back in detail, but he too nodded. Already he knew enough of the three Woodford women to guess that they would cope very well with the new situation.

Jean-Claude was an accepted part of the menage now. He travelled from Paris most weekends, and when he was on an overseas assignment he invariably flew home directly to Marseilles and was met by Cass or her mother.

Cass could never take his safety for granted. During the Paris riots—which he covered for *La Planète*—she was certain he would be killed. Although his old imperialist ideas had mellowed a long time ago, he was still publicly known for them, and could easily have been a target for the new liberalism sweeping France. When de Gaulle was returned to power and began to remodel the constitution, Jean-Claude wrote a leader in support of the new policy and was granted an interview with the President. As one of the war-time Free French, he managed to break through the stiff-necked reserve of the statesman.

Cass was partially reassured by this contact; as a supporter of de Gaulle he could no longer be seen as a threat. But, deep in her subconscious, there still lurked a belief that she must pay fate somehow for the unexpected gift of happiness which was so well and truly ensconced in the little shepherd's house in Provence. The fact that Bessie and her mother both loved Jean too crowned everything and made it perfect. Bessie, particularly, liked to get him to herself. "Jean, I've drawn the inside of an anemone. Would it do for a flower book, d'you think?" Carol realised the child was asking a professional for an opinion, but there was more to it than that. She saved special things for Jean: the first of the Northfield beans, the crop of tiny onions "for his soup," a poem she wrote about freedom. The immediate rapport she had felt for him in New York had ripened into love. Carol felt—physically—overflowing with this happiness. She told herself it was worth whatever price she might have to pay.

They used the same donkeys as before, and as Pierre did not come with them, the animals would remain this year and enjoy good mountain grazing.

"Let's hope we can stay yonks this time," Bessie said as she cut down one of the bean sticks for a staff. "We had to come back early last year because of that book you found, Jean!"

"I beg your pardon, Bessie," Jean said gravely. "But if it had not been for the book, I would not have seen Carol again. Which would have meant I would not have seen you. Or Mary." He grinned at Boris. "Or Boris."

Bessie nodded. "Or Aunt Mon. Or Aunt Hildie. Uncle George. Leo and Ossie . . . oh no, they were at camp."

Boris said, "Funny to think of all those people over there . . . funny that you know them, I mean."

Bessie said acutely, "Funny that I know them and you don't? But you know hundreds of people I've never seen, Borrie. And when you go into the Navy, you'll know thousands. I hate you going into the Navy. You'll be so . . . controlled. Not free any more."

He had said nothing about his call-up papers. "I hate me going too." He grinned at Bessie. "But at the moment I'm on my way up the Victoire. Which is wonderful!"

They reached the shepherd's hut and set about sweeping and fetching fresh hay for the palliasses. It was good to have the strength of the two men this year. Mary opened the shutters and went round with the Flit gun and left them to clean out the hearth and start a fire. She had worked out a menu for the whole of their two-week stay; if she could buy flour from the farm she intended making their own bread.

"Mother is in her element," Carol said to Jean as he fed kindling into the stove. "She feels she is turning the clock back when she gets away from her own kitchen. She says it reminds her of the war in the best possible way!"

Jean-Claude nodded. "Survival. In one way a challenge. In another . . . simplicity."

They smiled into each other's eyes. He did not touch her. He had made a point of not touching her at first in case it was an affront to Mary and Bessie. Now there was no need. Their union was absolute.

Bessie lost no time in taking Boris to the tiny climbers' hut which she and the Metier girls had discovered the previous year. It proved to be further than she remembered, and the knapsack of food which she had insisted on shouldering knocked awkwardly as she scrambled up the scree.

"Must have been in better shape last year," she panted, accepting Boris' hand at the top. "Now I'm in my teens I'm ageing!"

"Poor old thing," Boris commented. "Already decrepit. And what on earth have you got in that sack? It's all lumps and corners."

She flopped on to the grass plateau; it was as she remembered, like a box at the theatre.

"Well, food for a start. Grannie showed me how to make Cornish pasties yesterday, so I did four." She ignored his theatrical groan. "And my drawing stuff. And a paint pot."

As if reminded, he unhitched his camera and removed it carefully from its case. It was one of the new ones with a telescopic lens. He squinted through it, already seeing the enormous panorama in terms of photographs and frames.

Bessie coughed loudly. "I said 'and a paint pot.'"

"You're going to paint as well as draw?" he queried without lowering the camera.

"No. It's an empty paint pot."

She waited for his surprised eye to appear, and grinned smugly.

"Thought that would intrigue you. We're going to bury it. Right here. Or next to the hut. Anyway somewhere on this plateau."

He tried to retrieve his sang-froid.

"Before or after the Cornish pasties?"

"I could kill you!" But she was giggling. "Hasn't Aunt Myrt told you about the paint pot? It's like a family heirloom really. And it's sort of connected to my mother and your sister, so I asked Cass if I could bury it again on the mountain. And I wanted you to be in on it." She frowned. "It's not really like an heirloom. More like a symbol of eternal friendship."

"You sound like a schoolgirl comic. And what's this about your mother?"

She said flatly, "Carol is my mother. Didn't you know? Even Solange and Brigitte guessed, so I thought you probably knew from Jean-Claude, or your parents, or someone."

Boris stared at her for a long time without speaking.

She said, "Don't look like that. I know what you're thinking. I'm illegitimate. All that stuff. I'd rather be illegitimate a million times over and have Cass as my mother. Surely you can see that, Borrie? She and me—I—we're—we're blood sisters! All that love . . . it had to mean that we were from the same body. Yes?"

Her acquired Frenchness took him aback. He stammered, "Bess. Are you certain about this? Has Cass actually said—"

"Of course not!" She was impatient. "I don't want her to have to—to *confess*—nothing like that. I've told her I know, and that is enough!"

Again he was silent. He had heard his parents talking, and he could remember Monica at Bessie's age. They could be identical twins.

"And of course," she went on, "I've said nothing about Jean. Immediately I saw him, I knew he was my father. I've asked questions since then, and it fits in. He came over to join the Free French in 1940. He was only sixteen. I expect he met Cass at a dance. They used to go to a lot of dances in those days." Her eyes took on a far-away look. "They fell in love. Then Paris was liberated and he was trapped into marriage by Gaby." She flashed him a look. "That's his wife. Remember he was still only twenty." She crooked her knees and hugged them. "It's obvious. Cass would love just one man. Only one. So when she told Grannie and me about Jean, it didn't take me long to realise that he must be the one. And then when we met at the airport in New York, I just knew." She waved a hand airily.

Boris swallowed. "I see." He had heard only vaguely about the business with Monica in New York; Myrtle no longer talked to him as she had done, and Bessie herself had been reticent.

They sat spine to spine. The sun was hot but the air was very clear and cold: a heady combination. Bessie knew that if she leaned further, the top of her scalp would fit into the nape of Boris' neck.

Especially if he, too, lifted his face to the sun.

She said in a low voice, "Boris. When can we get married?"

His spine tightened against hers. But at least he did not move away or laugh at her.

After what seemed to her like a year, he said, "I have to report to Corsham. On September 10th."

She said, "Oh."

"Bessie." His voice was rough. "You are thirteen years old!"

"Fourteen in three months. And I shall get older."

"You'll meet boys. Men."

"Of course. You'll meet girls."

"I'm different."

"Because you wanted to be a monk for five minutes? I knew why you wanted to be a monk, Borrie. You were disgusted. That night Myrtle had Mallie. That was the end, wasn't it?"

"Oh God. How did you know? You were nine!"

"Don't keep telling me how old I was. I started to love you at Myrtle's wedding. So where you're concerned, I've always been grown-up."

"Yes. But . . . it's not the same. Being married needs something extra to . . . love."

"It'll be all right, Borrie. Because we're so close to start with. We've always played at mummies and daddies. We've had . . . practice."

He managed a laugh then, and his back seemed to relax a little against hers. He said, "I love you, Bess. I want to protect you and look after you."

"That's all right then. You're like Jean-Claude, you don't know about these things. Women do. Cass knew. I know. That's why I want it settled before you go away." She took a deep breath. "I want us to be engaged, Borrie."

"Oh Bess. One minute you sound like a woman of thirty. And the next you're such a *kid!*"

"I know it sounds like that. I can't help it. I've got to have it out in the open, cut and dried. That was one of the reasons for the paint pot. And for this."

She did not move her back from his, but her hand reached behind her and found his. He took the gold bracelet from her.

"Aunt Mon bought it for me in New York last year. It's the only valuable thing I've got. It's real gold, you see. I want you to keep it. You could wear it on a string around your neck. No-one would see it underneath your shirt. Anyway, keep it. Somehow. It means you belong to me and you can't get married to anyone else. Is that clear?"

"Oh Bess. I can't do this—"

"Is that *clear*?" Her voice was fierce.

He looked at the bracelet in his palm which had been bought by her real mother; and she did not even know it. One day she might need him properly; there were so many dangers, so many shipwrecks . . . He closed his fingers over the gold.

"Yes. That's clear."

She smiled sightlessly at the pearly view. Gradually her head tipped back. His came to meet it. They sat in the sunshine supporting each other easily and naturally. When they eventually stood up to eat their lunch, the grass was flattened evenly and there were no visible joins.

Liv was not surprised by Myrtle's letter. Monica showed it to her almost accusingly.

"What has been going on?" she demanded. "I thought you and Malcolm were up to something. But Myrt and Reggie? It doesn't make sense."

Liv stared at the flimsy airmail paper without a great deal of interest. She said unemotionally, "I was very stupid, Mon. I've always been stupid about boys, haven't I? D'you remember I used to notch up how many had asked me out? Like the fighter pilots used to clock up victories?"

"We're talking about men, Liv. Not boys."

"That's it, you see. I still thought of them as boys. To be won. To be notched up." She let the single sheet of paper fall to the carpet. "I went down to Cheltenham that day, to notch Malcolm up." She shrugged. "I suppose I didn't think that when you're grown-up, you . . . you . . ." She flushed slightly.

Monica finished for her. "Malcolm went a bit far for you, Liv, didn't he? You wanted a kiss. You wanted him on his knees, begging for you. You wanted to be able to turn him down." She picked up the letter and folded it with a deep sigh. "Oh God."

Liv said, "I wish Myrtle had known that. But Myrtle has grown up. And when she rang the Cheltenham number and I replied, she thought . . ." a tear formed in her right eye. It was Liv's misfortune that it looked theatrical. She swallowed. "Anyway. She and Reggie . . . Reggie is so good at—at being kind. And he must have been angry with me. And it started from there."

"That's why you came out here," Monica said flatly.

"I had to get away. You don't know what it was like, Mon. He is obsessed with her. He can't live without her. I mean . . . Myrt! Of all people!"

Monica was silent, staring through the window at the enormously expensive view. She remembered Nancy. It had been her pride that had hurt then; that was all. Was it the same for Liv?

She said at last, "Has it ever occurred to you, Liv, that you and I haven't got much love in us? We were the ones who played around when we were at school. Perhaps we've gone on playing around ever since. Carol and Myrtle were different. Even then I knew that Cass was special. And Myrtle was so—so—*giving.*"

Liv snorted a laugh which turned into a sob.

Monica said, "You're not interested in men. Not really. Are you? Material things come first for you. Admit it."

"All right. But I do love Reggie. Or I did love him. Oh, I don't know. He was so insulting, Mon." She began to cry in earnest. "At one stage he said that if nothing came of him and Myrt, I could have what was left! I tried to scratch his eyes out."

"Really?" Monica asked with interest.

"Yes. I hated him so much at that moment. Myrtle is my friend. And she's not even pretty. Both of them—both of them—were betraying me! I couldn't bear it!"

Monica patted Liv's shoulder almost absent-mindedly. The objective side of her reviewed the whole scenario with complete detachment. Somehow she could not see it as a tragedy, unless poor Reggie and Myrtle were eventually consumed with guilt. They had fallen in love and gone away together. That was the only fact that mattered. Once that was accepted, the problem to be dealt with was Myrtle's family, and Liv.

She waited until Liv was dabbing at her eyes, then she stood up and began pacing.

"The thing is . . . are you coming with me?" she asked briskly.

Liv blew her nose miserably. "Where are you going?"

"To England of course. Cheltenham. To look after the boys." She made a face. "And Malcolm I suppose. He's going to be more trouble than the other three put together."

"Me? Come with you to Cheltenham? Myrtle's home? Don't be silly, Mon. How could I do that?"

"With great ease. Come on, Liv. What else can you do? You can't stay here. If we go together, it will shut Bob up. It will shut up most of the Cheltenham gossip. And, as you want to get back at Myrt and Reggie, I should think it would heap coals of fire on both their heads!" She began to smile. "From where I'm standing, it looks the ideal move to make."

Liv stared, mouth slightly open. "You're so cold-blooded, Mon! It's not a game of chess, you know!"

"Might be better if you tried to see it in that light!" Monica paused and looked down at the big eyes. "Listen, Liv. You're not that badly hurt. You might not have Reggie. You might not have poor old Myrtle. But you've got me." She sat on the arm of a chair and stared right at Liv. "I'm pretty strong you know, Liv. I was only seventeen when I had Bessie, and I worked for eight years getting the Albion on its feet. The only person I've ever really wanted is Bessie, and I gave her back to Carol last summer. You can lean on me till you learn to stand on your own two feet."

Liv was shocked at the sudden confession. Her eyes seemed to focus anew. After a long pause she said merely, "Thank you, Mon."

Monica stood up again, energy tingling through her.

"I want to go to Cheltenham. I want to look after Myrtle's kids. It's a terrific challenge."

Liv focused on another thought.

"What about Bob?"

"Yes. It might be the end for Bob and me. I don't know. He's pretty tied up with Rosa at the moment. So he won't object too much if I go home with you."

"What about if he does object?"

Monica flashed a smile over her shoulder. "He's given me an ultimatum before. He thinks he won then. He thinks I gave up Bessie for his sake. I didn't, of course. Well, he'll know this time that he's lost."

"You can't do it, Mon. You can't give up . . ." she spread her hands ". . . all this."

Monica looked around the room calmly. "I shall miss it. And America. Hildie and the boys and the new baby." She smiled. "But for a while, I shall be much too busy to think about that."

Liv began to cry in earnest. She dropped her face into her hands. Monica said, "I'll make some tea. Have a good cry in peace, then you can make up your mind what you're going to do."

She left the room and Liv wept on for a while obediently, then dabbed at her eyes. Her voice catching childishly, she said to the empty room, "You're not just cold-blooded, Mon. You're hard." Because after all, there was really no decision to be made. Monica was right, she couldn't stay here with Bob and she didn't want to go back to Birmingham and the total shame of being a deserted wife. Maybe later she could go to Carol, but not yet. She'd have to stick to Monica. She'd have to.

By the time she'd drunk a cup of tea, she had accepted the preposterous idea of living in Myrtle's house and looking after Myrtle's husband and children. It had its ironies. It might even embarrass Reggie and Myrtle.

Slowly over the damp summer, Myrtle learned to love Reggie. There had been no doubt about their physical attraction in Barnt Green; it had been difficult to keep their hands off each other once they were committed. Even that frightful afternoon when Liv had discovered them together had not ended the affair. They had thought it was the end, but that night Reggie had crept into Myrtle's room again, and after the first shocked refusal—"I can't, Reggie darling, not now that Liv knows"—she had welcomed him into her arms until dawn. But if she hadn't been with him that early evening, she might have known that Mallie was in the garden on his own. Reggie assured her it was not so; how could she have known that the boys had climbed the fence on to the golf course and left Mallie to his own devices? If anyone was to blame, it was himself. He always played with the boys for an hour when he got home from work. But his time with Myrtle had been running out, he had known that. And Liv was sitting on the terrace relaxing before dinner.

Myrtle was adamant about the holiday.

"I really cannot sleep with you, Reggie. I'm terribly fond of you. I'd rather be with you than anyone else in the whole world. But I can never sleep with you again. You do realise that?"

"Darling girl. You know how I feel. Whatever you want . . . whatever."

If she wanted to be with him more than anyone else, it must mean that beneath that awful frozen exterior she loved him. He was certain of it. For him, last summer had not been merely a crazy sexual fling. He had always seen Myrtle as a "good sort," uncritical and easy-going. He had liked her from the moment he had met her at the wedding. Later, he had seen her as a good influence on Liv. Her careless happiness with her three boys must surely show Liv that families need not be the fraught, destructive units she thought they were. And then, later still, he had felt a strong sexual attraction. The attributes which Liv thought disgusting drove him mad with desire. The breasts made pendulous by three avid babies, the distended abdomen, the thighs diagonally marked with stretch marks, gave her a reality Liv had somehow lost. And then she had turned to him for comfort. As they had made love that first time he had thought of a phrase in the marriage service: "mutual comfort." They had given each other mutual comfort.

Maybe it could have ended there if Mallie hadn't drowned. He might have transferred his heightened feelings to Liv and battered down her primness somehow. Myrtle would certainly have returned to Malcolm and taken a kind of pride with her; pride that another man had found her beautiful and irresistible.

But Mallie had drowned. And everything had been turned upside down.

They drove north that early June, along the interminable A1 past Scotch Corner and Newcastle and signs announcing Newbiggin-on-Sea and Seahouses. Reggie turned back there, and they had a high tea at a little cafe overlooking the workaday harbour with the boats leaving for the Farne Islands.

"We'll go there one day," he told her, smiling into her inward-looking eyes. "We'll see the puffins and the seals and pretend we're marooned."

She said, "I'd like that, Reggie. To be marooned. Away from everything."

"I know, darling. But you are away from everything now. With me. You'll realise that quite soon."

"Reggie. You're so sweet."

"Only you think so, Myrtle. But then, your opinion is the only one that matters to me."

She knew that Malcolm didn't love her like that, had never loved her like that. She tried to respond by reaching across the table for Reggie's hand. He took her wrist and eased off her glove and held her fingers in his warm ones. It made her wish for an instant that she hadn't made the gesture in the first place. Then she thought that it didn't really matter because nothing really mattered any more.

But when they drove into Alnmouth that night, she liked it. The few houses and hotels, huddled behind dunes from the north sea and its winds, had a friendly look about them. They promised sanctuary. Reggie signed the register and pushed it over to her; he had booked separate rooms. Their hotel was called the Lobster Pot. He explained that everyone in the Hardfanger working party had booked their own rooms. They would work as a team, but they were by no means tied to each other. She need not meet anyone if she did not wish it. He would introduce her as a family friend so that she need feel no embarrassment either. She could mix, or she could be private.

"I'd prefer to be . . . private," she said as they sat over a drink in her room.

"All right, Myrtle. That's all right."

She liked her room, too. She could hear, very faintly, noises from the bar below, but nothing intrusive; just a reminder that her isolation was chosen rather than forced. The room itself was small with two deep window embrasures where she could sit and look at the sea. The walls were an aged cream colour, dissected randomly by beams. After she'd unpacked she ran her fingers over some of the beams. They were split and pitted and she could smell the tar in them. They gave her comfort.

She told Reggie she didn't want anything else to eat.

"That boiled egg filled me up. Where did we have that?"

"Seahouses. D'you remember me saying we'd go to the Farne Islands?"

"Oh yes." She smiled at him. "I think I'll have an early night, Reggie. If that's all right."

He smiled back. "It's all right." He took her face in his hands and kissed her forehead. She stayed very still. He said, "Would you like to walk to the seashore before you settle down? Have some fresh air?"

"Yes. That would be nice."

"And would avoid me kissing you again?" His smile deepened. "Myrtle, please believe me. I am not going to force anything. Anything at all."

They walked down the sandy road and came upon the shore unexpectedly. The white beach rolled away into the distance and the waves came greyly along it, pounding it indiscriminately. The air was damp and cold on their faces. Myrtle shivered.

"Come on. Let's run!"

Reggie took her hand and pulled her over the sand. Her legs moved leadenly. She was immediately out of breath.

"Reggie, stop! I can't—"

"Do you good, Myrt! Come on—down to the sea with you—"

"Reggie, we shall get wet!"

"That's the idea! Jump that rock! Come on!"

He did not realise that her sobs were in earnest. She never cried. Her white strappy sandals sank into the sand as it grew damper. Suddenly a wave came up the beach and soaked them both to the knees.

Myrtle started to scream.

He picked her up and held her closely against his shoulder.

"It's all right, Myrtle. It's only the sea. I was trying to make you feel like a child again. Running into the sea on the first evening of the holiday!"

She held him so tightly he thought he might suffocate.

"Oh, Reggie. That's how it was, wasn't it? For him. For Mallie. And it crept up and up and then he fell down."

Reggie carried her to a rock and leaned her against it. She could not stop weeping.

"I'm sorry. So sorry, darling. I should have thought . . ." he kissed her hair. "It's good to cry. You haven't done enough of it."

She calmed down at last and they went slowly back to the Lobster Pot. As she said goodnight to him at her bedroom door, she smiled directly at him for the first time.

He whispered, "Goodnight, Myrtle. Get out of those wet shoes quickly and snuggle down like a good girl."

She went into the room and noticed that the floor was uneven. How Mallie would have loved it.

"The first day of the holiday," she murmured.

He did not go to work immediately. He took her to Bamborough Castle and Alnwick. In the tiny, expensive shops of Alnwick she bought herself a new dress and shoes. He chose them for her: a lime green linen dress, sleeveless, with a mandarin collar and gored skirt. Ridiculous shoes with heels that gave her height. She had always worn gathered skirts and flat shoes. The tailored dress made the most of her slim waist and big bust, the gored skirt kept her hips smooth, the plain green court shoes did wonders for her legs if not her balance. She wore her new things and held tightly to his arm as they toured the castle. He thought of another phrase from the marriage service. "With my body I thee worship." His body worshipped Myrtle's. It was much more than a sexual feeling.

The next day he went to look over Hardfanger and meet his fellow workers. Myrtle had decided to stay in her room, but after lunch she changed her mind and went for a stroll. It was a grey, windy day and unless she strode out for a long walk there was not much to do in the tiny village. She wasn't up to striding out, so she went into a cafe and ordered tea and cakes. The elderly owner brought them on a silver salver.

Myrtle was suddenly inspired.

"Is there a hairdresser in the village?" she asked.

"Aye, pet. Two of 'em. Jeannie does home perms if that's what you were after."

"I don't know what I want. Something different."

"Then Meggie's the one for you. She's just above the gown shop, a few steps down the road. Aye, Meggie's the one with the imagination."

The words were spoken without much approval, and Myrtle wondered what Meggie would do for her. It did not worry her unduly; she knew that a visit to the hairdresser would please Reggie. Reggie was so kind. She wanted to please him.

As it happened, Meggie was inspired when it came to Myrtle's dry and frizzy mop. She cut out all the old perms that had built up over the years and got down to Myrtle's fine, schoolgirl hair that lay flat to her head like a cap. She shampooed the inch-long locks and styled them layer on layer in the popular urchin cut. Suddenly Myrtle was emerging as a small girl, no longer flabby and overweight. Since the birth of Lennie, she had lost interest in eating and was in any case much slimmer than she'd been for years. Now, with her close-cut hair and tailored dress, she looked quite different. She surveyed herself in the mirror with a feeling that was almost pleasure.

"Madam is pleased?" asked Meggie in her careful voice.

"Reggie will like it," Myrtle replied.

Reggie was delighted. It was a positive sign of her recovery. That evening he spotted one of his colleagues in the hotel dining room. He risked introducing Myrtle, and she took it well, shaking the man's hand and smiling politely. He then suggested that the next day she should go with him to Hardfanger to see the library which he and Alan Forrester were cataloguing. She agreed to that in the same way she had agreed to come away with him, like a small obedient child taking medicine she didn't much relish. But once in the tall library with its beautiful mobile staircases on the ground floor and gallery, she changed. It was such a subtle change that Reggie did not recognise it for a while. He explained the system they were using and showed her the entry books and the catalogue cards. Her absorption could have been the same politeness she had shown before; it was not until they broke for coffee that he realised she was turning pages and checking the entries in his handwriting with the relevant file cards.

He said, "We'll go and find a pub for lunch, Myrtle, shall we?"

"Didn't you say that the housekeeper prepared a snack lunch in the kitchen?"

"Yes. But I rather assumed you wouldn't want to mingle with the others."

"I'm not keen. But you can mingle and I can have a look around. Would that be all right, Reggie? This castle belonged to the King of Northumbria when the Danes were here—did you know?"

"Yes. That's why it's such an important gift." He tucked her hand in his arm and led her through the vaulted hall to the staircase. "See. It's like an upturned boat. All the architecture around here of that time seemed to be based on the sea."

"There's some stuff about Bede entered in your writing."

"I'll look it out for you this afternoon. Would you like that?"

"I won't understand it, Reggie. I was hopeless at school."

"There are notes to go with it." He led her down a narrow passage incongruously ribbed by metal gas pipes. His voice was suddenly husky. "Darling. Don't ever call yourself hopeless. Not to me. You see . . . you are my hope."

Unexpectedly, tears came into her eyes again. She said nothing and had blinked them away when they emerged into the enormous cellar-kitchens, but she felt suddenly as if she might be starting to melt. Quite literally and physically.

She went to Hardfanger with him most days. There were other women in the party: wives of the curators, secretaries and administrators. They would have liked her to join them occasionally for shopping and exploring, but they were not offended when she declined. Myrtle discovered that she had a talent for not giving offence. She thought back and realised how often she had smoothed the ruffled feathers of Malcolm's patients—and the husbands of patients. She smiled at the motley collection of people she met in the castle kitchen most days, and asked them whether they had enjoyed their trips to Lindisfarne or Scotland, or even the Lakes; and they seemed to respect her isolation and told her she really must go before the summer was over. Meanwhile she was actively helping Reggie: transforming his scribbled notes into legible entries, sorting cards for him, enthusing when he showed her a first edition or a handwritten manuscript.

"I'm beginning to understand how Carol feels about books," she said one day when they drove through Hexham towards Hadrian's Wall. "Perhaps it's one of the ways we can get inside people's heads. Share thoughts." She smiled at Reggie. "Those books bridge time. They almost make you feel you're beginning to understand eternity."

Reggie nodded. "You remember what Carol said to us about that book she was editing? The one smuggled out from Algeria?" He returned her smile tentatively. "She said something about it being the author's immortality."

Myrtle was silent for a long time. She asked at last, "What are you trying to say, Reggie? Mallie couldn't write his name. He couldn't hold a pen." Her voice was as steady as a rock.

He said, "But you can write. You could write about Mallie."

"No. No, I couldn't do that. I couldn't bear to do that."

He did not push it and there was another silence. They came to Haltwhistle and found a car park. The weather had improved in the last three weeks, but it was still blowy, and Myrtle's new haircut blew around her head like a cherub's halo. They clambered up a rise and surveyed the view of the Wall and a distant fort.

Myrtle said, "Let's walk along it. Let's pretend we're from one of the Legions." It was the first positive suggestion she'd made; he let her take the lead, though his instinct was to go ahead and help her over the rough places. She climbed a rickety ladder and turned to smile at him. "Wouldn't Nicky love this?"

He paused, his hand on the top rung of the ladder. They looked into each other's eyes, and for the first time he faced the possibility that her "cure" might also mean she would return to her children. She took his hand.

"I could write to you, Reggie. I could write to you about Mallie. About everything."

Almost immediately, she turned and walked along the grass track on top of the wall, leaving him to scramble up and follow her. He wanted to shout, "You won't have to write to me. I shall be with you. You can talk to me." But he said nothing, and they walked on until they came to the round buttress of the fort. She turned then, and gave him the Roman salute. But when she saw his face, her fist dropped to her side and she came to him, put her arms around his waist, and pressed her head against his shirt front.

She said very seriously, "I love you, Reggie."

They were the words he had wanted to hear. He did not know why he kissed her short silky hair as if they were saying goodbye.

She spent some more time alone. She went into Newcastle, driving the car cautiously, parking on the outskirts and taking a bus into the shopping centre. She bought some more clothes and made a phone call home. Monica answered and was her usual brisk self. She said, "Why don't you have a word with Malcolm, Myrt? He phoned your hotel about six times last night and you weren't there."

"I was there, actually. I go to bed at eight o'clock. I'm still very tired." She looked through the glass of the phone box. She could see the gilded cupola of the university building and the long length of Newgate Street. She should have felt disorientated and lonely, but she didn't. "How are the boys?"

Monica said, "First time you've asked that. Liv has taken them out for a walk."

"Why aren't they at school?"

"Holidays, idiot. Can you speak up? You sound a million miles away."

"Three hundred, almost." She'd forgotten about the holidays. "Are they all right?"

"What, with Liv? She's not going to suffocate them or anything if that's what you mean."

Myrtle flinched. But of course Monica did not know that she had put a nappy over Lennie's face.

"I just meant . . . are they all right?"

"Fine. I'll say this for Malcolm, he's a good father."

"Yes. He is. I know."

Monica said, "And you're a good mother. Don't worry, I make sure they know that."

"Oh, Mon."

"I'm loving it. I'm properly tired at night. When you come home I could stay on if you like. Help you."

"What about Liv?"

"She wouldn't stay on."

"Is she . . . very unhappy?"

"Of course."

"It's awful, Mon. Isn't it?"

"Depends what you want from life. Most of us aren't wonderfully happy. Liv will be okay."

"Mon. I can't thank you enough. I'd have ended up going mad."

"Yes. But you're all right now. Aren't you?"

"I think so. I haven't wanted to know about the boys before."

"Quite. Well, my offer stands. I'll help you when you come back."

"I . . ." Myrtle looked at the golden dome and tried to picture Malcolm and the boys and the sitting room overlooking Imperial Gardens. She said, "I don't know about that, Mon. I'm different. I don't belong to the boys any more. I certainly don't belong to Malcolm."

"You belong to Reggie?"

"No. I belong to myself."

Monica's voice became suddenly stronger. "That's good. Then you can choose. You can make your own choice." There was a pause. Then she said, "Goodbye, Myrtle. Ring again." And she was gone.

Myrtle replaced the receiver carefully, and waited for a pang of some sort. Guilt, or maternal anguish, or plain homesickness. Nothing happened. Further down Newgate Street was a bookshop, she wondered if they had anything interesting about Bede. She looked in the small mirror above the telephone and checked that her nose wasn't shiny, then she pushed the door with her shoulder, and stepped into the sunshine.

Malcolm rang before she was in bed that night; he sounded jovial and assured her everything was fine and Monica had everything under control.

"Don't want to cut your holiday short or anything, bunny rabbit, but can you give us some idea . . ."

"No, Malcolm." She was surprised at the steadiness of her voice. So was he, and his joviality became hectoring.

"Look here, old girl, it's not right going off with your best friend's husband! She's stuck here looking like a yard of pump water. It's embarrassing to say the least. And Monica's a good egg, but she's bossy."

Suddenly Myrtle wanted to laugh. She said, "So long as she's taking care of you and the boys—"

"Dammit Myrtle! You're my wife! It's your duty to come home! I don't care if the place is like a pigsty if you're here! I order you to come back—tomorrow! The next day! By the end of the week at the very latest!"

She said gently, "Malcolm, I'm tired. Good night." And she passed the phone to Reggie and went upstairs.

After that, Reggie took all the calls that came for her. If it was Monica he would pass the telephone over, but most evenings he would hunch a shoulder and listen hard for a long time, then make a few remarks before saying goodbye.

June went out in a blaze of sunshine and July came in with a thunderstorm and then sultry weather that made Hardfanger's thick walls very welcome. Malcolm's phone calls became less frequent. Myrtle rang Monica during the day when she knew he would be in the treatment room, and Monica said that he had been in touch with Reggie's firm of auctioneers and knew that his work was coming to an end.

Myrtle said, "Next time Malcolm rings, Reggie, let me speak to him."

"Really? I don't want him to upset you, darling. You're looking wonderful. You're almost better."

"I am better. Thanks to you. I'll talk to him next time he phones."

Reggie looked at her. "Tell me first, Myrtle. Are you going back to him?"

"No."

"But you are going back to Nicky and Martin and little Lennie?"

"No. Monica will stay on. Perhaps eventually she will be divorced from her husband, and she might marry Malcolm. But she will be a good mother for the boys."

He couldn't believe it. "Myrtle. Does this mean you're staying with me?"

"Do you want me?"

"Myrtle—"

"Yes. All right."

He had to be content with that for the moment. It was not the sort of wholehearted commitment he had hoped for. But she did not wait for Malcolm to ring her; that evening she got through to trunks and asked for the Cheltenham number. He made a move away to give her a spurious privacy but she put a hand on his sleeve and kept him near her.

She said directly, "Malcolm. It's Myrtle. My dear, I'm sorry, but I'm not coming home. I thought I'd better tell you the minute I'd made up my mind."

Reggie could hear sounds but no words. Malcolm could have been spluttering with rage; he could have been weeping.

Myrtle said very calmly, "Why? Because I love Reggie, that's why. You must have guessed that."

She continued to listen with strange politeness for a very long time, but she did not speak again. Eventually she put the telephone down.

"He is confused," she said, not looking at Reggie. She turned and went upstairs and he followed. At the door of her small and very private room, she paused as if considering something. Then she said, "We'll be together now, Reggie. Shall we?"

He could have wept. He said, "Only if you want that, Myrtle."

She nodded briefly, went through the door and held it open for him.

It wasn't as it had been before, there was no crazy abandonment. Afterwards, Myrtle pillowed his head on her shoulder and ran her fingers from his forehead to his chin.

She said again as she had said that day on Hadrian's Wall, "I could write to you, Reggie. You wouldn't mind about my spelling and grammar, would you? I was terrible at school."

He said throatily, "I wouldn't mind, darling." He held on to her tightly and pushed his cheek into her shoulder as if he could weld himself to her. After a while he whispered, "But Myrtle, you won't need to write. You can tell me everything you want me to know."

She stilled her fingers and cupped his face to her.

"I know," she said.

But she was seized with the idea of writing. She began to write to Carol, short letters at first, about Hardfanger and Alnwick and the white sand at Alnmouth. One day she added a postscript: "Mallie would love it here, it's so empty and there is so much water. Do you remember Miss Edgeworth saying that all life came from the sea? Perhaps Mallie was going back to the beginning of everything when he kept going into Liv's fishpond."

Just before they left Alnmouth, she had a reply. "Myrtle, I am in love with a married man and so are you. How strange life is. I think you, too, feel a sense of temporary happiness only and that is why you write to me: to record this happiness and make it eternal whatever happens. In the same way you are remembering Mallie, cherishing him still. Myrtle, Bessie did this sketch of Mallie during your stay in Barnt Green. It comes with great love, and a belief that it will not hurt you. I make no comment about Liv. It is obvious that Reggie loves you very much and had to do his best to protect you. You are lucky, Myrtle. I am too."

Sandwiched between pasteboard was Bessie's sketch. She had drawn a back view of Mallie, but it was unmistakably him. In the raised hands, the bowed head, the hunched shoulders, it was possible to see delight as he dipped one sandalled foot into the scribbled water.

13

*I*n a strange way the summer of '58 was the happiest period of Monica's life. She was coping with an impossible situation which involved no personal heartache; she was making normality from abnormality; she was daily dressing invisible and unhealing wounds. She felt like a nurse for Liv and Malcolm, and a mother to Nicky, Martin and Lennie. She organised Malcolm's professional life so that gossip and speculation were kept to a minimum. Most of his regular clients had known that Myrtle was ill after the loss of Mallie, and the birth of the new baby, so to mention discreetly that she had gone away to convalesce was logical enough. That she and Liv were Myrtle's best friends and had stepped in to help was no less than laudable.

If anything, Malcolm's popularity increased. Favoured lady patients who thought that Myrtle had gone into a private lunatic asylum hoped that they might step into her shoes eventually, and made more regular appointments. Local doctors, who had held out against his paramedical status, were sympathetic and charmed by Monica. They began recommending him to their own incurables. Malcolm might not be able to effect a cure any more than the doctor could, but he had a definite facility, and his soothing hand and high bills convinced people they were improving.

Luckily, Nicky and Martin had liked Monica's straight and open approach when they'd met her at Aunt Liv's. Now, after the uncaring chaos of their mother's recent rule, they welcomed her wholeheartedly. As Nicky said one day, "If we can't have Mummy, we might as well have you, Aunt Mon." And Monica took that as the enormous compliment it was.

But Lennie was the real joy for her. He had been born at almost the same time of the year as Bessie, and she felt she was living the time she had missed then. Every day she saw a difference in him; when she arrived he lay flat in his cot or pram, doing amazing press-ups when he was on his tummy, lifting his head with agonised grimaces when he was on his back, but flopping sideways if she propped him up. Within two weeks of her arrival, he was sitting up in the pram when they went across the park to meet the boys. After a month he could sit on the floor scuffing his legs ecstatically and clutching at the air with pudgy hands. By the time Myrtle rang Malcolm to say she was never coming back, he was crawling everywhere, lifting his arms to Monica when she came into his line of vision, finding his mouth and filling it with whatever came to hand.

Monica looked at Malcolm's haggard face and said, "Don't worry, Malcolm. Myrtle won't be able to stay away from the children for ever. She'll come back. And until she does, I'll stay."

Until she saw him flinch she did not realise she had been cruel. She added quickly, "It's a temporary thing. After losing Mallie. And having the new baby. She is still your wife, Malcolm."

He allowed himself to be rallied; he was easily convinced because he could not really believe anyone would prefer Reggie Bradbury to himself.

Liv was different.

"I can't stand it much more, Mon. It was different when they were officially on holiday. But now . . . And they don't *care* that I'm here—they don't care who is here. They're obsessed with each other—totally and absolutely obsessed!"

"Listen, Liv. It'll burn itself out. Can't you see that? These intense affairs always do. Myrtle will come home, and so will Reggie."

"Don't *you* see that I wouldn't want him again? Not after . . . Myrtle."

Monica was tempted to ask what alternatives there were; but she did not. She did not look into the future herself. She had had the perfect excuse for returning to England. Bob had understood that her friend was ill and needed her; besides, he had Rosa Palmer in mind. But there was a limit to Bob's understanding, and his letters were becoming short, terse and infrequent. Monica's happiness had not entirely suppressed the calculating side of her nature, and she thought there might come a time when she would want to return to Bob. She might not love Bob passionately, but she was very fond of him; and she felt part of his family.

So their odd, triangular life limped into August. The boys were starting a different school that autumn, and Monica and Liv took them to Cavendish House to be fitted out in the wine-red uniform. Monica carried Lennie on her left hip and held Martin's hand. Liv walked by Nicky's side and waited ostentatiously for him to open doors for her. It was very hot and Lennie was unusually fractious. The boys stood in front of mirrors in their new blazers and said they itched all over.

"Just let's get you fitted out," Monica told them briskly. "And we'll have tea at the Gloucestershire Dairy and go on to the lido. How does that appeal?"

"Haven't got our swimming stuff," Nicky objected instantly.

"If it's too far for you to get it, then we won't bother," Monica said in a friendly voice. "Aunt Liv and I will take Lennie, and you two can help Tom in the garden."

"We'll come," Martin said quickly.

But on the roof garden of the cafe, eating ices from metal sundae cups with flat spoons, it was Liv who became recalcitrant.

"I'll have Lennie. You take the boys. I can't face all the noise. It'll be packed out."

Monica looked at her sharply; she was pale and her lovely Shirley Temple curls were sticky with sweat.

"We can manage Lennie. All the stuff will go in the pram anyway. You go and lie down, Liv."

So in the end they left Liv in her room; Monica put a swimsuit under her dress, collected all the necessary paraphernalia and stuck a scribbled note for Malcolm under the tea-tray in the kitchen.

Really, it was easier without Liv. The boys walked either side of the pram and chattered without restraint. Monica chipped in now and then, but mostly she smiled at Lennie and made noises at him when he gurgled at her. It was less than a mile to the open-air swimming pool, and at that time in the afternoon the queues had disappeared and people were beginning to leave to go home for tea. Monica bought the tickets and waited for the gate to be opened for her to take the pram through. The boys insisted on using the turnstile, and somehow Martin got stuck halfway through. She rescued him and they walked through to the grounds around the pool and found themselves a base. Lennie began to whimper again. The boys put on their trunks and went off to the children's pool while she undressed Lennie. Then she slipped out of her dress and piled everything on to the pram. The boys crowded delightedly at the edge of the pool when she slid in with Lennie in her arms.

"He likes it, Aunt Mon!" Nicky peered into the baby's surprised face. "He's stopped crying!"

"It'll just cool him down." Monica dangled him experimentally. "I think he might have a touch of the sun."

"Will you wait for us at the bottom of the chute, Aunt Mon?" asked Martin.

"You don't need to be *caught*, do you?" scoffed Nicky.

"He wants to make sure Lennie and I get splashed," Monica covered for him. The boys went off, honour satisfied, and Monica waited at the bottom of the chute and dipped Lennie now and then. Yes. Yes, she was happy. She did not want Myrtle to come back. Ever.

Liv could not sleep, she could not even lie still.

Monica had explained that her unhappiness was due merely to wounded pride, but it did not seem to make much difference what caused it. It was perpetual and debilitating. Sometimes she felt ill with it.

She got up and went to open the window wider. The clock on the parish church struck five. Malcolm would be finishing off his last patient and going into the kitchen for his tea. It was a pity she could not face him unless it was in a crowd, because she and he had something in common now. He looked as she felt, haggard and frightened, and utterly bewildered. It was two weeks since Myrtle had telephoned him from Alnmouth and announced she wasn't coming home. He had gone downhill badly since then. He had cancelled three appointments at very short notice and shut himself up in his room.

Her window overlooked the walled back garden. Old Tom did his best with the raised borders, and there was an ancient apple tree in one corner with a swing suspended from it, but otherwise it was simply a square of grass bounded by the high wall of the old mews. Down the centre of the grass was a worn line where the boys kicked their footballs against the wall, and under the swing another worn patch. Next door they had a pergola and roses everywhere and a hammock. Liv had had roses and a hammock. Her eyes filled with tears.

The kitchen door opened and Malcolm came into the garden holding a cup. Liv drew back, but watched him with morbid curiosity. It was like watching herself, or at least, her own actions. He wandered around the garden aimlessly, pausing now and then to stare at a clump of flowers as if admiring them. When he got to the swing, he put the edge of his bottom on the seat and sipped at the cup. Liv moved to the windowsill again and put out her head. He had taken off his white coat and where his braces crossed his back, his shirt was darkened with sweat. She'd never noticed Malcolm perspire before; nor herself. Yet her hair was stuck to her head today and though she wore dress shields she knew that her Moygashel suit was ruined.

He took another token sip from his cup then stood up again and walked down the other side of the garden. His head was bent, the sun glinted on the immaculate waves, and the reddish-coloured hairs on the backs of his hands were burnished. They were large, competent hands. She remembered them searching the bones of her back last year, and closed her eyes on renewed pain. If she hadn't left home that day . . . if . . . if. Malcolm stopped suddenly by a blazing bed of godetia, stared at their colours as if offended by them, and suddenly tipped the cup of hot tea over them. They crumpled where it fell, instantly spoiled.

Liv must have made a sound because his head came up and he saw her. They looked at each other, both frowning as if at intruders.

Malcolm said, "Have you had any tea? Monica's left it ready in the kitchen."

"No. I was resting."

"Come on down. Let's have a cup together, shall we?" He looked at the scalded flowers. "I've just spilled mine."

She did not want to be with him, but something made her nod. Guilt or pity, she did not know which it was. She picked up a comb as she passed the dressing table, and ran it from the nape of her neck to the crown of her head. For a moment the hair stayed glossily loose, then fell back again. She would have changed her linen jacket for a blouse, but nothing seemed worthwhile.

At least the kitchen was cool and cavernous. Monica and Liv between them had organised it beyond recognition, and with the door open on to the garden it was pleasant and homely. Malcolm was at the gas stove, making fresh tea. Strangely he was more domesticated than Reggie. Perhaps it was because his work kept him in the home. Or perhaps she had never given Reggie a chance.

She fetched two cups and saucers from the dresser and set them out; poured milk into each. He brought the teapot to the table and sat down heavily.

He said, "Why didn't you go to the lido with Monica and the boys?"

"I felt too tired. Couldn't face the people." She looked up at him. "You know."

He snorted a mirthless laugh. "Oh yes. I know. We both know. We can't help each other, but at least we both know."

She was surprised at his empathy. She had always thought it was just animal attraction that kept Myrtle tied to this man, but sometimes lately she wondered.

She swallowed. "It was my fault. I know that. I'm sorry, Malcolm."

"I wondered about blame too. Wondered if I should have sent you packing that day. But . . . dammit, Liv. Myrtle. I could have trusted her with anyone. And *Reggie*—he was my best friend!" He stood up violently and his chair fell to the ground with a clatter. "I'll never forget last May when he told me he was going to take her on holiday. He made it sound so bloody reasonable. But . . . he was *ruthless!*"

She put her elbows on the table and looked at the backs of her hands. "I know. That's how he was with me. Ruthless."

"Myrtle didn't stand a chance, Liv." Malcolm paced to the sink and back again. "She was ill. He was determined. I should have kicked him out then and there. Never let him in the house again. I thought she'd laugh at him. But she didn't have the will to do it. He—he practically abducted her!"

"Yes." It still stuck in her throat. Myrtle. Of all people.

"She told me there was nothing in it. All those weeks in that blasted hotel up there. Nothing, she said. She helped him with his stupid work, and he looked after her. She let me think she'd be back. Just a holiday. She'd come back and be her old self again. And then . . . oh *God!*"

She said dully, "I know."

He kicked at the fallen chair and winced with the pain of it.

"Liv." He leaned on the table and stared at her. "She's gutted me. I can't live without her, d'you know *that?*"

She said nothing. In one way the thought of living with Reggie again was repulsive.

He said tensely, "I haven't touched a woman since Myrtle went off with Reggie. I've lost . . . that. It's as if she's castrated me!" Tears suddenly flooded his eyes. "No-one can help me, Liv. Only Myrt. Only Myrt. Only Myrt . . ." He was sobbing, almost hysterical. She had to do something.

Quite suddenly she knew what to do. She would give herself to Malcolm. She would allow him to take her this time. Fully. And with that one action she would prove herself an attractive woman again, and she would help Malcolm to realise that he could indeed live without Myrtle. She would make the sacrifice now. She put a hand over his as she stood up.

"It's all right, Malcolm. All right. Don't cry. We're both in the same boat. But they'll come back. And we'll show them that we don't care. We're all right. That way they'll come back very quickly! Oh yes, they're not going to give everything up for some silly attraction . . . you'll see." She moved round the table as she spoke, not removing her hand from his, massaging his knuckles gently. When she stood in front of him she lifted the hand and turned him towards her.

"We can help each other, Malcolm. Myrtle hasn't . . ." she could not bring herself to say the word "castrated" and searched for a frantic three seconds for an alternative word. "Myrtle hasn't damaged you. Of course she hasn't. You're a very attractive man. Very attractive."

She released him to reach in her pocket for a handkerchief. She dabbed at his eyes and less efficiently at his nose. He put his hands on her shoulders to steady himself. She remembered his touch all too clearly and an unexpected tremor centred itself in her pelvic area.

He sobbed breathlessly, "You and Mon. So good. But you've taken me over. I'm no-one any more. Nothing. Nothing."

She let him lean on her, reached up and touched her lips chastely to his. She knew again what he meant. But together they could restore each other.

He was startled and held his breath on another sob to stare at her.

"Liv?"

"Yes. I know," she whispered as if they were magic words.

"Liv. You can't. Don't you remember? Before?"

"It's different now. We need each other."

He went on staring for a long moment, still leaning heavily on her shoulders. She dabbed again, more effectually, and touched his lips with her fingers. Automatically, his mouth opened and he held them gently with his teeth. Then he lifted the padded shoulders of her jacket and wrenched hard. The buttons flew off and the jacket slid down her arms. He took her wrists and held them down. The jacket fell over the chair.

Liv was startled. It was so practised, so sudden, so violent. Thoughts of them comforting each other were gone. This was to be a fierce, animal coupling. She told herself wildly she didn't care. This time she would do all that was expected of her. The jacket had been spoiled by her sweat anyway. Before he could tear the straps of her petticoat and brassiere, she slipped them quickly from her shoulders.

He cupped her small firm breasts and bent quickly to them. Her pelvic tremor spread to her legs and she would have collapsed if he hadn't held her so firmly. He knelt before her and stripped her expertly. His hands were on her buttocks, his thumbs in her groin. She couldn't bear it. Yet she could not stop him, did not want to stop him. She took his leonine head in her hands and turned his face upwards, afraid of what he might do next. And that was her mistake. His eyes were closed, screwed up like a child's. He was breathing fast through his mouth, panting fiercely as if he were racing time. He might have gone through with it if she had let the race continue. But she had interrupted it. He opened his eyes and saw her. His face twisted in agony. She fell to her knees too, trapped by her own clothes. The fallen chair scraped her bare back.

She babbled, "It's all right, Malcolm. I don't mind, honestly. Whatever you want to do. Whatever—"

But he was crying again, this time like a dog, head thrown back, howling at the moon.

She deciphered words and put them together in some sort of order. "No good. Only Myrtle. Can't do it. Myrtle."

He pushed her quite hard so that she fell back against the upturned legs of the chair, then he was up, scrabbling his braces back over his shoulders, still howling incomprehensibly. For some reason he banged his fist on the table and the teapot skidded across the scrubbed surface. He must have been burned, because his voice rose still further; then he stood up and bowed his head. "She burned me. With tea. Once."

And he stumbled across the kitchen and was gone. She heard the door of the treatment room close. She was left with dripping tea, her clothes in tatters around her feet, her body indecently exposed. And completely unsatisfied.

When Monica returned, Liv had tidied everything and gone to bed. She lay on top of the covers, bathed and in her best nightie. She wondered whether she was going mad. She recalled once before when she had obliterated something from her mind—though she could not remember what that something was—and she tried to do it again. What had happened in the kitchen must be torn out of her life somehow. Otherwise she could not bear it. She must not—she must never—remember that she had tried to seduce Myrtle's husband. She must never remember that he had rejected her. She must never picture the upturned chair, the slavering man, the dripping tea, the naked depraved woman. Never. She put her fist in her mouth and bit down hard, and as the pain registered like balm, so Monica knocked on her door.

"Liv, are you all right?"

"Yes. Fine." Her voice sounded completely normal; it was amazing.

"Are you coming down for supper?"

"No." She could not think of an excuse, so repeated, "No."

Monica sighed audibly and called through the door again, "I'm a bit worried about Lennie. He seems very hot. And Malcolm won't come out of the treatment room to look at him. He just shouted at me to go away."

Liv said, "Come on in." She swung her legs to the floor. She should never have left her own house. At least she could have had some privacy there. Mon came in looking not her usual calm self.

"What's going on, Liv? Surely you're not going to bed yet?"

"You told me to lie down!" Liv felt her head throbbing alarmingly. She tried to pull herself together. "Tell Malcolm about Lennie. That will bring him to his senses."

"What do you mean? Have you talked to him? Is there something the matter?"

"I really don't know, Monica. I'm not a doctor." She felt with her bare feet for her slippers. "I'll come and help you to put the boys to bed."

"No. No, it's okay. You're right, I'll have to tell Malcolm about Lennie. If he's ill *he* should have a doctor."

"I'll see to Nicky and Martin. You see to Lennie."

Nicky and Martin were hard work and did not obey Liv as they obeyed Monica, but if she was up with them in their room she would not have to face Malcolm.

They were tired anyway, and thoroughly clean after their swim. She stood over them while they cleaned their teeth, folded their clothes while they got into the pyjamas, opened their window as wide as it would go to catch some of the cooling air.

"D'you want a story?" she asked grudgingly.

"No thank you, Aunt Liv," Martin said. And Nicky asked, "Can we look at our books by ourselves for ten minutes?"

"Yes. All right."

Martin said, "Aunt Liv, when is Mummy coming home?"

"Soon." Liv let her mind think of Myrtle and Reggie. They were behaving cruelly . . . evilly . . . but if only they would come home everyone would forgive them. Even she herself. "Soon, I hope," she said.

She trailed out on to the landing. She was wearing her old dressing-gown because putting the boys to bed was not always a pristine activity, but the sight of the over-ironed satin depressed her unutterably. She went into her room and slung it over the bed. She had worn this nightie when she'd gone home from Cheltenham last year . . . to please Reggie. It had been packed in tissue since.

She heard Monica coming along the landing and climbed quickly into bed. Nothing would make her face Malcolm across the supper table. Monica was breathing rather heavily. She burst into Liv's room without knocking. Her face looked muddy.

"What—"

"Quickly . . . Liv . . ." Monica could hardly speak. She hung on to the door handle. "I've phoned the ambulance. Come down quickly!"

"Oh my God. Is it Lennie? Not again . . . please not again . . ." Liv shoved on her slippers once more and grabbed the dressing-gown.

"No. It's not Lennie. It's Malcolm." Monica bent low and sucked in a deep breath, then straightened. "Oh Liv. He's taken a bottle of the painkillers he gives his patients and locked himself in the treatment room. He told me it's too late to do anything! I didn't want to start screaming . . . the boys mustn't know anything is wrong . . . kept knocking on the door. Tom and Doris aren't anywhere—"

"It's their day off. It'll be all right."

Quite suddenly Liv felt almost her old self; slightly impatient with Malcolm for making such a fuss, rather surprised at Mon for going to pieces. She clutched her old dressing-gown around her again and ran down the stairs and across the wide hall to the treatment room. She tapped lightly.

"Malcolm! It's Liv. I want to talk to you about this afternoon. Let me in, please."

She put her ear to the door. The silence was thick.

Monica panted behind her, "He hasn't spoken for ages. That was why I phoned the ambulance. Liv, if anything happens to him—to any of them—it will be my responsibility. D'you realise that? I practically forced my way in here—I didn't ask him whether he wanted me to come—and I dragged you with me. My God, I never realised before . . . I never thought . . ." Her beautiful dark eyes looked haggard. She took Liv's arm and her nails dug through the crinkled satin. "Liv—I've been happy! Can you believe it? While you've hated every minute, and Malcolm has been slowly sinking into this state, I've actually been happy!"

Liv said, "Yes, I know. The thing is, how are the ambulance men going to knock this door down? It's mahogany or something."

"It's too late. He said it was too late."

"He didn't mean it. Not Malcolm." Liv frowned. "The waiting room. It looks over the garden. Maybe in this hot weather one of the windows will be open."

"He'll have closed all the windows."

But he hadn't. Liv wasn't surprised. She wasn't angry with him either. If she'd known more about drugs, she might well have done the same thing. She grabbed a trowel from the trug outside the door, kilted her dressing-gown and nightie and pulled a bench beneath the window and scrambled on to the sill. The sash was open at the top. She stood up and closed it with difficulty—the windows were six feet high and very heavy. Her nails broke and her slippers came off at the heel. She kicked them behind her and pushed at the lower window with all her might. It came up half an inch. Grimacing with triumph she squatted on the sill and levered the sash with the trowel. She scrambled inside; there was no sign of Malcolm. If he'd locked the inner door they were no better off. She pushed her head out of the window.

"I'll let you in from the hall, Mon. You'd better unlock the front door. See if the ambulance is coming."

The hall door was bolted. She opened it wide, then went to the inner door. It was unlocked. She went inside.

Malcolm was lying on the treatment table. The Venetian blinds were closed against the evening sun and it was unbearably hot in the room. Instruments lay everywhere. On the soap dish at the wash basin was an empty bottle. She looked at the sleeping face.

"You covered every angle, Malcolm," she said.

He did not move. His breathing was stertorous and saliva ran from a corner of his mouth. Monica came in with a rush. She took in the scene at a glance and groaned aloud.

Liv said, "It's all right. He's still alive and he's left the bottle for the medical people to see, so probably there's an antidote."

"What can we do? There's no sign of the ambulance!"

"Get him to wake up if poss." Liv took one of the flaccid arms and hauled hard. "Give me a hand. He's too heavy for one of us."

Somehow they propped him up. His head lolled alarmingly. Liv did the things she'd seen in films: talked at him, moved his body, and—not at all reluctantly—slapped his face. It was terribly hard work; she and Mon were breathing as heavily as Malcolm, and it was some time before they realised that the sounds coming from him contained complaining notes.

"He's coming round," Monica panted. "My God—Liv—you've done it!"

"We have to keep it up." Liv delivered a stinging blow across his cheek and shook his arm. "Come on Malcolm! Wake up!"

"I think I heard a bell." Monica stopped breathing to listen. It was the bell of an ambulance. The next moment two uniformed men appeared, bringing sanity with them. There was a stretcher and another man. Someone said, "Will you come with us, madam?" He spoke to Monica as she was dressed, and she looked helplessly at Liv.

"I'll see to things here," Liv assured her. "He won't want to see me when he comes round."

And then they were all gone, and the house was blessedly silent. Liv did the rounds of the boys. They were asleep. Little Lennie looked like an angel. Liv hung over his cot for a moment, feeling a very slight maternal pang. Suddenly she knew quite definitely that Myrtle would have to come back to the children.

Liv went to her room and began to dress again. When Monica got back they would need to talk. But she had already made up her mind. She'd had enough of inactivity, of running away from her problems. She would go up to Alnmouth tomorrow and see Myrtle.

Monica was not sure it was the right thing to do, but then, Monica was not sure of anything any more. She had no time to wonder about Liv's decision however, there was so much to do. She sat for two hours with the appointment book on her lap, telephoning Malcolm's clients while Doris took the boys for a long walk and Tom painted the window which had been scarred with the trowel. She visited Malcolm and tried to talk to the blank face without success. He was kept in the General Hospital for the next day only, and then, because he was not fit to be seen by his sons, she arranged for him to be transferred to a private nursing home in the Park. Seizing the opportunity, she spring-cleaned the treatment room, sterilised the instruments, boiled the sheets from the table, booked professional cleaners to steam-clean the carpet and curtains. She tried to telephone the hotel at Alnmouth and got through eventually, but was told that Mr. Bradbury and Mrs. Lennox had left there a week ago. She asked about Liv. "Yes, Mrs. Bradbury stayed overnight here the night before last. I believe she was then travelling south to catch the ferry."

Monica could hardly believe her ears. "Ferry?"

"Mr. Bradbury left a forwarding address in Paris."

The voice was withdrawn and disapproving. Melodramatics were not encouraged in small northern hotels, and Liv's arrival must have made it obvious that Reggie and Myrtle were absconding.

"Could you give it to me, please?"

"I'm sorry—"

Monica said with a return to her old authoritarian voice, "I am looking after Mrs. Lennox' children. Her baby son is not well and her husband is in hospital. I think she should know."

"Um. Yes. Just a moment, please." Muffled sounds of consultation came across the wires. Then the voice said huffily, "Hotel Crillon. Place de la Concorde."

"Thank you." Monica replaced the telephone and stared down the hall. The Crillon. It was like the Savoy or the Ritz. What the hell did Myrtle think she was playing at?

A key turned in the lock and the door opened to admit Doris with Nicky and Martin. They clamoured towards her.

"Can we go swimming again, Aunt Mon?"

"I want to go down the chute head first!"

They felt that their father's mysterious illness and Liv's departure warranted a relaxation of all rules amounting to anarchy.

Monica said, "Perhaps. Let's get lunch first. Salad in the fridge, Doris. I just want to book a call to France."

"Salad?" howled Nicky. "Rabbits' food! Ugh. And double ugh!"

Doris rolled her eyes at Monica. "Shall I do them a few chips, Mrs. Gallagher?"

Monica felt so helpless. She shrugged. "All right. Tom is still painting and keeping an eye on Lennie in the pram. Could you check on them first?"

She booked a call to the Crillon, and one to Carol who had recently had a phone installed at the Bergerie. Then she went down to the kitchen. Lennie had graduated to Mallie's high chair and sat up there squawling for his lunch, rubbing the soles of his feet together convulsively and banging with a spoon. Tom was washing his hands at the sink, ignoring everything. Nicky and Martin were pouring salt on to the table and throwing it over their shoulders with much laughter. Poor Doris was trying to fry chips at the stove.

Monica stood in the door and shouted at the top of her voice,

"Shut *up!*" which certainly worked with the children, but probably damaged Doris' heart. Tom did not flinch. The only sounds to break the startled silence were the running tap and sizzling chip fat.

"That's better." Monica removed the salt cellar and Lennie's spoon. "Go and wash your hands up in the bathroom while your chips are cooking."

"We've already washed, Aunt Mon."

"Then do it again, and this time use the nail brush on your fingernails. Also comb your hair." She moved to the dresser and began to open a tin of baby food. "Any future trips to the lido depend entirely on your behaviour."

The boys disappeared meekly.

Tom turned off the tap and dried his hands laboriously. "Well done, Mrs. Gallagher. Lick 'em into shape early, I say."

But Doris, obviously still suffering from shock, was less approving. "Mrs. Lennox never has any trouble with the lads," she said, banging the wire chip basket on the side of the pan with unnecessary force.

Monica tightened her lips as she approached Lennie.

"Then the sooner she comes home, the better," she said. It was the first time she had wished Myrtle back. Lennie looked at her as if she were Pontius Pilate, and turned away from the proffered spoon.

The lines to France were hopeless. The Crillon did not have anyone by the name of Blackberry, whether they came from Chester Lennox or Timbuctu. Baffled, Monica asked for someone who spoke better English than her French, and when a cultured voice said, "The English secretary here," she spelled Bradbury and then Chester Lennox. "We do not have a Mr. Bradbury. Nor Mrs. Lennox. But Mrs. Bradbury has booked a room. She is out at the moment. May I ask her to telephone you when she returns?"

"Yes, please." Monica gave the Cheltenham number without much hope.

Her call to the Bergerie was more successful. Mrs. Woodford answered the phone and sounded clear and immediately understanding.

"Carol has gone to the village for some groceries, Mon dear. We have just come back from camping in the mountains. Yes. Delightful. Bessie? She enjoyed it very much. Boris Denning was with us. They are very close. I wonder if perhaps, later . . . Cass calls me the ancient romantic!" Her laugh sounded blessedly normal. She resumed more seriously, "Mon, we realise how difficult it must be for you and Liv over there. Carol would like to help. She writes to Myrtle, you know. She thinks Myrtle will soon be well enough to return home."

Monica told her the latest developments, and Mrs. Woodford's horror was consoling.

"You're there on your own? Oh, Mon, I am sorry. How rotten. Listen, Jean-Claude is in Paris at the moment. Perhaps he could contact Myrtle? Yes, but I do not think Liv is the best person to act as conciliator, do you? All right, my dear, I'll tell Carol exactly what has happened, and she will contact you as soon as she can."

That meant they could not go to the lido that afternoon. Monica did not feel she could ask Doris to take the children out yet again. Instead, as if to prove something, she gave her the afternoon off, and lugged Nicky's inflatable pool into the garden. Tom tipped the bench across the window so that no-one could climb up and touch the wet paint, and disappeared without suggesting that he could fill the pool via the garden hose. She organised a chain with buckets from the sink and tried to ignore the puddles all across the kitchen floor. The boys pretended to slip in the water and spilled even more. They ran in and out and turned the lawn into mud. Lennie sat in his pram and bawled. The phone rang and Monica left the sink and ran for it.

"Carol? Is that a call from France, operator?" she babbled.

"This is Mrs. French from next door. I'm sorry to be a nuisance, Mrs. Gallagher. I do realise that you are doing your best. But I have a tea party for the Ladies' Circle this afternoon, and I wondered if you could possibly make a little less noise?"

Monica almost sobbed her apologies and ran back to the kitchen to find Martin sitting in the sink splashing Nicky whenever he approached.

Somehow she had organised them into making paper boats, when Carol's call eventually came through. At least that offered some hope.

"I'm going to Paris myself, Mon. I've got hold of Jean-Claude, but obviously he does not know Liv—he doesn't know any of them—and if they've signed under false names, we can only identify them on sight. I think Liv has made a mistake to chase after them, but I suppose she couldn't sit and take it any more."

"No." Monica felt guilty again. "I didn't realise it was telling on her so much, Cass. She was so different when Malcolm took those tablets—she seemed to know what to do—she absolutely took over."

"Yes, but it means you're there on your own. Too much for you, Mon." She paused but Monica did not contradict her. She went on, "Boris could come and help out, but he has to go to Corsham next month. And Mother needs to be here to look after Bessie—"

"I'm all right, Cass. Honestly."

"No, you're not. I can tell. I'll come over from Paris. Hopefully I'll bring the others with me. But I'll come anyway."

"Oh, Cass. Could you?"

"Of course. It will be compassionate leave. Don't worry."

Monica could only say, "Oh, Cass."

She replaced the phone and listened to the sounds from outside. Mrs. French's tinkling teacups were almost submerged beneath yells from the boys. The paper boats were engaged in a naval battle. Monica sorted them out and stood on the bench to look over the wall.

"I'm terribly sorry, ladies. We won't disturb you any more." She gave them all her sweetest smile, but melted very few hearts. When she looked round and saw Martin had righted the bench and Nicky was climbing on it and hanging on to the wet window like grim death, she could have wept all over again.

"Right. That's it. Inside. Baths and bed."

"It's not tea time yet, Aunt Mon," wailed Martin.

She scooped Lennie out of his pram and he yelled again.

"I don't care if it's breakfast time. In you go."

She herded them before her, ignoring their protests. Just let Myrtle come back and she'd tell her what she thought of her. She was so tired her head ached, and she felt thoroughly alone.

The door bell rang just as they turned to climb the stairs. With Nicky holding his paint-stained hands high, Martin as naked as the day he was born, Lennie raising Cain under his arm, she opened the door.

Bob stood there.

She said, "Bob! What in heaven's name . . ."

He blurted, "I had to see you. Rosa Palmer is pregnant. I want a divorce."

It was as if he had hit her across the face. She flinched and grabbed Lennie with her other hand as if afraid she might drop him. Suddenly Martin started to cry.

"Don't go away, Aunt Mon! Please don't go away! We won't be naughty any more."

Nicky put his paint-hands around her skirt and held her hard. "We love you, Aunt Mon!" he shouted.

She began to cry.

14

The room at the Crillon overlooked the Place de la Concorde and was vast. Myrtle could not get over it.

"Reggie, how will you afford it?" She went from canopied bed to Empire escritoire, feeling materials, sliding across the rosewood with her fingertips. She opened a door into an enormous and elegant bathroom. "Gold taps! Oh, Reggie, I do believe they are gold taps! And this thing—what's this thing?"

"A bidet, honeybun."

He was delighted his extravagance was so successful. She was moving quickly, like a girl. She wore a slim linen suit with a bolero-type jacket that flattered her full bust. He loved her so intensely that he could have wept when he looked at her and saw her happy and carefree again.

She noticed him watching her and came to him.

"Darling. I do love you." She rubbed her cheek against his with a familiarity that surpassed a kiss. "I never knew it could be like this, Reggie. You give me so much."

"You give me more than I could ever give you, darling."

"No. It is an equal giving." She cupped his face and looked at him intently. "For a long time it wasn't. You gave and I received. Now, I think it is equal. It is as if I was born for you, and you for me." She kissed him. "I am not talking about this room, Reggie. You know what I mean."

"Of course." He put his hands to her waist and drew her body towards his. "I was nothing until I loved you, Myrtle. All that stuff about being an empty vessel—dammit, it's true!"

She smiled into his eyes. "For me too. More so, perhaps." She laughed, a sound which was still unfamiliar and which entranced Reggie. "Oh darling, Reggie. Shall we? On the bed? Now?"

They did.

Last year at Barnt Green, Reggie had had to remind himself that Myrtle's expertise in bed had been learned from Malcolm. But since her calm declaration of love a month ago in Alnmouth, he had gradually known that their love-making owed nothing to anything or anyone. The Myrtle he had coaxed from the ashes of despair, brought a kind of innocence to their bed. At first it was passive; she would lie on her back looking just past his head, and when he roused her she would cling to him desperately, panting his name as if she were drowning. Then she had started to watch him as he undressed; she had touched his appendix scar: "I didn't know you had that," she said, as if it were important to her. Later she said, "I need to know you, Reggie, every inch of you. Without you I am nothing at all, so I must know you." Her investigations, even of his fingernails, had been at once the most erotic and spiritual experience of his life. She made him conscious of the sanctity of his own body. When she responded to him it was a sacrament.

But in Paris, the canopied bed took away any seriousness from their coupling. They romped on it like children and he tickled her until she giggled helplessly.

Reggie had made up a name for them to use in Paris. They had driven to Dover, inventing and discarding the most ridiculous identities. Myrtle had wanted the Honourable and Mrs. Dalrymple. Reggie had suggested Alf and Gladys Mudd. In the end he had phoned a booking from the Railway Hotel in Dover where they left the car. Mr. and Mrs. Turner Stubbs. "My two favourite artists," he explained to her on the boat going over.

It seemed to impress. They were given what Reggie called pre-war treatment. His tweeds and brogues made him the archetypal English gentleman, and her round femininity was indefinably French. They had the best of both worlds: the reluctant respect accorded to the indomitable British, and the courtesy given to a womanly woman. Reggie hired a car and they "did" the countryside around Paris. So it was that when Liv enquired for them at Reception, they were at Versailles and did not return until she had gone to bed. They slept late the next day, breakfasted in their room, and walked in the Tuileries while Liv enquired at neighbouring hotels. The Crillon was so vast they could have been in the foyer together and not known it. For three days they lived in the same building and came and went at different times. On the fourth day, Carol arrived from Provence, and enquired for Liv. She was out again, roaming art galleries, sure that Reggie would want to see all the pictures he could. Liv was feeling a sense of purpose she hadn't experienced for a long time.

Carol waited for her in the long blue and white gallery of the hotel. She drank coffee and corrected proofs and thought of how she would surprise Jean-Claude that evening at the Reine Blanche. He had told her that he ate every evening there, in memory of that first meal together; they had promised each other that they would go back one day and drink onion soup again, but they had not done so. Until now. She turned back a page of her manuscript and nibbled at her bottom lip, feeling suddenly guilty that her mission to Paris was not entirely disinterested.

She glanced up, hoping that Liv would appear and enmesh her in the tangled web that had spun itself so inexorably since Mallie's death last year. She was becoming selfish in her happiness, and somehow she was still haunted by the feeling that she was in debt to fate. It had come so easily: Bessie as a daughter, Jean-Claude as a mate; the love between Bessie and Jean-Claude and between Jean-Claude and her mother. She still wondered, every time he left the Bergerie, whether she would see him again. She could never forget the terrible anonymous hatred behind that fire bomb.

A waiter hovered, and she ordered more coffee. It was no good, she could not concentrate on the manuscript. The train journey had been tiring; she had picked up the Côte d'Azur at Marseilles with a boatload of sailors going to Paris on leave. One of them had been sick in her carriage and the smell had lingered until they ran into the Gare du Nord.

She slid the sheaf of paper into its folder and made room before her for the tray of coffee. She forced herself to think of Monica alone in Myrtle's house, coping with Myrtle's three children and suicidal husband. It was all so awful. Yet she could not condemn Myrtle as the others must be doing. Myrtle's letters came regularly now, at least one a week. They had been disjointed at first and full of unconscious pathos; now they were full of Reggie. Anyone else might have found them unbearably immature. Carol did not.

She poured coffee and reached across the damask-covered sofa for a copy of *Paris-Match*. There were some graphic illustrations of the student riots around the Sorbonne. She stared at them intently. Jean-Claude had another appointment with General de Gaulle to discuss these very issues. She wondered when they would ever be resolved. Britain appeared to be giving up her colonies more readily than France. Perhaps that humiliating surrender in 1940 had hardened France's innate nationalism into a canker. Jean-Claude prophesied a lot more trouble before the Algerian problem was settled.

She shivered and turned a page to the fashion spread. Yves St. Laurent had taken over the house of Dior and was shocking the world with his mannish designs. Carol smiled at a picture of a girl dressed in black leather. Then stopped smiling and peered closer. The model was Gaby Durant. Jean-Claude's wife.

She leaned back and stared unseeingly down the gallery. Gaby. The same Gaby who had sat beneath the window in the office on Avenue Foch and typed so busily; who had prinked at her Brigitte Bardot hairstyle in the tiny mirror. Before Carol had known of Jean-Claude Gaby had been a colleague, and the sight of her in a newspaper should be a shock. No more than that. Nothing more than that. Just an insignificant coincidence.

But she felt cold in spite of the weather, and she took a gulp of coffee as she might have taken medicine. She glanced at her watch. Almost midday. At least six hours before she could go to the Reine Blanche.

And then she saw them. It was incredible. All three of them. Liv was several yards in front, obviously looking for Carol after getting her message in the foyer. Reggie and Myrtle had no idea that their secret hideout had been discovered, and were wandering along the gallery on their way out, or to lunch, their hands linked loosely; they had eyes only for each other. Reggie looked exactly as Carol remembered him last year, tweeds and white shirt, dark blue tie; Myrtle was quite different, slimmer, smaller altogether, her head erect and neatly framed in a Byronesque haircut not unlike Gaby's, a straight linen strawberry-coloured dress with a mandarin collar making her look taller than she really was.

Carol half rose and Liv saw her and hurried forward. Myrtle's attention was caught by the sudden flurry of movement: she switched her gaze from Reggie and saw Carol and Liv embracing. Frantically Carol signalled to her to go away. For a split second Myrtle hesitated, then she turned to Reggie and said something urgently; the next minute they had disappeared through the doors to the foyer.

Liv said, "Cass—my dear—what on earth are you doing here? Did you know?" She withdrew and smiled up at the familiar plain face. "Oh of course. Mon phoned you. I suppose she's worried to death?"

"Well, yes. She is rather. Oh, Liv . . ." Carol shrugged with Gallic helplessness. "Sit down. Have this coffee—I've only just poured it. No, I'm awash with the stuff. Oh, I'm glad to find you. I wasn't sure if you'd come back before tonight." She watched Liv settle herself with her usual fussy movements. "My dear, you look fine. I thought—I was afraid—Mon did not know how you'd be."

Liv finished smoothing her skirt.

"I'm better now actually. I shouldn't have run to Mon like I did. It was just so awful, Cass. And I've never had to be on my own . . . oh, you wouldn't understand of course, you're so independent—"

"Not any more."

"No, but . . . anyway, I did go to Mon. I sort of plonked all my worries on to her. I don't know what I expected her to do. She produced some answers of course, but they weren't the right ones for me. It's been a dreadful summer, Cass. Like some waking dream in New York which turned to a nightmare in Cheltenham." She sipped her coffee and dabbed at her lipstick with the monogrammed napkin. "Mon thought me being there and helping to look after Myrt's children would bring Myrt back quickly. Guilt. That sort of thing. All it did was to make her throw in her lot with Reggie officially." She sighed, opened her bag, fished out a compact and snapped it open to look at her reflection. "You heard about Malcolm?"

"Yes. He's going to be all right, Mon says."

"Oh, of course. He had no intention of committing suicide. Not really." She snapped the compact shut. "God, Cass, it's such a *mess!*"

"And why are *you* here? That's what I cannot understand." Carol let her eyes flick towards the double doors. There was no sign of a strawberry linen dress. She sat back on the sofa again.

Liv shrugged. "I had to do something. Off my own bat. I know Reggie is besotted. Even now I can't bear to remember some of the things he said to me, Cass. But Myrtle . . . surely she intends to go back to the children and to Malcolm? I want to tell her about Malcolm myself." She leaned forward. "I know how he is feeling, Cass. He told me."

Carol was at a loss for words. She could not see that anything Liv might say to Myrtle would help anyone.

Liv drank her coffee and put the cup down with a click.

"Strangely enough, now that I'm . . . on the trail . . . I feel better." She lifted her brows at Carol. "I know it sounds utterly heartless, Cass, but there was nothing I could do until Malcolm took that overdose. The inactivity was simply terrible. I knew that Mon was half despising me too. Oh she's been kindness itself, don't get me wrong. But sometimes she would look at me in a way that I knew was . . . well . . . critical. After all, look at the terrible knocks she's had to take. No family, nothing."

Carol felt like protesting; there had been herself, her mother, Dilly and Gander Gosling.

Instead she said, "What *about* Mon? How long will her husband put up with this situation?"

Liv shrugged. "She doesn't love him. She and I, we're quite similar in that way still." She laughed mirthlessly. "Unloved, and unloving."

"Rubbish," Carol said without conviction. She leaned across and put a hand on Liv's arm. "*We're* still friends. All of us."

Liv laughed again. "Speak for yourself! Oh, you can speak for Mon, I suppose. But Myrtle has opted out of friendship, I'd say. Wouldn't you?"

"No." Carol's voice was strong. "No. I certainly wouldn't say that. Our friendship is still there. Remember last summer? Finding the paint pot?"

"Oh, come off it, Cass."

"I mean it. It wouldn't matter what happened. We four would have something left. Something."

"Well, if you mean Myrtle would have my husband, and Mon would have Myrtle's kids, and you would have Mon's kid, and I nearly had Myrtle's husband . . ." Suddenly and unexpectedly, Liv's eyes overflowed with tears. "Oh damn! I thought I was over all this soppy stuff. I thought I'd pulled myself together by now."

"You have. That's why you're crying. Because it's hit you that you've still got Myrtle. And me. And Mon." But Carol was white-faced at the brutality of that summing-up. She said desperately, "Liv, I know it sounds crazy, but in a strange way, what you said just now . . . doesn't it show that we still share those things? Oh God. I don't mean that we should share our husbands. I don't mean that. I don't know what I mean. But there is something, Liv. Something."

"You're upset now." Liv passed a handkerchief. "God. Here. In the swankiest hotel in Paris."

"That doesn't matter. What matters is that we don't hurt each other more than we can help. Listen." Carol blew loudly and smiled. "Not to that!" She tried to laugh as she tucked the ridiculous square of cambric into her sleeve. Then she stopped laughing and looked very serious. "Liv. I don't think you should see Myrtle. Not this time."

Liv stared at her. "Surely she has a right to know about Malcolm?"

"Yes. But he can tell her himself when she's back in England. She's been very ill, Liv. Close to a complete breakdown. She's been writing to me and I've been able to chart her recovery. If you confront her with this news, other things will be said—they're bound to be, Liv, you won't be able to control your words once you start. Forgive me, my dear, but you are the worst person to tell Myrtle. You're doing it for the wrong reasons. You want her to go back to Malcolm so that you can return to Reggie."

Liv protested angrily. "No such thing! I thought I'd explained to you—I thought you realised—I cannot go back to Reggie, ever!"

Carol looked down at her hands. Like Monica she could see no other future for Liv. She said quietly, "I wasn't criticising the idea, Liv. Not at all. I was just saying that this is not a good way to bring it about."

"Haven't I just said—!" Liv half rose as if to flee, but Carol put out a hand and she subsided again. "Cass. I don't want to talk like this. Please. I felt better—coming out here—I had a—a mission—" she sobbed a laugh—"sorry. But you know what I mean. Something definite to do. I don't want to lose that feeling. Don't try to talk me out of it. Please."

Carol swallowed. "All right. Pax. For now." She took Liv's hand and held it tightly. "Will you give up your 'mission'—just for a few hours? Let's go and have lunch somewhere. Let's talk about . . . anything. I think whatever your motives it was terrific of you to look after Myrt's children. Tell me about them. And New York."

"Mon was in charge of the boys. Well, I suppose I put them to bed sometimes. Nicky is quite a little gentleman—he opens doors . . . that kind of thing." Liv looked helpless and lost again.

Cass said, "That's what I meant about sharing things. We share the children. You and I have none, Liv. But it doesn't matter because we share Mon's and Myrtle's. Does that make sense to you?"

"I suppose so." Liv managed a wry smile. "But I'll give you this, Cass. I don't think I could have got through the last few months without Mon. And now you. After what Myrt has done to me, I needed to feel your support."

Carol thought about Myrtle: the Myrtle she had known in baggy dirndl skirts and blouses and the Myrtle who was in the Crillon with Reggie Bradbury, using a false name and wearing a straight dress with poise.

She said, "Don't hate Myrt. It . . . happened."

"You've always been an idealist, Cass."

"Not really. Most friendships are based on sheer pragmatism. I like to think ours isn't." Carol stood up, then bent to pick up her bag and added softly, "I know I'm going to sound like the manuscript I'm reading, but I actually believe this—the more love you give, the more you get."

Liv did not reply. But when Carol proffered a crooked elbow, she pushed her hand through it affectionately, and they walked through the swing doors and the foyer and into the Place to find a cafe for lunch.

Reggie and Myrtle, sitting in the foyer behind a screen of palms, registered the linked arms with foreboding.

Myrtle said, "What does it mean? Liv here. And Carol too. What are they doing? They must be looking for us—they must be! But then, why did Carol wave us away?" She pushed a hand through her careful urchin cut and it stood on end. "Reggie. I'm frightened. I'm really frightened."

"I know, Myrtle." He stared after the two women, frowning. He knew that of all four friends, Carol Woodford was the most reliable, the most staunch, the most faithful. All those years ago at Malcolm's wedding he had wanted to know her, and when finally they had met last summer, his first impressions had been confirmed. "Those letters she has written to you, darling . . . Carol is on your side. I'm sure of it."

"She understands. Yes." Myrtle's initial panic had abated. "But she won't be on anyone's side, Reggie. Carol isn't like that." She looked at him. "It might be something to do with the children. Carol wants to stop Liv blurting it out."

"Rubbish. If there was anything wrong with your family, Carol would be the first to come and tell you so. You know that."

Myrtle swallowed. "Yes. Yes, you're right of course. Then Liv is going to try and get me to go home, Reggie. Or to make you . . . Reggie, what are we going to do? We've never talked about the future properly. I know I said I was leaving Malcolm . . . but I didn't say that I was leaving the boys."

It was Reggie's turn to be frightened.

"You wouldn't—Myrt, you couldn't—we're everything for each other. You've said that—"

"And I've meant it. I still mean it. Now and in the future."

"You wouldn't feel you had to make any sacrifices? You know that if you sacrifice your happiness, you sacrifice mine too."

"Yes. Yes, I know."

She met his eyes but looked away before they could make their usual connection. He had no children. He loved hers, but they weren't his. If Liv and Carol had come to tell her that something was wrong with one of the boys, she might have very little choice.

Bob lay propped on pillows in Malcolm's bed, wearing Malcolm's pyjama top and watching Monica give Lennie his early-morning bottle.

"He should be sleeping properly now, hon, surely?" he asked, running his hands through his hair. "And I thought babies had their own rooms these days?"

"Not when I'm looking after them." Monica tore her gaze away from Lennie's blissfully closed eyes and frantically bellowing cheeks, and glanced at Bob. He grinned at her, but she did not grin back. She knew how he felt; the feeling of a secret shared, the secret of their love-making. It convinced her—even more than his admitted infidelity with Rosa Palmer—that it was over between them. Bob saw absolutely nothing wrong in sleeping with his wife after he had asked her for a divorce so that he could marry a woman he had made pregnant. Monica hated herself for surrendering so abysmally to his blandishments.

She said abruptly, "The trouble with me is I'm too good in bed."

He laughed. "You are, hon. But that's no trouble. Take it from me."

The teat of Lennie's bottle turned suddenly inside-out and he opened his gums to yell. She lifted him expertly on to her shoulder while she released the vacuum in the bottle. She resettled him.

She went on as if Bob had not spoken. "I can't relate love and sex. Love is something I feel for Lennie and Martin and Nicky. And Carol and Liv and Myrtle. Sex is something else."

He was affronted.

"Are you saying you never loved me, Mon baby?"

"I'm not sure."

"What about last night?"

"That's what I mean. I certainly don't love you now. I might have done earlier. I simply do not know."

"You're saying this because of Rosa. Okay, so I have to marry her. I want to marry her, dammitall—she's carrying my child. But I still love you. There. If I can admit it, so can you!"

"Bob . . . for goodness' sake. I'm trying to be honest. I don't want you going into this new marriage with an albatross around your neck! You're free! And you're lucky—you're going to have a family!"

He returned stubbornly to his point. "And what about last night?"

She looked him straight in the eye. "Bob. I'd had an awful day. An awful week. I felt totally alone. Any man would have done."

For an instant she thought he might hit her. His eyes narrowed coldly and his right hand clenched on the bedspread. Then he shook his head as if to clear it. She could almost follow his train of thought: Monica was making it easy for him . . . good old Monica . . . typical English sportswoman.

She finished winding Lennie and put him back in his cot, smiling down at him reassuringly as she smoothed the covers around his shoulders. He should sleep again until nearly nine; long enough for her to get breakfast for the boys and send them off with Doris for a walk. She felt a renewed energy as she thought about the coming day; her smile became wry, perhaps that was what last night had been about. He misinterpreted the smile.

"Christ, Mon. What will you do? You're bored enough when we're up to our eyes in the sports club and the theatre and everything. What are you going to do here? Your friend, Myrtle, whatever her name is—she can't stay away for ever. You've got yourself in the middle of a godawful mess. How are you going to get out of it?"

She shrugged. "I stay in it until it solves itself. I'm not in the solution business, Bob." She transferred the smile to him. "You should know that."

He smiled back, reassured, relieved . . . enormously relieved.

"You're a nice woman. You're a stunner. If only . . . But anyway, Mon, I'll always love you. If ever you need me, just yell. Okay?"

"Okay. That's the nicest thing you've ever said to me actually, Bob. And I'll yell. In fact I'm yelling now."

He reached for her. "Again? Christ, you're insatiable. But then, so am I—"

She slapped him away. "Not that! Idiot. I want you to shave and dress now, while the bathroom is free. Then I want you to have breakfast with Nicky and Martin and take them out for an hour. It'll be good practice for you."

He pretended to be henpecked and grumbled all through getting dressed. She watched him. It was the last time. There was something very intimate about lying in bed watching a man tuck his shirt into his trousers and fit a tie beneath his collar. When he was ready she put on her dressing-gown and kissed him chastely on the cheek.

"You're a nice man. Completely amoral, but nice."

"Immoral? I'm no such thing . . ."

She didn't explain the difference. They trailed downstairs, bickering like any old married couple. When she saw how good he was with Nicky and Martin she could have loved him properly, but she wouldn't let herself. It was too late. But the one thing about being too late was that you had to make new beginnings. Carol would be phoning today.

Carol did not tell Liv that Myrtle and Reggie were staying at the Crillon.

They ate lunch together and talked about the past, and gradually

Liv was able to reveal her pain and unhappiness as if it were a running sore to be healed by the clean air of Carol's understanding.

They walked down the Champs Elysées to the Tuileries and sat in the gardens in the sunshine. They had so little in common, yet there was no difficulty in talking. Carol spoke of her feeling for Jean-Claude and Liv admitted for the first time that Reggie's defection had made her realise how deeply she loved him.

"When he comes home you'll be able to show him that. So that he isn't consumed with guilt."

"Oh, Cass. He won't come back. That was why I came here . . . yes, you were right of course. I can't get him back like that. But it's still the only way. He'll never come back to me of his own accord."

"I think he will. You see, he'll want to be with someone . . . make someone happy. If you were at home, waiting for him . . ."

Liv laughed uncomfortably. "I wanted to be independent. Tough. Like Mon."

"You're not like Mon. You're Liv. There's a lot to Liv Baker— show Reggie the side he hasn't met yet." Carol shifted the fine gravel with her toe. "You've found out that Reggie is a very passionate person. Can you fill that need in him, Liv?"

Liv stared. "You've changed. You couldn't have said that when we were girls!"

"No." Carol blushed faintly and smiled at her friend. "Jean-Claude has made the difference, of course. But I think Bessie would have done, anyway. She is very . . . frank."

They both laughed.

Liv said, "You're so lucky, Cass."

But Carol said quickly as if touching wood, "Happiness is only on loan, remember, Liv. Like Bessie. Only on loan."

"Rubbish. You'll never lose Bessie. Oh, I suppose one day she'll learn that Mon is her real mother, but she won't forget you and your mother. Never." She tipped her head back and closed her eyes on the sunshine. "Any more than I can forget Reggie and Myrtle."

Carol stood up briskly. "Come on. Enough of that. Let's find somewhere and have a cup of tea. I'm meeting Jean-Claude this evening to tell him what is happening. Then tomorrow you and I will go back to Cheltenham and help Monica." She pulled Liv to her feet. "Listen. If Reggie and Myrtle had been—say—victims of an earthquake—you would nurse their injuries. That's what they were. Victims of an earthquake."

Liv tried to laugh.

Arm in arm they walked back towards the Place, unmistakably English, though so different. If they noticed the small knots of students hurrying in the direction of the Bastille, they did not find it remarkable. President de Gaulle was even now discussing the future of Algeria, where he had kept alive the idea of a Free French Government all through the war years. If anyone could sort out the muddle it was he. Student groups were always volatile, whether they were French, English, American or whatever.

In their room at the Crillon, Reggie wondered whether there might be a demonstration in the offing. The traffic, whirling around Concorde at high speeds as usual, was diverted, even halted momentarily, by strings of young people like threads of molecules, running between the cars. Reggie fetched his binoculars and in an effort to divert Myrtle from her constant worrying about the sudden appearance of Liv and Carol, watched them carefully, reporting back to her where she lay on the bed.

"They've got some kind of banner, darling. Black. I can't see what it says."

Myrtle turned on one side and pillowed her cheek on the palm of her hand.

"Could that be why Cass is here? Maybe she is with that reporter—Jean Durant—and she asked Liv to come for a holiday and they—"

Reggie seized on this explanation gladly.

"Of course that's it, Myrtle. Why didn't I think of that? It's obvious, isn't it? Nothing at all to do with the boys. Liv was with Cass in Provence. Durant was given this assignment in Paris. They thought it was a good opportunity to show Liv the city—"

"But why come to the Crillon? I mean, it's not Cass' sort of place. And she didn't seem surprised to see us, Reggie."

"But she couldn't have known we were here, darling. If she'd known—I mean, if she was looking for us—she'd hardly wave us away like that, would she?"

"No. She wouldn't want Liv to see us. But supposing Liv had come to find us. To tell us something about the boys. Or Mon. And Cass saw her by accident. And—"

"Honey. Cass knows we are here. She doesn't know what name we're using, but she knows we're here and she'll find a way to contact us. All we have to do is sit tight. Which is okay by us, yes?" He smiled over the binoculars, then put them to his eyes and swept the enormous circus again. "Those youngsters seem to have met up and gone into the Métro. I'll ring down for some newspapers."

"We could switch on that wireless."

"Can't understand the lingo unless it's written down, can you?" He steadied the binoculars and concentrated.

"Let's go down for dinner, Reggie. We shall pick up more from the waiter than from the newspaper."

He watched carefully. It was Liv. By herself. She was beneath them now. He went to the window and saw her disappear under the awning.

"Let's have dinner sent up, Myrtle." He came over to the bed and kissed her ear tenderly. "I don't want to share you with all those people." He moved his lips from ear to cheek and murmured, "If I never saw you again, my love, I'd always remember the feel of your skin under my mouth."

She turned and tried to focus on him.

"You're just as frightened as I am," she whispered. She put her arms around his neck. "Ah, Reggie. Don't be. We're here and it's now."

And she held him to her.

Carol's taxi crossed the Pont Neuf at six-thirty and was stopped in the Rue Madeleine by a column of people in the road, waving a banner proclaiming *"Liberté pour Algérie."* She wound down the window and heard them chanting the words like a mantra.

"What is it?" She spoke in English after being with Liv for so long, and the taxi-driver replied in English too.

"They are young and impatient. Not willing to wait. There is much ill-feeling." He leaned on his horn and received some black looks. "They are congregating around the Sorbonne. Also the Bastille. Do not be out late, *mademoiselle.*"

"Thank you. I do not expect to be."

But the hold-up continued and by seven-thirty she was beginning to wonder whether she might miss Jean-Claude.

"I'll walk." She leaned forward to pay the driver. "I am sorry, you are well and truly caught in this crowd."

He let her alight with many warnings which she hardly heard for the sheer press of people around the vehicle. However, as soon as she went into the crowd, there was a furious honking behind her and she saw the taxi do an about-turn and honk its way back towards the river. Unexpectedly she suddenly felt isolated and very foreign among the motley collection of students.

A young girl with hair and eyes as black as Bessie's spoke to her. "You are English? You would join us?"

Carol hated crowds and could hardly think straight. She tried to work her way diagonally to the other side of this impenetrable mass.

"I'm trying to find a friend," she panted.

"Ah. One of us?"

"Yes. I suppose so."

"*Bien.* Then come—come—venez ici—"

The girl took her arm and wormed her way between two young giants labelled "Maquis." She shouted something at them and they shouldered another opening, and the next minute Carol was among the stragglers on the other side of the column.

"Thank you. Thank you so much," she gasped at the dark-haired girl. But she had already gone and the young giants roared *"Vive la liberté!"* and marched on.

She moved on down the Avenue, and leaned against one of the acacia trees to watch the last of the demonstrators. She hoped Liv had got back to the Crillon all right and that she would not see Reggie and Myrtle. Perhaps she should have told her that they were in fact staying in the same hotel, presumably under a false name. But she hadn't, and it was too late now.

She took some deep breaths and relaxed her stiffened spine. She was wearing a blue dress with a deeper blue cardigan, both rather the worse for wear now. She straightened the cardigan self-consciously. Jean-Claude would say it was typically English, but it seemed to her that on a summer's evening there was really nothing else to wear. Certainly Liv had worn a linen suit and Myrtle appeared to be wearing something vaguely Chinese, but such fashions were no good to Carol.

She began to walk towards the Reine Blanche. If Jean-Claude wasn't there, she didn't know where to find him. She hoped very much—in fact with all her soul—that he would be there. She was experiencing a strange sense of déjà vu. As if there might be another explosion, another fire.

But he was there.

She paused in the little side street where he had left the Renault that time, and saw the familiar outline of him in the same seat that he'd occupied that night. She could see the shape of a bowl before him, and there were other bowls too. She wondered how many he had managed tonight. She walked along the wide pavement towards the entrance, picking her way between the outside tables, transferring her bag from one shoulder to the other, thinking he would glance up and see her and come running to meet her. She looked up again. He was with someone. Of course he would be. There would be other reporters, and some of them would be women.

But this woman was vaguely familiar. Carol stopped beneath an umbrella and blinked her eyes clear. The woman was leaning over her bowl, laughing, spooning soup into her mouth. Carol had seen her picture just that day.

It was Gaby.

There was an instant's hiatus of thought and action. And then small things clicked into place. Gaby was happy. She was actually laughing at this man who was her husband—laughing with him. Yes, he was laughing too. And Gaby had never laughed all the time she had worked with Carol in the Paris office; she had been secretive and mysterious and entirely without laughter. And all those soup bowls. Six soup bowls. They were on the last two. They had shared six bowls of onion soup. Gaby was a model now, featured in *Paris Match*, used to more exotic fare than onion soup.

Carol turned and walked quickly across the road and behind the screen of acacia trees. She closed her eyes and told herself she was being a fool and it was all right. But she couldn't face them now. She couldn't look as if she'd followed him here.

She began to walk briskly, intending to go back to the Crillon to find Liv, eat dinner with her and be normal again.

At the Pont Neuf she met up with the column of marchers. She turned away, almost sobbing with frustration, wondering how she could get across the river. Coming towards her was another column of people. Gendarmerie. They appeared to be carrying dustbin lids in front of them. She glanced from them to the marchers. They had seen the police and were turning to meet them with a concerted howl that sounded animal-like. Carol searched their anonymous faces for the familiar one of the dark-haired girl, but could see only open mouths and aggressive flags.

She was suddenly possessed by an unnatural terror. She knew

it stemmed from that previous incident four years ago and was activated by everything that was happening to her here and now: Myrtle and Reggie, Liv and Monica, Jean-Claude and Gaby. She tried to use mental logic to calm herself, but the only logic she knew was Jean-Claude. She should have stayed at the cafe and seen him. She had to get back there quickly.

For some reason the police were beating the dustbin lids with their truncheons. The noise from the marchers had escalated to a near-scream, and they were moving towards her.

She began to run towards the police.

At the Reine Blanche, Jean-Claude offered Gaby a Gauloise and sat back in his chair. He wondered what he had ever seen in her. She was so pretty, so smug and self-satisfied, so egotistic.

He said, "Are you sure you'll be all right, Gaby?"

She smiled again, showing perfect, pointed teeth.

"Certainly. Marcel is a film star you know, *chéri*. He understands that I, too, am in show business. He will get me a part quite soon." Her smile widened. "Oh yes, I shall be very all right."

He lit her cigarette and nodded slowly.

"You know I have wanted a divorce for some time now. I am . . . grateful."

"You would not have it if it did not suit me, Jean-Claude!" At least she was honest. She exhaled smoke through parted lips. "Though I refused before, *chéri*, for your own sake. I did not think your infatuation with the English Carol would last. She is not suitable for you, *chéri*. She is not . . ." she searched for a word, her eyes narrowed in concentration. "She is not *amusant*."

Jean-Claude considered for an instant trying to explain to Gaby what fun it was to be with Carol, then gave up the idea. She would never understand.

He said, "Well. Perhaps you know her only in one way." He must be diplomatic. She was capricious and could change her mind on a whim. "After all, Gaby, in the office it was a little different."

She shrugged. "It is of no importance." She smiled again. "It has been *amusant* for me"—she waved her cigarette to indicate the small cafe. "Meeting like this—so *mystérieux* . . . you must have wondered who wanted to see you. And when you got here, why there were six bowls of onion soup all ready to be eaten!" She laughed deliciously and leaned forward. "Or did you recognise my voice on the telephone and wish to see me again, Jean? Was that it? A double secret?"

He smiled obediently. He had known his anonymous caller was Gaby, and he had come here tonight in the ever-present hope that she wanted to marry someone else. At last it had happened, and now he could ask Carol if she would marry him.

He said, "You were always up to such tricks, Gaby. I should have remembered."

"It was why you fell in love with me first, yes? You called me your taste of happiness!"

"Yes. Yes, I did." The recollection made him suddenly sad, as if he had been disloyal to Carol.

She was serious. "And you saved me from much unpleasantness, Jean. I am still grateful for that. I had enjoyed the war. There were people who resented me enjoying myself. Then you came along— the brave Free Frenchman—and you married me! Who could criticise me then?" She shrugged again. "Pouf! There are still people who resent me enjoying myself. I do not care a fig for them!"

He waited until she finished the cigarette, then said, "Gaby, I told my photographer to meet me here at eight o'clock to cover the student demonstration. When he arrives I must go. The lawyers will send me the papers no doubt?"

"It is all organised." She stood up. "Get me a taxi, Jean. I am having a proper dinner with Marcel later." She smiled roguishly. "My days of onion soup are over!"

It seemed a fitting epitaph. He waited with her beneath the pavement umbrellas until the taxi arrived. Down towards the river there was a constant noise from the demonstrators. They must be crossing the Seine to meet up with others from the university. He wondered where his photographer had got to, and wished he had brought his own camera.

"Listen." Gaby looked up at him in surprise. "Is it drums? They must have a band."

He frowned, then said, "It is police batons. Beating their shields. They're trying to disperse the students before they can become threatening."

"Young fools," Gaby said unemotionally. "Causing inconvenience to good citizens." She looked the other way. "Ah. Here is my taxi." She got in and slammed the door. "Au 'voir, Jean. We shall meet again. Of that I am certain."

He did not watch her drive away. He began to run towards the noise. He was used to violence and he could smell it in the air, hear it in the muttered roar of the students and the beating of the police shields. If there was a story he had to be there to report it. But it was more than a journalistic urge that sent him accelerating along the Saint-Germain; he did not know what it was. His heart was hammering in his chest and his head was filled with a nightmare terror that he had never experienced before.

He saw the backs of the police, a solid phalanx across the boulevard. Beyond them there was a mass of people and the usual array of banners; not waving in the slight breeze as they would have done if held still, but jerking spasmodically as their bearers became aggressive. He saw the whites of faces and gesturing hands and knew that they were all young people. Probably unwise, even foolish, but idealistic and with the terrible power of idealism.

He came to the police guard as the first stone crashed among them.

"Let me through," he panted. "*La Planète*—I can talk to them—they will listen to me. Let me through!"

"*Retirez monsieur!*"

An angry face was turned on him, and someone—obviously an inspector—came and took his arm.

Then another hail of stones caused a momentary gap in the line of police, and he saw someone running towards him. He could not believe, for an interminable second, that it was Carol. She was back in the safety of the Bergerie with her mother and Bessie. The girl running so desperately in his direction wore a blue frock very like Carol's, and a blue cardigan identical to the one Carol had bought in London last year. But it could not be Carol.

And then something hit her. He could not see what it was, but she went down in a sprawled heap, her arm stretched out, her shoulder back at an angle to her body. And he saw that it was Carol.

In the sudden shocked silence, his cry filled the air. He was through the gap and running towards her. The police inspector shouted a warning, but if the stones had been machine-gun bullets it would have made no difference. He was on his knees, skidding to a stop by her head.

"Cass—my Cass—" he heard his own voice, high, like a child's. Blood was oozing from the back of her head and darkening her sun-striped hair. The hair hung in loops from its pins and he pulled them out frantically, frightened that the pins themselves might have impaled themselves in her scalp. She was unconscious, but she was breathing.

"Get an ambulance!" He lifted his head. He knew he was weeping but did not care. *"Vite!* An ambulance!"

Someone knelt by him.

"She was with us earlier, *m'sieu*. She was looking for you."

He glanced sideways and saw through his tears the wavering face of a young girl not much older than Bessie.

He said, "She'll be all right, won't she? It's just a surface wound—she'll be all right?"

But the girl had disappeared, wrenched away by official hands. The police, doubtless trained in first aid, were all around. There were blankets and a white box with a red cross printed on it. And then the blessed sound of the ambulance.

He said, "I must go with her. Let me through . . ."

But there was no need for further struggle. The crowd had magically dispersed and the way was clear. The stretcher slid on to its shelf and he followed it in and knelt again, his arms protectively over the blanketed figure.

They told him she would be all right. The ambulance man who travelled inside tried to help by saying that she had done the police a great service because the demonstration was over without anyone being hurt. Then he realised what he had said and tucked the red blanket around Carol's neck carefully, Jean-Claude found himself abandoning the enormous question of why Carol was there at that precise time, and asking himself whether the red blanket was to disguise bloodstains. He tried to recall how he had dealt with emergencies on his many travels, especially in Suez where he had taken over an ambulance and driven twenty miles through enemy territory. He remembered feeling very calm, almost detached. Not like this. Not weak and shaky and completely helpless.

He said suddenly, "She's wet—oh God—she's wet! She's bleeding somewhere else!"

The ambulance man pushed him out of the way and flipped back the blanket.

"Urine."

It sounded simple enough, but still the man crouched above her clamping an oxygen mask over the white face.

"Hold this if you please," he said to Jean-Claude brusquely.

Somehow they changed places in the cramped confines of the van. Jean-Claude knew suddenly that this was an emergency. He felt the weakness in his limbs drain away, and he became very cold. He leaned close to Carol's ear and said quietly, "My strength is going into you, beloved. Feel it. Know it."

The ambulance man was pounding on her chest. The ambulance took a wide turn somewhere and they all swung inwards. For a moment Jean-Claude imagined that Carol was leaning on him responsively, and his right arm went beneath her head to hold her to him. And then, with terrible certainty, he knew she was dead.

He pushed aside the mask and held her face to his in a spasm of grief that seemed to explode his soul. At his left shoulder the ambulance man had given up his attempts at artificial respiration. He said quietly, "I am sorry, *m'sieur*. Very sorry." Jean-Claude made no reply. He was conscious that something was happening. He held Carol to him quite gently and knew that they were in a void together. They were still together. Then he was alone, yet not alone. He was filled with her. She had told him once that he had become Jean-Claude-Carol and he had thought he had known what she meant. He had not known. He did now.

Very gently he laid her head back and took away his arm. He remembered that void and wished himself back there; yet knew she was no longer there. She was here.

Even so his voice said, "She cannot be gone. It is not true." The ambulance man responded instantly to the new emergency and pushed him firmly back on the other stretcher. And then everyone else took over. It was in their behaviour that Jean-Claude knew of his own outward state. Inside he was calm and whole. Nobody else knew this. He sat very still and let Carol's being fill him again and again. He was lifted and taken into a hospital and heard someone say the word catatonic, and thought how amusing it was.

Liv waited in the foyer at the Crillon until ten o'clock, when she knew she and Carol had missed the train. The old fear and isolation began to overtake her. She wondered whether she had dreamed the whole episode of meeting Carol yesterday. It was possible. She had read an article in one of Malcolm's osteopathy magazines about something called psychosomatic pain and hallucination. She tried to remember exactly what it had been about, but could not. She could barely remember why she was in Paris at all. When she looked up and saw Myrtle and Reggie coming towards her, she thought they really were part of the dream she must be having. Then she saw that Myrtle was weeping and Reggie was holding out his arm to her as if to include her in their grief. She held back, telling herself she hated them both. Myrtle did not look like Myrtle at all, she was small and smart and strangely French. But Reggie was the same, and Reggie had been cruel.

Reggie said briefly, "We telephoned Mrs. Woodford. The girl—I expect you've heard about it—it was Carol."

Myrtle took her by the upper arm; her weeping was uncontrolled and embarrassing.

"It's our faults, Liv. All our faults. And Carol . . . oh God, Liv, Carol is innocent!"

Liv said, "What has happened to Carol?" At least it wasn't a dream. None of it was a dream.

Reggie said, "She's been killed. During the riots last night. Mrs. Woodford said you were here and Carol had come to see you. We thought you must have heard."

Liv drew back slightly and looked at them both. The news was at once unacceptable and inevitable. There had had to be a sacrifice. It had not been Mallie; Mallie's death had caused the events that followed, not atoned for them. It had not been Malcolm; his suicide attempt had been almost ludicrous. No. It was Carol.

Nevertheless, she said, as Jean-Claude had done, "It isn't true—it can't be true!"

Reggie tried to gather her in again, but she held back. "We've asked for a taxi. We're going to the hospital. Come with us, Liv—"

"No! I have to meet Carol!"

He repeated gently, "Come with us. We should be together now."

The realisation that she would not be meeting Carol and going home with her hit Liv like a blow in the solar plexus. As she bent with the pain of it, Reggie's arm encircled her at last and drew her to him. She felt Myrtle's hand on her shoulder. They stood together. Carol's death had brought them together.

essie survived. She did not want to survive. For a long time she thought quite seriously about trying something like Uncle Malcolm had tried that awful summer—and making it work. But there were things that stopped her. There were people who stopped her. Grannie, Boris and Jean obviously topped her list of people, but her aunts came close behind. Especially Aunt Myrt. She did not know why, but her feeling for Aunt Myrt changed with Carol's death and became painful and protective. Aunt Liv and Aunt Mon had to be protected too, but she knew instinctively that if she did an Uncle Malcolm on them they would cope with it eventually. Not Aunt Myrt. Aunt Myrt needed them all now: her husband and her children, Uncle Reggie and Aunt Liv, Grannie, Aunt Mon, Bessie herself, even Jean-Claude. Then when she thought she must go mad with her unhappiness, she discovered a way to deal with it. She invented a yellow curtain—manufactured it quite carefully in her mind—and drew it with a circular motion right around the events of that September evening. She did not think Carol would return, she did not fool herself or live in some childish make-believe world, but she simply did not look at the actuality of Carol's death, and thus it was possible to live almost normally.

She tried to share her imagined curtain with Jean-Claude and Grannie. They all stayed at the Bergerie, but not because they wanted to, just because they did not know what else to do.

Jean-Claude said, "I like that colour, *chérie*. I think always of Carol being bathed in sunshine."

But that had not been Bessie's intention at all. Her memories of Carol were strong, often monochrome. She had no wish to blur them in any way. She flung her arms around him and hugged him hard as if she could drive the terrible unhappiness out of his soul. He suffered her embrace and returned it only half-heartedly. She knew that he still loved her, but that he had also distanced himself from her. She did not know why. Sometimes she considered blurting out that she knew he was her father, but something always stopped her. Something to do with Aunt Mon. Something which she had also shrouded in her memory.

When she told Grannie about the yellow curtain, she had a much better response.

"It's like bandaging a sore leg, darling. Isn't it? You know it's still there, but it helps to make it better."

Grannie obviously used the same method. Together they limped along as best they could.

Everyone survived.

Myrtle knew she had to, not even dear Mon could look after Nicky, Martin and Lennie as she could. She agreed with Reggie that it would be a temporary arrangement, until the boys were grown-up. But she knew neither of them could make that gigantic leap together again.

She wrote to him every week. In the autumn of 1962 Lennie started kindergarten. Myrtle left him there with a strange feeling of release. He could no longer be seen as substitute for Mallie; Mallie had never gone to school. Lennie had a life of his own now. She watched him run confidently into the playground with the other children and wondered whether she might even make friends with him.

That afternoon she wrote to Reggie.

Lennie started school this morning. I waited by the gates and watched him. He is so like Malcolm. It never occurs to him that people might not like him. He rolled across the playground like a small red barrel in his new red blazer, grabbed someone's hand and had organised a game of Poor Mary before the other kids had said goodbye to their mothers. I never worry about him like I worry about Nicky and Martin. Sometimes, Reggie, I think Mallie took most of my love and concern with him when he died. You started to resurrect it during our time together and if it hadn't been for you I could never have come back to Malcolm and cared for the children again. I think you knew that at the time, Reggie. Didn't you? In a way you always knew you were making me better in order for me to go back home. And if it hadn't been for my illness, Reggie, we would never have gone away together in the first place, would we? This is such a difficult letter, my darling. I shall always love you, but can we be really honest, Reggie? Will either of us be able to hurt Liv and Malcolm all over again? I don't think so. Perhaps in a year or two we might be able to spend some time together without hurting either of them. Just a day. Just to talk—nothing else—just to look at each other. Darling, when Lennie went off to school, without a backward glance, my thoughts came to you. My dearest love. I am so hopeless at writing letters. Carol understood them, and I can only pray that you will too. Now that all three boys are at school, there are some hours in every day which are my own, and in those hours my thoughts will always be with you. Not with Mallie. Not with Cass. But with you. I bless you for this because it means I want to live. Dear Reggie, I hope so much that you want to live too. Ever yours, Myrtle.

Liv knew that the letters which arrived so regularly were from Myrtle. She would pick them up from the hall floor and put them carefully on the table for Reggie to find when he got home from work. She was surprised that she felt so little resentment or jealousy at their regularity. Perhaps she no longer looked on Reggie as hers; certainly they did not sleep together and though they would spend evenings at home companionably enough, they never went out together either.

The love which had flared when she lost him was quite different now, changed by Cass' death into a concern for him and his wellbeing. In an odd way she would worry if Myrtle's letters stopped.

This time when she placed the envelope meticulously next to the clothes brush, she felt that it was heavier than usual. Letter-writing was anathema to Myrtle—Liv remembered only too well from schooldays what Myrtle's spelling was like—and her notes to Reggie were usually as flimsy as airmails. This one was not exactly bulky, but it had some substance.

That evening she waited until the dinner things were stacked in the dishwasher and they were sitting at right angles to the television ready for a serial called "A for Andromeda," then she said, "Everything all right down in Cheltenham?"

Reggie glanced at her warily. "Fine." He cleared his throat, then shifted in his seat. Then he added, "Lennie started kindergarten yesterday apparently."

"Oh."

She had known that, of course. Monica had rung from Exeter to say she was sending him a school satchel and it hardly seemed like three years since they had wheeled him along the Prom, did it? Liv had agreed, but she hadn't sent Lennie anything. The science-fiction serial was announced and the credits rolled up.

She said, "So Myrtle is free again."

Reggie became still.

"You read her letter?"

"No. I've never read one of Myrtle's letters to you, Reggie. Surely you know that?" She was hurt more than angry.

He breathed normally and stared at the screen. "Sorry."

She said, "Look. Reggie. If you have to go to see her . . . then go. I mean it. I came back to you to try to make something else— not what we had—neither of us wanted that back again." She sighed sharply. "And I certainly did not expect you to fall in love with me." She leaned forward. "Reggie, I know you loved Myrtle. I know you still love her."

He was almost shocked by her honesty; she had indeed changed.

"You came back to make something else? What do you mean by that, Liv? What were you trying to make?"

"I don't know. I still don't know. Carol's death had to mean something. It brought Myrt back to her children—you can't deny that."

"No. I don't deny it. But I think she might have done that anyway. Quite soon."

"Well . . . I don't know. Maybe. But we wouldn't have joined up again—I'm sure of that. I was too bitter, too . . . oh I don't know. It doesn't matter now, I suppose. I just want you to know that if you have to see Myrtle, you do not need to—to pretend you're playing golf."

He remembered the lie he had lived that frightful winter when he had thought Myrtle would die.

"Liv . . . I'm sorry."

She was surprised. Since Carol's death three years before, he had never apologised to her.

She said slowly, "I'm sorry too. It was an earthquake. We were all injured in one way or another."

"I meant . . . the lies. But, I suppose you're right about the earthquake."

"Carol said that."

"Ah."

They watched the screen but saw no more than moving shapes.

After the news, Reggie stood up and switched off. He said quietly, "I want to see Myrtle. But she doesn't need me like she did before. I'm not going to Cheltenham."

Liv closed her eyes momentarily. When Reggie was at the door, she said huskily, "If you have to go—at any time—will you tell me?"

He paused and looked back at her. For the first time he noticed that the baby curls were pale with grey threads. He said, "Yes."

Monica survived better than any of them. In 1962 she was State Registered and working in the Children's Hospital in Exeter.

Before Carol's death Monica had been determined to become a nurse, but when she had the frantic telephone call from Liv that glorious September morning her decision had become resolution. Hard work had got her through tragedy before, and she knew it would again. For perhaps ten minutes she examined the idea that now Bessie would need her. Then she discarded it. She had less right to Bessie than ever now. And if she tried to offer herself, Bessie might well end up hating her.

Monica was the ideal nurse. She was not sentimental, but her compassion was limitless—or at any rate she had not yet reached its limit. She could supply what the patient needed, from a bedtime cuddle for homesick toddlers, to tough tactics with the convalescents.

One night she nursed a five-year-old from this world into the next, and went off duty two hours late.

The night sister followed her down the ward.

"Thank you, nurse. Are you all right?"

"Yes." Monica was surprised at the question.

"Would you like a sleeping tablet?"

"No. Thank you, sister." Monica smiled, reassuring her senior. "I never lie awake." She nearly added "when I sleep alone" but luckily did not. But it was true. She went to her tiny cubby-hole in the nurses' home, and fell into bed. If she thought of the child who was now being moved into the mortuary, it was with deep thankfulness that he had escaped all pain and distress for ever. Once, she had found herself murmuring, "Another one for you, Carol." But only once. In Monica's opinion, so much of religion was akin to whimsy.

Mary Woodford knew that one day her grief would catch up with her and she would be quite literally pole-axed. She postponed that day by some pretty desperate methods. Bessie's "curtain" was one; work was another; the reasons for the postponement were, in themselves, yet another.

Those reasons were, simply, that Bessie and Jean-Claude needed her. Bessie's need was obvious: the child could not manage alone, and though Monica would provide a home for her at the drop of a hat, any kind of transferral—physical or mental—was out of the question. Mary prayed constantly for life and strength until Bessie finished school.

Jean-Claude's need was perhaps less obvious. His life went on much as it had when Carol was alive. He spent blocks of time abroad or in Paris, and then would come home to the Bergerie and take up a domestic life with apparent relish.

But Mary knew that although he wanted to be with her and Bessie, the relish was entirely forced. He had nowhere else to go, nothing else to do. Gaby and he were divorced. He was free ... and lonely. He had no official capacity at the Bergerie. He was not a grieving widower, nor a loyal son-in-law. He was, as he had always been, just a friend.

Mary could think of no solution. Bessie's eventual career—or marriage—would make things worse. She wondered what the future could hold for him, and knew that he too, being an intelligent man, would wonder also. She shivered. There would come a time when she could do no more for Jean-Claude. Carol had always thought he would be the one to be killed. It had happened the other way round. And Carol would have managed far better than he could.

■

Boris Denning spent two very boring years learning how to be a signalman and was determined never to lose his freedom again. In the autumn of 1961 he managed to visit Bessie in France, and they talked as naturally and as easily as they always had done.

"I'd shoot my foot—like they used to in the Great War," he said to Bessie. "Or be a Bevin Boy. Anything."

He'd met her out of school as a surprise. She was nearly sixteen then, leggy and very beautiful. He was more like his father than ever. They made a striking pair, and Bessie's friends hung back, whispering and giggling. She put her nose in the air and ignored them.

"It would be different if there was a war, or another emergency like Suez," she said wisely. "At least it wouldn't be a waste of time, then."

"I was worried about you," he explained. "Oh God, Bessie. When all that happened just as I'd gone in—"

"You wouldn't have got compassionate leave however long you'd been in," she said matter-of-factly. "We're not related, you see. Jean-Claude told me that."

"I would've," he maintained stubbornly.

They swung into the track and walked between the massed chrysanthemums; the smell was pungent and very autumnal.

He said, "How are you? D'you realise I haven't seen you for a whole year, and that was only a four-day leave?"

"Of course I realise it, idiot." She glanced sideways, unsmiling. "Have you still got my bracelet? Did you keep it with you all the time?"

"Yes. And yes." He produced it from a pocket and made to return it to her. She pushed it away.

"It's our engagement thing!" She sounded annoyed. "If I take it back it means we're not going to get married!"

He laughed uncomfortably. He was twenty and she was still only fifteen. But he replaced the bracelet in his pocket and was thankful. He had wondered whether Carol's death might have changed their relationship. However unsuitable it might be, he couldn't have borne that.

He talked to Jean-Claude about his career. They had always got on well even when Bessie wasn't around: they had a lot of interests in common.

304

Jean-Claude approved his plans to go back to art college and specialise in camera work.

"So much design work will be redundant in a very few years, my friend." Jean-Claude shook his head regretfully. "But the accuracy and immediacy of the photograph . . . especially the television film. How would you feel about that?"

Boris grinned. "Bessie and I used to talk about travelling the world filming."

Jean-Claude did not return the smile. "Bessie has her education to finish, Boris. You must understand that."

"Of course . . ." Boris found himself almost stammering or calling Jean "sir" or something equally silly.

"I might be able to get you something. A trainee cameraman with a film crew. Yes, it would certainly mean travelling."

Boris stammered in earnest; he was overwhelmed. "Could you? Really? It would be marvellous."

"It would mean being away. For long periods."

"I . . . understand." Boris looked at the older man frankly. "You want me out of the way. While Bessie grows up."

Jean-Claude lifted his shoulders. "I am not as definite as that, Boris. But the crew I have in mind produce films of exotic locations. Pearl-diving. Primitive tribal living. It would mean being away for a year. Perhaps more."

"No holidays at the Bergerie for a while."

"Probably not."

"You know that I will come back? You know that I love Bessie?"

"That is understood." Jean-Claude inclined his head as if bowing to the inevitable.

"She will be . . . thrilled."

"Then try to angle your course towards filming. And I will see what I can do."

"That's . . . wonderful. I can't thank you enough."

In 1962, he went to say goodbye to his sister.

Lennie had been at kindergarten for two weeks and already Myrtle was taking a few patients in the old waiting room and talking of making it into a second treatment room. It was as if her letter to Reggie had released her in some way and though Boris knew nothing of that, he could see the re-emergence of his down-to-earth commonsensical sister. This time with something added:

305

an independence; a freedom from all kinds of fetters.

It was good to see her enthusiasm when he told her about his job. He had secured a trainee position with one of the new commercial television companies and was being sent to Australia to do some underwater filming around the Barrier Reef. There had been several interviews with film companies, overtly arranged by Jean-Claude. Boris was not absolutely certain how much influence Jean had exerted in this case; as the project entailed at least fifteen months' filming at the other end of the world, he assumed—wryly—that Jean had pulled quite a few strings.

He said diplomatically, "I think it was something to do with Jean-Claude. There were about forty applications from all the art colleges in the country—they interviewed fifteen and I didn't have the qualifications of some of them!"

"Rubbish!" Myrtle told him stoutly. "You've always been able to do anything with a camera. Besides, how would a Frenchman know anyone in British television?"

"He's an international journalist, Myrt! He told me he would pull a few strings."

Myrtle smiled. "Bessie's been nagging him then. I sometimes think the only reason she took to Jean was because she saw him as being a help to you!"

He said quietly, "She thinks he is her father, Sis. That's the real reason she is so devoted."

"My God! You're joking, Borrie!"

"No. She told me before Carol was killed. It has been her one consolation."

Myrtle was appalled. She stared at her brother who was so like his father. Yet so completely different.

"You'll have to tell her the truth, Borrie. You're the only one who can. You do *know* the truth, do you?"

"That she is Monica's child. Yes. I think she knows it too. Something happened in New York, when she went there . . . she never talks about it, but I think in her heart of hearts she must know."

"Yes, but do you know who her father really is? Obviously you don't. No-one does except us girls, I suppose. It's Giles Cook. Monica's adoptive brother."

It was Boris' turn to be appalled.

"That . . . layabout? Bessie's father? Oh no—Myrt, are you certain?"

"Monica told us herself that summer. It's true."

Boris was silent, assimilating this unwelcome news. Finally he said, "Well, I couldn't have told her about Jean-Claude before. I certainly can't now. The only way to convince her that he's not her father is to tell her the name of her real father. And I'm not telling her that it's Giles Cook!"

Myrtle saw the point of that.

She said, "Well. I suppose it doesn't matter. Not really." She glanced at the clock. "It's time to meet Lennie, Boris. Are you coming?"

Bessie would be seventeen that Christmas and she wanted to leave the convent and join the staff of *La Planète*.

She had expected resistance from Jean-Claude, but not the complete barrier put up by her grandmother.

"It's the most ridiculous idea I've heard of!" Mary looked at Jean-Claude. "Tell her, Jean. She has always wanted to use her drawing skills—there is no place for that in journalism!"

"Grannie—I wanted to draw flowers when I was a little girl! Now I want a career! Cass worked with books and Jean-Claude works on newspapers. Surely it is obvious—"

Jean-Claude interrupted calmly. "Listen, *chérie*. The day of the cub reporter is gone. Now you need to go to journalists' college and learn all there is to learn about newspapers. And in order to get there, you will have to stay at school for at least another two years."

Mary said, "But in any case, Jean—"

"That is necessary whatever Bessie eventually decides to do, Mary." Jean looked at the older woman meaningfully. "If she should then decide to turn to botanical research—"

"I only wanted to do that because I thought Boris and I could work together," Bessie declared hotly. "Now I know that is impossible, surely it is natural I should wish to work with Jean?"

Mary said carefully, "Perhaps it is natural in our circumstances, darling. We are very close. Perhaps too close. You know that you are adopted, so that legally you and I belong to each other. But—"

Bessie began to feel desperate. "Then if it's natural, that's all right. Isn't it?"

"What I meant was, *we* understand how you feel. We think it is natural. Outsiders will not agree." Mary folded her hands. "I'm sorry, Bessie darling. But I think it would be much better if you went into something else. And botanical research sounds just your thing."

"Grannie—stop it!" Suddenly Bessie could bear it no more. She stood up. "I know Cass was my real mother! I understand that! And I know Jean is my real father! I am not a child any more—I can understand how it happened! I want to follow in their footsteps, Grannie. I want to work with my father. Why can't we bring it into the open—I know when I was a child you wanted to shield me . . . but—"

Jean-Claude too stood up. His face was chalk-white and his voice, when he spoke, was hoarse.

"Bessie! Stop! You do not know what you say." He took a deep breath. "Let us be clear about one thing, child. I am not your father." He made for the door. "I am not Carol's husband. I am nothing. Nothing to either of you." He opened the door and turned to look at Mary. "I think you should tell her. And then I think you should finish her education in England among her friends."

Mary said, "Jean—please! Do not go! I think of you as Carol's husband and my son—you must know that—"

But the door closed quietly after him.

Bessie made to follow him and then stopped and looked around at Mary. She was shaking, near tears.

"What did he mean? Grannie, what is happening?"

And so . . . wearily . . . Mary began to tell Monica's story.

In spite of Mary's reassurances, Jean-Claude moved out the next day. Only a week later he applied for, and got, a post as correspondent in Algiers. The country had at last gained its independence, and Jean-Claude, as de Gaulle's unofficial envoy, had been responsible for many of the negotiations. He had seen his work there as a tribute to Carol, but he knew that this new post—to report on the country's progress—was nothing to do with her. This was self-inflicted banishment.

Mary and Bessie went home. It was as if all the things that had happened came home to roost at last and they could no longer face the Bergerie. They spent two weeks packing up all the things they wanted to keep and arranging for them to be put into store. Bessie cast a thought to the mountain plateau where the symbolic paint can lay buried, but it was meaningless now. She felt empty and utterly helpless; all her schoolgirl energy and enthusiasm had gone. She was reading Shelley's poetry and the life of Byron, and she wondered whether she might be going into a decline.

Mary had plans for buying back the old house in Northfield and sending Bessie to the grammar school at Kings Norton, but the house was not for sale and the autumn term was well advanced: Bessie would need to do a lot of reading at home to qualify for the university entrance course. They stayed with the Dennings and though Bessie had Boris' old room, she could not settle to any books. She missed the view of the mountain terribly, but had no desire at all to go back there. She was in a curious no-man's-land where nothing much mattered and though she wasn't ill she certainly wasn't well, either. She took to walking in the park where she and Boris had met so often and so coincidentally when she had been a small girl.

Mary rang Monica and told her that Bessie knew everything.

"She's taking it badly," Mary reported. "Will you come up and talk to her?"

On the other end of the phone, Monica studied her red nurse's hands carefully. Life was so damned ironic; at one time she would have leapt at such a chance, but now . . . what could she offer a girl of seventeen? Did she really want to give up her nursing and make a home for her?

She said, "Has she asked to see me?"

"No. It's the lack of curiosity that has me bothered, Mon. It's not natural."

Monica said astutely, "She's known inside her head for some time. She's angry with herself."

"Perhaps that's it. It's more than that though. She's losing Carol all over again." Mary began to weep. "Sorry, Mon. It's . . . awful. We'd got something together between us in France . . . we didn't dream—Jean and I—that she was seeing him as a father. A father figure perhaps. But not a real father. She's lost them both, Mon. Something has to fill the—the vacuum."

"Yes, but if I force myself on her . . . listen—will you ask her outright if she would like to talk to me? She can ask me anything she likes. I'll come then."

Mary swallowed her tears. "Yes. All right, Mon. Thank you." She knew what Bessie would say. And she was right. Monica was the last person Bessie wanted to see.

■

It was the worst winter for years. The snow began before Christmas and by the middle of January was piled everywhere in drifted, abstract shapes that bore little relationship to the objects they covered.

Bessie had still not started school, still not started a serious course of work. She hated everything now: hated the snow, hated living at Dr. Denning's big house on the Bristol Road, hated the old familiar Brummy accents all around her, more especially hated herself. She knew she was making Grannie ill and Mrs. Denning even more anxious than usual. Mrs. Baker had called yesterday and Bessie had heard her say that it was a case of sparing the rod and spoiling the child. When Bessie went into the lounge she pretended she had been talking about her eldest daughter's little boy, but Bessie knew that was not true. She wondered whether she really did need a good beating; impossible to imagine Jean administering punishment, but supposing he appeared and suddenly smacked her across her face as if she were hysterical. Would it snap her out of this dreadfulness? If so, she would willingly put up with it. But not from anyone else. Not even Boris. Especially not Boris.

She went for her usual afternoon walk in the park. No-one had used the swings that day and the seats were three feet thick with snow, the chains solid white ropes. She swept one of the seats with her forearm and shook the chains vigorously until they emerged from their sheath, then sat down and began to swing idly. Her breath vaporised before her; already her fingers and toes were numb and her nose hurt. She'd have to go home again and make another pretence at doing some work.

Then a voice said, "What's a pretty girl like you doing out of school on a day like this?" And she looked up to see a man just beyond the rank of swings, blowing on his gloved hands, red with cold, short and rather fat and not attractive, but grinning at her cheekily as if they were old friends. She had never seen him before.

She said, "Killing time. Feeling fed up." At least with this stranger she could be honest.

"That won't do." His grin became wider. He moved closer, beating his arms around his barrel chest now. "You're playing truant, aren't you? Nice girl like you too. What's the world coming to?"

She knew she should brush him off now; pleasantries had been exchanged and that was that. But in spite of his unprepossessing appearance she felt strangely at ease with him. She said, "Oh, it's not really like that. I haven't started school yet."

He laughed. "Not started school? Where's your trike then? Where's your dolly's pram?"

And she laughed too. "Oh, I wish I had them still!"

"Do you?" He leaned against the supporting posts and looked at her, still twinkling. "D'you know, that's something I never wish for. Going back. Oh I've had some good times—don't get me wrong—I've had some great times! But there's better ones yet, I reckon."

It was her own philosophy; or it had been until last September. She nodded sadly.

He said, "Come on now, girl. Give us a smile. That's better! I can't abide long faces—life's made for fun, I reckon."

She smiled again, nodded again.

He said, "Listen. Let's go to the pictures. What d'you say? I've just come off early shift—give me ten minutes to get changed and I'll treat you to fish and chips and Cliff Richard down at Longbridge."

"Cliff Richard?"

"His latest. *The Young Ones.* Come on, what d'you say? I'm nearly old enough to be your dad, so there'll be no hanky panky. And I reckon it's about time I was seen around with a really pretty girl again!"

She had to laugh; he was so frank and open.

She said, "I don't even know who you are. My grandmother would have a fit if she thought I was going to the pictures with a stranger!"

He sketched a ridiculous bow.

"Giles Cook at your service, madam. But you can call me Gilly."

She stared at him speechlessly for what seemed a long time. He kept laughing and flailing his arms and repeating, "Come on now, say yes. No strings attached."

It was so strange. She had considered looking him up, but not seriously and not for long. She didn't want a new father; she had a new mother and that was too much. She wanted Jean-Claude to be her father.

But here he was. Aunt Mon's adopted brother. Her natural father.

She said, "All right then. If you're sure it will be okay. I love Cliff Richard and it's too cold to stay out for long."

"Never a truer word spoked!" He crooked his arm and she took it. She didn't know why she was doing this, why she wasn't telling him that she was his daughter. It was as if she were trying to punish someone. Monica. She was trying to punish Monica for having her in the first place.

Amazingly, she enjoyed herself. Afterwards when she had left him at the edge of the snow field which was really the school playground, she tried to analyse why that had been. Grannie had described Giles Cook as an "ordinary man" which had sounded damning to Bessie's young ears. But it was his very ordinariness that made him such easy company.

She told him her name was Lizzie Durant; as far as he knew they were complete strangers. So there was none of the tangled string which made life with Grannie and everyone so tricky. She didn't have to think about what she said: quite stupid remarks, like "the snow makes lots of things private," went down with him like Einstein's theory. He came back with, "In the summer I miss my hot-water bottle," and she knew just what he meant. Especially now when going to bed was a kind of escape from everything.

Walking back up the long hill to Turves Green, they had talked about the film. He must be about the same age as Jean-Claude, yet he had enjoyed seeing Cliff and Hank and Una in their improbable story, and they had discussed it from the same standpoint. Perhaps it wasn't complimentary to him to think he was so immature, but it certainly made him easy company.

They had reached the colony of bungalows past Kalamazoo, when the rooks, disturbed from their roosting by the laughter, squawked a protest. Giles immediately parodied the title song of the film: "The young ones, always want the breadcrumbs . . ." It had been ridiculous, not a bit funny, but they had laughed uproariously.

"Let's do this again," he'd said impulsively. And she smiled secretly and said, "Let's."

Grannie was waiting anxiously for her.

"Darling, where on earth have you been? I went round to the park—it's been three hours—so dark tonight—"

"I met someone and we went to the pictures." Bessie felt better still. Somehow, all powerful. She had been a puppet for too long. "Don't be cross, Grannie. It was Cliff Richard and it was great."

Mary looked at the sparkling eyes and rosy cheeks and decided against asking questions. It was wonderful to see Bessie looking her old self again. She would find out more about the new friend in due course.

But Bessie was strangely evasive. She disclosed that the friend was male and that he lived in Northfield, but more than that she kept to herself. Mary respected that. Outside the convent, Bessie's friendship had been limited almost exclusively to Boris. And because she had always been happy, everyone had thought this was perfectly all right; but perhaps it had not been. Girls of seventeen usually had a host of boyfriends. Perhaps Bessie was merely reverting to normality.

Mary said tentatively, "Listen, darling. I hope I don't sound over-protective at this late date, but you will be careful, won't you?"

For some reason Bessie flushed bright red. "Sometimes, Grannie, adults can be . . . disgusting!" she said unexpectedly.

Mary persevered. "I am thinking of your safety, Bessie. Not the proprieties—though they are set basically for safety reasons."

"Grannie. Take it from me. I am as safe as houses with this particular friend."

Mary spread her hands. "All right. But if you go to the pictures again, I would like to know about it beforehand. And I would very much like to meet this young man."

"I'm dying for you to meet him, actually. And Aunt Mon, too."

"Really? Darling, Aunt Mon would love to come and see you—and any of your friends. You know that. She is in a very invidious position where you are concerned—"

"*She* is in an invidious position! That's rich!"

Mary frowned slightly. That was not the sort of thing Bessie said. She hoped the new friend was not going to be a bad influence.

They went to the pictures again. Then they met in a greasy little cafe run by his mother. It came as a shock to Bessie to realise that Mrs. Cook was her real grandmother. She began to feel a tiny sympathy towards Aunt Mon which she suppressed quickly, reminding herself that somehow everything was Aunt Mon's fault and all this was by way of sweet revenge.

Revenge or not, Giles Cook's company was consoling. She found that with "project Giles" in mind, she could actually begin to study properly. She took to spending mornings in the little library at the top of Turves Green hill. It got her away from the irritation of the Dennings and the constant reminder of unhappiness which showed in Grannie's anxious expression. When Giles was on nights at the factory, he would sleep all morning and often see her in the afternoons. He would sit opposite her in the small reading room and make faces at her until she succumbed to stupid, schoolgirl giggles and was glared at by the librarian. Then they would go outside and throw snowballs at each other all the way down the hill. One day he said out of the blue, "This is crazy. I haven't had a friend like you since . . . oh, a long time ago." And she responded automatically, "Nor me." And then realised she meant it. She wasn't thinking of Boris either. She was thinking of Jean. Maybe she had fooled herself for a long time now where Jean was concerned; maybe that's what he had been, a good friend.

But she didn't want to soften at this stage, and she said quickly, "Would you like to come and have tea with us one day, Gillie? My aunt is coming for a weekend soon. I'd like you to meet her."

He flushed with pleasure. "Say when, girl, and I'll be there," he accepted promptly.

She never achieved the vindictive pleasure she had been working for.

She planned it all carefully: Monica arrived just before lunchtime from Exeter, she had left at the crack of dawn and had to change trains at Bristol and was exhausted. Mary had planned a quiet afternoon in front of the fire. Just the three of them—Mrs. Denning had been prevailed upon to go visiting. At three o'clock, when she could see Monica's eyelids begin to droop, Bessie sprang her surprise.

"I've invited my new friend to tea," she announced brightly. "I want him to meet you, Aunt Mon, and as Mrs. Denning has gone out, it seemed the ideal opportunity."

"Why on earth didn't you warn me?" Mary was not so much flummoxed as disappointed. She excelled herself at afternoon teas. "I would have made some potato scones or something nice."

"Oh, he's not coming for the food and drink. Just to meet you." Bessie smiled as the knocker sounded. "I'll go. Just relax. You'll feel as if you've known him all your lives. I promise you."

It was Monica she wanted to hurt. Not Grannie. Not Giles. But it was Monica who threw back her head and burst out laughing when she registered who the "new friend" was, and it was Grannie and Giles who looked at her as if she'd stuck a knife into the pair of them.

Monica saved the day by being so frank it made Bessie feel small.

"Well. You certainly exploded a bombshell here, Bessie," she said as if it were a Christmas cracker. "Let me have your coat, Gillie. Is it snowing again?" She went behind him and pressed his arms as she slid the coat sleeves down over his jacket. "Did you know about it?"

It was obvious from his face he hadn't known a thing.

"You said your name was Lizzie," he said accusingly to Bessie.

She was defiant, her plan in ruins. "It's Elizabeth. And you—" she threw Monica a challenging look. "You never liked Bessie. You wanted to call me Lizzie once."

"So I did." Monica put Giles' coat over the back of a chair and came forward, still smiling. "I've grown up a lot since then." She indicated a chair. "Sit down, Gillie. Don't look like that. After all, what's in a name? I'm glad you and Bessie have made friends."

But Giles had had enough of being conned. He looked from Monica's determinedly smiling face to Mary's ashen one.

"We haven't. I don't make friends with people who lie to me." He picked up his coat. "I don't know what's going on here, our Mon, you always were a devious one. Looks like she's the same too." He jerked his head at Bessie with something like contempt. "I'll be on my way. And I don't want to hear anything more about this. Is that understood?"

Even Monica was silent at that. Mary began to apologise. Actually to apologise.

Bessie cut across her stammering words. "And we don't want to hear any more of *you*, either! I haven't lied—I don't *know* what my proper name is, do I? I told you Durant because that's the name of the man I thought was my father until six months ago! I just wish he was . . . oh God, I just wish he was!"

And she left the lounge precipitately and went to her room which was bitterly cold in spite of the central heating. And would never be home. She heard Giles leave shortly afterwards and got off her bed to watch him trudge through the snow to the front gate. She hadn't wanted to hurt Giles Cook, her new friend. But oh, she had wanted to hurt Giles Cook, her natural father.

It was an hour later when Monica knocked on her door and said briskly, "I think you'd better come down. I don't seem to be able to console your grandmother."

Bessie called, "She's not my grandmother. My grandmother runs a horrid little snack bar along the Bristol Road!"

And Monica said, "It's not that bad, actually. Have you tried her sausage and chips?" And then, even more aggravatingly, she did not wait for an answer, but went back downstairs.

Bessie went down too because in another hour Mrs. Denning would be back and life would be even more intolerable. And she wanted tea and toast and the warm fire.

Mary and Monica were talking about the weather. Monica was telling a story about them airlifting a pregnant mother from Exmoor to the maternity unit at Exeter. And Mary said yes it was really incredible, though of course there had been fairs held on the frozen Thames in Elizabethan times, so . . .

Bessie interrupted rudely, "Well? What are you going to do about me? A reform school? Pity I haven't got an aunt in the country somewhere, isn't it?"

Mary looked down at her lap. And Monica said thoughtfully, "Actually, you have got an aunt in the country. That's a good idea, Bessie."

"I'm not going to Aunt Myrt's. Not without Boris. Besides I want to go to your old school. Cass' old school." Bessie was suddenly white-faced and determined. "I know I've made a bloomer, but you can't take that away from me!"

"I was referring to Aunt Liv, actually. Plenty of countryside around there. Good train service to Kings Norton. Lots of peace and quiet for studying. And . . . I rather think Aunt Liv needs you."

"Needs me? You mean Grannie."

"Grannie too. But I meant you."

"Why?" Bessie's self-esteem was so low she could not imagine anyone needing her.

Monica paused, then said bluntly, "Because if she hadn't gone over to find Myrtle and Reggie in Paris, Cass would probably be alive now."

Bessie was wide-eyed. "That's a terrible thing to say! You might as well blame Aunt Myrt for going off to Paris in the first place! And Cass never blamed *her* for anything! She said that if Myrtle hadn't gone with Reggie, she would have died!"

Monica said calmly, "I'm just telling you how Liv feels. Not how I feel." She looked at Bessie. "I've been to see Aunt Myrt, Bessie. And I've talked to Grannie about it all. You're more than welcome there. And I don't think you want to stay here much longer, do you?"

Bessie swallowed. At the moment she did not want to stay here another minute.

"No," she said.

Monica drew out her cigarette case. "Then that's settled." She smiled at Mary reassuringly and turned again to Bessie. "Look. I know you're very miserable at the moment. Everything has gone wrong—or so you feel. You're raw and it's awful. There's a cure. And it's work. Quite simply, work. Get yourself settled at Liv's—Reggie will love it and he'll be Giles and Jean rolled into one. You'll fill a gap for Liv, believe me. And then start school, work hard at it. This time next year, you'll wonder what this was all about."

Bessie said soberly, "No, I won't." She looked at Mary, still big-eyed and white-faced. "I don't want to forget. This is . . . important."

And suddenly she began to cry and cast herself on the woman she had always called Grannie. Not for the first time, they comforted each other.

Mary and Bessie settled in to the Barnt Green house very easily. They gave Liv a purpose in life; she enjoyed cooking—she enjoyed housekeeping—but the days of being houseproud were over, she needed a reason for making a home now. Reggie was his usual gentle self, but she knew that if she put fish and chips in front of him every day he would not notice. Half of him was still with Myrtle.

Reggie too was delighted to have them in the house. His taste for family life was still there, and they filled a yawning gap for him. He timed his homecomings for when Bessie got off the train each afternoon, and he ran her home and heard how her day had gone.

An unexpected bonus was the way they could talk about the past; the past before Mallie's and Carol's deaths. Reggie spoke of his childhood with Malcolm: football and paper chases and camps in Scotland.

"We ought to take a holiday in Scotland, Liv," he suggested. "It's completely unspoilt, you'd love it."

She looked at him in surprise, but all she said was, "Yes. Yes,

I'm sure I should." It was the first time she realised that he was missing Malcolm as well as Myrtle; perhaps more than Myrtle.

For her part she spoke of the Haunted House and Monica's complicated hair-do's and their days at school.

"You're in time for the tennis, Bessie. The courts are so lovely. There's a little grove of lime trees just beyond them where we used to sit and talk, and Cass would read us the Shakespeare sonnets, and Myrt would tell jokes, and Mon and I . . ." Her voice died and Bessie said, "Go on. Please, Aunt Liv."

"Oh, nothing really. Mon and I used to talk about boys. That's all." She sighed. "Mon must have been so unhappy. Finding out she was adopted and had no family that she knew about. She'd never been one of the Cooks."

There was a silence. Then Mary picked up her knitting.

"Mon loved Giles. Let's get that straight. She loved him as a brother, then she loved him as a man. And while she made no demands on him, she was wonderfully happy."

Reggie said, "I've never thought about it before. It must have been an impossible situation. If only Giles had had the gumption to leave Northfield and take her with him. Make a home somewhere else."

"She knew he couldn't—wouldn't—do that." Mary dropped a stitch and spent a long time picking it up. Her gaze flicked to Bessie and back to her knitting. "D'you know, on V.E. day she was on her way to London to find an American who would marry her and be a father for you, Bessie. Luckily she called in at the Haunted House to say goodbye to Cass, who persuaded her that we could help."

Reggie said strongly, "Thank God. Talk about a happy ending . . ." He cleared his throat. "She gave you what she hadn't had herself. An enormous family!" He tried to lighten his voice. "We've shared you, for a start, Bessie Woodford!"

Everyone laughed obediently. Liv said, "Cass was saying something like that. The afternoon before she . . . before it . . . happened."

Bessie, who had been staring at Mary's knitting, looked at Liv, then got up and went to sit on the arm of her chair.

"If she'd died any other way—" she too cleared her throat— "she wouldn't have had that time with you, Aunt Liv. I'm so

318

glad she had that. It sort of connects us all together again, doesn't it?"

Liv bowed her head. Almost as if receiving absolution.

Much later, when she was sitting up in bed reading, there was a tap at the door.

She smiled, certain it was Bessie.

"Come in," she said, "I'm not asleep."

The door opened tentatively and Reggie was there. She put down her book and sat away from the pillows.

He said, "Liv. Until today—tonight—I didn't realise how you felt. About Carol."

She was bewildered. "Carol? You must have known how close we were. The four of us."

"Yes. Of course. But the way Bessie spoke to you . . . surely you do not feel responsible for what happened?"

Liv swallowed. "I . . . of course. You know I was responsible, Reggie. You all knew. If I hadn't come over to Paris to look for you, Carol would have been safe at the Bergerie when those students marched that night." Her throat muscles worked convulsively.

Reggie closed the door and came further into the room.

"Come off it, Liv. Ask yourself why you were there. You can trace responsibility any way you like."

She gripped the sheet and closed her eyes. "Doesn't it all come back to that day before Mallie? When I went to see Malcolm and threw you and Myrt together?"

He said strongly, "No. You and I . . . we weren't a proper couple, Liv. If that hadn't happened, something else would have triggered off the train of events."

He sat on the edge of the bed.

"Listen. Liv. It's almost four years since . . . all that. I'm not suggesting the wounds are healed, my dear, but even if we're limping along—surely we're limping in unison?"

She heard the smile in his voice and opened her eyes. She thought how strange it was to fall in love with one's own husband; and to accept that she would always come second for him.

She whispered, "Don't feel . . . sorry for me, Reggie."

"Why not? I hope you're sorry for me, Liv."

She sobbed suddenly. She was sorry for him; it was true.

He held her and stroked her hair.

He said, "May I come back here, Liv? Are you as lonely as I am?"

She did not stop weeping for a long time. She had not imagined that making love could be an act of intense compassion.

Much later still she whispered to him, "Oh, Reggie. Bessie was right. I am so glad I had that time with Carol before she died. So glad. So . . . thankful."

16

*T*hat summer, Mary and Bessie went back to the Bergerie for a holiday. In response to a carefully worded letter from Mary, Jean-Claude suggested that he join them for a week at the end of August.

Bessie thought she was all right. She had survived a year back home with the frightful knowledge of her true parentage gradually settling into some kind of sense. The move to Barnt Green had been a good one: in Reggie she had found at last a father figure worthy of the name, and she knew that Liv was comforted by the presence of Mary and herself. She respected Monica for the way she had dealt with her confrontation with Giles Cook, and when Liv and Reggie spoke of her, she began to feel a certain pride that this woman was her mother. And of course Myrtle was always there when she was needed; a Myrtle who was different, stronger and more independent, but still full and overflowing with love. And a link with Boris, who was, after all, Bessie's assured destiny. Yes, she had grown up, she was certain of that. She and Grannie, they were all right now.

She was a loner at school, but she was not lonely. The sixth form was small and friendships had already been made when she arrived in the spring term. But she was respected for her difference; her wide knowledge of French literature and history set her apart from the others. In some ways she was younger than her peers; in others much older. She knew nothing of sex, and many of her contemporaries had gone "almost the whole way" with their boyfriends. On the other hand she was used to the company of males and able to hold a conversation with them without embarrassment or giggling.

She thought she probably felt as Monica felt: not so much independent as sufficient within herself. Yes, she was fairly certain she had negotiated her particular valley of shadow.

And then Mary announced that Jean was coming home for a week.

"It will be like old times," she said brightly, knowing that old times had gone for ever. "We'll make lots of onion soup and you can bake that favourite cake of his."

"Marble cake," Bessie said, swallowing.

"That's it. Marble cake. D'you remember how you used to play that silly game to see if you could eat one colour at a time?"

"That was ages ago, Grannie. When I thought he was my . . . that was ages ago."

Mary looked out of the window at the Victoire soaring over the little house. "Darling," she said slowly. "The three of us . . . we're a family. We're not united by blood ties, but we're still a family."

Bessie nodded and swallowed again. "We're united by Cass, Grannie. Aren't we?"

"Yes, darling." Mary's eyes were full of tears. It was the perfect answer. They would always be a family because of Cass.

But though Bessie had provided the answer, though it seemed obvious to her, it did not bring the pleasure it should. She had adored Cass; now, unexpectedly and shockingly, she felt that Cass might come between them in some way. It was ridiculous and she pushed the thought away quickly.

But there was no ease any more with Jean. He arrived a day before they expected him, driving up the track in a new Citroen that looked like a police car. Bessie knew he was inside it; she saw it turn off the village road and bump between the clumps of chrysanthemums, and she sensed that it contained Jean. She did not move from the hammock where she and Mary were sitting shelling the second crop of peas.

Mary said, "What can the gendarmerie want with us, I wonder? It cannot be news from England. They would phone us direct now."

"It's the Renault," Bessie confessed quickly, as if she could change the occupant of the car somehow. "Pierre's cousin who is a policeman saw me driving it through the village yesterday, and he knows I am not yet eighteen."

"Bessie! How could you? Well, you'll have to eat humble pie and hope for the best." Mary put down her colander and stood up as the car swirled to a halt outside the door. "My God." She looked wildly at Bessie. "My God, it's Jean!"

It was only then that Bessie realised how much Mary had missed the man who had been almost a son-in-law to her. The older woman flew to the car and pulled Jean-Claude from it, laughing and crying at the same time. Belatedly, after she had hugged him soundly and scolded him for not telephoning ahead, and telling him he had lost weight, she realised that Bessie had risen from the hammock but not moved one step forward.

"Bessie—it's Jean—look how brown he is!"

He was very brown, and had somehow acquired an Arabic look. His black eyes were perpetually narrowed against the sun and his hands seemed longer and thinner than ever.

They stared, and he protested quickly. "Please. I am not used to so much attention." He glanced at Bessie then swiftly back to Mary. "It is good to be back. Thank you for asking me."

Mary was confused. "I didn't mention it to Bessie. I wasn't sure you'd come and I wanted it to be a surprise."

"Ah. I wondered at the state of . . . shock."

He smiled and his long intelligent face was transformed. Bessie held herself against crying out.

He said, "Mary tells me it has been hard, *chérie.* But you have come to terms with . . . everything."

She managed to nod. She had thought she had. Now she knew she had not.

He held out his hand. "Come. Do not hold it against me. I am here for one week. Let it be a good one."

At last she came forward and took his hand. It was warm and dry and blessedly familiar. She felt tears behind her eyes and did not know why.

Her happiness that week was poignant and painful and almost too much to bear. He was determined to behave as if nothing had happened, and up to a point, he succeeded. But the spontaneity had gone from their relationship. She was a woman now and she knew he was not her father; she could no longer throw her arms around his neck or sit by him on the old leather sofa and jabber to him insouciantly. Yet he was so precious to her, so dear, that she wondered how she would exist when he went back to Algiers. He talked to her about his work as he had always done, but when the conversation became more personal he spoke indulgently as if she were still a child.

"What would you like to do, *chérie*? Shall we drive to one of the *parfumeries*? Or go down to Antibes for a day? Whatever you wish."

"I'd like to trek up the Victoire," she said.

Mary pulled a face. "I can't spend a whole day walking, like you two. Count me out."

Jean hesitated then gave his wry upside-down smile.

"Very well, Bessie. A trek it shall be. How far?"

"As far as we can. We'll start at six and be back before dark."

His smile became a laugh. "I asked for it, I suppose. I am an old man now, Bessie. How can you ask this of me?"

"You are not old. You will never be old in that sense. You are . . ." she searched for a word to describe him. "You are universal."

"*Mon Dieu!* I thought you were going to call me ageless! I must be thankful for small mercies I suppose." He lifted his shoulders. "Only at sixteen could the word 'universal' be made to apply to age!"

"I am nearly eighteen, Jean," she reminded him, but without undue emphasis.

He had genuinely forgotten. "You were sixteen when we parted so unhappily, *chérie*. To me you have not changed at all."

She too gave a Gallic shrug. "I also am universal," she told him. "Age has very little relevance sometimes. It is simply a . . . convention."

His smile died as he looked into her serious dark eyes.

They went, lightly loaded with small haversacks and sticks.

It was a splendid morning; September was a few days away and the sun held a different warmth: gentle and golden. Jean had switched on the wireless before they left and pulled a face because the main item of news concerned the Beatles and their latest hit record.

Bessie said, "It's so much better than war and disasters, Jean. You have dealt too much in them. You should listen to the Beatles."

"Yes, *ma vieille*," he said pseudo-solemnly.

They walked until eleven, and then stopped for their sandwiches. They had passed the tiny shepherd's hut some time before, and were well on the way to the slide of scree and the mini plateau.

Jean fetched water from the stream that was fed by last winter's snows. He gave the beaker to Bessie and watched her drink.

"Do I gather this is a sort of pilgrimage for you, *chérie?*" he asked. He drank himself, and waited for a reply. She nodded.

"Ah. I have to guess, is that it?" He was using his indulgent voice again. "Now. Let me see. Boris." She nodded again. "The summer we all camped up here."

She said, "The Metier girls first of all. We found this special place. Then I brought Boris. I'll show you why, when we get there."

"Ah. A secret. A mystery." He drained the water and put the beaker away. "Come then. En avant."

She went ahead. She did not know why, but sometimes the feeling she had for him was liberally mixed with anger.

They reached the plateau at midday and rested, heads against the haversacks, while the sun spent its noon heat and settled into a lazy afternoon. Bessie sat up at last, opened her sack and removed a trowel. Jean watched her, surprised and amused, as she began to dig. She could not remember the exact place and had to make several attempts before the trowel clinked on metal. At last, after a tussle with the springy turf, she resurrected the paint can.

He said quietly, "I know about it, Bessie."

"I thought you might," she panted. "Well, this is it. I want you to have it."

He stared at the battered tin and his eyes were no longer smiling. "No. It is for you girls. Not me."

"I am not one of them."

"Then give it to Myrtle. It was she and Cass who took it in the first place. Give it to her."

She sat with it between her legs, staring at it. For some reason she had wanted to get rid of it. She did not know why. But she was glad Jean-Claude did not want it.

She said, "All right. Perhaps I will." She knelt again and packed it carefully away. Then she sat down once more.

He said, "This . . . ritual. With Boris. It was special? Perhaps though you were so young, he asked you to marry him?"

She smiled into the sun.

"No. We've always sort of known we would get married one day. I engaged myself to him a long time ago. With Aunt Mon's bracelet." She looked into the past. "My mother's gift to me. I didn't know that at the time, of course. Or perhaps I did."

The silence stretched between them until Bessie was breathless with it.

Then he said, "You are angry with me. Because I arranged work for Boris that would take him away for a long time."

She was surprised out of her tension.

"No. I did not realise . . . no. Not angry."

She had missed Boris of course. Often. But there had not been the anguish she associated with missing Jean-Claude.

He seemed to feel the need to explain.

"I knew how it was between you two. And I wanted very much for you to finish your education, *chérie*. To look around. To see other things. I told Boris this."

"What did he say?"

"I think he understood. But he said that one day he would come back and marry you."

"He said that?"

"Are you surprised? I thought it was settled between you?"

"Yes. But I was the one who had to settle it." She was pleased Boris had said that. She felt enormously flattered.

Jean said very dryly, "Ah. Yes. I can imagine that."

She looked at him, and for the first time they laughed together wholeheartedly and without inhibitions.

As they wandered down the mountain and into the warm dusk of the flower farms, she knew that part of her pleasure had been because Jean had taken a hand in her fate. He had sent Boris away. He had kept her . . . safe.

The agony of parting was upon her before she was ready for it. She extracted a promise that he would come again at Christmas, but he made provisos about his work schedule, and she did not trust him.

Then she had an idea.

"Grannie will stay on here—won't you, darling? It's only three months till Christmas . . . just over. Why don't you stay? Jean would come home much oftener then, wouldn't you Jean? Like you used to."

Mary's refusal was automatic.

"Bessie, I wouldn't dream of leaving you in your A levels year!"

But Bessie was adamant. This was her link with Jean-Claude. The few letters they exchanged meant nothing. But if he came regularly to the Bergerie, she would get news . . . he would be joined to her by Mary.

Unexpectedly he too thought it a good idea.

"The English winter does not suit you, Mary. And you love this house and the kitchen and the garden."

"I'm all right with Aunt Liv and Uncle Reggie, Grannie. I'll be able to work much harder if I don't have to worry about you!"

Mary laughed reluctantly. The idea appealed to her very much; Liv shared her house as best she could, but it was still her house.

Bessie warned, "I'm going to keep on at you, Grannie, until you agree!"

Mary groaned. And so did Jean-Claude. And then they laughed. It was almost like old times. Almost.

She got her way. And back in Barnt Green she continued to take Monica's advice and worked furiously. Time flew. Christmas was wonderful; to be reunited with Mary and Jean-Claude was enough. But Jean had arranged a party for practically the whole village. She met again with Solange and Brigitte, was introduced to Grandmère and danced with all the young men there. Jean did not dance. He watched smilingly and helped Mary to give out the presents.

As they walked back up the track that night, he said quietly, "It is all right now, yes?"

Mary replied immediately, "Oh yes, Jean. It is all right."

Bessie said, "What is all right?"

"We are a small family again. We go our separate ways. We come together and pool our *contente*—is it not so?"

She did not answer. The stars were brilliant; she stared up at them until she stumbled and would have fallen if Jean had not grabbed her elbow.

He said quietly, "She is not up there, Bessie. She is with us here. You know that."

"Of course. Yes."

He was right. In everything he had said, he was right. She was surprised it did not give her more pleasure.

As soon as Bessie's examinations were over, Monica went to stay at Barnt Green. Mary Woodford was already there—had come back with Bessie after the Easter holidays and stayed ever since. Liv's four double bedrooms were filled again and she obviously enjoyed it. Monica smiled, remembering the old Liv.

Reggie escorted all of them to the school on the last day of term to see Bessie receive her leaving gift: a copy of the controversial New English Bible. Afterwards they waited in a queue to be introduced to the headmistress. Thankfully Monica saw that old Miss Jenson had been replaced by a fairly young woman who even smiled now and then.

"My grandmother," Bessie murmured. "Uncle . . . aunt. And my mother."

Monica took the proffered hand, but could no longer see the face. Somehow, with an enormous effort of will, she controlled her tears. Bessie took her arm and led her towards a display of work.

"It's lucky in a way," she said in Monica's ear. "I've never called anyone Mother. So now, I can learn all about it."

Monica knew that Bessie had thought about it carefully, it wasn't a spur-of-the-moment thing. She remembered the barren years when she had so much wanted to possess this girl and call her daughter. By letting her go, pushing her away almost, it had happened.

She held on to the young arm very tightly. Without it she thought she would probably fall down.

That night they were to have gone out for a celebratory meal, but it was raining and the house was warm and cosy.

"Let's stay in," Bessie begged. "We could play Monopoly. When I went to see Aunt Myrtle at Easter, the boys had a craze for it and it was such fun."

Liv rose to the occasion. "Why not? And I've got some steaks for tomorrow. I could do steak and chips. And we could have a bottle of wine. Shall we?"

Suddenly it was a party. The rain ran steadily down the French windows and the sunken rose garden which had been the fish pool filled with water. Inside Liv produced a wonderful meal and they played Monopoly.

"The last time I played this so-and-so game was at Rhyl. D'you remember, Mary?"

"Yes. I remember." Mary smiled into the eyes of the girl who had at last taken her rightful place. "You won immediately of course."

Monica gave her old wicked grin. "I think I cheated actually. I often did."

"I can vouch for that," Liv agreed, shaking the dice so vigorously it flew on to the floor. "Ooops. Sorry everyone." She shook again, moved, then said, "You know, you two should adopt each other. You get on so well, you've got Bessie between you—you're made for each other."

Reggie said quickly, "Happy endings are for books, Liv."

Liv flushed. "Oh I didn't mean . . . I'm sorry."

Mary said calmly, "You didn't mean that Monica could replace Cass. Of course you didn't. Monica has always been an extra blessing. I think that's a marvellous suggestion, Liv." She smiled again across the table. "Anyway, Mon, you haven't got much choice. You are Bessie's mother and I am Bessie's grandmother. So it follows—"

Bessie chanted from her literature syllabus, "as the night the day . . ."

Monica said, "My God! Have I got a mother and a daughter now?" She tried to laugh. "It's too much."

Bessie was grinning like a Cheshire cat. "What she means is it's two more birthday presents to buy!"

That night Monica talked to Cass as she so often did when she was alone.

"Darling, I was going to thank you for Bessie. Now I have to thank you for Mary too. I don't know what to say. I'm not too good at being deep, am I, Cass? Never was. But . . . well, you know that my one fear was having no-one of my own. Later. When I can't work any more." She laughed. "Yes. I'm being morbid, darling. Sorry." She grinned into the darkness and took a deep breath. "Thing is, Cass, I'm a great one for believing that there's a way of saying thank you for these sort of things. Cass, I want to do something. What can I do? I mean, in one way I'd like to go and see poor old Giles and tell him that everything is all right now. But . . . well, I can't do that, Cass. It still wouldn't work between us—never will—but he can still melt my heart with that crumpled smile of his. So what can I *do*?" She waited a few moments, then sighed. "Okay. I'll sleep on it. But . . . it's been the best day of my life, Cass. It really has."

The next morning she sought Liv out in the kitchen. It was still raining and the others were discussing a trip into Birmingham to buy presents. Boris was coming home that summer and Bessie was paying her usual visit to Myrtle and Malcolm to see him. She wanted to buy a cricket bat for Lennie and fishing tackle for the other two boys. She had been going to get a special lens for Boris' camera, but was now deciding to buy an umbrella. "He'll need it. And he won't have one. And it will make him laugh," she was saying to Reggie and Mary in the living room.

Monica said, "Liv, it's been a wonderful time. Thank you."

Liv looked round, surprised. "Mon. You've made it wonderful. You always do. You're so full of energy. You take us all and—and—make us into something!" She laughed. "I don't know. I always feel better for seeing you. And it was lovely for Bessie."

Monica leaned against the new freezer. "I suppose you're thinking up something to replace the steaks for today? And we shall have a marvellous lunch produced in minutes. And the dishwasher will do its job—"

Liv said quickly, "I know. Same old Liv. I can't help it, Mon. I enjoy it."

"My God, I wasn't criticising! And you're not the same old Liv. You didn't used to enjoy it, my girl. Admit it." They both laughed and Monica said seriously, "Liv. I don't want to step on any toes, but couldn't you forgive Myrtle now? It's been six years. A long time. And I think Cass would like it if we got together again, don't you?"

Liv looked round. She still had her baby face, but paradoxically it was no longer young.

She said simply, "Yes. Yes, of course she would. And I would too. And obviously so would you. But . . . there are obstacles, Mon."

"Reggie."

"I don't think he could bear it."

"It would be a shock, but I think it's the answer, darling. She was

330

a dream, that's all. She's not the same now, Liv. She's no dream. She is very, very real."

Liv said nothing for a long time. She forgot her meal preparations and put her back against the sink to stare into the past which appeared to be just left of Monica's knee.

"I just don't know. He wouldn't agree to it. But even if he did, there's Malcolm. He has had nothing to do with Reggie since then. Nothing at all." She looked up and smiled slightly. "Actually, Reggie misses him very much."

Monica smiled back. "Incredible."

They both laughed, then Monica straightened.

"Well, that *is* something I can do. I'll go down to Cheltenham with Bessie and Mary and stick my oar in there."

"Steady on, Mon. You might get hurt."

"That doesn't matter." Monica gave her indefatigable grin again. "If I've inherited Cass' mother and Cass' daughter, then I've got to do what she would have done. And the sooner the better!"

She walked into the hall. "Is everyone ready? I suggest we go now and treat Liv to a slap-up lunch at Rackham's. Everyone in favour say—"

Bessie yelled, "Aye!"

Boris had changed. Bessie had expected him to be different after two years in the outback of Australia, but not in this way. He was more . . . enclosed . . . than before. Where she could have expected a confidence and a free-and-easiness from his outdoor life, she was met with a strange self-containment that did not exactly exclude her, but was nevertheless impenetrable. For one thing he accepted the umbrella as if it were the Holy Grail instead of a bit of a joke.

"I'll treasure it always," he said.

"I thought you'd probably wear one of those special hats to keep off the rain."

"Hat?"

"You know, the kind the Australians wear. Like a cowboy hat with corks all round."

"Oh. Yes. They're to keep the flies off, actually."

"I know *that!* Idiot." She laughed and aimed a kiss at his cheek and the boys, who were dancing around with fishing rods and cricket bat, gave knowing catcalls and wanted to know if they were going to play mummies and daddies again like they used to.

Boris turned bright red and Bessie missed his cheek and

rounded on the boys and chased them out of the room. Myrtle was just seeing off her last patient. She herded them down to the kitchen where Monica had started a meal.

"Give Borrie and Bessie a bit of peace," she ordered, laughing. She stuck her head around the door before closing it. "For goodness' sake talk him out of this latest thing, Bessie. If anyone can do it, you can!" And she left.

"What's this? A new job?" Bessie was so pleased to see him she could hardly stand still. She took one of his hands and swung around him as if they were still children. "Come on, tell Bessie!"

"Later. It's something to talk around. But not now, not here."

She respected that and knew it must be serious. But still she pestered him, enjoying reverting to their old camaraderie.

"Give me a clue. Is it work?"

"Oh, Bessie."

"Come on, come on. Is it a different life?"

He looked at her dancing around him like a gadfly.

"Yes. If . . . it would be a different life. But . . . I just don't know, Bessie. Leave it for now. Please."

She stopped and stared at him, not laughing any more.

"Will it be the end of us, Borrie?"

She saw his Adam's apple move as he swallowed. Then he said steadily, "You know that I will never stop loving you, Bessie."

She said just as solemnly, "Nor I you. So that's all right then. Let's go and have tea with everyone. And laugh again."

He smiled and pulled her hand through his arm in the old companionable way. As they went into the hall, Malcolm emerged from his treatment room.

"Ah. The heavenly twins," he greeted them. He kissed Bessie chastely and shook Boris' hand. "I feel safe with you two." He shook his head. "My God, you've seen us through some tough times, haven't you?"

He put his arms around their shoulders and led them down to the kitchen. And it was the same as ever, darkly cavernous and inconvenient, and totally homely.

After two days, Mary decided she would go and see Dilly Gosling and then return to France, and Mon took over the kitchen. Like Bessie, she enjoyed its old associations, and the challenge of making it nearly efficient again.

Nicky was almost twelve and he and Martin had inherited their father's domestic streak; they were pressed into service. Lennie, a fully-fledged horror now, had been recruited into as many organisations as would have him, so was not much in evidence. Monica packed him off in Doris' care most mornings, and left his room till last.

Myrtle bemoaned the fact that it was no holiday for Monica.

"I'm in my element, Myrt!" Monica folded and turned her puff pastry. "Next month I get my own little place. This is great practice."

"Oh Mon. You're marvellous." Myrtle unconsciously echoed Malcolm's words. "You've seen us through it all, haven't you?"

"I've certainly been around." Monica floured the rolling pin and paused. "I'd like to be around more in the future, too."

"My God. You know you're always welcome here, darling. Any time at all. I mean that—"

"I'd like us all to be around in the future." Monica rolled out an oblong piece of pastry and folded it again into three. "You. Me. Liv. The others of course. But we're the middle. We're important. We should be together again."

Myrtle pulled out a chair and sat down quickly.

"I'd like it more than anything. But how can I expect . . . ? After what happened . . . Liv could never . . . And Malcolm hates Reggie. Hates him."

"I don't believe that. And Liv wants to heal the breach. And Reggie misses Malcolm."

"Liv would actually be willing to see me? Be friends again?"

"She is worried about Reggie. Naturally. What do you think?"

"It's gone—like Mallie—like Cass. Gone."

"I agree. So it's just Malcolm."

Myrtle stared as Monica put the pastry over a bowl full of apples and began to crimp the edges.

"Are you going to have a go at him, Mon?"

"Why not? I've got nothing to lose and a lot to gain."

"Yes. Well. If you really think . . . It would be marvellous if we could . . . . I miss Liv. They used to come down quite often. And occasionally she'd invite us up there. Without the boys of course."

"She's different now. She'd have the boys. Even Lennie."

They both laughed.

Monica said, "Look, Myrt. No time like the present. Tell Malcolm his coffee is ready."

"Oh my God."

333

But Myrtle stood up and went to fetch her husband. Then she tidied away her own instruments and wished she'd remembered to tell Monica about Boris. He and Bessie had gone for a walk to the Devil's Chimney, an outcrop of rock on Leckhampton Hill. She wondered what would be the outcome of that. And of Monica's interview with Malcolm.

They sat on the side of the hill, the whole of Cheltenham and Tewkesbury spread below them. For once they were without Nicky and Martin. It was an overcast day with a chilly wind blowing; the boys had decided to go to the Gaumont where *Summer Holiday* was showing.

Bessie took a deep breath of the wind.

"It's a splendid view, but it's not in the least like the Victoire, is it?"

"No. The air tastes differently and there's no sun."

"It's very English. And the Victoire is very Provençal. The taste is because of the flowers."

"Will you go up the Victoire next week? When you and Mary go back to the Bergerie?"

"What do you mean—me and Mary? You're coming too, aren't you?" Bessie was dismayed. She turned on her wrist and looked at him. He lay on his side, his jacket turned up at the collar, his eyes on the grass by his supporting elbow.

"I'm not sure. I have the chance to go to Prinknash Abbey. A sort of retreat."

She waited for more and when it did not come, frowned her puzzlement. "Prinknash is Roman Catholic, Boris. You won't be able to go there."

He glanced up. "Bessie. It is one of the things I want to talk about. I was accepted into the Roman Catholic Church last January."

"You never said anything. In your letters. Nothing." She was hurt at the omission, but not surprised. Borrie had been attracted to that religion for many years now. She leaned down. "Why didn't you tell me? It's not a secret or anything, is it? You're not ashamed of being a convert, surely?"

He sat up quickly. "Of course not. I am proud, my dear." He picked some grass and examined it carefully. "I could not tell you what was happening, Bessie, because I did not know. I still do not know. I wanted . . . whatever was happening to my soul, to happen. Not to be influenced by . . . anything."

"Oh, Borrie. I wouldn't have tried to influence you. I went to a convent. My friends in France are all Catholic."

He nodded but was silent. He began to discard the blades of grass, piece by piece.

She said, "It's more than that, Borrie. Isn't it? You wanted to be a monk before. Is that what it is?"

She saw by the contraction of his ear that he smiled briefly, but all he said was, "You know me very well, Bessie."

She took another breath. The wind filled her chest and seemed to give her courage.

She said, "You thought I would hold you to our—our engagement, Borrie. Was *that* it?"

He laughed then. "No. Of course not. That is not your style, Bessie Woodford." He turned and looked at her and she saw so much love in his eyes she gasped. "I can see that already, now, you are preparing to . . . what is it called? Give me my freedom?"

She could not return his smile. For so long she had counted on Boris for her future. For so long.

She said, "We were children, Borrie. It was nothing. You have always been free, you know that."

He continued to look at her until she dropped her own gaze. She thought in a sudden panic, I do not love him like that . . . I could not give my life for him . . .

He said quietly, "I want to marry you, Bessie. God needs me. He has called—if you like. Quite literally called. It happens. But I cannot give you up. I love you more than I love God. Will you marry me?"

It was such an enormous thing to happen; she felt her heart beating—thumping—in her chest, the wind lifting her hair, an incipient blister on her heel beginning to sting; and inside herself and Boris, in their souls, there was this awesome statement. To be loved more than God.

She was not conscious of making a decision. She was not conscious of sifting thoughts and feelings and coming to a conclusion. Boris was there, infinitely dear to her, always special, always different. And here was she; understanding him because she had acquired so much sensitivity from Cass; yet irrevocably Monica's daughter, her feet always on the ground.

She said matter-of-factly, "Darling Borrie. I do love you. I've always loved you and always will. But I cannot marry you. Oh Boris, I'm in love with Jean. Help me. Help me if you can. I did not know till now. Oh Boris . . . Borrie . . ."

And she crumpled where she was on the short grass. And after a very small hesitation, he gathered her up and held her tenderly. Like a shepherd holding a lamb.

17

*I*t was a week later. Mary and Bessie had gone to France without Boris. He was still with Myrtle and Malcolm and gradually moving out of the curious limbo-state in which he had been for some time. Bessie's "confession" had released him in many ways; he knew worldly love was not for him. Probably he had known it since that ghastly day Myrtle had given birth to Mallie. Now, quite suddenly, the horror he had felt for some time at the outward manifestation of that worldly love was dissolving. It was something to do with Bessie, but he didn't know what. In turning him down, Bessie had quite literally set him free. It was curious. Like Alice, he felt it was becoming curiouser by the minute. Also fascinating and interesting and almost overwhelming. There was nothing ethereal or otherworldly about the love he felt for God. It was tremendously exciting. He waited impatiently for a reply to his letter to the Brotherhood.

Monica had gone back to Exeter feeling such intense irritation with Malcolm she would dearly have liked to smack him.

"I haven't given up," she warned Myrtle. "And neither must

you. Immediately you see a chink in his armour, attack! I am absolutely determined we shall get together again. It is my mission in life."

Myrtle felt almost sorry for Malcolm. She said, "He can be very stubborn. And after all, when you think what happened—"

"He brought it on himself!" Monica wouldn't give an inch. "How about withholding conjugal rights?"

Myrtle correctly concluded Monica was fishing. She laughed. "Blackmail, Monica."

Monica reverted to her American days. "Oh, shoot," she said. It was strange that her irritation with Malcolm did not extend very far at all. She was so happy these days she thought she might write to Bob and ask how his son was doing now. Or maybe . . . just maybe . . . get in touch with Gilly. No, not that. But it was a pity. As she had said over and over again to Malcolm, they were all getting too old to harbour grudges.

Liv stood, like Sister Anne, waiting at the window for Reggie's return from the farm sale in Malvern. Immediately the roof of the Humber Snipe appeared, gliding along the top of the privet which bounded the front garden, she whipped into the kitchen and began on the hollandaise sauce. The salmon lay on its dish. The meringue was drying in the oven, the cream whipped and in the fridge. She would leave the wine to him; she did not know whether this was a celebration or not.

She saw immediately that he was tired and her heart sank. He had been subdued since Mary and Bessie left; different. She wondered whether he was finding the house intolerable without them. Whether he was thinking of Bessie . . . with Myrtle.

He stood in the kitchen doorway, loosening his tie.

"D'you mind, Liv? It's so damned hot. Do I stink? It turned out to be mostly sheep to be auctioned. Can't get the smell out of my nostrils!"

"You don't smell at all, Reggie. But why don't you have a bath before supper? Go on. I'll bring you a cup of tea if you like."

"Will you?" He sounded surprised, though it was a long time since Liv had ruled that no food or drink went in the bathroom. "I must admit that sounds good."

Even so, he sat on the kitchen stool and watched her stirring the sauce as if he did not have the energy to climb the stairs. Her heart went six inches lower. He was going to tell her something. It could only be that he could not live any more without Myrtle.

He said, "D'you mind me collapsing here for a few minutes, Liv? There's something soothing about watching you cook."

"Of course not. Here." She left the pan and wooden spoon to reach inside the fridge for a carafe of lemon juice. She poured him a glass. "Have some of this. Fresh lemons. Mary showed me how to do it. They used to drink it in France."

He accepted the glass gratefully, but she wished she hadn't mentioned Mary. She went back to the sauce. It was unnerving the way he was watching her. He sipped, looked, sipped, looked. He was trying to find the courage and the moment to tell her something.

She said brightly, "It's your favourite. Salmon with hollandaise sauce."

"Lovely."

"I thought we might sit in the garden afterwards. The television is a bit . . ."

"That would be nice."

He stood up and reached around her to put the glass on the work surface. At close quarters she could smell the sheep. She wanted to throw her arms around him and hold him to her physically. Force him to forget everything that had happened.

He sat down again. "Liv. How you've changed. Do you realise how much you've changed?"

"Yes." Her voice was stifled.

"Oh I know. We've all changed. Some of us more strikingly than others. But I don't think anyone realises about you. They think you're the same. And you're not."

She said in the same muffled voice, "I know."

But he wanted to tell her anyway. He said, "You're an artist, Liv. Did you know *that?*"

She did not know that and she glanced up in surprise.

"I thought you meant my hair going grey. And all my lines."

He actually laughed. "If you're looking for compliments . . . you have all of twelve grey hairs, and they seem to be making you look blonder than ever. And there are no lines, Liv. You are far more beautiful than when I knew you first. Then you were pretty. Now you are . . . beautiful. Yes, beautiful."

"Oh, Reggie. Reggie." Her eyes suddenly filled with tears and he forgot what he had been going to say.

"What is it, Liv? What's the matter?"

"Nothing. Nothing at all. But . . I know you're building up to something. Go on. Finish now, Reggie. Please."

"Finish? I was just thinking about you, love. How different you are. You would have swept me out of the kitchen at one time. Got me into a bath before I could fill the house with the stink of sheep!" He laughed; but without condemnation. "Now, all that—that—what do you call it—house pride? You've refined it, Liv. You're a home-maker now. You've made a home—a sanctuary—for Mary and Bessie. And for me before that. When we got back from Paris. I didn't realise it then, of course. I could only think of Myrtle. But when I saw you looking after Bessie, then I knew what you'd done for me, Liv." He smiled right at her. "Yes, you're an artist."

She swallowed and moved the saucepan from the ring.

She said in a small voice, "When Bessie goes, for good I mean, will you stay? I mean, will it be the same, Reggie?"

He did not answer for a long time. He knew suddenly that this was an important moment, and he needed to choose his words.

At last he said quietly, "I'll stay for as long as you'll have me, Liv. You must know that I love you. Surely—now—you know that?"

She said, "Myrtle?"

"Liv. Myrtle is part of me. I cannot wrench her out. But I couldn't *live* with her. I couldn't live without you, now. I can't explain it, my darling. Can you . . . take me on trust?"

She tried to laugh. "I trust you to be honest. I know you would be."

He knew she was thinking of his . . . brutal honesty . . . about his love for Myrtle.

"Oh God. I'm sorry, Liv. I'm sorry."

"No. Don't be. We wouldn't be here now if anything had been different. We mustn't waste time on regrets."

He made no attempt to touch her, and she wanted him to put his arms around her very much indeed.

He said, "It's six years now. Six years ago. Would your Carol be disappointed, d'you think?"

She kept her head turned from him, tears dripped into the sauce. It would be inedible.

"Not altogether. Bessie will marry Boris. Myrtle is working. Monica is happy—very happy."

"What about you, Liv?"

She whispered, "Reggie, I don't want you to feel . . . tied. Or anything like that. But, I'm pregnant."

He didn't shout or jump, or react in any way for a long time.

Then he stood up slowly behind her and put his arms right around her and held her against him. She could feel his breath moving the curls on top of her head.

He said, "Darling. Listen. I know you don't want this, but believe me, you will be happy. You will be the best mother in the world. You've got talents, Liv, and those talents need other outlets, not just me. Please be happy, Liv. Please. This is the most wonderful thing that has happened to either of us."

She howled then, lifting her head and letting cries burst from her. He turned her within his arms and held her tightly against him so that she could hardly breathe.

She babbled through his soothing words, through her own tears, "You idiot. You absolute idiot. I'm so happy I could burst. But I thought—I thought—you'd be thinking of Myrtle and I couldn't bear it! I want this baby more than anything in the world, Reggie. But not unless you want it too. It's yours. At last—at last—I am giving you something! Can't you understand that?"

He smoothed her curls, then held her away from him so that she could see that he, too, was weeping.

Somehow, saltily, they kissed. And then they kissed again. And then they held each other as if they might be drowning in their own tears.

The year before, Bessie had arrived at the Bergerie assuring herself that she was "all right" and had discovered over the holiday that she was not all right. She had not known why, but it had been a fact. She had gone home to follow Monica's instructions and work through it.

Back in the refined and perfumed air, she knew at least that she was most definitely not all right. And she knew why.

She wondered how long she had been in love with Jean-Claude. She remembered the instant connection she had felt with him when she met him in New York and wondered if it could have been then. She wondered if it had been her love for him that had made Cass into some kind of barrier. She wondered how it was that Boris' love differed from hers. She wondered why she was happy one minute and bewildered and frightened the next. She wondered what she should do. She wondered whom she could tell.

The last question was the only one she could answer. She could tell Monica. She had told Boris and he had come up with no answers. She could not possibly tell Grannie . . . because . . .

because of Cass. Solange or Brigitte would treat it as a giggling secret and that would be unbearable. Liv and Myrtle were pretty hopeless when it came to being in love. And on the surface so was Monica. But only on the surface. Bessie knew by now that Monica would always—hopelessly—love Giles Cook. Monica would understand. And would come up with some practical answers too.

Meanwhile Bessie was on the see-saw of emotions; delirious one minute when Jean-Claude talked to her properly, or laughed with her and not at her, or was simply there; derelict the next when he saw her looking at him with her shining dark eyes and became immediately avuncular.

She found herself resorting to ploys she'd read in magazines. They went to Nice for the day and swam in the tideless, rather murky Mediterranean. She wore one of the new bikini two-piece costumes, named for the atoll in the Marshall Islands where the Americans were testing nuclear bombs. When they sunbathed afterwards, she passed the sun oil to Jean-Claude without a word and rolled on to her front.

Obediently he smeared some on her back, stopping short halfway down her spine.

"Legs too, please Jean," she said, her voice muffled by her arms. And while he tackled her calves, she reached behind her and undid the ties of the bra.

When, half an hour later, she rolled on to her back, he did not look at her for a long minute and then was suddenly furious.

"Cover yourself, Bessie! Do you wish to be arrested?"

She felt like a defiant schoolgirl.

"I don't see why I can't do it. Lots of others—"

"What would Mary say? If she had not gone to the shops you would never have dreamed—"

"You're so old-fashioned, Jean!"

"Certainly I am. Especially where you are concerned."

She put on a towelling robe and hugged her knees.

"There is no shame in the human body."

"The shame is when it is used provocatively."

Her face flamed. She thought he had guessed the reason for what she had done. But when he said no more, she had to conclude otherwise.

After that he made sure they were rarely alone together. When Mary left the room to cook or simply to walk in the garden, he

342

would get up and follow her, offering her his help even though she patently did not need it.

Mary herself noticed something was wrong.

"Have you and Jean had a row?" she asked bluntly one morning when they were picking the last of the tomatoes. "He hates shopping, but he offered to go down this morning as if he couldn't wait to get away from us."

"Well, in that case, perhaps he's had a row with you?" Bessie said pertly.

Mary tightened her mouth. "No. He has not had a row with me. How about you, I ask again?"

"Oh, Grannie. He's just a bit cross with me about something."

"What?"

Bessie had the decency to blush. "I took off the top of my costume when we were on the beach in Nice. I wanted to get one of those all-over tans. You know, like Bardot."

Mary did not display immediate disapproval as Bessie had expected. She rubbed the bloom off a tomato with the palm of her hand and placed it carefully in the trug.

"Darling. This is difficult to say. I think—I am certain in fact—that Jean-Claude sees Cass in you."

Bessie did not like that at all. "I'm not a bit like Cass," she protested.

"No. Perhaps I don't mean it quite in the way you think." Mary bit her bottom lip then tried again. "He reveres you, darling. He's put you on a pedestal. You are the part of Cass that must be kept . . ." she ran out of words.

"Pure?" Bessie was incredulous. "Mon *Dieu!* Should I get inside the china cabinet or something?"

"Don't be silly, Bessie. It's just that anything like that would make him—er—react strongly."

"Yes. Certainly." Bessie's face was suddenly set and determined. "Well, I must get off the pedestal, mustn't I? He must see me as I really am." She glanced at Mary. "And that is not even Bessie Woodford, Grannie. It is Bessie Cook."

She put a tomato in the trug as if physically making a point, then she turned and walked down the garden, over the wall and through the roses that were even now being cut for the perfume factories. One or two of the pickers called to her, but she ignored them. Mary watched as she reached the boundary of the cultivated land and started on the real mountain. She had been wearing a hat, but she took it off and swung it by her side. Her hair—black like Monica's and curly like Giles'—fanned out behind her almost down to her neat waist. She wore an old cotton frock and espadrilles, but there was nothing childish about that figure.

Mary sighed, then to her own surprise she began to laugh.

Bessie walked until she could walk no longer. Her heel, which always blistered unless she wore proper walking shoes, was burning protestingly. It was late afternoon and there were goose pimples on her arms in spite of all the exercise. She found the stream they always used for drinking water, and sat above it, hypnotised by the rushing glitter as it passed over stones and made miniature weirs and waterfalls. To wake herself up she got down the bank on her bottom, and dabbled her feet, but then she felt really cold and her shoes wouldn't go back on and the scramble back up the bank was difficult and when she got there it was almost dusk.

"Damn, damn and double damn!" she said loudly. She wanted to throw back her head and scream her resentment and frustration to the skies, but sound carried a long way on the mountain and there were a few farms not far below her.

She crammed her feet back into the espadrilles somehow, crammed her sunhat on until it covered her ears, and started back down. And, like her mother, she talked aloud to Cass.

"I don't want to take him away from you—I don't want that! I don't know what I want! I don't want him to think I'm you, either. I'm not you, Cass. We were like blood sisters—spirit sisters, but we weren't alike. I want him to see me as me. But if that means he has to forget you, then he can't. Not ever. Can he?" She stopped and lifted her head and said as loudly as she dared, "*Can* he, Cass? *Can* he? Oh why don't you answer me—just put a thought in my head or something! Don't you see what is happening, Cass? You are haunting us! Just like Mallie haunted Myrtle! I want to stop it, yet I don't want to send you away, Cass." She began to weep. "I love you, Cass. I love you and always will love you. But I love Jean-Claude too. What am I going to do, Cass?"

She huddled down, clutching her cold legs to her, letting her tears drip on her knees. But there was no answer and after a very short while, feeling slightly ridiculous, she stood up and began to plod grimly on. If Cass couldn't help she would have to take matters into her own hands.

344

It was quite dark when Jean-Claude met her almost on the Lassevour boundary. She was limping badly and her face was streaked with tears, but he could not see that and his anger was cold and cutting.

"You think you are grown-up, yet you have no consideration whatever for your grandmother, have you! She will tell me nothing but I suppose there was an argument and off you go like the spoiled brat you are!"

She would say nothing to excuse herself, but she fumed with the injustice of it, and tried to walk tall and make her silence dignified rather than piqued.

He jumped over the wall and waited for her to do likewise. She sat on the top, swung her legs over and promptly collapsed in a heap, catching her bare arm on some rose thorns. She could not hold back a cry.

"Let me see."

She tried to struggle up but he practically shoved her back down, found a torch in his pocket and shone it on her.

"*Mon Dieu!* You are in a state, are you not?" For a moment his voice softened, then he saw the blood oozing from the back of her espadrille. "You wore those for walking on the mountain? You deserve everything you got! Little fool!"

She could stay silent no longer.

"How dare you call me names? What right have you got to—to disapprove of me! None at all—you have made that quite clear over and over again! I realise you are here on behalf of Grannie—well, now you have found me so you can go back and tell her everything is all right!"

She tried to stand up and immediately collapsed again. He wasted no more time on words, but bent and picked her up as if she were a sack of potatoes. There was nothing romantic about it; nothing she could look back on later and enjoy in retrospect. Her head hung level with his waist, her hands clutched the top of his trousers in panic. He hoisted her back slightly to balance her weight, and ripped off both her shoes. The cold air on her bleeding heel was bliss. She closed her eyes momentarily, surrendering to the inevitable, and the next minute they were trudging between the roses and she was jolting up and down and from side to side, trying to brace herself, failing, losing every scrap of dignity, hating him more with each step.

Mary took her gently from Jean's bowed figure and laid her back on the sofa. A bowl of water appeared and she put her feet in it. Somewhere there was another bowl and Mary bathed her face and hands. When she opened her eyes, Mary's were smiling at her without reproach.

"Well, darling. You walked it out of your system well and truly, I should think. Bed now. I'll bring you some cocoa and a sandwich. Supper in bed. You always enjoyed that."

She wanted to decline it if only to prove she was no longer a child, but she was famished and the thought of bed and food at the same time was delightful. She avoided Jean-Claude's eye. He sat at the kitchen table, a book open in front of him. He did not say goodnight when she limped past him so neither did she. The stairs were difficult to negotiate and she would dearly have liked to go up on hands and knees. The sight of her bed, turned down neatly, the pillows arranged like an armchair, was too much and she started to cry again. She hardly ever cried now, and it was, of course, all his fault. When Mary came in with a tray she had mopped herself up, but it was no good.

"Bessie . . . Bessie. Don't force it, darling. Something will happen and he will realise you're a woman."

"What—what do you mean?" Bessie was startled out of her self-absorption. "What's he been saying? Has he been moaning about me behind my back?" She pushed back the clothes, already recovered enough to go down and do battle.

Mary laughed as she put down the tray. "He has said nothing at all—though his face is grim enough for anything." She shook her head gently. "He was very anxious, Bessie. He said it was for my sake, but it was for his own. I knew you would be all right—the Victoire is your mountain and you would have called for help if necessary." She went to the door. "He loves you very much, darling," she said quietly. And was gone.

Bessie stared at the closed door. Even if Mary had not disappeared so quickly she could not have asked her for further information. But surely she must mean that Jean *loved* her?

She ate her supper appreciatively and thought how she would get up early tomorrow and light the fire in the range and make breakfast and be . . . wonderful. Then she wondered if Jean-Claude would notice; or if he would just see her as a penitent child trying to get back into everybody's good books. She bit her lip and flung back the clothes to examine her heel. He hadn't even looked at it properly.

346

She needed to clean her teeth and go to the lavatory. She got up quietly and crept across the landing. Below in the kitchen, Mary and Jean were talking. Mary's voice was soothing and reassuring—as usual. Bessie hardly heard it, she knew what it would be saying. But then Jean spoke. "She is just a child, Mary. In many ways we have over-protected her. She is more than just innocent—she is naive."

It was the way he said it. Not exactly with contempt, but certainly not affectionately. There was a weariness in his voice. As if he were sick and tired of the whole problem.

Bessie went into the bathroom, did what was necessary, and went back to her room. She sat bolt upright in her high French bed, listening. First Mary went to bed. Then Jean. Then the old house creaked into a kind of silence. Outside, a little breeze got up. It would be cold on the mountain. Bessie shivered.

At midnight precisely she got out of bed, ignored her slippers and dressing-gown, and padded silently over the bare boards to the door. Unfortunately they, and the door, creaked at the slightest pressure, but by the time she had got herself on to the landing nothing was stirring. Jean slept in Cass' old room. She lifted the latch millimetre by millimetre, then pushed on the door. It swung inwards quite silently. Sitting up in bed, a book on the cover in a pool of light from the bedside lamp, Jean-Claude looked at her. He said nothing. Anything would have been better than nothing. For a few moments of indecision, she was paralysed.

Then she said in a high voice, "My heel hurts."

He did not move but he said levelly, "Go back to bed, Bessie. Now."

She said, "But Jean, my heel hurts. And I can't sleep." She advanced into the room and pushed the door shut behind her. He flung back his bedcovers and swung his legs to the floor. He was wearing ivory-coloured pyjamas that she had seen often on the ironing board, but they looked different on him. She could hardly breathe and a sensation developed in her pelvic area and spread down her legs.

He snapped, "Go back to your room immediately, Bessie!"

She whispered, "No. I'm not a child, whatever you think. I'm grown-up. I'm a woman. I want to sleep with you."

He stopped feeling for his slippers and looked at her in total disbelief.

"You what?" His voice was dangerous, but she refused to back down now.

"I don't care what you think. When I took off my bra I wanted to do it for you. Look—I'll do it again!" She dragged her nightie over her head frantically. The buttons got caught in her hair and pulled it unmercifully, but she ripped them away and flung the whole thing on the floor. Then she had to hang on to one of the brass knobs at the foot of the bed because she thought she might collapse with the nightie.

He stared at her, his black eyes burning. He did not move, but she was suddenly terribly conscious of her body. It was as if he touched her, ran his hands over her. Like Eve, she was ashamed of her nakedness.

He said very quietly, "Put your nightgown back on, Bessie. Go to your room. We will never speak of this again. But I would like you to try to imagine how Cass would view it." He got back into his bed and picked up his book.

She was totally dismissed. Her love, her desire, rejected. And because of Cass. She could not fight a ghost.

She shook like a leaf as she struggled into her nightie. And when she got outside the door she had to go to the bathroom again. She leaned over the basin and brought up her sandwich and cocoa. Her own actions had made her sick.

She arrived at Exeter before her letter. But Monica knew she was coming because she had received a frantic phone call from Mary the day before. It seemed Bessie had left the Bergerie very early in the morning, taking with her two thousand francs and a bag containing two cardigans, a mac, a pair of shoes and a toothbrush. She had written a garbled note for Mary, saying merely that no-one was to worry, she was quite old enough to travel by herself and she was going to see her mother.

Monica had reassured Mary and promised she would telephone as soon as she had some news of Bessie, but as she had no idea by which route the girl would come, she had to sit tight and wait. Mary had phoned twice when Monica was out, and the porter reported that her phone had rung several times while she had been on duty. As a sister, Monica now had a flat in the grounds of the hospital. It was in a block of alms-houses built in the last century, and she felt a positive sense of homecoming as she opened up and went into the tiny lobby after being on duty all night. It was a quiet grey morning, windless, full of the scent of stocks from the little cottage garden around the block. She took a long breath before closing the door and leaning against it with her eyes shut. She was tired in her very bones, but knew there was no hope of sleep.

She went into the kitchen and plugged in the kettle.

"It's all very well," she said aloud. "I haven't got the experience. Yes, I know it's marvellous—running home to mother—just marvellous. But I don't know what to do about it, Cass."

The kettle bubbled and she made tea, laid a tray and carried it into the little sitting room. It was chilly in there, and she switched on one bar of the electric fire and pulled her cardigan closer over her uniform. Then she sat down and poured her first cup of tea. It tasted wonderful. She closed her eyes against the steam and inhaled with the same pleasure with which she'd breathed in the flower scent ten minutes ago.

"The trouble is, Cass, I'm so damned content! We've got a little outbreak of meningitis—towards Barnstaple—quite a country district. Two children came in during last night. Took lumbar punctures . . . results just been confirmed. Told the parents . . . got them tea and toast. Told them it will be all right—kids already responding to penicillin—thank God for penicillin, Cass." She sipped, still with eyes closed. Then went on. "You know, Cass, if ever I get time, I'd like to do a paper about the necessity of nursing the whole family in these cases. Kids respond so much quicker if ma and pa are there. D'you know, in Africa, the patients invariably bring half a dozen close relatives with them when they're admitted."

She sipped again and opened her eyes quickly before she nodded off.

She said, "Cass, why has she run away? That's what I need to know. She'll tell me something of course, but it might not be the truth. And I need to know the truth, Cass. Otherwise what can I do?"

She drained her cup and poured another one.

"I know what you'd do. Listen. Not advise, not interfere. Just listen. But I'm not like you, Cass. I want to do something. And it's often the wrong thing. I mean, I shouldn't have married Bob. And maybe I shouldn't have taken over Myrtle's family. Or lugged poor old Liv along with me. Maybe if I hadn't done that, you wouldn't be dead now, Cass."

349

The second cup of tea did not taste as good as the first one. She needed to go to the bathroom and clean her teeth and maybe take a shower.

"Oh, shoot," she said wearily.

And the door knocker thumped.

Bessie did not look too bad. Her hair was combed and her face and hands were clean. She wore French espadrilles, one pencilled with the name "Paul," the other "Ringo." There were traces of blood around the top of one of them.

She stood in the doorway clutching a small zipped bag and looking chilly.

"Did you get my letter?" she asked by way of greeting.

"No." Monica stood aside and guided her into the sitting room and the one-bar fire. "I knew you were coming of course. But no letter yet."

"Do you mind? I had to get away. And Boris is still with Myrt, and I couldn't possibly tell Liv after what happened to her and Uncle Reggie."

"I don't mind. I'm on night duty so after tonight I shall have four days off. If that helps."

"Yes, it does. I want to go up to Liv's and get my results. But . . . I don't know what to do, Mon. I just don't know what to do." She sank down on the floor by the fire and shivered. "I've done something awful. Really awful."

"Mary didn't say. So it couldn't have been that bad."

"She doesn't know."

"Oh, I think she'd know."

"No. It's got nothing to do with her really." Bessie put her head on her knees. "Except . . . except now I think of it, it would probably kill her! Oh God, oh God!"

Monica took the cosy off the teapot and felt the outside. It was still very hot. She poured Bessie some tea in her own cup and handed it down saucerless.

"Drink this. I'll get some food. I suppose you're starving?"

"No. I mean, I'm not hungry. I'm probably starving though. Mon, don't go. I have to tell you straightaway." The head came up and the eyes were black in the white face. "Listen. When Boris told me he was going to be a priest, I didn't mind. Not at all. It was right—I could see that. Boris has always been different. Trying to get away from the things people do. He should have gone into that monastery when he wanted to . . . ages ago."

"Boris, a priest? I didn't know." Monica wondered whether she'd got hold of the wrong stick altogether. "Are you sure you didn't mind? I mean, you've always . . . you and Boris . . . only kids, I know, but it's amazing how these things grow up . . ."

"I was sort of relieved. And of course, once that was out of the way, I realised the truth." She slurped some tea and wiped her hand over her chin. "I must have known all the time, of course. It was so obvious. When I was in France before . . . I should have known then." She drank more tea. "The trouble is . . . Cass. Oh, Mon, I never thought I'd want Cass to go away—right away—" she began to cry and Monica leaned down and took the cup away from her, then crouched opposite her. She wondered whether she should take the girl into her arms, then decided against it.

After a while, she said briskly, "You haven't told me yet. Just why do you want Cass to go away? Or shall I guess?" She took a breath; Bessie did not speak. Monica said bluntly, "You're in love with Jean-Claude. And you think Cass would mind? You're an idiot, Bessie Woodford. You're an absolute idiot. Cass would be over-joyed. The people she loved best in the world coming together? Use your head, girl!"

Bessie looked up, startled. "How did you know? Oh my God, is it that obvious?"

"No. But the only reason you might see Cass as an obstacle is if you thought you were on her territory." Monica leaned towards her daughter and took her face in her hands. "Darling. You do Cass such an injustice."

She continued to hold the head that was so like her own, while Bessie's tears began again. Then at last she put her arms around the shaking shoulders and held them close.

"Don't cry, Bessie," she whispered. "It's natural. And beautiful. Nothing to cry about."

"He—he—he thought I was disgusting! I *was* disgusting! I had to make him see me—really see me! And I went into his room and took off my nightie and asked him if I could sleep with him. And he said—he said—what would Cass . . . oh, Mon . . . I was so ashamed! I wanted to die! I was sick. Then I tried to sleep. Then I went downstairs and wrote a letter to you and to Grannie, and then I left. I got a lift to Marseilles and there was this horrid old ship coming across to Plymouth and I—"

"My God! Bessie—you fool—you could have been abducted—"

"White slavery?" There was a tiny hint of a smile in the girl's voice. "Mon, I'm not that much of an idiot! When I said horrid, I meant it stank. It was full of salted fish. It was quite respectable otherwise. There was a vicar on board."

Monica tried to take into account that she had worked all night; even so, the conversation was more than just bizarre.

"A vicar?" she asked faintly.

"He'd done the whole of ancient Greece on fifteen pounds. Of course he was pretty thin by then."

"Bessie. Can you sit up in the chair now, darling. I need some food. Toast or something."

"I'll make it. Really. I love your little house. I'm so glad you've got . . . something . . ." She began to cry again.

"Oh for goodness' sake!" Monica struggled to her feet. "Listen, my girl, I've got everything. And if you end up without Jean-Claude, you can still have everything. It's there for the finding, for the . . . listen, Bessie. Stop crying a moment. You might have to do without him. But you might not. He knows now how you feel. Give him time. If you're still free in two or three years—"

"Two or three *years*? Besides, he hates me. I disgust him. I—"

"Bessie. Shut up." Monica went to the door. "I don't want you to help me. I want to do it by myself. We'll eat, then we'll sleep. And then, perhaps, we can talk properly."

She went into the kitchen and began to make toast and scramble eggs. She wondered how it was possible to want to laugh and cry at the same time. It could be hysteria of course. But she didn't think it was.

She said quietly, "You know all about it, Cass, don't you?"

As she took the tray of food into the sitting room, the post dropped through the door. She recognised Bessie's round handwriting. It reminded her that she must telephone the Bergerie immediately.

The girl looked up as she went into the room. Her face was streaked, but she was no longer crying.

"I know what you're going to say, Mon. I did it before—worked, I mean—and you're quite right, it's the only thing to do." She took the tray and put it on the floor in front of the fire. "But I'll never forget him. Just as you've never forgotten your Gilly."

Monica stared. Then gently sank to her knees and began to serve the eggs on toast.

18

Two days later, refreshed and subdued at the same time, Bessie went to St. David's station in Exeter and caught a through train to Birmingham. She telephoned Monica to announce her safe arrival and to say that her results were very good and she could go to Bristol University to read Zoology. It was where Cass had gone.

Two hours later she rang again.

"Aunt Liv says I can tell you, Mon! They're having a baby! Isn't it marvellous? Yes, of course you can speak to her. Hang on." Monica duly spoke to Liv.

There was a lot of laughter amidst the congratulations, then Monica said quietly, "So it's all right now, Liv? It was worth it?"

"I can't answer that, my dear. But it looks as if something good is happening for most of us, doesn't it? And . . . and I couldn't have done anything without you, Mon. And Cass of course. And Myrt . . . yes, Myrt especially."

They talked almost incoherently for ten minutes, then Bessie came back on the line.

"Listen, Mon. Will you tell Grannie? Somehow, this makes the—er—situation—seem better. It's so great it kind of dwarfs all that—drama—at the Bergerie. D'you know what I mean?"

"Yes. I think so. It might make all the difference to Malcolm, too."

"Malcolm?"

"I meant to tell you, I tried to arrange a big reconciliation. Nothing doing. Malcolm is too insecure, too frightened he will lose Myrt again. But now . . . Bessie love. If I can get Mary over here for a spell, how would you feel about meeting up at Cheltenham? All of us?"

"Well, fine. If it's okay with everyone else."

"You're certain that Boris—"

"I told you. I'm glad about Boris."

"But before that, you said you couldn't go to Myrt's—tell Myrt—because of Boris."

Bessie actually managed a little chuckle. "Can you imagine me confessing to Boris what I'd done. And him about to enter the brotherhood?"

"Sorry, love. That's fine then. I'll see what I can do. Perhaps you can work on them your end?"

Monica replaced the receiver. It would give Bessie something to think about at any rate. If nothing came of it, it was worth it for that.

She made her phone call to France with an enormous sense of déjà vu. Events seemed to be piling up as they'd done before. Somehow she ought to have more wisdom than she'd had then, and knew she had not.

She had postponed her nights off in case she might need them for the future. Bessie had slept for twenty hours after they'd breakfasted, and Monica had gone on duty at eight as usual and napped for three hours the next morning. Today, she was beginning to wonder if her eyes were focusing properly; she had already dropped two cups of tea and burnt her toast.

Jean answered the call. Monica had met him twice: once in Connecticut at Hildie's farm, and once at Cass' funeral. She felt she knew him intimately because of Cass and now because of Bessie, but she could so easily be wrong.

She said, "Is Mary there? This is Monica Gallagher."

"She is here." He covered the receiver but she heard him call

Mary. Then he came back to her. "Monica, we were so glad . . . Bessie must feel very close to you. It is good she had somewhere—someone—to go to."

"It is, isn't it?" Suddenly Monica forgot all her qualms about rushing in where angels feared to tread. "As she was forced to run somewhere—anywhere—it is very good she could come here." She heard her own voice, fierce with anger and sarcasm. It wasn't the way to do it. But she could not stop now. "It was clever of you to find the one way you could really cut her down, Jean. But then, I suppose you are trained to do just that."

There was a pause. She wondered if he had walked away and left the receiver dangling somewhere. But then his voice came on the line again. "Monica. Mary is here. I would like to talk. Afterwards. Shall I telephone you?"

She said crisply, "That is entirely up to you."

Mary's voice came next. She did not sound anxious.

"Mon. I've telephoned Barnt Green, so I know Bessie has arrived safely. My dear, she sounds so much steadier. Thank you."

"Nothing to do with me. She has common sense and as you know, I'm short on that." Monica tried to laugh. She said, "Mary, did she mention anything else to you? About Liv and Reggie?"

"No."

"Liv's pregnant."

Mary's joyous comments echoed resonantly. The kitchen at the French cottage must be big, or maybe stone-flagged.

Monica said, "The thing is, Mary. It might make it possible for us to get together again. And I'd like that. I feel it would be . . . right. I wondered if you could come over too? Go straight to Myrtle's—I'll fix it all up. Just for a few days. What do you think?"

"Well . . . yes. Why not? I was coming over anyway to be with Bessie obviously. And Myrtle can always do with help. That kitchen . . . and Lennie . . . Mon—leave it to me. I'll ring Myrtle. Good idea."

They made their farewells. Monica put down her receiver and sat by the phone, waiting for it to ring. She drank more tea and made more toast. If he didn't come through in the next half an hour she would have to go to bed and that was that.

After thirty-five minutes, it rang.

"I had to wait for Mary to go into the garden. It was necessary to speak privately, Monica. Obviously Bessie has told you what happened and you are very angry with me."

"Obviously," Monica echoed icily.

"It was cruel. Yes, I see that it was the cruellest thing I could have said. But it had to be done quickly. Finally. In the end she will thank me."

"In the end? What end is that, Jean? Your end? Or hers?"

"Monica, please. I am twenty years older than she."

"So you think you might die sooner than she dies, then she will be glad she's not a widow? Is that what you mean?"

"Monica, you know what I mean. The child still loves me as a father."

"So she tried to seduce you?"

"She is confused. The point is one that is still escaping you." His voice no longer pleaded for understanding; it was stern. "I do not love Bessie Woodford as my child, Monica. I love her as a woman. If I had not sent her away very quickly the other night, I might have indeed taken her into my bed. And that would have been unforgivable."

Monica was silent. She closed her eyes.

Jean's voice came across the wires again.

"Are you still there, Monica? You are disgusted perhaps? You too are thinking of Cass?"

"No. I was thinking of Giles. My adopted brother. Bessie's father." She took a breath. "Jean. Bessie is my daughter and I know her instinctively. She does not love you as a father, she loves you as a woman loves a man. She loves you even more because you were Cass' man. If you truly love her, you cannot leave her in ignorance. I mean it, Jean. You can go to Timbuctu afterwards. But first you have got to tell her that you love her."

"That is exactly what I am trying not to do."

Monica said levelly, "And I am trying not to interfere in this. Sometimes when I interfere, things do not work out properly. But I say this to you, Jean. If you do not tell Bessie, then I will. Goodbye."

She replaced the receiver once more, and began to clear away her breakfast things. Later she would ring Myrtle and Liv. Later on still she would arrange to have next week off and she would buy a new dress to wear in Cheltenham. But now . . . she had to sleep.

The first reunion was a stilted affair to begin with.

Liv, Reggie and Bessie arrived at Imperial Square a week later to find Mary already there. It was tea time and the boys were dressed in their best; Malcolm was with a patient, Myrtle had just finished her appointments for the day and was frantically trying on dresses in her bedroom. It did not matter what she looked like, yet she wanted to look . . . all right. Not beautiful as she had looked for Reggie; she would never look like that again. But she wanted to look . . . all right. She actually tried to get into the lime green dress she had bought in Alnwick, but it would not pull over her bust any more. Probably just as well.

By the time she had decided on her usual gathered skirt and V-necked top, Malcolm had joined her.

"I don't know whether this is a good idea." He looked as nervous as a schoolboy. "You should hear them in there, laughing and talking as if they're quite at home!"

"That's what we want, darling. We want to be natural. Normal. Don't worry. The boys are there. And Mary. It will pass off easily. And by the time they've been here a couple of days we shall feel easier."

"It's ridiculous filling up the house with visitors at our busiest time!"

"It's not a busy time by any means. I had to cancel just two appointments and Doris and Tom will put up the double bed in there this evening—it will be no trouble at all."

"Not to you. You let everything like that sail over your head. But I'm still working, trying to see patients—"

She came close to him and kissed him. "Darling. I'm just as nervous as you are. But do it for my sake. Please. You and Reggie were good friends and I came between you—"

"It was him! The bastard! Even now when I think of it, I could bloody well kill him!"

She kissed him again, sensed him beginning to feel heavy against her and realised there wasn't time for that.

"Come on, sweetheart. It'll soon be tonight."

"Oh, bunny rabbit, I do love you. I'm doing it for you, then. Is that quite clear?"

"Perfectly clear."

They went downstairs holding hands.

Unfortunately, Mary rounded up the boys and disappeared with indecent haste as soon as they came into the room. Lennie, who had a summer cold and could not go swimming, whined a protest which Nicky amputated with a surreptitious clip. The two couples were left facing each other across a loaded tea-trolley. Liv and

Reggie had scrambled to their feet as soon as the door handle turned, Malcolm and Myrtle appeared to have forgotten where the chairs were placed in the room. They all stood and stared.

Myrtle hardly glanced at Reggie, her eyes were all for Liv. On Liv depended everything as far as Myrtle was concerned. And Liv was scared; Myrtle could see that. Liv was still scared that she might whip Reggie away. Oh God.

Myrtle said, "Liv. I'm so sorry if I hurt you. And I'm so pleased—so very, very pleased, about the baby."

It was as if a spring was released in the region of Liv's shoulders. She gave a gasping sigh and ran at Myrtle. They embraced thoroughly, laughing and weeping and rocking from side to side so that they appeared to be doing a strange sort of dance.

Malcolm cleared his throat.

"Well, Reggie."

Reggie said, "It's good of you to invite us here, old man."

"I know it bloody well is. But actually it wasn't me. It was Myrtle."

"Well . . . you must have agreed to it."

"Suppose I must."

"The baby. Amazing what babies can do, isn't it?"

Malcolm looked at him. "Yes. Amazing."

"Sorry, old man. Look, can't we—somehow—be friends again?"

"Don't know. Not very likely."

The girls had finished their foxtrot and separated, laughing sheepishly.

Myrtle said, "Let's have some tea. Sit down, Liv. Relax every moment you can, it's terribly important." She risked a quick look at Reggie. "Do you still take sugar, Reggie?"

Malcolm said, "They've had tea already. I heard them at it when I came out of the treatment room."

"Then we'll have some, darling."

Myrtle sat down by the trolley and began to pour. Liv sat too. Malcolm and Reggie remained standing.

Then the door opened and Bessie's head came around it.

"Okay? Sorry to disappear like that. Boris and I went for a walk. We're going down to the kitchen to help Grannie."

Malcolm turned quickly. "No. Don't do that, Bess, old thing. Come and have tea with Myrtle and me. Is Borrie there? Get two more cups, Borrie, and join us." He almost carried Bessie into the room. She had been a friend to everyone all through. With her sitting next to Myrtle, the two men could also sit down.

Myrtle smiled at Liv. It wasn't going to be easy. But they'd made a start.

That night as she got ready for bed, Myrtle let herself think about Reggie and the time they had spent together. She was not introspective, and soon after Lennie started school she had known that she could no longer continue to cherish her time with Reggie as the perfect relationship. Its perfection relied entirely on its brevity and its complete lack of responsibility. Reggie had probably saved her sanity; he had made her well; and when Myrtle was well she did not dwell on the past, she lived in the present. Myrtle saw those three months now as lived by other people—actors in a drama— nothing to do with the Myrtle who was undressing here and the Reggie who was undressing downstairs.

She only hoped that Reggie felt the same way.

She sat on the edge of the bed to roll down her stockings; gone were the days when she slopped around bare-legged in the summer. Her legs were more veined than ever. She held one of them out and wondered whether she might have the veins stripped soon. They did not ache or trouble her in any way. She remembered Reggie tracing them from thigh to ankle. Dear Reggie. If he could see them now he would realise that she was not the same girl.

Malcolm came into the room with a rush. She smiled at him over her shoulder. He was looking better these days; celibacy had not suited him.

"Myrt—honey-bun—there are noises coming from your treatment room!"

She looked at him in surprise.

"Well, of course, Malcolm. Reggie and Liv are sleeping there. Have you forgotten? It's so that Monica can have the—"

"I know they're *sleeping* there, Myrt! But these noises . . . it's disgusting, darling."

He was genuinely shocked. She began to laugh.

"It's not a laughing matter, Myrt! Under our roof!"

She could not control herself. She rolled about on the bed like the old Myrtle, convulsed with schoolgirl giggles.

"You! Of all people, Malcolm Lennox! My God! That treatment room was more like a boudoir—"

"They're in *your* room, Myrtle! Not mine! And it's many years since . . . Myrtle, will you kindly stop laughing! In the circumstances you have to admit it's in pretty poor taste."

She got off the bed and went to him.

"Darling. They're having a baby. So they must have done it before." She kissed him. "Did you tell me so that you could gauge my reaction? Well, it's this . . . I'm glad that Reggie and Liv are making love under our roof, Malcolm." She kissed him again. "Would you help me with my brassiere, please, darling? And are you too tired to give me a massage?"

"No." His voice was hoarse. He slid her shoulder straps to waist level and kissed her breasts very gently. There was a reverence in his love-making that had not been there before.

He whispered, "Oh, bunny rabbit. I do love you."

She looked at his handsome head, touched the crisp hair and the outside edge of his ears.

"I love you too, Malcolm."

Monica arrived the next day in time for lunch.

"Why didn't you telephone?" Myrtle fussed around her like a mother hen. "We'd have met you at the station or something."

"I didn't come by train. I had a lift. Practically to the door."

"Isn't this wonderful—all of us together after so long. And Liv having a baby. And everything." Myrtle seemed in a state of euphoria.

Liv said, "You look tired, Mon. Bessie told us about the meningitis."

"It's not the worst kind. I think it's all right."

Bessie said mock-soberly, "It's motherhood. It's tough for Mon. You'll come to it gradually, Aunt Liv. Mon tends to jump in at the deep end."

She was referring to herself but suddenly realised there had been another time when Monica had taken on motherhood. But they all laughed, which was a good sign.

They went upstairs and helped Monica to unpack. Lennie jumped on the bed and Nicky and Martin held him down.

"Where are Malcolm and Reggie?" Monica asked, wondering whether a week would be too long in Cheltenham. Her head was already aching; she had worked everything out with great care and forgotten the children.

"Boris and Reggie have gone to see a photographic exhibition at the town hall, and Malcolm has appointments today." Myrtle put a navy-blue dress on a hanger. "You do sound rather done up, Mon. Is everything all right?"

"I hope so. I wondered if we could have a day out. Weather permitting." Monica smiled brightly at Liv and passed her some underwear. "You see, I've got a friend with me. The chap who gave me a lift, actually. And I said I'd show him Stratford—you know how foreigners are, they always want to see where Shakespeare was born."

"One of your American in-laws?" Liv laid the underwear in a drawer and closed it. "It would be great fun, girls, wouldn't it? We lived so near but we only went with boring school parties to see productions of the plays we were reading."

Myrtle groaned. "D'you remember Donald Wolfit in *King Lear*? Cass thought it was too marvellous for words and you got off with one of the actors, Liv—"

"We could go on the river!" yelled Lennie. "Super-duper! I'll row. I know how to row!"

"We could have a picnic," said Martin a little less exuberantly. "Cold sausages and ham sandwiches and strawberries from Evesham—"

"It's September, idiot!" said Nicky. "But there'll be plums. Pershore plums. And Victorias. And—"

"Who is your friend from America, Mon?" asked Bessie.

There was a little pause, then Monica turned and faced her daughter.

"It's Jean-Claude. He's staying at the Queen's."

"Jean? Cass' Jean?" Myrtle was astonished. Neither Mary nor Bessie spoke of him often. "I didn't realise you knew him, Mon! Whyever didn't you bring him here? We could have managed."

"He wouldn't do that. But he wanted to see us all." She turned again to her case. "He has to go back to Algeria for at least a year."

Bessie said, "When? When is he going to Algeria?"

"Next week."

"So you asked him to come over," Bessie concluded flatly.

Monica smiled. "No. As a matter of fact, I didn't ask him to come over. We spoke on the phone. Then he turned up on my doorstep. Rather like you did."

"Why?"

"He had a rather marvellous idea he wanted to put to me. He assumed you'd get your place at Bristol all right. And he thought

I might try for a job at the Children's Hospital there and join you and Mary." She turned her smile on Mary. "I don't know what you think about it, but it sounded good to me."

Mary beamed. "And to me. And meanwhile he'd like to see Stratford." She hauled Lennie off the bed. "Come on boys. Let's go and see what's in the larder. We shall need at least four loaves and an enormous picnic hamper."

"We could take a tent in case it rains," Lennie suggested.

"Can we swim?" Martin asked. "Aunt Mon used to take us swimming—"

"Shut up, Martin." Nicky ordered tersely. They went off and the room was quiet again.

Bessie said, "I can't face him."

"Rubbish."

Myrtle said, "Why not? Has there been a row?"

Bessie said, "Yes."

Monica said, "No."

Liv said, "Don't let there be any more rows. Please."

Monica said, "He wants to talk to Boris. He hasn't seen him since he came home from Australia. Then he simply wants to say goodbye to you and Mary, Bessie. That's all. He doesn't want to disappear without a word like last time. We'll all be with you, don't worry. Just be there. If nothing else, it will paper over the cracks. And that's important just now, isn't it?"

Liv said, "It is. It is, Bessie."

Myrtle said, "So there was a row."

Bessie sighed. "No. Not really. Monica is right, there was no row. And . . . I suppose . . . if everyone else is there, I will be too."

Monica hugged her. "You'll be glad. Afterwards, you'll be glad," she assured her.

Nicky lost no time in detaching Lennie and persuading a willing Martin to come with him to the Queen's. At twelve years old, he was suddenly curious about adults and there was a mystery somewhere which he had been unable to solve. It could well be that Monsieur Durant was the missing link.

They presented themselves at the reception desk with aplomb and were taken into the lounge where Jean-Claude was drinking tea and looking disappointingly English. Nicky introduced himself and his brother and graciously accepted a place at the low table.

"We thought we'd better come and tell you about the picnic tomorrow," Martin explained. "Lennie wants to row but of course he can't—he's only five. But after you've seen the town and everything, the river might be a good idea. Before the whole thing gets boring."

Jean-Claude inclined his head. "It sounds enchanting. A picnic by the Avon river. Yes."

Nicky said kindly, "Actually it's called the river Avon, not the Avon river, monsewer. And it won't be exciting like Algeria of course. I saw a film that took place in Algiers. There was this man with a knife who captured English ladies and sold them to—"

"It certainly has an exciting history," Jean-Claude agreed. "The Kasbah is intact still. It was the headquarters of the old pirates."

"Golly," said Martin. "Are you allowed in there, monsewer?"

"Yes."

The boys were momentarily dumb. Jean-Claude took the opportunity to order more tea and some buns. His popularity kept rising.

After more conversation about the Algeria of the deys and pirates, Martin said hopefully, "I think you might be some relation of ours, monsewer. If you were married to Aunt Carol, then you're sort of Bessie's stepfather. And—"

"Bessie was adopted," Nicky interrupted scornfully. "And anyway, she's not our real cousin."

Jean-Claude added gravely, "I was not married to Carol unfortunately. We were to be married."

"Ah." Nicky looked apprehensive. He'd thought men never cried, but he'd seen his father in tears not long ago and that had been connected with Carol in some way.

He said quickly and without giving his words due consideration, "Of course, if you were to marry Aunt Mon, then you would be Bessie's real stepfather, and—"

Martin said triumphantly, "But she's still not our real cousin, so monsewer wouldn't be related to us."

Jean-Claude passed the buns again. "Actually, I am not going to marry Monica. But I could still invite you to see Algeria when you are a little older."

"Golly. That would be great," said Martin without bothering to swallow. "Thank you tons, monsewer."

Jean-Claude brushed crumbs from his shirt front and Nicky said, "Sorry about that, monsewer. Martin is a pig at times."

But all Jean-Claude said was, "I think you had better call me Jean. You can pronounce it as John if you prefer."

"Oh jolly good. French is stupid really, isn't it?"

The next day was Saturday and Malcolm had no appointments. It was slightly overcast but nothing was going to stop them now. Jean-Claude had hired a car in Exeter; he managed to pack in Boris and the three boys. Reggie's Humber Snipe took Malcolm, Mary and Bessie, leaving Myrtle to drive Malcolm's car with Liv and Monica. They stopped at Broadway for coffee at the Lygon Arms. Bessie did not look at Jean, and he did not look at her. But, as Monica had said, they were together, and that must count for something.

They went slowly through Willersey so that Jean could see the ducks.

Boris said, "The first time Bessie and I came to stay with Myrtle, my father drove us this way. We stopped and fed the ducks. It doesn't seem very long ago."

"It is not very long ago. Nine years. No more."

Martin said, "That's a lifetime, monsewer . . . John. Lennie wasn't even born then. Crikey, imagine life without Lennie . . ." There was a skirmish on the back seat during which Boris said quietly, "Time is so relative. Nine years for you is not long. For Bessie it is the difference between childhood and maturity."

Jean-Claude murmured, "You know."

It wasn't a question but Boris replied. "I know she loves you. And . . . actually . . . I know quite a bit about love. So I really do *know* that she loves you."

Jean sighed. "To think I got you that job in Australia to keep you apart. And all the time . . ."

"You kept yourself fairly apart too. You must have known subconsciously that you loved her. You do love her, Jean, don't you?"

Martin said, "Who? Who do you love, monsewer . . . John? If you've changed your mind about Aunt Mon, we'd better tell you that she is very strict."

"But very nice," Nicky added.

Boris turned in his seat.

"Shut up, boys," he said pleasantly.

They parked the cars and walked to Shakespeare's birthplace. The boys were restless. They went on to the church and the boys were more restless still.

"We'll save Anne Hathaway's until after our picnic," Myrtle decreed.

They took out three skiffs. Skimming past the Memorial Theatre and beneath overhanging willows, they felt suitably Arcadian. Bessie and Monica sat in the stern of the first skiff, trailing their hands and smiling at each other. Boris sculled the boys; Malcolm and Reggie took on the other two boats.

They stopped for lunch at a jetty upstream.

"Someone else can row back," Boris panted.

"Me—me!" Nicky offered.

"I'll do it," Lennie said. "We've gone canoeing with the club and it's easy-peezy."

Martin said, "Well, you're only five, so hard cheese."

They went off across the grass, wrangling amicably, while Boris and Bessie began to lay out the picnic. Jean-Claude put some bottles to cool at the edge of the river. It was halcyon. And still very easy to avoid any kind of confrontation.

After lunch it clouded over. "Thunder," Myrtle forecast. "Lennie will have a fit."

"Lennie?" queried Jean incredulously.

Malcolm said, "He's like his father, all front and no back." Then he realised what he had said and started to laugh. So did Reggie. They went so far as to punch each other on the shoulder. Myrtle looked at Liv and smiled. "Filthy devil," she commented.

They began to pack up hurriedly.

The boys were playing French cricket. It amused them greatly that though he was French, Jean-Claude had never heard of the game. Lennie had been in for a long time simply because the bat completely protected his small knees. Nicky and Martin were fed up with him, and glad the game had to end.

"You're cross because I'm so brave," Lennie mentioned matter-of-factly. "I've got the heart of a lion!"

"And the brains of a donkey," returned Nicky tartly. "Mother is packing up because it's going to thunder, Lennie the Lionheart!"

Lennie's reaction was craven, much to the joy of his two brothers.

There was an immediate scrabble to load the skiffs and embark. Jean-Claude waited his turn politely, and somehow Bessie got behind him. He passed the last basket.

"I would very much like to walk along the bank. Malcolm, it will make the boat lighter and you will be able to get Lennie back more quickly. We will meet you in the hotel by the car park." He turned and took Bessie's arm. "Come. We can be back as soon as they if we step it out."

She thought it an obvious ploy, but everyone seemed to accept it naturally; Monica pushed off the last skiff and Malcolm sculled into midstream. The boys were catcalling from ahead; Lennie hid in his mother's arms.

"So. Do not be distant, Bessie. You must know that I came to Cheltenham with Monica especially to see you."

"I thought . . . just to see each other . . . papering over the cracks Monica called it." Bessie could feel her heart jumping around quite wildly. She managed to disengage her arm fairly casually and went ahead of him. "Personally, I think it's a case of least said soonest mended."

"I do not agree. I am going away next week—"

"Monica told me. Not even the occasional weekend back at the Bergerie?"

"No. And in any case the Bergerie is only home for me when you and Mary are there."

"Oh. But it was yours and Cass'." She picked a huge frond of cow parsley and sniffed it luxuriously. It smelled rankly of river.

He said, "Cass is dead, Bessie."

She took a breath and swallowed it.

He said, "I wish to congratulate you. And I hope the three years at Bristol will be very happy. I like to think of you and Monica and Mary making a home together and sharing your experiences."

She said lightly, "You sound like the complete stuffed shirt, Jean. What you mean is, you hope that we will make another life, that I will meet suitable young men, and not embarrass you again."

He said, "I do not hope that. No. Because I am very selfish. But if it happens then . . . I will dance at your wedding. Is that the saying?"

She flung away the cow parsley. "Oh, shut up," she said rudely.

Incredibly, he laughed. She wanted to turn round and hit him. Instead she increased her pace until she was almost running.

She heard him panting and laughing behind her.

"Bessie, if you are trying to prove that I am much older than you, you have succeeded. I cannot keep this up for long!"

She stopped abruptly and he almost ran into her. She said, "I think I hate you, Jean."

"Ah *chérie*. Do not say that."

"I do say it. Because you are playing with me. You are treating me like a child again. You know I love you. You know that I want to marry you. You know that I feel terrible because of Cass, but that I still want you. You think because I am nineteen, I am a child. I loved Boris, now I love you, next week I shall love someone else. But it is not like that, Jean. I have always loved you. Ever since I saw you first at the airport in New York, I have loved you. I thought you were my father and I loved you as a father. But I know now, it wasn't for that reason at all. I fell in love with you when I was twelve years old, Jean-Claude! And I didn't even know it!" She turned and looked at him. "I cannot force you to love me. But surely I deserve something more than a pat on the head and good wishes for the next boyfriend?"

He bowed his head as if he expected—wanted—her to strike him.

He said, "Bessie. I cannot look at you. You are too beautiful and it hurts too much. When you came to my room . . . I had to send you away. Otherwise I would have made love to you as you wanted me to. And *chérie,* it would have been wrong. Not because of Cass. But because for so long I *was* a father to you. You must understand that, Bessie. It would have been the betrayal of a trust."

She hardly heard his last words. She whispered, "What do you mean? What are you saying, Jean?"

He did not look up.

"I am saying I love you. I am saying I want you. And I am saying that I am going away and giving you time . . . giving us time. Because that is the right way to do things."

She breathed, "You love me. Say it. Look at me and say it."

He lifted his head. His black eyes met her black eyes. He said, "I love you, Bessie. I am twenty years older than you. But I cannot help myself. I love you."

She sensed his helplessness, amounting almost to a fear of this second total commitment. She put her arms right around him and held him tightly.

"Then that is all right, my darling. All right. There will be no other boys, Jean. I will wait. I will work and you will be proud of me. And then, if you still love me, we will be together." It was strange that the crazy joy she should be feeling was suddenly muted to this protectiveness. She tightened her grip. "Trust me, *chéri*. Trust me. This is right. There will be no more pain."

She felt his tears before her own. And then his arms came around her and held her to him, and her joy began.

19

*J*ean-Claude and Bessie were married in 1967. The ceremony took place in the same church as Myrtle's wedding fifteen years before, at the top of the hill in Northfield overlooking the enormous housing estate where once had stood the Haunted House.

Boris gave her away. He had not yet entered a seminary, choosing to spend a few years with the Franciscan order in a small friary near Bristol, and in his brown robes and sandals he brought an air of simplicity to the packed church. He had of course returned the bracelet, and Bessie was wearing it over the white cuff of her wedding dress. He put his hand over it lightly as they walked up the aisle together. He had arrived at his happiness as tortuously as the others, and the bracelet was a poignant reminder of how near he had come to another life altogether. He smiled sideways at the exquisite gypsy face beneath the froth of lace. She had not changed that much from the girl he had danced with at his sister's wedding; and she was as much his sister as Myrtle—more in many ways.

Nicky and Martin had refused to be attendants, but had agreed to the less embarrassing tasks of ushering. Lennie followed Bessie up the aisle, resplendent in velvet and jabot. Behind him, Liv, as matron of honour, carried Helen instead of a bouquet. Bessie had insisted on it. "We can't leave her out, Liv. She's got to carry the torch for all of us." And Helen, at two and a half, seemed to accept this responsibility. She had her mother's curls and her father's warmth; she eyed the guests carefully and smiled happily at a selected few.

Myrtle, frankly dumpy again, stood next to Malcolm and smiled all the time. She had been sorry that Boris and Bessie had never made a match of it; like her mother, Myrtle felt they had all "lost" Boris. But his presence today went a long way to banishing this conception, and it gave more meaning to Bessie's marriage to Jean-Claude. Somehow they were all part of this match, even Cass. Cass would be so pleased; it made the wastefulness of her death have some kind of meaning. When the rector intoned, "If there be any just cause or impediment why these . . ." she felt Malcolm's hand fumbling for hers in the folds of her full skirt, and she took it and squeezed it gently. Malcolm was so emotional, so dependent on her; sometimes it was like having a fourth son; almost like having Mallie back again. She leaned forward slightly to smile at her mother who was standing next to her doctor husband, looking as anxious as ever. No, Myrtle hadn't wanted to follow that particular family pattern, and she hadn't. And neither had Borrie. Some time she would talk to Mother and try to reassure her about Borrie going into a monastery. It was so right for him. He was special. She hadn't seen it before, but that's what he was, special.

Reggie had opted to sit on the groom's side as Jean had no family. He too smiled, looking at his wife and daughter, then Bessie, then Jean-Claude. Reggie was almost certain it would be all right. The man did not even look French, and though he was so much older than Bessie, there was no generation gap. Bessie had come midway between the two generations. Reggie did not want to be fanciful, but he could almost imagine the very English Carol drawing them together, bridging any gaps there might be. He blinked and smiled across the aisle at Mary Woodford. What must she be thinking? Eight short years ago at Carol's funeral, her life had been shattered. And yet she had carried on somehow and put the pieces together. It was so good that she had had three years of Bessie and Monica; the trio had made up an odd little household in their flat off Whiteladies Road in Bristol, but how would she manage now? He had to remind himself that eight years ago his life too had been in ruins. That affair with Myrtle . . . how had it happened? He looked further down the church and saw Myrtle and Malcolm holding hands like a pair of lovers. Myrtle was forty and looked older; she also looked competent and in control of everything, Malcolm included. He recalled the lost and terrified girl on Alnmouth beach; the tremulous mistress in the room at the Crillon. They had gone. This was the real Myrtle.

Malcolm looked across heads and saw Reggie staring. For a second he was startled, almost frightened. Then Reggie smiled and lifted a hand, and Malcolm relaxed against the stalwart shoulder so near his breast pocket. Well, he would never take Myrtle for granted again, he hardly needed Reggie to remind him of that. And he hoped that Reggie would never take Liv for granted either. Malcolm looked back at Liv, standing small and slim by Lennie. Helen had moved in her mother's arms so that she could see her father. Malcolm was a loving father, and seeing the link between Reggie and that baby girl melted his defences. Neither Reggie nor he deserved their happiness: let them both remember that. As if to underline that thought, the rector's voice boomed out, "Those whom God hath joined together, let no man put asunder."

Mary listened to the words too, and felt a deep thankfulness that Cass and Jean had never actually married. She remembered Cass' conviction that her union with Jean-Claude could not last. Well . . . it had not, but in a way Bessie was continuing it. Mary dared not let that train of thought go further. She heard the awe-inspiring words and knew that if they'd been said before, they would have stayed in Jean's head for ever and come between him and his love for Bessie. They were words that should be said only once in a lifetime.

She moved to the vestry slowly, forcing Monica to go ahead and sign the register first. She looked around her smilingly and caught Giles Cook's eye. So he had come to see his daughter married. On an impulse she went back down the aisle and took his arm, urging him up.

"Would you walk with me?" she whispered. "Then Mon can go with Boris."

371

He flushed bright red with pleasure. And, better still, when Bessie saw him in the vestry she beamed at him and said, "Oh, I'm glad you're here. Are you all right?" And he nodded, quite unable to speak.

Monica felt strange; apart from all of it. For three years now, she, Bessie and Mary had shared a flat in Bristol and lived in almost perfect harmony. She and Mary were to continue living together. Everything was working out well. Yet she stood in a corner of the vestry, watching the smiling faces, feeling like an observer and not knowing why.

When Mary walked in with Gilly, she felt the usual soft squeezing of her heart muscles, a tenderness oozing through her insidiously, and wondered for a moment whether Giles might, after all this time, be her true destiny. But the very next instant she knew it was too late; had been too late even before Bob.

Liv came up and gave Helen to her.

"Bessie wants me to sign too. Hang on to Nellie, will you, Mon?"

Monica took the child, her godchild, and was rewarded by a smile and a quick, snuggling hug. And quite suddenly she knew what she wanted to do. She couldn't wait to tell Mary all about it. Mary loved children too. If she felt up to it, she'd be as keen as Monica herself.

Giles came up to her.

"Nice little kid," he said awkwardly, standing stiffly to attention. "Whose is that, then?"

"Liv's. You remember. Liv Baker that was." Monica waited until Helen turned and said hello. Giles chucked her under the chin too familiarly and she buried her head in Monica's neck.

Monica said, "I've wanted to look you up, Gilly."

"Aye aye," Gilly said. "What have I done now?"

Monica said, "I hoped you weren't too shattered by that business four years ago. Is it too late to apologise?"

Unexpectedly, he grinned. "She did that already," he said. "Couple months after it all happened. Didn't she tell you?"

"No."

"She's quite a gal. Invited me to the wedding too. Prob'ly didn't think I'd come, but I couldn't've missed it."

"No," Monica said again. She never cried, but she could have cried at that. Bessie was special, so very special.

Giles said frankly, "Reckon she's giving us plenty of chances to get together again, our Mon. But I don't think we could, do you?"

Monica swallowed and pressed her cheek against Helen's curls. "No," she said.

"I mean. If you've got leanings that way—"

"No."

"That's all right then. 'Cos I'm a bit set in me ways now. Couldn't really fancy anyone else after you, our Mon, but couldn't be bothered either. Know what I mean?"

"Absolutely."

He said, "Right. Then it's just as well I'm walking along of Mrs. Woodford. We don't want to give no-one ideas."

"No."

They gathered around the car which was to take Bessie and Jean to the airport.

Mary said to Monica, "Are you sure we'd be allowed to foster children? I thought there had to be a father figure somewhere around?"

"Short-term fostering . . . difficult children . . . that kind of thing we can do. What do you think?"

Mary said thoughtfully, "We'd have to buy a house somewhere of course. Or maybe a bungalow would be better."

Monica smiled and squeezed the older woman's arm. "It would be fun to do something together, wouldn't it? Make a family again . . ."

Mary said, "Mon, you're not suggesting this simply for my sake are you? What about your nursing career? You're doing so well."

"I'm suggesting it for my sake. Selfish to the end, you see. But I can't do it without you, Mary. And we can offer so much—a foster mother and a foster grannie!"

They both laughed.

Bessie had changed into trousers and shirt. She and Jean would be in the Bergerie within three hours. Their goodbyes were laced with instructions: most of the people there were coming out for their holidays before the end of the month.

"Don't do a thing, darling," Mary told her. "I'll give the place a good clean and do masses of cooking—"

Monica said, "You'll want to get away from all of us! Are you sure—"

Jean said smilingly, "We're sure. And perhaps in any case we shall not be there. Bessie is taking me up the side of the mountain—tomorrow morning very early. I believe we shall be accompanied by a mule."

Everyone laughed. Then Bessie looked at Boris. "I've got something here. Something Borrie and I buried a long time ago and Jean and I dug up. We all think it's too important to be kept in one place. It's going to do the rounds. Like a talisman."

"What is it?" Myrtle asked curiously.

Bessie transferred her gaze. "It's your paint pot, Aunt Myrt. It—it's a sort of proof. Of Cass. Of Mallie. Of everything."

Myrtle looked and said nothing. Suddenly Liv went to her and put her arms around her. And Mon followed suit. The three women were quite silent, standing there in the sunshine. Then Myrtle held out an arm for Bessie.

She kissed each one in turn. And then went to Mary. It did not surprise her to find that Jean was there before her, holding Mary gently to him. It was he who said, "Cass is still here. In each one of us. We shall never lose her."

They got into the car and drove away.

For some reason, Mary heard herself say, "It's not finished. It will go on and on."

Monica asked, "Do you mind?"

Mary said, "No. There are so many kinds of happiness. I have one kind in abundance."

Monica said, "So have I."

Liv said, "So have we." And, instead of looking at Reggie and Helen, she added, "Haven't we, Myrt?"

Myrtle took out a large man's handkerchief, wiped her eyes and blew her nose. "Yes." She grinned, and was her old self, the Myrtle who had scrambled up the bank of the brook with Cass' help. They looked at each other anew. None of them had changed at all. They could have been still thirteen, with all of life before them.

"Of course," she said emphatically.

Bessie placed a tureen of onion soup on the kitchen table next to the basket of rolls. It was a heavy tureen and her hands trembled slightly as she sat down. She put them quickly onto her lap.

Jean-Claude said in a low voice, "I am frightened too, Bessie. Do not let us hide our fear from each other."

She swallowed visibly, then tried to smile.

"You are frightened that I will come between you and Cass. I understand that, my darling. I will never do that, Jean. I will never . . . usurp . . . Cass. This—thing—this love between you and me—it is something different. Something separate."

He said nothing, but he smiled at her and lifted his shoulders as if helpless to explain the deep flow of their feeling for each other.

She said briskly, "Let's have your wretched soup while it's hot enough to scald our tongues! And—and—just—take it as it comes."

He held his plate, his smile widening. She said, "What? What have I said?"

"Nothing. It is the way you speak. So like Monica. How could anyone have imagined you were Cass' child!"

She flinched and gave a little cry and he leaned forward and grabbed her wrist.

"Darling! Bessie—I did not mean to hurt you. She was closer to you than a mother could have been!"

The tears flooded her dark eyes. "I know. I know. I know. But . . . if I'd actually belonged to her—been her daughter—you could have loved me—sort of—through her . . . don't you see?"

The grip on her wrist tightened painfully.

"No. I don't see! It would not have been like that, Bessie. Not a bit. It would have been wrong—practically incestuous!" He pushed back his chair and came around the table, not releasing her wrist. "Listen, *chérie*. What you have just said . . . it makes sense in an upside-down way!" He lifted her and held her tightly and she pressed her face into his shoulder and let the tears flow. "Ah . . . listen, Bessie." His mouth was close to her ear. "You think you need to be one with Carol for me to love you. But it is the other way round, my darling. I have to tell you something . . . and I cannot find words." He laughed briefly. "Jean-Claude Durant, bereft of words! *Mon Dieu, c'est incroyable!*"

He was trying to make her laugh, but she could not. It was as if all her grief and love had come together at once and fountained from her in tears. He cradled her, smoothing her hair back from her hot forehead. Then he carried her to the old settle by the range and pillowed her head on his shoulder. And gradually she became quiet.

He said softly, "Darling Bessie. I want to talk about Carol's death. Can you bear it?"

For a long time she did not speak or move. Then he felt her head jerk up and back. He kissed the parting in her hair.

"I have never spoken of it to anyone, dearest. They thought—at the time—that I was suffering from shock. And perhaps I was. Who can tell? It seemed to me then, and still does, that those moments of Cass' dying, were the most real of my life. Until now."

Her hands which had been clutching his shirt front, slid slowly around his chest and held him.

He went on very quietly. "Bessie. I wanted to go with Cass. I wanted to die with her. But she would not let me. She sent me back. For a reason of course. We know why, don't we?"

Another pause, then Bessie's head nodded again.

And again he kissed her and went on.

"I came back to this life, not . . . empty. Not without Cass." He sighed. "This is the difficult part to explain, Bess. Yet is so simple. Cass and I were one. We are still . . . one. The person you love, my darling, is not just Jean-Claude Durant. It is Jean-Claude-Carol Durant. That is why I tell you that your words were upside-down. Can you understand that?"

Her hands held him tightly. She nodded.

He whispered, "Do you see that Cass can never come between us, yet never be dismissed into the past? Can you see why our love is amazingly strong?"

She cleared her throat. "Yes," she said hoarsely.

They were still. Neither of them spoke. They held each other tightly as if afraid one would fall down without the support of the other.

Jean-Claude said, "I have put it badly. You are more frightened than before."

At last she sat up. Her eyes were still shining with tears, but he could see into their depths and was instantly reassured.

"I am not frightened, Jean," she whispered. "I am just . . . amazed. I was thinking back. Thinking of everything that has happened. And it seems to lead . . . here."

It was his turn to weep. She held his head in her hands and kissed his eyes. And then the bridge of his nose. Finally his mouth. And then they came together. Without haste, or embarrassment; with perfect naturalness, they undressed and made love on the kitchen floor while above them, the tureen of onion soup grew cold. And congealed.

And it was as if all the roads from the Haunted House so many years ago, had indeed led to this place, and this time. A real time. A time when all the laughter and all the weeping were given a wonderful significance. An even more wonderful immortality.